praise for

Dust Settles North

"Deena ElGenaidi's stunning debut masterfully weaves the personal and the political to tell a story of resistance, loss, and displacement—all while tracing the undying bond between siblings. I would follow Hannah and Zain wherever they go." —Zaina Arafat, author of *You Exist Too Much*

"A beautiful meditation on grief, family, and the ties that bind. I was wholly absorbed by this atmospheric novel of transformation after mother loss, and the apt exploration of the way that loss reshapes the world. *Dust Settles North* will speak to anyone who has ever chased belonging, both with family and in the world, meaning this book is for everyone. Gorgeous." —Chelsea Bieker, author of *Madwoman* and *Godshot*

"*Dust Settles North* is a remarkable character study that accomplishes the rare feat of being truly honest with its messy, imperfect, frustrating protagonists. The novel is a raw, insightful look at the effects of grief, secrets, and upheaval on a family split between two worlds, richly detailed and filled with compassion. ElGenaidi has crafted a stunning debut." —Vaishnavi Patel, *New York Times* bestselling author of *Kaikeyi* and *Goddess of the River*

"A beautifully wrought, tender story of familial ties across time and place with characters that leap off the page." —Gabrielle Korn, author of *Yours for the Taking* and *The Shutouts*

"*Dust Settles North* is a moving account of the way grief knocks down life's edifices, making difficult truths impossible to ignore. This is a story of reckoning: with self, with family, and with the world and a powerful reminder that when everything falls apart, there's a chance to build something new. A magnificent debut." —Lilly Dancyger, author of *First Love*

"*Dust Settles North* is an unsparing exhumation of the untruths that keep a family together, of the small sins and glaring hypocrisies that can quickly drive them apart. This gritty debut will have you thinking about inheritance and legacy, grief and loss, and perhaps most especially that central question: What does it mean to be truly honest and vulnerable with the people we allegedly love the most? A powerful meditation on family and belonging that will stay with readers long after turning the final page." —Jeanna Kadlec, author of *Heretic*

"*Dust Settles North* by Deena ElGenaidi weaves familial hurt, grief, and religious guilt into one beautifully written, tear-inducing tapestry." —Kay Synclaire, author of *House of Frank*

"ElGenaidi expertly explores themes of faith, becoming, and the consequences of freedom at the individual, familial, and geopolitical levels. Using the metaphorically rich backdrop of an Egypt fighting to forge its own future, *Dust Settles North* asks the question of how to balance what we owe community with what we owe ourselves.

“*Dust Settles North* is sure to be a five-star read that will challenge readers with its sharp cultural commentary while also comforting readers with the heart of a family struggling to love and, infinitely more difficult, trust each other.” —Micaiah Johnson, author of *The Space Between Worlds*

“An enduring and heartfelt story of a family coming apart at the seams—and the bridges they build to find themselves again. ElGenaidi writes about destructive grief, crumbling identity, and the double-edged sword of familial loyalty with breathtaking compassion.” —S. Hati, author of *And the Sky Bled*

Dust Settles North

Dust Settles North

a novel

Deena ElGenaidi

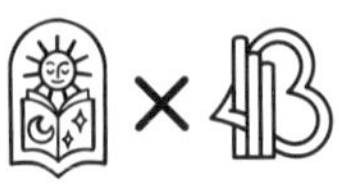

Published by Boundless Press, an imprint of Bindery Books, Inc., San Francisco
www.binderybooks.com

Quotes on pages 12, 130, 149, and 150 taken from the Quran.

Acquired by Jananie K. Velu
Edited and designed by Girl Friday Productions
www.girlfridayproductions.com

Cover design by Charlotte Strick
Cover illustration by Cecilia Carlstedt

ISBN (paperback): 978-1-964721-16-3
ISBN (ebook): 978-1-964721-18-7

Library of Congress Cataloguing-in-Publication data has been applied for.

First edition
10 9 8 7 6 5 4 3 2 1

Printed in China

For Sasha

SUMMER 2012

Hannah

Two days ago, Hannah was walking down a busy Brooklyn street when she felt her phone buzz in her pocket.

"Have you started packing yet?" her mom asked in a tone that conveyed she already knew the answer and was only calling to give her a lecture.

"I have, like, a month left until I need to move, Mom." She adjusted the tote bag of groceries slipping from her shoulder.

Hannah was moving out of her Brooklyn apartment to a place closer to Columbia for law school. And sure enough, her mom's lecture began, telling her she needed to start packing now—that she wouldn't have time later. Sometimes, Hannah thought her mom just liked to find reasons to be stressed and that she wouldn't be satisfied until her children were equally stressed.

As Hannah walked down the sidewalk, beads of sweat dripped down her chest, this New York summer being even more humid than the last. A man sped past, knocking her bag off her shoulder so that a bundle of oranges fell to the ground and rolled along the pavement. She stood still for a moment as her mom's words continued buzzing in her ear, then looked up at the sky, exasperated.

"Mom, I have to go." Hannah hung up before her mom had the chance to say goodbye.

That was their last conversation.

Her mom wanted to be buried in Egypt, on family burial ground, next to grandparents and other dead relatives Hannah didn't care about, so she and her family were flying out right away. In Islam, the body has to be buried as soon as possible.

Just a few months earlier, the whole family was supposed to visit Egypt, but they'd canceled their trip, her parents wanting to wait until the political situation stabilized—was less dangerous, they'd said. This, now, wasn't the family trip they were supposed to take.

At the airport, Zain was hungover, it was obvious. He arrived separately from Hannah and their dad, his usually coiffed black hair disheveled, dark circles under his eyes, his T-shirt stained with last night's drinks. He reached in for a hug, smelling like alcohol—not fresh like he was still drunk, but stale and mixed with morning breath. Hannah hugged him and said nothing, and their dad didn't seem to notice as they silently walked through airport security, avoiding the glances of TSA agents.

On the plane, scrunched into a middle seat between two strangers, Hannah shut her eyes, hoping to sink into darkness, the backs of her eyelids pulling her away from the world until she didn't exist anymore. They couldn't get seats together since the trip was so last minute. Hannah shifted her legs, crossing and uncrossing them until she could get into a comfortable enough position, with the little airline pillow as a cushion behind her back. She wanted to sleep and never wake up, her dreams preferable to this waking nightmare.

When the news broke, her boss at Legal Aid had told her to take as many days as she liked, but she only had about a month left before law school. Could she take off the entire month and never return? Two years of work just to end in tragedy and a disappearing act.

She woke to the sound of the pilot announcing their landing—a reminder that she couldn't sleep forever—then a thump as the wheels released beneath her, her body bouncing as the plane hit the ground.

When they stepped foot in Egypt, the smell, as they walked toward customs, was of cheap cologne and sweat mixed with something familiar: dust, but dust specific to Egypt, with lingering remnants of cigarettes and musk.

Her mom usually complained when they landed. "The flight was horrible." Then more complaints when they went through customs. "This line is a mess. They're so disorganized. Egyptians don't know what they're doing." She was the first to defend Egypt against slander but also the first to insult it. "I could never live here again." And when the revolution had started—the protests in the streets—she'd said she wanted to be a part of it. That it was inspiring. But when the topic of visiting in that time was broached, she'd rejected it flat out. "Are you crazy?" she'd said. "It's dangerous."

Hannah joined her dad and brother in silence as they waited in line. They moved forward as though in a dream, reality melting into a bad acid trip where nothing was real—nothing made sense. How could her mom be dead? Hannah half expected to wake up in a sweat, consumed by nothing more than a nightmare, but this wasn't a dream.

Now, watching her dad rush them through customs, collect their bags, and usher them outside to hail a taxi, she felt nothing—numb, a body detached from a soul. As they walked through the doors, a burst of dry heat hit them and the smell of cigarettes permeated the air. In the past, familiar faces in the crowd had greeted them, leaving lipstick-stain kisses on both cheeks, squeezing them with unwanted hugs. This time, people they didn't know embraced one another and smiled. The three of them walked past the crowds, embracing no one, and stood at the curb.

"In the cab, don't say anything," her dad said, raising his hand toward a small black-and-white taxi. She knew the routine, and yet one of her parents warned them every time, worried they'd open their mouths and in English or broken Arabic give themselves away as tourists.

Hannah sat next to Zain on the sticky, cracked leather seats. She looked up at the Arabic street signs, slowly reading the calligraphy with her elementary reading level, only attained because when they were growing up, their mom had forced them to take lessons. Hannah and Zain, attempting to rebel, wouldn't have their homework done in time for their lesson, and each week the teacher would report back with fresh complaints. It was Zain's fault, really. Hannah just followed his lead until, one day, their mom ended the lessons entirely. She and Zain cheered, but their mom was disappointed, her muted anger more powerful than their dad's yelling. Hannah never talked about it with Zain. Instead, she celebrated the victory silently and knew he did too.

As they drove, they passed the familiar billboards—Vodafone

and Nike. The driver had his window open, and Hannah looked down, blinking the dust out of her eyes as pools of water formed in the corners. She couldn't tell if the tears were allergies or grief—if grief, then the numbness must have been wearing off as reality sank in. They slowed for traffic, eventually coming to a full stop, and the driver leaned his hand on the horn, mumbling, "Ibn el kalb." Cars swerved in and out of lanes, but there weren't really any lanes in the first place, just faded lines no one paid attention to. They began to move again, but a moment later, the driver hit the brakes, stopping inches from the car in front. Next to them was an old brown station wagon with a group of teenage boys on the roof. They were smiling and singing some song in Arabic, and briefly, Hannah made eye contact with one of the boys. His eyes were lighter than her own dark brown. His were a hazelish-green color, not typical in Egyptians. His coral T-shirt had holes in the sleeves, and he smiled and waved. She looked away.

Hannah shut her eyes and leaned back, the gentle vibration of the car against her head lulling her in and out of sleep. Sleeping was easier than thinking. People always complained that they couldn't sleep when they were stressed or sad or anxious, but Hannah never had that problem. The only way she knew how to deal with this grief was to sleep through it—if she could just get the chance. There were shouts in the distance now.

Tahrir Square. She recognized it almost immediately. The grassy traffic circle with the Egyptian flag poking out of the center. Tents from previous months of protests lined the outer edges, and crowds held up signs, Arabic writing illegibly scrawled across. But the revolution was over. A new president was in place. What was this about? The shouting wasn't quite clear—something about *"water"* and *"light,"* distinct repetitive chants. A few weeks ago her mom had said something about power outages across Cairo. Maybe this was related. They drove past the square, and the chants quieted. Hannah leaned her head back again, and they drove for a while more as she began to doze, until finally, the car came to a complete stop.

Outside was the apartment she'd been to a handful of times over the years. It was the apartment her mom had grown up in, old now, covered in a layer of dust so thick that you almost couldn't see the chipped paint and graffiti underneath. This was supposed to be a nice neighborhood, quieter than much of the city. As they stepped out of the car, the dry heat hit like a concrete wall, blocking the dreamlike path she'd been gliding along, waking her up to the fact that they were here for her mom's funeral, her dead body on its way to the mosque at that very moment.

She gasped. Her lungs felt like they were collapsing, being crushed under the weight of grief. She hoped her dad and brother didn't notice. She wanted to disappear, to stop existing, for this moment to end altogether. She wanted something drastic to happen—perhaps a sandstorm. They were in Egypt, after all. A rush of wind enveloping only her, pulling her away from here until she became part of the sand herself.

At the building entrance, a young boy in tattered clothing arose from his lawn chair and grabbed their luggage, saying he'd take it upstairs. Before anyone could protest, they followed him into the building, which had no elevator. They trekked up the un-air-conditioned stairwell, and Hannah watched as the boy balanced three bags in his arms and over his shoulders.

"Dad, he's a kid," Hannah whispered, her voice echoing off the concrete walls. "We can carry our own bags."

"He wants to get a tip," her dad said. "Let him."

Hannah looked up at the boy, who was several steps ahead of

them, barely breaking a sweat, while they carried nothing, their breaths growing heavy as they followed. The stairwell was dark and stuffy, with slivers of light shining in from the tiny windows, square openings with no glass or screen.

They reached the fourth floor, and as Hannah looked at the green wooden door, she began to bite her chapped lip—an old habit her mom hated. She'd always scolded Hannah for her chapped, peeling lips that would sometimes bleed from picking at them. Her dad knocked, and a few seconds later, her grandmother opened the door, dressed entirely in black, with a black headscarf covering her hair. She held a tissue up to her pink, puffy eyes. This would be excruciating—the whole grieving relatives thing. Hannah had no idea how to act or what to say, or what performance of grief they expected, and all she wanted was to be alone.

Hannah's grandmother tucked away her tissue and pulled her forward, kissing both cheeks without saying a word, then did the same with Zain and their dad.

"Yasmeen is on her way," her dad said, pulling some cash from his wallet for the boy who'd carried their luggage.

"Shukran, ya basha." The boy grabbed the cash and ran back down the stairs.

Yasmeen is on her way. Like her mom was just in another car, running late.

Inside, the walls were covered in family photos—of her and Zain, of their cousins, their mom, their aunt and uncle. Hannah scanned the room and held her breath. One of her great-aunts came out of the kitchen and greeted them with a kiss on each cheek. Seeing the whole family made it real, and while it still seemed like a dream, the wet kiss, the sweet perfumes, the lipstick she wiped from her cheek were all more vivid than any dream she'd ever had. Knowing this was real was like falling—the floor disappearing beneath her feet, and despite it all, she had to keep standing.

Her dad turned to Hannah and Zain. "We should change. We don't have much time."

When her mom arrived at the mosque, the funeral would begin, no embalmment, no waiting period. That was the way Muslims did it.

Hannah looked down at her blue jeans and gray T-shirt. She hadn't thought to dress in black on the plane. Clothes weren't even on her mind.

In the bathroom, she held a black dress in her hands and looked in the mirror, her large round eyes pooling with tears. She could see her mom in those eyes, and in her cheekbones, and even in the little pout she made with her lips. Her face now was dewy, her brown skin glowing with its summer tan. The dress she held was one she wore to work, usually. Professional-looking, just above the knees, but she put some black opaque tights on to cover her legs, her hands shaking the entire time.

Zain

Zain was in a bar when he got the news their mom died. At first, he thought maybe he hadn't heard correctly, or that this was some kind of twisted joke, but his dad didn't seem to be joking. Everything happened in slow motion after that. Emily asked what was wrong, and they went outside. His dad was crying on the other end of the line. He couldn't understand everything being said. There had to be some mistake. Some misunderstanding. It was like time had ceased to exist, and the world was folding in on itself, the night sky and the sidewalk beneath his feet bending toward one another at an angle that wasn't real—the bar outside turning sideways into the atmosphere. He could barely stand, but later, Emily told him he was pacing back and forth the whole time, repeating the words "Dad, no, no, no, no." He didn't remember any of this. He only remembered the pain, the feeling of a brick dropping in his stomach, the weight of it bringing him down, its sharp edges scratching against his insides.

A little later, the rest of his friends were outside too. They all hugged him, said they were sorry. It was like a scene in a movie, and Zain knew how he was supposed to act. He should have been crying as he accepted his friends' condolences. He should have been saying how much he loved her, how he couldn't believe she was gone. He'd seen enough movies. But he was frozen. He hadn't yet shed a tear.

"Why don't I take you home?" Emily asked, rubbing her hand against his arm as he stared at the empty street in front of him.

The rest of his friends insisted on coming along, saying he'd feel better if they were all there—support or some shit like that. They all walked back to his apartment together and, when they got inside, almost immediately continued to drink. Everyone said they'd be there for him, that they loved him, that it would all be okay. But how would it be okay? His mom was dead. And maybe she was watching him getting slowly drunk instead of sobering up and going home to be with his dad and sister.

His friends eventually left, but Emily stayed. With everyone else gone, he finally broke down—lying next to her in bed, his shoulders shaking as he sobbed into her chest. She cried too, until just a few hours later, it was morning, and she drove him to the airport.

Now, they were in Egypt, and still he could barely believe it. He changed quickly, into a black suit and tie—one his mom had bought for him a couple of years back for a relative's wedding. He remembered going with her to the store, where they'd argued for a minute over the fit, Zain insisting on a slimmer cut to match his slim stature, his mom criticizing him for being too thin. Though he'd bulked up slightly since that time, the suit still fit, but he'd never imagined back then that she was helping him shop for her own funeral.

As he stood in the apartment's foyer, waiting for everyone to finish getting ready, one of his mom's younger cousins, Hatem, approached. Zain nodded at him and looked down at his phone, hoping Hatem wouldn't have anything to say—or at least that his dad or sister would show up, saving him from having to make awkward small talk.

Hatem didn't say anything right away, and instead looked over his shoulder twice, then came up and stood close to Zain, who leaned back as his personal space was being invaded.

"This is very hard for you and Hannah," Hatem whispered.

Zain just nodded, taking a small step away.

"Do you like hashish?"

Zain looked up quizzically. There was no segue, no normal transition. It felt like a trap—if he said yes, he'd be caught, and Hatem would run back to tell the rest of the family. But Hatem continued speaking in whispers before Zain could even respond.

"I have some." He pulled a box of cigarettes out of his back pocket, and in the box was a small ziplock bag of what looked like weed, along with some rolling paper and matches. "Here, take it."

Zain reached out slowly. "Why are you giving this to me?"

"To help," Hatem said.

Hannah

They went straight to the mosque, an ornate building with a domed rooftop, once white but now the same color as everything else in Cairo: dusty tan. The inside wasn't shy of color, though. Red wall-to-wall carpets with a gold flower trim covered the floor. The walls were a mosaic tile pattern of blue, gold, and purple, with intricate designs and Quranic verse all around. Everyone took off their shoes at the entrance and stepped onto the soft, plush carpet, which felt like a cushion beneath Hannah's feet. She put on a black cardigan and covered her hair with a black scarf. At the entrance, her grandmother pulled her in another direction.

"Dad—" Hannah turned her body to face him as her grandmother tugged on her arm.

"It's okay." He nodded. "We'll meet you after."

She'd known this was coming, but she wasn't ready, wanting to stay with her dad and Zain. Zain looked at her, a pained expression on his face, and he walked over and pulled her in for a hug. They rarely hugged, and when they did, it was quick and careless—goodbye, hello. This hug was different. Zain squeezed tightly. It was the way her mom used to hug her—warm, enclosing her in her arms like they wouldn't see each other again. Her grandmother pulled her by the shoulder, and they split apart.

On the second floor, they stood at a balcony above the men, like the upper level of a theater. At the front of the mosque was a plain wooden box, covered in a black velvet sheet with gold Arabic letters stitched in. A verse from the Quran. Hannah could see her dad and Zain down below in the front row, just a few feet from the coffin. She clenched her teeth, tightening her jaw. It felt as though someone was pounding on her chest, trying to wake her from this nightmare.

It wasn't fair that she couldn't be up front, closer. She'd argued with her parents about these rules when she was younger. Why should the men be in the front, women in the back? "Because we bend over to pray," they'd both say, as if it were a rehearsed speech with set answers. "Men shouldn't be looking at women bent over when they're praying. They should focus on the prayer." There was no way her parents really bought that rhetoric, but they sure as hell sold it. Now, she was standing at her mom's funeral, not allowed at the front for fear she'd distract the men.

In front of the coffin stood a microphone. A man in a black traditional galabiya and a white rounded cap walked up. The Imam. He began by reciting the opening verse of the Quran, his voice echoing through the room, musical in its tenor.

"Bismillah al-rahman al-rahim."

Relatives and friends, both familiar and not, stood shoulder to shoulder, all looking down, their hands folded across their stomachs as prayer began. Under her breath, Hannah recited those words her mom had had her memorize so many years before.

"Alhamdulillahi rab al-alameen . . ."

Her mom would sit across from her in her bedroom, having Hannah repeat those verses over and over. Each night after learning a new verse, Hannah had to recite it until it became a habit. She still remembered most of the prayers.

Now, though, she could barely focus, her mind racing with images of her mom, one after another, like a film reel. Her mom teaching her to pray, telling her to bend, stand, bend, kneel. She remembered standing in the women's section of the mosque every year during Eid, next to her mom, who instructed her to focus on God. She wasn't focused on God in this moment, though. Instead, she wanted to scream. And then the prayer was over.

As soon as they stepped back outside, she removed the scarf from her head and took off the cardigan, and her uncle drove them to the burial site, the other cars following behind.

When they arrived, they stopped in front of a courtyard with dusty gray walls enclosing her family's burial site. They stepped out, and her dad and Zain walked toward the car that held her mom. Her dad had explained all this at the airport. The four closest male relatives would carry the coffin into the graveyard. That meant her dad, Zain, her uncle, and, it appeared now, her mom's cousin. Together they'd go down into the grave and place the body.

Zain's face looked so pale. He was always the sensitive one between the two of them—the one who wouldn't be able to handle carrying their mom's body into a grave. But he was the boy. It had to be him. Hannah could do it, though. She *wanted* to. The men pulled the coffin out, a simple wooden box, no longer covered in fabric. Her dad grabbed one end first, along with her uncle, and then the cousin. Zain was last, only reaching forward when their dad said, "Zain, yallah."

Hannah walked behind them, and other male relatives tried to push ahead and help. She kept close, but they told her to step back. Her dad never mentioned that she wouldn't be allowed near the front for this part too.

"Why?" she asked, quickening her pace so that she was at the front with her dad. He looked forward, the front of the coffin resting on his shoulder, and Hannah, keeping pace, turned to him for an answer, knowing that he couldn't possibly have one. No one said anything, so she stood amid the group of men, close to her mother's body, as the women in the family followed behind. They weren't inside the mosque, so there was no need for separation here. She wasn't doing anything haram—she wouldn't let them push her back for this part.

When they stepped inside the grave area, it was nothing like those in America. The tombs were spread out, and instead of gravestones, each grave was covered in a large stone block bigger than a coffin. There was no grass, just dust and sand. They were walled in—protected. A man in a white galabiya stood watch at the entrance. Guardian of the graves. They stopped before an empty rectangular hole. Hannah looked up. Sweat dripped from the men's foreheads as they struggled to keep the box upright. A second or third cousin, Hannah didn't know which or even really the difference, stood next to her.

"They say if the coffin is light and moves fast, then God loves you, and you are blessed."

Was this cousin saying her mom was blessed? How would he know if the coffin was light? He wasn't carrying it. The men lowered the coffin so that it sat on the ground directly next to the grave. Hannah stood close by, but her grandmother pulled her back.

"Just the men."

The anger hit all at once, like a separate entity that controlled her movements. Her legs shaking, she ripped her arm away from her grandmother's grasp. She wouldn't cry or make a scene. She had to prove she could handle it. They opened the coffin, and as she inhaled, dust flew into her nostrils. Zain looked away. Her mom was wrapped in white linen. Hannah kept her gaze focused, unable to look anywhere else, imagining her mom's face beneath the cloth. Her brother stepped back and stood next to Hannah. He was crying, not looking.

Her dad and uncle lifted her mom's body from the coffin and gently placed her in the ground. The coffin wasn't going in with her. Her mom would hate that. Lying in the dirt.

2005

Hannah

"This is disgusting," her mom said the first time they visited Zain's apartment in college.

He was no longer living in a dorm, having graduated to campus apartments instead, where he lived with two other roommates. The family had come to Philly for the day, and Hannah was excited to see his college life—to see what it might be like for her in a couple of years, away from home for the first time.

When they walked into Zain's kitchen, Hannah immediately clocked the dishes in the sink, the crumbs on the countertops, dirty plates left out on the table. She knew right away her mom would have something to say about it.

Her mom was militant about cleanliness—keeping the house spotless as she vacuumed every day—and made sure everyone took their shoes off immediately upon entering, something Zain's and Hannah's white friends would sometimes forget as they dragged their street dirt inside. Hannah always reprimanded them, afraid she'd later get blamed when the floors weren't spotless.

And sure enough, here in Philly, her mom spoke up.

"How could you live like this? You've lived in a clean house all your life, and now you're in this disgusting place?" She looked down at the kitchen counters and shook her head.

"Mom, it's fine," Zain said.

The place was messy, sure, but not as bad as her mom made it out to be.

"This is really, really disgusting, Zain. You have to clean. I'm horrified."

She insisted on using hand sanitizer when they got back into the car.

SUMMER 2012

Hannah

Her mom's body would just lie here in the dirt, with no clean box, no decorum. It was part of the religion. Everyone began stepping away from the grave, but Hannah wasn't ready to go. Leaving her mom there would mean the end—it was over, and she wouldn't be back. Hannah couldn't accept that yet, and her feet stayed glued to the ground, the dirt, the earth, like she was a part of it now—she and her mom.

"Come on, Hannah." Her dad's voice was soft and somber, and he reached over to grab her arm.

"We can't leave her here." She was shaking, her voice cracking, so her dad stopped for a moment and held her.

"We can't leave," she repeated.

"Hannah, it's okay. She'll always be with us."

It wasn't okay. She was gone.

Her dad pulled her gently by the arm and began walking her away from the grave as she dragged her body along. No twenty-three-year-old was supposed to lose their mom. She was supposed to live so much longer. Tears blurred Hannah's vision, but she soon noticed everyone watching her. She wiped her face with her hand and ran it along her black dress, leaving behind streaks of dirt.

There were shovels next to the open grave, and her dad and a few of the men began to shovel the dirt over her mom's body, the white linen turning a dirty brown. Zain stood back, but Hannah reached for the shovel in her dad's hand, and he gave it to her. She had to do this. She couldn't let these men bury her mom on their own. Here she was, a crying mess, likely adding fuel to their idea that women couldn't handle this kind of thing, and so she had to prove them wrong.

A few minutes later, the gravedigger motioned for them to put their shovels down, so they stepped back, watching him complete the task himself. They watched until they couldn't see her anymore, until her body was fully submerged in the ground. People began to leave, starting with the women, but Hannah couldn't step away. It was like there was a magnetic pull on her body. If she could just get a moment alone with her mom, without all the other relatives surrounding her, maybe—

"Dad, can we stay for a bit?" Zain asked, as though reading her mind.

"We have to go back, Zain. Everyone will be waiting. But we can come back tonight."

"Dad, you go." Hannah kept her eyes on the mound of dirt that covered her mom's body. "Zain and I will catch up."

She could feel her dad's eyes on both of them, and she knew how she must look, sweating and covered in dirt, dried-up tears staining her cheeks, her nose runny from crying.

"You two can't stay here alone. It's dangerous. How will you get back?"

"Taxi," Zain said.

"No, not alone. Especially with Egypt being the way it is right now. The political situation—"

"Dad, we've both traveled alone before." Hannah looked up at him now. He was watching them with concern, squinting to keep the Cairo sun out of his eyes. "Plus, I have that pepper spray you gave me. And we can handle taking a taxi."

"Will you be okay?" He looked from Hannah to Zain. They both nodded.

He told them to be careful and gave Zain specific directions on what to tell the driver. Their uncle gave them his cell phone. They were adults, but the family treated them like children—teenagers who couldn't fend for themselves—and it was easy to just accept it. Technically, they *were* the children.

Their dad left with the group, under obligation to sit with guests in the apartment. Zain and Hannah were left alone, looking down at the plot of dirt. As they stood there, she asked Zain if his hangover had passed. She was provoking him. They were Muslim. They didn't drink. That was the lie they told their parents. It was the lie they told each other.

"What?" His hands were in his pockets, and he looked toward her, feigning ignorance.

"Your breath smelled like alcohol before the flight." She wasn't crying anymore.

She didn't know why she was bringing this up, here at the funeral. Zain's drinking wasn't a surprise, but she was tired of them pretending to be good Muslim kids, lying even to each other. They didn't know one another, not really. And now, with their mom gone, they had to build their own relationship outside of her.

"Fuck. Hannah—" He took a step back and reached his hands up toward his face.

"I'm not judging you," she said, looking at the ground and making a circle in the dirt with her foot. "I'm just sick of the secrets."

They both stared down at the gravesite.

"Do *you* drink?" Zain glanced back up at her.

She clenched her jaw. They were standing over their mom's grave, and maybe it was guilt or shame or a combination of both because their mom would be so disappointed. She had ingrained in them a sense of values that couldn't be broken, and as hard as Hannah tried, she couldn't escape that. People talked about Catholic guilt, but Muslim guilt was real too.

Hannah nodded.

She and Zain had been lying to one another for years. She didn't know when he'd started, but for her, the lies had begun in sixth grade, when Adam Harrison asked her to be his girlfriend and she started a two-week relationship with a boy, afraid her parents or brother would find out. Since then, it had been one lie after another.

"I just don't want to keep secrets anymore," Hannah said.

2002

Zain

"Nour found alcohol in Sayeed's room," his mom said over dinner.

Sayeed was Zain's age, but they went to different high schools. Zain was never stupid enough to bring alcohol home.

"Sayeed *drinks*?" Hannah said, wide-eyed.

Zain looked up from his plate. "What did his mom do?"

"She threw it away, and he said it was his friend's, but she doesn't believe him." His mom reached forward and scooped some rice up from the serving platter, adding it to Zain's plate unprompted. "I told her to send him back to Egypt." She laughed.

Zain looked down at the overabundance of rice in front of him.

"Mom, that's a little extreme."

"I know, but she doesn't pay attention to who his friends are," she said between bites. "Of course this happens if he spends time with the wrong crowd."

The wrong crowd. What was the right crowd? Zain's friends were no different, but somehow, he'd managed to hide that.

"Those kids have no religion," his dad said. "Nour and that idiot she's married to don't teach them anything. What did she expect?"

Zain swallowed a mouthful of rice, keeping silent. Just a few days earlier, he'd gotten almost blackout drunk at a friend's sleepover, despite the religion he'd grown up with.

"So what are they gonna do to him?" Hannah asked, gleefully soaking up the drama.

SUMMER 2012

Zain

Zain looked down at the plot of dirt that held their mom. The fact of Hannah drinking didn't surprise him, though he always saw her as the wholesome one—or maybe he just didn't think of her as having a life outside of their family at all. As kids, they were taught that alcohol was a sin, raised to judge American culture with its loud, obnoxious drinkers, as if all of America consisted of frat boys holding a Budweiser. At restaurants, his parents would hand back the drink menu with a sense of superiority as they said, "No, we don't drink." Growing up, Zain bought his parents' rhetoric. When he was ten, he'd proudly declared he'd never drink, just as most ten-year-olds rocking their D.A.R.E. T-shirts declared they'd never do drugs.

But in middle school everything had changed. Friends who'd once spent their days trading Pokémon cards were now sneaking into their parents' liquor cabinets, and by eighth grade, Zain had already had his first beer and his first kiss. When he went home that afternoon, four pieces of gum in his mouth, he looked over at fourth grader Hannah on the other side of the dinner table, eating their mom's stuffed grape leaves and breaded chicken, and felt he wouldn't be able to explain himself to her. Now he was twenty-seven and still hiding.

"When did you start drinking?" Zain asked Hannah, looking out toward the street at a man passing by in a galabiya.

"College. Freshman year."

She was straightforward, quick to answer, but kept her gaze on their mom's grave. Unlike him, it seemed Hannah had remained innocent through high school. He wanted to ask more questions, afraid of what she'd tell him. They kept so many secrets from one another.

"When did *you* start drinking?"

Hannah turned her head toward him, and now it was his turn to look down at the grave.

"Middle school," he replied, avoiding eye contact.

"Jesus."

Zain shifted his stance, rocking his body forward and back. "Mom and Dad didn't watch me as closely."

"Yeah, I remember."

He looked up at Hannah, then back down at the plot of dirt in front of them. "Maybe we shouldn't talk about this over Mom's grave. She wouldn't want to hear this."

They were supposed to believe in life after death, in heaven and hell, and if they believed in that, they should believe she was watching them from heaven. Maybe all that was left was her body, flesh and bones, cold now, soon to be consumed by maggots. Maybe he should pray for her? That was what you were supposed to do, but he couldn't. Something about it seemed insincere. Like praying sacrilegiously would be worse than not praying at all.

He and Hannah had never been super close, but she was the

only one who could understand what they'd lost—what their mom meant. No one would ever love them that much again. Last time he'd been home, he'd been working in his room when his mom had walked in without a word and handed him a bowl of cut strawberries and a cup of tea, like only a mom would.

"Don't stay up too late," she'd said, tousling his hair on her way out.

They decided to head back to the apartment, where their dad and the relatives would be waiting. Though that was the last thing he wanted—their condolences. Their judgment. Before the funeral, when he'd walked in wearing jeans and a green T-shirt, his forearm tattoo visible, they'd looked down at his arm and wouldn't look away. It was as though he'd committed a sin right there in front of them, and his mom's death didn't matter because he'd marked up his arm and marked himself for hell, despite the fact that his tattoo was a crescent moon and star.

He'd gotten it on a whim one day while out with friends, though he'd been thinking about it for a while. Afterward, he'd called his mom because this was a secret he wouldn't be able to keep. She'd yelled, told him he was an idiot, that he would regret it when he got older. When he saw her one week later, she'd calmed down, probably accepting that more yelling would be futile.

"Huh," she'd said, her eyes resting on his arm. "It actually looks kind of neat." Zain had smiled and hugged her. She'd never approve, but that was enough.

As they left the gravesite, he pulled at the front of his shirt, stuck now to his sweaty skin. It was upward of eighty degrees, and he still wore his suit and tie. The sweat dripped down his chest, so he peeled his jacket off, looking down at the stains on his pressed white button-down. They walked toward the street and hailed a cab. Men passed by and glared at Hannah but said nothing. Zain stood closer to her. Maybe with a man by her side, she wouldn't get harassed. He was thin, with a face others said was young for his age, so he never felt all that threatening.

"Hello, very pretty," a man said in English as they passed. A small black-and-white taxi stopped in front of them, and Zain pushed Hannah inside first.

The smell of their sticky, sweet sweat filled the cab, and their black clothes were now stained with spots of brown dust. Streaks of dirt sat on Hannah's face. As they drove, there were shouts in the distance. They were passing Tahrir again.

"What do you think they're protesting?" Hannah asked, looking out the car window. "I thought the revolution was over."

"I don't think they're very happy with Morsi. They had two bad choices for president."

He had been following the situation in Egypt closely, dreaming that he could be in the field reporting on it—or just that his boss at the newspaper would assign him something substantial to work on for once.

When they arrived back at the apartment, relatives sat in the living room, drinking tea and sharing stories. They immediately bombarded Zain and Hannah with their pity, saying sorry and that their mom was in a better place. It was suffocating, like the air had stagnated with a cloud of bitter despair. Hannah finally said she needed to rest in the other room, and he immediately followed, grateful to his sister for finding a way out.

In their mom's childhood bedroom that she had shared with their aunt, each of them sleeping on a separate twin bed, Zain lay down above the polka-dot blanket that had probably been there since the '60s. He could breathe in here, without the circling crows asking if he was okay, if he needed anything, talking about how sad they all were.

Zain couldn't remember which bed was his mom's and which was his aunt's, but on the headboard of the bed he was lying on were stickers of Disney characters—Mickey and Minnie and Cinderella. He shut his eyes and tried to picture his mom as a kid putting stickers on her headboard.

"Hey, what is this?" Hannah held out a photo and a packet of papers she'd taken out of the nightstand drawer that sat between them.

Zain sat up.

"This picture," she said. "And these papers. AWSA?"

In her hands was an old picture of their mom with a group of women—probably in the '80s by the looks of everyone's outfits. They were all wearing T-shirts that read "AWSA," holding up posters and smiling.

"Arab Women's Solidarity Association. That's what this pamphlet says."

"Let me see." Zain grabbed the pamphlet out of Hannah's hand. "Arab women's liberation? Was Mom in some kind of activist group?" He smiled as he scanned the pages of the pamphlet, yellowed with age.

"She never said anything about it." Hannah pulled out a few more pictures from the drawer.

The pamphlet Zain held was filled with information about the rights of women in Egypt, statistics about injustices by the government, and what AWSA was trying to change.

"This is pretty cool." Zain could hear himself getting more animated now as they uncovered some of their mom's history, which she'd never spoken of. "Maybe it was, like, something she did in college."

When the revolution had started, his mom had obviously cared about what was going on—about her country—but never enough to want to get involved in anything. And before that, she'd never once talked about politics and women's rights in Egypt.

"There's a lot of pictures here." Hannah handed Zain a stack of photos.

Their mom was so young, smiling with her arms around her friends. In some of the photos, they were making posters.

"Yo, check this out," he said. "Did Mom go to protests?"

"No way." Hannah looked at the picture in Zain's hand.

Their mom had followed the news, had opinions, but she'd never been one to get involved. She'd studied law, but after they'd moved to America, she'd never taken the bar exam, instead working part-time at various office jobs as a receptionist and eventually a paralegal. Zain had always assumed she wasn't actually interested in law or politics—that it was just something she'd studied in school and then pressured Hannah to do as well. In fact, Zain was sure the first time she'd ever even voted was in 2008. But she'd never wanted to attend the Obama rallies with him and Hannah.

"I don't want to stand for that long," she'd said.

And yet here she was, making posters for a protest.

They flipped through the rest of the pictures, and more than anything, he wanted to run out of the room, find his mom sitting there with the family, and ask her about them. He wanted to laugh with her as she reminisced. But they'd never get that. All they had now were these pictures. His heart began to hurt, like fingers were slowly squeezing until the pressure was enough to make it implode. He couldn't call her anymore, couldn't reach out whenever he needed something. She was really just gone.

Zain leaned back on the bed. "Hey, this is gonna sound crazy, but do you wanna smoke?"

Hannah squinted, looking confused.

"I mean, I don't know if you smoke," he added quickly, "but I have some hash. Hashish. Pretty sure it's just like weed."

She leaned forward at the edge of her bed. "What the hell, Zain? Where'd you get it?"

"Hatem." He smiled.

"Mom's cousin?"

He told her the story from that morning, and she laughed.

"No way, this did not happen."

"I swear, it did." He pulled the bag out of his pocket. They were both laughing now. He hadn't thought they'd laugh today. "So, do you want to?"

She didn't say anything. Maybe he shouldn't have brought it up. It would be odd, smoking with his sister, when an hour ago they wouldn't have even admitted to one another that either of them smoked.

He shifted his body in his small bed. "Look, if you don't want to do it, we don't have to."

"I never said that," she answered from her own bed. "It's just such a weird thing to have happened. I didn't think Hatem was the type. And also, how will this even work? Logistically, I mean. Our entire family is right outside." She pointed toward the door, where they could hear the buzzing of voices from the living room.

"Well, if we crack a window . . ." Zain looked behind him at the shut window, but Hannah shook her head.

"No way, they'll still smell it. And someone might come in. Too risky."

"Stairwell?" Zain offered.

"Maybe the roof?"

As kids, they'd visited their grandparents and sat up on the building's rooftop balcony. No one else would be up there now.

They opened the door to the bedroom as quietly as they could and headed into the foyer. The chatter from the living room and the tape of Quranic verse would cover the sound of the apartment door opening and shutting. Even if the family did hear them, they could simply say they wanted to go out on the balcony for a bit. No one would bother them.

On the roof, they sat side by side on the floor with their backs leaning against the cement balcony walls. This was strange, letting Hannah in on a part of his life he'd kept secret for so long. His stomach rumbled, a physical manifestation of some kind of guilt, maybe, like he was the bad older brother, but it wasn't like Hannah was a little kid. It wasn't like she didn't smoke weed. They just didn't do it together. He'd certainly never imagined smoking with Hannah in their mom's childhood home.

The ground was dirty, but neither of them cared that their black clothes, already soiled from the morning, would be stained with the dust that had piled onto the rooftop floor. Zain pulled the ziplock bag from his pocket and glanced at Hannah, who was watching his hands.

"Maybe this is a bad idea," he said.

Hannah looked up at him. "Yeah, it is."

He shook his head and looked back down at the bag of hash. "Fuck it, let's just do this."

He hadn't felt bad for smoking since high school. He was always careful back then. His friends would get caught by their parents, but they'd simply get a quick lecture—maybe get grounded. If his own parents ever caught him, though, they'd be angry, sure, but more than that, they'd never trust him, never look at him the same way. He'd be the disappointment. His mom would cry and feel like she'd failed with him. That was just how it was with Arab, Muslim parents.

Now, this guilt—this was new. Or old, really—a familiar stomach-churning sense of unease that he hadn't felt in years. If their mom was watching, if there really was an afterlife, she would be so disappointed.

Zain opened the bag, releasing the familiar skunky smell, though not as strong as that of weed in America. He rolled and lit the joint, took two puffs, and reluctantly handed it to Hannah. She was always the baby of the family—his kid sister, even if she *was* twenty-three now. He leaned his head back and listened to the chatter and car horns from the streets below.

He shifted his body, placing one leg under the other. The concrete floor pressed up on his bones as he sat. Hannah passed the joint back, and he took another hit, shifting his position again. Weed usually relaxed him, but now there was something foreboding in the air, in the sounds of the city, harsh and grating with each car horn, each shout, each jovial chant from down below. He and Hannah weren't talking. Maybe there was nothing left to say. His heart began to race. Their family was sure to notice they were missing.

"We should go soon." Zain passed her the joint. "They might be looking for us."

Hannah took one final puff and put the finished joint out on the ground, then wiped her hands on her now-filthy tights.

"We should talk more," she said as she began to stand, and Zain's heart slowed. "I don't know anything about you. Are you also in an activist group I don't know about?"

He laughed. Where to even start? Their conversations were always superficial—about movies or TV shows. Hannah was right. She didn't know him, and he didn't really know her either.

"We'll talk more," he promised.

He meant that. They would be a part of one another's lives now, especially since their mom could no longer be the bridge bringing them together. He was the older brother. He would make an effort. He would call his sister on the phone, for starters.

They sat in silence for a while more before heading back down. Inside the apartment, everything remained the same. Hannah immediately got into her bed, as Zain stood in the doorway. Their mom was dead, and they were just meant to sleep in her old room. His heart was beating fast again, and he couldn't sit down.

"What are you doing?" Hannah asked.

He shook his head and saw Hannah watching him, so he walked to his bed and sat. Everything was moving in slow motion, and that feeling of the room bending in on itself was back—just like the night he'd found out about all this. He needed to be somewhere else. He lay down and shut his eyes. Maybe then the room wouldn't shift and fold.

"I wonder what else is in here?" Hannah asked.

Zain opened his eyes and saw Hannah sitting up now. "What do you mean?"

"I don't know—Mom's stuff."

She was standing, opening more drawers, flipping through articles of clothing. If he went through his mom's things, the entire room would collapse in on itself, he was sure. He couldn't bring himself to be as curious as Hannah. She should just leave it alone.

Suddenly there was a knock at the door, and Zain jolted upright. It was their dad, coming to tell them the ceremony would continue in the mosque.

"Zain, are you ready?"

He nodded. Would his dad smell the hashish on them?

"Hannah, the women are staying here," their dad said from the doorway. "They're listening to Quran in the living room."

"What?" She looked ready to fight, her face contorting into outrage. "No, I'm going with you."

"This is men only." Their dad shook his head.

But Hannah ignored their dad, picked up her phone, and stood up.

"I'm coming. She's my mom."

Her voice was shaking. Meanwhile, Zain was still sitting in bed, his head cloudy, eyes practically begging to shut. He'd give anything to be in her place—the one allowed to stay home.

"Dad, let her come," Zain said, his sense of balance slightly off as he stood up. He didn't know how he'd get through the rest of the day.

Sighing, their dad nodded, motioning for the two of them to follow him. He'd explained this part to Zain at the airport. They weren't going to the mosque just for prayer. They would also sit and accept people's condolences while an Imam read from the Quran.

Shuffling behind their dad into the apartment foyer, where the men waited, Zain watched Hannah walk with determination, as though ready to defend herself against the others, who would surely comment on her decision to join them. Zain, though, trailed behind, shutting his eyes for a moment as he walked, taking in the scent of garlic and herbs that filled the apartment.

"She's coming with us?" his uncle said when they reached the rest of the group at the door.

"Yes, she wants to come," his dad said, resolute and offering no other explanation.

No one protested, and they headed out. Zain watched his

dad, whose face looked more like he was angry than grieving. He didn't make eye contact with anyone as he shuffled into the front seat of the car.

"Is the air okay?" his uncle said, slicing through the silence.

"Mm," his dad said, nodding.

Their dad had barely said a word to him and Hannah since they'd landed. Even before, at the airport, they'd just sat together in silence. It was impossible to tell how he was taking it, and Zain didn't know how to bridge the gap between them, so he just looked out the window and kept on with the silence.

They entered the mosque from a different door this time, walking into a room with blue walls and the same red carpet, with plastic chairs for them to sit in. The Imam from this morning stood at the front of the room and began to recite a verse from the Quran in his melodic, musical voice. The chairs were hard, like the concrete floor on the balcony. Zain looked at his dad, whose hands were cupped together as he said a prayer under his breath. When he finished, he looked up at Zain and Hannah.

"We'll be okay," he said with tears in his eyes. "I love you both so much, and I know we can get through this together. Your mother would be so proud of you both." It was the first thing about their mother he'd said to them in a while.

Zain looked down and adjusted his body on the uncomfortable chair. He couldn't help but think that "proud" was not the word he would've chosen. They were high at her funeral, after all.

Eventually, people began to flow in, each person stopping to say their individual condolences.

"We loved Yasmeen."

"Yasmeen was so kind."

"One of the kindest women we've ever known."

Some of them he knew, and others he hadn't seen in years.

"You were this tall last time I saw you," they'd say, gesturing to some arbitrary height.

Zain leaned forward in his seat and pushed his palms to his forehead. He couldn't breathe, suffocated by condolences and well wishes—too many people breathing too much air. He needed to get out.

"How much longer, do you think?" Hannah whispered to him.

He looked up and shook his head slowly, watching a few more people enter the mosque. "No idea."

His dad abruptly stood as a man and woman entered together, the man in a black suit and tie, the woman in a long black flowing dress and a black headscarf. Zain looked up at his dad, who furrowed his eyebrows, his face expressing a combination of anger and alarm.

"What are you two doing here?" he said in Arabic. His voice was deeper in register than what Zain had grown used to.

Zain and Hannah sat up straighter and looked from their dad to the two strangers.

"Yasmeen was our friend," the woman said. Her eyes were red and puffy. Something about her seemed familiar, like he'd seen her face before. The man too. Zain stared, trying to recall where he'd seen them before.

"You shouldn't have come." His dad was still standing, as though trying to intimidate them into leaving, however unlikely, given that Zain's slim stature was a carbon copy of his father's. "You haven't spoken to Yasmeen in years."

Their uncle stood too and placed his hand on their dad's shoulder.

"Yousef, it's okay," he said. He gestured with his other hand for him to sit. "Let them say goodbye."

"We're sorry," the man said, almost in a whisper. The woman glanced at Hannah and Zain, and Zain quickly looked down.

"Are these your kids?" She pointed toward them.

Their dad nodded, and the woman approached. Zain stood, while Hannah remained seated next to him. "We were friends with your mom in university." She smiled. "My name is Noha, and this is Hamada."

Hannah got up now too, and they shook hands with the couple, who offered their condolences, saying how much they loved Yasmeen and how they wished they could have stayed in touch over the years. Zain looked over at his dad, whose body remained stiff and unwelcoming. Looking back at the smiling couple, it dawned on him. Zain had seen their faces just recently, in the photos from his mom's bedroom. But of course, they were all younger then, without the wrinkles that now formed around their eyes and foreheads, or the gray hairs that peeked out from under the woman's hijab and were sprinkled atop the man's head.

Before Zain could even think to question them further, they offered their condolences one last time, apologizing to their dad for disturbing him on this day as they made their way out of the mosque, the woman wiping her eyes with a crumpled tissue she held in her hand.

Hannah

Hannah was at the airport when she made the decision. Her dad and Zain were checking in at a different area, flying to Philly, while she was supposed to be in line checking in for her New

York flight. Her knees began to shake, like they sometimes did in the cold. Only now, it was summer and the airport AC was incredibly weak. From there, her stomach seemed to flip on itself, like her organs were fighting to climb out, and a wave of nausea began to rise, stopping just below her throat.

What was the point of going back? Fly to New York, start law school, and then what? Maybe law school, this whole time, was just to make her parents proud, and now her mom, the person who had pressured her to apply in the first place, wasn't even here to see. Maybe Egypt was where she needed to be, and her body was trying to tell her. Law school was just three years of studying for a job she didn't really want.

She made the decision without even thinking, really—her body acting independently. She knew she couldn't get on the plane, couldn't leave her mom here. It was almost like she was on autopilot when it all happened, like someone else was in control. She pulled out her phone and quickly searched Airbnb. She couldn't go back to her grandmother's house, because her relatives would just call her dad, who would be on the next flight over, dragging her back to New York, so she found a small apartment that she could book immediately for a price way cheaper than anything back home. When making the reservation, she felt nothing but the magnetic force pulling her away from America. This was the right decision. It had to be, because the shaking in her knees stopped and the nausea subsided. Her stomach was at rest.

In the minutes that followed, it was like a part of her brain turned back on, but not the part with feelings and emotions. Just the part that wanted to survive—wanted to make this work. She didn't have enough clothes for more than a week. Maybe Zain could send her some stuff. And her apartment. Someone would have to pack up all her shit. But it was fine. She would worry about all that later.

For now, she would map her way to the just-booked apartment while she still had Wi-Fi, and she could take a bus back into the city so as not to waste money on a cab. The next bus would arrive in thirty minutes. She searched her bag and found the pepper spray her dad had given her when they landed—a "safety precaution" in case they got separated—and shoved it into her back pocket. Outside the airport, she stood at the bus stop next to a man that appeared to be her age, though she attempted not to make eye contact. Best to be wary of men in Egypt, given all the catcalling.

"Amrikaniya?"

"Huh?" Hannah looked up at the man next to her, who was distinctly Egyptian-looking, with large eyes and curly hair, tan skin sprinkled with little beads of sweat from the summer heat.

"You are American?" he repeated in English, pointing to the passport she was shoving into her bag.

"Oh, yeah."

It was hard to tell if he was just making friendly small talk or if it would progress to him hitting on her. She expected the catcalls, the possible grope from behind, things that occurred everywhere but even more so on the streets of Cairo. The bus, for this reason, made her nervous, but she knew she could handle it.

"Are you visiting?" he asked.

She wasn't sure how to answer that anymore. "Sort of. I don't know how long I'm staying." He nodded but looked confused. "My family is from here," she quickly added.

"Ah, Musriya?" he said.

"Yeah."

They continued to make small talk, and it didn't seem like he was hitting on her. Maybe he was just a nice person. He introduced himself as Zakaria and let her know that he was returning from a trip to Sharm El Sheikh, stuck on a different flight than his friends due to an error in booking.

He shuffled through his backpack and pulled out a pack of cigarettes.

"You want one?"

She didn't smoke, at least not when she was sober, but she said "Sure" and reached her hand out. She put the cigarette up to her lips and heard the scrape of match hitting matchbox as Zakaria held the fire near her mouth, hand cupped. She leaned forward and inhaled. What better way to fit in with Egyptians than to take up their habits—their bad ones, at least?

"You know," he said, shoving the matches into his pocket and taking a drag from his cigarette, "there's a street here in Cairo. It's the most dangerous street in Egypt, but instead of guns, everyone has samurai swords."

"Samurai swords?" Hannah smiled.

He ran his fingers in a scratching motion atop his tuft of curly black hair. His skinny jeans were surely tighter than hers, just like all Egyptian boys with their skinny jeans.

"That sounds cool." She wiped the beads of sweat from her forehead, and with her other hand, tapped her cigarette in the air and watched as bits of ash fell onto the dusty concrete. She hoped the cigarette would prove to be a sufficient distraction, something to hold besides a cell phone, hers now useless outside without Wi-Fi. She took another drag.

Her mom would disapprove of the cigarette.

She could hear her dad in her head too. *Stop talking to strangers at bus stops.*

"If you want, I can take you to the samurai street one day,"

Zakaria said. She faked a laugh, and he continued. “Or no, I will show you how to go there, and you call me if anything bad happens.” He paused and took another drag of his cigarette, then looked back at Hannah. “Actually, no, you won’t be able to call me because they’ll take your phone.”

This time, she laughed for real, flicking some more cigarette ash onto the ground, flecks of gray blending with the light brown dirt beneath her feet.

The airport bus finally arrived, fifteen minutes late, and they shuffled in, packed between other riders with hardly any room to breathe. Hannah’s shoulders leaned into Zakaria’s chest as they held the handrail above them, the scent of his cologne wafting through her nostrils and floating through the sweaty bodies that surrounded them.

The bus dropped them off in the middle of Cairo on a crowded street she wasn’t familiar with. She should have researched this area more carefully. The air smelled of cigarette smoke, and she sniffed her shirt to see if the scent was coming from her, only to be accosted by a puff of smoke from a man standing a few feet away. She looked around. The buildings were all the same dull tan shade, their former colors barely visible underneath the dust. Cars honked all around her, and music blasted from the speakers, the sounds of some new Arab pop she didn’t recognize. On the sidewalk where she stood, people scurried past, rushing off to work, school, the nady, or wherever. Hannah turned around and saw that the bus had already sped away, and she could see it in the distance swerving through traffic with no regard to lanes or laws. She pulled up a predownloaded map of Cairo on her phone, but it all looked the same to her—just an endless maze of roads and alleys in a city she didn’t know.

Zakaria was standing next to her, looking down at his own

phone, and in the midst of her silent worry, she barely noticed when he glanced over her shoulder at the map and asked if she needed any help.

Hannah looked up at him. "Um, maybe . . . what street is this?" Her nose crinkled as she looked back at her phone and zoomed in on the map.

"Where do you need to go?"

She pulled the address up from her phone's notes section. Maybe she should just take a cab there and give the driver the address. It was better than letting this stranger know where she was staying. She'd seen enough movies to know that was stupid.

She looked up, squinting in the sun. "You know, I could figure it out. I'll just take a taxi."

"Why? I know this area," Zakaria said. "Taxi is expensive. I can help for free."

Hannah pressed her lips together and nodded slowly. He seemed okay, like just a nice guy. Not everything was a movie. She showed him the note on her phone, hoping that her instincts were right on this one.

He nodded. "I know this street. Busy street. Famous for prostitution. I'll take you."

She looked up at him. Was he joking?

"This way. We can walk."

He pointed to the left of her and began pulling at her suitcase.

"I got it." She grabbed the suitcase from his hand. "But wait, famous for prostitution? Are you serious? Is that safe?"

"Eh, it's Egypt." He waved his hand in the air dismissively and trudged forward. "Not safe to walk alone at night but safe."

He gestured for her to follow him. A man bumped into her and shoved her slightly to the side. Zakaria kept walking. The street was crowded, and her shirt, now sticky with sweat, clung to her body as she zigzagged along the sidewalk, dragging her bag along behind her. She quickened her pace to keep up. Anytime she fell behind, men shouted something in her direction. Zakaria looked back.

"Let me take this for you." He reached for her suitcase. This time, she let him. She could do it herself, sure. She didn't need a man to help her. But the bag was heavy, it was so fucking hot, and she already had a backpack on. She thanked him, and without the suitcase, she could keep up. Men looked at her but remained silent. Maybe her black V-neck was too tight, the neckline too low? She pulled the shirt up slightly.

"You speak Arabic?" Zakaria asked, glancing at her walking beside him.

"Yeah."

His language switched then. *"So if I spoke to you in Arabic, you'd understand me?"*

The words strung together so seamlessly, so smoothly. There was something different in his Arabic than in her parents', even though the dialect remained the same. His tenor sounded almost musical, so that the language was more beautiful than she knew.

"Yeah, I can understand," she answered in English.

She could speak Arabic, but it was broken, accented. Her parents spoke to her and Zain in Arabic all the time, but the two of them always responded in English. When speaking to relatives in Egypt, she and Zain would sometimes make an effort, but their attempts were met with laughs and jokes. "See how she said that?" they'd say. Then they'd follow with an impression, saying the word in a sort of obnoxious American accent. It didn't seem to bother Zain as much, despite usually being far more sensitive to ridicule than Hannah. He'd just laugh and carry on speaking, but Hannah would always answer them in English, not wanting them to hear her butcher the words. She knew she could be head-strong, defending herself when necessary, but she also knew her Arabic was weak, and she wanted to hide that weakness whenever possible.

"Almost here," Zakaria said. English again.

They turned a corner down a more crowded street, Zakaria still dragging her suitcase. If he was a murderer, she'd be safe in these crowds, at least.

"This building, right here." He pointed toward a gateway up ahead. As they walked up to the door, someone tugged on her backpack and she stumbled backward, colliding with the man who pulled her, turning to face him.

"Hi." The man smiled and grabbed her shoulder strap as she leaned back. He was balding and smelled of cigarettes and sweat.

"What are you doing?" Zakaria shouted in Arabic. *"Get out of here."* He pushed the man away.

"What's the problem? I just want to talk to this pretty girl over here." His hand was on her shoulder. She pulled away from him, tugging her backpack hard enough that he released his grip.

Hannah fumbled through the back pocket of her jeans. Nothing. Other pocket. Her hand gripped the small container of pepper spray, ready to pull out at the right moment as her index finger rested on the trigger. Zakaria was still shouting, but she didn't know what he was saying anymore. No one else on the street seemed bothered, and people walked past with mere glances. The man grabbed her shoulder again, and Hannah pulled the pepper spray out of her pocket and sprayed, causing him to jump back screaming, his hands reaching for his face.

"Bint el kalb!" He grasped at his closed eyes, rubbing them and shouting expletives in Arabic as Hannah stood frozen, in disbelief that she'd even done that.

Zakaria pulled her arm and led her toward the building, opening the door and waiting for Hannah to go inside first. She looked back for a moment and saw the man still shouting, his eyes shut, hands over his face as a crowd started to form around him.

Zakaria turned to face her once they were inside. "You sprayed his eye?"

"Yeah." Hannah held up the small bottle of pepper spray. "He deserved it."

Zakaria laughed. "Alhamdulillah. He was crazy. We used to carry this in Tahrir, but it wasn't so dangerous in the beginning." He shook his head.

"You protested in Tahrir?"

"Yes, before Morsi and the Muslim Brotherhood took over, but I stopped going after the army came in and created problems. Too dangerous then." He waved his hands in the air near his face, as though brushing the memory away from him.

Hannah opened her mouth to ask more, but Zakaria interrupted before she could get the words out.

"So this is where you're living? Nice building. You will be safe. Just keep spray with you."

There was a man sitting at the front desk in the lobby. He seemed unperturbed by the chaos outside and barely glanced at Hannah and Zakaria when they walked in. The two of them approached the desk.

"I'm supposed to be staying in Imane Sayid's apartment for the next month," she told the man in her best broken Arabic.

"You're the American." He glanced up at her and reached into a side drawer to pull out a key. *"Number 34, floor three."*

He didn't even check her ID or reservation.

"Do you want help or you're okay?" Zakaria asked.

He'd been trustworthy and reliable up to now, but she wasn't about to let him up into the apartment.

"I'm good, thank you so much."

"Here, take my phone number if you need anything. And I can show you around Egypt," he said, grabbing a piece of paper and a pen from the desk. He scribbled the number down, smiled, and handed the paper to Hannah. "You can send me a text when you get Egyptian phone."

As he waved goodbye and walked out, the line between Egyptian hospitality and flirtation remained unclear. She couldn't tell if he'd just slipped her his number for a date, or if he genuinely wanted to show her Egypt and be a friend. She'd keep his number, though. Zakaria seemed okay, and she needed friends. Plus, she wanted to hear more about Tahrir.

Upstairs, Hannah was pleasantly surprised to find a layout much more modern than what she was used to at her grandmother's place, and furnished with clean sheets and towels. There was a living room, kitchen, bedroom, and bathroom, all much bigger than anything you'd find in New York at this price—if you could even find anything at this price in the first place. Hannah still wasn't sure about the neighborhood, but it wasn't like she knew the neighborhoods in Cairo anyway.

Hannah sat down on the blue plush couch in the living room, different from the gaudy Renaissance-style furniture often found in Egyptian homes. That's when it sank in, like someone had shaken her awake. She was here—not on her flight back to the US. She was giving up Columbia Law. The room began to spin, like she was drunk, only she wasn't. Everything had happened so quickly, as though someone else had made all the decisions as she'd floated along. Maybe it was her mom, keeping her close, pulling her to this place. There was something to be done here—some reason she couldn't go back.

She wouldn't go to law school. She was here, in Egypt, and she needed to settle in. Then, in twelve hours, she could talk to Zain. Twelve hours was enough time to come up with an explanation, surely. Something to make this sound less stupid, less impulsive. Despite it all, she knew in her bones that this was the right decision. But now, sitting here without the forward momentum of a few moments earlier, she wanted to disappear again—to not exist and instead sink deeper into the couch she sat on, enveloped by the cushions until she was just a part of the fabric, nothing more. Maybe here, in this country where she knew almost no one, she actually could disappear, escaping her old life and the grief that came with it.

Zain

When Zain arrived at his South Philly apartment, everything looked clean. Someone had taken out the trash. The piles of papers and newspapers that had been on his coffee table were neatly stacked on the bookshelf. His rug was freshly vacuumed. The air smelled of Swiffer wipes, and the hardwood floor glistened. Emily had to have been here. He heard a noise in his bedroom, someone moving. It seemed she was still here.

"Em?"

"Zain." She walked out of his room, lemon-scented Lysol spray and paper towels in hand. "I didn't think you'd be back so soon."

"What are you doing?" He dropped his bags on the floor next to him.

"I wanted to do something for you. I figured I'd clean your place."

He untensed and went to hug her, wanting to stay like that forever, grasping her to keep from falling. They were dating, but not really. It was hard to tell, their lives so intertwined. They behaved like a couple on most days but just friends on others. At one point, they did date officially. For two whole years in college.

Emily slept over, even though he told her she didn't need to, that he would be okay and that he had work in the morning anyway. But he was glad to hold her, the smell of her lavender shampoo lulling him to sleep.

In the morning, she was gone. For the first time in days, Zain had slept soundly. He hadn't heard Emily go and didn't wake up until the sound of his alarm at eight a.m. She'd left a note on the nightstand: "Left for class. Didn't want to wake you. Let's get dinner tonight."

Zain peeled his blanket cocoon off himself, and the shock of the harsh, air-conditioned air in his bedroom jolted him up, reminding him of the cold office he had to head into so soon after this tragedy. It was hard to believe life just went on. As he started to get up out of bed, his phone rang, the shrill ring of a FaceTime call. Hannah. He picked up and didn't recognize the room she was in. This didn't look like her apartment.

"Where are you?" He rubbed his eyes and leaned forward, sitting now at the edge of his mattress.

"I need to tell you something," Hannah said, urgent. "But don't freak out, and don't tell Dad. Not yet, at least."

His stomach sank. He couldn't take any more bad news.

"Okay," Zain slowly said, standing up and shuffling toward his closet.

"I'm still in Egypt."

"Was your flight canceled?" He stood in place now.

"No, I just—I didn't get on the plane. I felt like I had to be *here,*" Hannah said. "I got an Airbnb, and—"

"Hannah, *what*?" Maybe he was still asleep, dreaming. "Why—what about law school?" He walked back toward his bed and sat down.

"I don't think I want to go to law school." Her voice was calm, and Zain paused a moment before speaking again.

"Hannah, what are you talking about? You have to go to law school."

He didn't know what to say or how to process her words. He still wasn't even sure he was awake, hoping maybe this was just a weird dream—his unconscious mind giving him another thing to feel anxious about.

"You're not listening to me," Hannah said. "I don't want to go anymore. Maybe I never wanted to go at all."

"Hannah . . . you can't screw up your future because Mom died."

He knew as the older brother he was supposed to steer her in the right direction, but he was lost himself, floating through space untethered as the room began to fold in on itself once again.

"I've thought about it," she said, her face blurring slightly on the screen before shifting back into focus. "I applied to law school because it seemed like the next thing. It's what Mom and Dad wanted me to do, and that's not really a good reason to go."

Zain held the phone in front of him. He had to say something—to make her change her mind. She told him law school was a waste of time and money if she wasn't even sure she wanted to be a lawyer, and he couldn't argue that she was wrong. It would be stupid to go into debt for a career she wasn't even sure she wanted. But again, he was the older brother. He had to be the responsible one.

"Egypt isn't really the safest place to be right now," Zain said.

"I'll be fine," Hannah reassured him. "It's not like I'm going to Tahrir or anything."

"You just have to be careful."

It had been less than a year, after all, since the army had beaten and tortured protesters. Everything was still tenuous.

Once they hung up, he needed to lie down to properly take in Hannah's news, but there was no time, because now he was expected to saunter into the office and work on whatever boring fucking stories awaited him that day, like nothing was even wrong. His hands were shaking, but he picked himself up, showered, dressed, and tried to push the thoughts from his mind like a bad dream.

In the office, his desk looked the same as when he'd left, papers stacked in disorganized piles, notes on little yellow Post-its. There was a card: "Sorry for your loss" written across the front, with signatures from everyone in the office.

"Zain, buddy," a coworker whose name he couldn't remember walked over. "I'm really sorry about your mom. If there's anything I can do, let me know."

They could leave him alone for starters. But everyone he worked with eventually made their way to his desk, all saying pretty much the same thing, and Zain nodded and said "Thank you" each time. This was how people were supposed to act—accept the condolences and move on.

In the break room, his boss, Rachel, was making coffee. Every interaction with Rachel was always such a fucking nightmare. He tried to quickly turn around before she saw him, but it was too late.

She looked up mid-pour. “Oh, you’re back. How are you doing?”

“Not great but getting through it.” The words didn’t feel like his.

“I’m sorry,” Rachel said, pausing for a moment. She looked around the room, as though unsure what to say, and Zain hoped someone else would walk in to break the tension. But after a brief pause, she started to tell him about a story she wanted covered—some high school robotics team competing in a nearby suburb. She poured the cream into her coffee and stirred, barely looking up at Zain as she spoke.

“Hey, Rachel, I actually sent you a bunch of pitches before I left. Did you get a chance to look at any of them?” He leaned against the counter and shifted his weight from one leg to another, almost knocking the coffee maker over out of surprise when Rachel thanked him for the ideas, saying that Andrew would do great work on them.

Zain stood up straight now. “You gave the stories to Andrew?”

“Yeah, I mean, he’s our Philly politics guy.”

This was typical. She never trusted him to work on anything real.

“You were away,” she continued, probably sensing his dismay. “I just thought—”

“It wasn’t time sensitive. I could’ve taken it when I got back.”

She looked down, slowly stirring some sweetener into her coffee now. “Well, you don’t usually cover politics, Zain.”

“Yeah, but I pitched the stories.”

Rachel looked up and smiled. “Next time. Besides, you should take it slow, given everything.”

She grabbed her mug and walked out as he balled his hand into a fist and tried to blink away the impending tears. He was stuck in this job writing stories about high school kids in the suburbs, and any time he tried to move up, she derailed him. He pounded his fist against the counter.

"You okay, man?" Another coworker walked in.

"Yeah, sorry, just stressed."

"I'm sorry about your mom."

"Thanks." Zain nodded.

2001

Zain

His parents were always hosting barbecues and dinner parties. They usually invited their Arab friends. All the kids would run around the backyard, screaming for no reason at all. His mom was always the most social one at those parties. Usually, the groups would divide, with men sitting in one room and women in the other—Arabs putting on a show of respectability, like the genders couldn't mix. But his mom, she was different. She always tried to bridge those gaps, bringing the rooms together and insisting they all interact.

"This isn't the mosque," she would say. "We can sit together."

She would wave everyone into the same room, making them reluctantly socialize.

And Zain and Hannah were forced to entertain the kids. It was one of those situations where none of them were actually friends but their parents were, so they had no choice but to hang out. Zain sometimes tried to hide away in his room, chatting with friends on AIM to avoid entertaining the kids, but his mom would barge in.

"Zain, you're being rude," she once said.

"Mom, those kids are weird," Zain said.

"They're our guests. Go play with them."

"They're *your* guests."

"Go."

He couldn't argue with her in those moments, especially not with everyone right downstairs and her voice so serious and stern.

SUMMER 2012

Zain

His first weekend back from Egypt, a coworker was hosting a Sunday barbecue, and Emily had encouraged him to go—to get his mind off things, she'd said. She couldn't come because of some med school stuff, so he'd swept his grief into a separate corner of his mind, like dust mites under a rug, and pulled his body to the party. All the while, though, the dust mites crept slowly out, threatening to fill the space until he could no longer breathe. It was too soon for parties.

This was nothing like the barbecues his parents hosted. At this one, alcohol flowed freely, and the beer in his hand was almost finished, the bottle warm now. He took one last sip and went to grab another as the host waved and smiled from over at the grill.

Zain had made his way into one of the circles of people outside when Rachel came out and joined them. Before long, she was telling jokes about the higher-ups not in attendance, letting some of the ice melt off her. And her impression of her boss—the stuffy, tweed-coat-wearing editor upstairs—was actually funny. But he wouldn't laugh. He wouldn't give her the satisfaction. She made his job miserable and ruined the optimism he'd had as a journalism major right out of college.

"So, what's going on with you?" She'd walked up to Zain, who was sitting at a table alone now, scrolling through his phone as he sipped his drink. "You seem . . . off."

He looked up at her. "My mom just died."

"Shit, right." She took a sip of her beer.

The sun began to set, and a few people had left. Zain was several beers in and had to pee. He went inside without a word. In the bathroom, the smell of artificial lavender permeated the air. A basket of potpourri sat on a shelf above the sink. Something about this room smelled like childhood. His mom used to buy those plug-in air fresheners—this was the scent. He hadn't smelled it in years. She'd stopped buying them at some point.

Zain peed and washed his hands, then looked in the mirror. He hadn't shaved in a few days, his facial hair now scruffy and patchy. He hadn't even cared enough to put his usual oils and products in his hair, so his curls were unruly now, with flyaways going in every direction. His olive skin glistened a little from the beers and summer heat. He had to get out of here. He'd already had too many beers for a work event. How many, even? Five? Six? Outside the bathroom, he heard footsteps. Someone was waiting. He took in one last breath of fake lavender—the smell of home, or what home used to be—and opened the door to find Rachel standing there.

"Sorry," he said and started to walk out.

"What's your problem with me?" she asked.

He stopped. "What?"

"You don't like me."

He leaned against the wall. He didn't have time for this shit right now.

"That's not true," he lied.

"You still dating that girl? The med student?"

"Why? Sort of. I don't know." Rachel's face was close to his as he pressed his back to the wall. He hadn't even realized she knew about Emily.

In the narrow hallway, Rachel's breath felt warm on his face, and he could smell the beer they'd both been drinking, along with the coconut shampoo that wafted from her sleek black hair parted with precision down the middle. Zain moved his body, maneuvering himself to stand at an angle, slightly farther away. She stepped closer, and he leaned back against the wall until there was no place else to go. And then out of nowhere, her hand, soft but cold, wrapped itself around the back of his neck, her fingers sending shivers up his spine. Her lips were on his, and he pulled back.

"What the hell?"

"Sorry." She pulled away. "This is completely unprofessional."

"Yeah," he said, but neither of them moved.

She smelled sweet too, like a perfume that Emily wore, and the smell coming from the bathroom—that lavender scent—his head was spinning. She looked at him and leaned in, kissing him again, only this time he didn't pull back. She pushed him into the bathroom and shut the door, locking it behind her.

This wasn't right, but it felt right, and before he knew it, he had grabbed the back of her neck and his tongue was in her mouth. She put her hands underneath his shirt and gently glided her nails down his chest. Should he do something or let her take the lead? What was appropriate here? Really, none of this was appropriate. But where was the line? They'd surely crossed it already, and as her hand moved farther down his body, his elbow hit the basket of potpourri.

Zain stepped back, laughing at the mess of scented petals strewn on the floor. Rachel laughed too, and as they looked down, then at one another, she asked if he had a condom on him.

"Actually, yeah." He had it with him in case he went to Emily's later—as he suddenly remembered Emily, his stomach sank. He couldn't think about her now, though, and pushed her from his mind as he grabbed the condom out of his wallet while Rachel unbuttoned his pants.

When they finished, the potpourri spread all over, they put their clothes back on silently.

"We should go back out separately," said Rachel, straightening her pants. "You can go first."

Zain nodded and exited the bathroom. He quietly left the apartment without even a goodbye, still riding high from what they had just done.

At home that night, he lay awake in bed, staring at the ceiling. He'd had sex with his boss. In a coworker's bathroom. His boss, who he hated. She'd initiated. He'd let her. Should he have stopped it? What would work be like tomorrow? Maybe he should just call in sick. But no, that would only make things weirder. Maybe they could pretend it hadn't happened. And Emily. He should call her. Was it cheating if they weren't technically exclusive? God, he was such an asshole. He had to tell her what had happened. It was the right thing to do. But it would break her heart.

He barely slept that night, his mouth dry and head pounding by morning. When he arrived at work, he walked directly toward his desk without glancing into Rachel's office. Maybe she wasn't even in yet. He could just focus on work—on this bullshit story he was writing. Maybe he wouldn't even have to talk to Rachel. At around eleven, she came and stood over his desk.

"Could I talk to you for a minute, Zain? In my office?"

He nodded without a word, but his palms began to sweat. She would fire him, for sure.

"Yesterday was weird," she said once the door was shut. "You work for me. I shouldn't have done that. I'm sorry."

"Oh." Caught off guard, Zain slowly seated himself in the chair in front of her desk. He certainly didn't expect an apology. "I'm not, like, mad about it."

Rachel laughed.

"Okay, well, that's good to know." She began to bite on a pen.

"It was a little confusing, though." He shook his leg up and down. "I kind of thought you didn't like me."

"Me? I thought *you* didn't like *me*," she said. "I was freaking out this morning, afraid you were gonna sue me for sexual harassment or something."

He laughed. "I'm not planning on suing you." Zain leaned forward in his seat. "I had a good time."

He sounded ridiculous, and at this rate, he was definitely going to get himself fired, but Rachel just laughed and pushed a strand of straight black hair out of her face.

"Yeah, me too. Or like, I mean, I also—it was fun. Stupid of me, but fun."

Zain nodded, smiling. Maybe Rachel wasn't as bad as he made her out to be. Up until now, he saw her as the icy, stone-faced villain, but she seemed human, anxious about the aftermath of their tryst just like him. And with Rachel, for the first time since his mom died, he felt some excitement.

"I should probably go back to work," he said.

At home that night, he sat in bed and looked at a text from Emily.

You doing okay?

If she weren't so fucking nice to him, maybe he'd feel less like shit. He put his phone down and went to grab a beer from the kitchen. The alcohol would drown the guilt. He couldn't tell her. She'd be too hurt. It was better that she didn't know. Before long, he was on his fourth beer, and he couldn't get Rachel out of his mind. Her smell, her soft skin against his, made him forget, for a little bit, that he was grieving.

Once he finished his fourth drink, he texted Rachel. She answered quickly and came over within the hour. They hooked up again, and after, he avoided Emily's calls. Unlike Emily, Rachel didn't ask about his life, and they could just have sex and not talk.

At work the next day, he got a call from his dad, probably to ask about Hannah. She likely still hadn't told him the truth. Zain hit Decline. That morning, Hannah had called Zain to say she'd set something up with her roommate in Brooklyn and some professional movers to put all her things into storage. Zain was supposed to go there at some point to collect anything important and send it to her. She'd managed to do all that but not tell their dad. Focusing on work seemed impossible with everything going on, so he moseyed over to Rachel's office.

"What's up?" she said as he came in.

"Just taking a little break," he said, sitting down in the chair facing her desk.

"Zain, people are gonna wonder why you're in my office."

"Do you want to get dinner before you come over tonight?" he asked, ignoring her comments. This would be the third night in a row they'd be seeing each other.

"Can't," she said. "Garrett and I are meeting with our lawyers."

Garrett. Rachel's ex-husband. Or future ex-husband. Asking her to dinner was probably a mistake. Again, an affront to Emily. Sex was one thing, but he couldn't also go to dinner with Rachel.

As he walked back to his desk, his phone buzzed again. He picked up.

"Zain," his dad said. "Are you okay? I've been calling you since yesterday."

"Yeah, sorry, I've been busy with work. Can I call you back tonight?"

"Wait, have you talked to Hannah? I can't reach her for some reason. Her phone goes straight to voicemail."

"It's probably just dead." Zain was seated at his desk, shaking his leg up and down again. Hannah should have told their dad by now, not left him to cover for her with no real plan.

"Well, if you talk to her, tell her to call me. I'm worried."

"Huh," Zain said. "I'll try to call her later."

"Okay, thank you. Talk to her. I know she's having a hard time. We all are, but we need to be here for each other."

Zain was fidgeting with his pen now, clicking it up and down with his thumb. "Okay, Dad. I really have to go now."

When he hung up, he texted Hannah, but the text sent as green. Her phone was probably off or she didn't have Wi-Fi.

At 4:52, he logged out of his computer and got up to leave. As he walked past Rachel's office, she called out to him.

"You're leaving?"

"Yeah, it's five." He leaned in her doorway.

"It's actually five to five." She looked up at him from behind her desk.

"Are you kidding?"

"You were supposed to get those two articles to me today." Her face was serious and unflinching.

"Yeah." Zain shifted his weight off the doorway and placed his hands in his pockets. "I was just distracted with family stuff. I'll get them to you tomorrow."

So what if it put them behind schedule? It's not like she would fire him. The articles weren't even covering anything serious to begin with.

At home, his phone began to buzz again. Emily this time. He hit Decline. A couple of hours later, his dad texted:

Can't reach Hannah. Worried about her. Do u have her roommate's phone number?

His dad always texted like he was too busy to write out full words. "U" instead of "you," "r" instead of "are." And with just his index finger.

Zain texted Hannah again.

You ok? Dad keeps asking about you. Text ASAP plz

He waited. Maybe Facebook was a better bet. It's possible iMessage wasn't working. He logged in to Facebook and typed the same message, and as he hit send, his doorbell rang. Rachel was here. At that, his phone buzzed another time, his dad calling him now. He picked up and started to walk toward the door.

"Hey, Dad, sorry, my doorbell's ringing. Let me call you back?"

"Zain, you better call me in five minutes."

"Okay, okay."

He hung up. Still no response from Hannah. He could hardly think, but the knocking persisted, so he opened the door, and Rachel walked in holding two bottles of red wine.

"One for each of us?" she said, smiling.

"I've been drinking for too many days," Zain said, stepping aside to let her in.

"What's one more?"

Rachel, like him, seemed to be running from her feelings, drowning the stress of her divorce in booze, and Zain knew that it was only a matter of time until the two of them imploded in their own self-destruction and grief.

"I have to call my dad first." He held his phone up, as though showing her something on his screen. She opened her mouth to respond, but he walked into his bedroom and shut the door behind him before she could say anything.

Hannah still hadn't responded to his messages. It was late in Egypt now, but maybe she just didn't give a fuck. Why was he even covering for her? She should have come up with some kind of plan. Fuck it. He would just tell their dad for her.

"Dad, Hannah's phone isn't working because she doesn't have service," Zain said when his dad picked up. He was pacing back and forth in front of his bed.

"What do you mean?"

"Don't freak out, but she's in Egypt. She should have told you."

Rachel opened the door and came in with two glasses of wine and the bottle under her arm. His dad's voice rose. He asked if Zain knew she was staying there and if she was coming back and why he didn't tell him, and what about law school, and Egypt was dangerous.

"Dad, I said not to freak out."

He was repeating the words Hannah had said to him just a few days earlier.

Rachel sat down on the bed and began to sip her drink. She took off her shoes and started to slowly unbutton her shirt, keeping her eyes locked on Zain's. He stopped pacing then, standing in place as he watched Rachel undress, his dad shouting on the other end of the line. Zain shot Rachel a look and walked out of the room.

He was pacing back and forth in his living room now, attempting to talk his dad out of getting on the next flight to Egypt, and lo and behold, Rachel followed him in there too. Her wineglass was full again. She grabbed a belt loop on Zain's pants and started to pull him into the bedroom. Her shirt was completely unbuttoned. She kissed his neck, and he pushed her away, still holding the phone to his ear.

"Zain, I'm bored," Rachel said.

He squinted slightly and shook his head in an attempt to tell her she was being ridiculous and could wait, before she walked off in a huff toward the bedroom. He shut his eyes and tried to tune out his dad's yelling. He could just hang up, turn his phone off, and focus on Rachel. It would be easier to forget about his dad and Hannah and instead drink the wine Rachel had brought, allowing himself to sink into his bed, into her.

Emily had told him he'd been drinking too much since his mom died. She'd said he had to deal with his feelings, not just drink them away. She was right, but he could just ignore her calls too.

"Dad—Dad." Zain interrupted his yelling. "It's done. There's no point in following her to Egypt because you don't even know where she is. I'll call you as soon as I hear from her again."

He hung up without saying goodbye, shutting his phone off and heading into the bedroom. Rachel was sitting on the bed in her unbuttoned shirt, scrolling through her phone with the glass of wine in her hand. She looked up at him when he walked in.

"I didn't come here to listen to you have a conversation with your dad."

He was irritated with her but even more irritated with his dad for pestering him, and with Hannah for putting him in this position in the first place.

"What, like you're gonna leave now?" He didn't know why he was being rude to her, when he was the one who'd asked her to come over, after all, but something about their mutual annoyance and disrespect turned him on even more. Zain threw his phone onto a nearby chair, climbed onto the bed, and began to pull his shirt off.

"Don't talk to me like that." She smiled a little. "You know, it was really fucking rude today when you just walked out of my office."

He could tell that she was enjoying the back-and-forth just as much as he was, as she pulled her already unbuttoned shirt off her shoulders and began moving toward him. He grabbed his glass of wine from the nightstand next to her and drank most of it all at once.

"I don't care." He smiled back as she pulled him forward.

2006

Hannah

"You're just letting Zain have a girlfriend?" Hannah said from the back seat of her mom's SUV.

They were on their way to Philly, to once again visit Zain in college. Her mom shrugged from the passenger seat and gave a small "eh" of indifference.

"It's not about let or don't let," said her dad, keeping his eyes on the road. "Zain is twenty now. We can't tell him he can't have a girlfriend."

Hannah was seventeen, barely even allowed to talk to boys. Of course, she did, but she had to keep that from her parents. She also wasn't sure they'd reserve the same leniency for her, even at twenty.

Zain had recently revealed to the family that he was seeing a girl named Emily and that Emily really wanted to meet them, so they would take her out to dinner on this visit.

"I just think if I told you guys I had a boyfriend, you wouldn't be okay with it," Hannah said.

"Bas, ya Hannah," her mom said, her tone frustrated now. "You're younger than Zain."

Hannah, not wearing a seat belt, scooted to the middle seat in the back and leaned forward so that she had a better view of both her parents.

"Just admit it," she said. "He's a boy, so you're treating him differently. Emily isn't even Muslim. Isn't that like *so* important to both of you?"

"Emily, Emily, Emily," her mom said, visibly frustrated now. "To hell with this Emily. It's just a stupid phase. He's not going to marry her."

Hannah leaned back, satisfied that she'd at least gotten some kind of reaction. It wasn't that she wanted to make life harder for Zain, but it wasn't fair how they treated him versus how they treated her. He was always allowed to go where he wanted, do what he wanted, stay out as late as he wanted, and with Hannah, everything was an inquisition.

At that point, her mom began to rant about how maybe they shouldn't meet Emily after all. What was Zain doing with this white girl anyway? It was bordering on haram. Her mom always assumed the best—that Zain and Emily weren't sleeping together, that Zain actually cared whether something was haram or not.

SUMMER 2012

Zain

A bottle and a half later, Zain watched as Rachel put her pants back on and buttoned her shirt up.

"What happened with your lawyer?" he asked from his spot on the bed.

"That's none of your business." She didn't look back at him.

"Jesus, Rachel. I'm just trying to have a normal conversation. It doesn't mean I want to start dating you."

She ran her hands down the wrinkles on her shirt and brushed her hair out of her face with one hand.

"You asked me to dinner today," she said.

"Yeah, it was a mistake. It won't happen again. I can't do that to Emily anyway."

Rachel picked up the empty glasses.

"Because this is any better?"

"You know what I mean."

"Nothing happened with the lawyer," she said. "We just fought."

It was clear she didn't want consoling or follow-up questions. That was the whole point of this anyway. No feelings.

"I'm supposed to interview someone for my highway construction story tomorrow," Zain said, sitting up slightly in bed. "But I don't think I'm coming in. I need to go home and talk to my dad before he sends a SWAT team to find my sister."

"Zain, you can't miss work tomorrow." From the foot of the bed, she looked at him with irritation in her face. "You owe me two stories in the morning."

"Who even cares? They're bullshit stories."

She looked angry now but just sighed and rolled her eyes, while he slunk down farther into his bed.

"Zain, I'm serious. You can't keep blowing off work." She turned to leave, but before walking out added, "I'm sorry about your mom. I know it hasn't been easy."

Once she was out the door, Zain grabbed the remaining half bottle of wine and took another gulp. He hated himself and who he'd become. The grief was all-consuming, taking over his body and mind like a disease, turning him into someone he didn't even recognize. More than anything, he missed his mom. He let his tears fall freely then, his shoulders shaking with each breath. It felt like his body was being torn apart, his skin being ripped into shreds from the inside out. He was completely alone. If his mom could see him, she would hate him.

He woke a little after ten the next morning with a headache, chugged some water, and turned his phone on. Two voicemails from work. He'd only told Rachel he wasn't coming in, no one else. When he sat up, the smell of wine from the empty bottle on his nightstand triggered the slight nausea building in his stomach. He needed to eat, but there wasn't even any food in the apartment. He should just shower and head out. Go see his dad and try to explain about Hannah. But she still hadn't contacted him. She was fine. She had to be fine. He texted her again.

Where are you?? Are you alive? I told dad

Still nothing on social media. Not even a read receipt on his Facebook message.

His phone buzzed. A text from Emily.

Dinner tonight? Haven't heard from you in a few days

His insides churned—the hangover swooshing around like a whirlpool mixed with guilt in his gut. He was such a shitty person. He either had to end this thing with Rachel or come clean to Emily—or both, actually. But he couldn't think about that just yet. For now, he needed to figure out what to say to his dad. He could tell him that Hannah was an adult. She didn't want to go to law school. But really, it was up to her to explain all this. Why wasn't she answering? Maybe she didn't care. Maybe she was getting his texts and choosing to ignore them.

He should have just gone to work, said "Fuck it," and let Hannah deal with this on her own. But then, what if something happened? He didn't even have her address.

Zain grabbed his keys and headed out. During the hour-long car ride he kept the radio on, loud, listening to Top 40 music and singing along to distract himself. Halfway through the drive, he checked his phone. Still nothing from Hannah but another text from Emily:

How long you planning on ignoring me?

With one hand on the wheel, Zain typed:

Sorry. Seeing my dad today. Not sure if I'll be back by dinner

He looked back up at the road. A texting-and-driving accident would make everything easier. A crash. A fire. More death.

People would get over it. He probably wouldn't end up with his mom, though, wherever she was.

Eventually, he pulled into his parents' driveway. His mom's car was there, her new blue SUV parked like she was just inside. When he was last at the house, back when his mom was alive, the car had had that new-car smell—the smell of leather seats.

"I didn't want leather," his mom had said, opening the car door to show him. "It has that smell that makes me sick, and it's always so hot in the summer."

"Mom, leather seats are nicer," Zain had replied.

"I don't care. It's not what I like."

He sat in his own car for a minute, parked behind his mom's, pretending for a moment that she was actually home. But once inside, the illusion shattered. She wasn't there. She wouldn't be ever again.

"Dad?" he said, his own voice echoing through the empty house.

No answer. Maybe he was at work, though Zain thought he still had a few more days off. He figured he'd just wait, then, and maybe plan out what he'd say about Hannah. And he could continue pretending, for a little bit, that his mom would be coming home too. Being in that house—she was everywhere. The furniture. The photos on the walls. The way everything was so clean, so organized. The house continued to exist like she was here, and yet, somehow, she wasn't. Zain sat down at the kitchen table, at the seat he'd eaten breakfast and dinner at every day growing up. He leaned his face into his hands, his elbows pressing down on the hard wood. There was a gaping hole in his chest, down to his stomach, and he wanted to scream.

The home phone began to ring, and Zain glanced at the caller

ID. It was a number he didn't recognize, so he let it go to the machine, which his parents still inexplicably had even though it was 2012.

Then—his mom's voice.

"Hello, you've reached Yasmeen and Yousef. We're not home right now, so please leave a message after the beep."

At the sound of her voice, a wave crashed onto him, threatening to drown him in a sea of sorrow. Again, it was like she was here still. Everything was the same. Her accent, her softness. He wanted to listen to it over and over, hear his mom's voice forever, but then a different woman's voice came through the machine.

"Yousef, it's Vivian. I know you don't want to talk to me, and I understand, but I can't help but think Yasmeen's death is my fault. I need to talk to you. We made a mistake. I have to see you. We can't just end things like this. Please call me back."

Click.

Who the fuck was Vivian? Neither of his parents had ever mentioned that name before. Why would his mom's death be Vivian's fault? End things? What did that mean?

A moment later, he heard the garage door open. His dad was home.

"Zain?" his dad said, a bag of groceries in hand.

"Hey, Dad." Zain stood to greet him, and his dad immediately asked about Hannah.

Zain quickly checked his phone again before responding. This time there were notifications, proof that she was alive.

Zain! I'm sorry! Wifi wasn't working, but I'm good. I'm sending you an email with all my info here. DO NOT give it to Dad, but tell him I'm ok. I'll call him later today

Zain looked back up at his dad. "Yeah, she's fine. She's good. Hey, who's Vivian? She left a message on the answering machine."

His dad fumbled with the bag of groceries in his arms as Zain leaned against the kitchen table.

"What did she say?" he asked.

"She needs to talk to you. Blames herself for Mom's death."

"Vivian is crazy," his dad said as he began to put away the groceries. "Don't worry about it."

"Who is she?"

"She's Hank's assistant at the office. I was having a business lunch with her when your mom was taken to the hospital, and now she keeps calling me like some insane woman and saying if we weren't having lunch, I would have gotten Yasmeen's calls and then called an ambulance in time. She's crazy. Don't pay attention to her."

He wouldn't make eye contact, and the explanation was strange. Zain watched his dad pull his phone out of his pocket and place it face down on the counter.

"How are you doing, Zain? How are you handling all of this?"

"I'm okay." He looked down at the tile floor.

"I know this is hard," his dad said. "We have to be here for each other now. See each other during the week and on weekends. I don't know why this happened, but it was part of God's plan."

God's plan. Fuck that. He'd heard enough of that at the funeral. God's plan was bullshit. If God planned this, then God either made a mistake or was a sadistic asshole, because of all people, his mom didn't deserve to die. His dad was still talking, but Zain had stopped listening.

The smell of lavender was back in the air. Had she started buying those air fresheners again? He looked to the side, and sure enough, an air freshener was plugged in. Rachel was on his skin again, back in that bathroom, and a wave of shivers trickled down his spine. Above the air freshener, a family photo hung on the wall. They were in Mexico—back when he was in high school. They were all fighting that day. Zain and Hannah had resented the fact that their mom made them dress up for this photo, but she'd just wanted something nice, with all of them together, that she could hang on the wall.

His dad was still speaking, leaning against the kitchen counter as Zain's eyes glazed over. "Are you listening to me?"

Zain was jolted back to reality and took a seat at the table. "Yeah, you were telling that story about the Prophet killing that child who would turn out to be evil. I've heard this before."

"I was just making a point," his dad said, "that God knows things we don't, so she had to have died for a reason. We don't know what would have happened."

"Was she going to turn evil?" Maybe the sarcasm was too much.

"You know what I'm trying to say," his dad said. Zain just nodded. "I need to use the bathroom, but we'll continue this when I get back."

As soon as he heard the bathroom door shut, Zain sprang up from his seat and grabbed his dad's phone off the kitchen counter. It was password protected, but he always used the same password for everything: 5467. Unlocked. He clicked on Messages. The most recent text:

We shouldn't have been together. It's my fault you didn't answer Yasmeen. Please call back.

Zain kept scrolling. Static electricity propelled his fingers.

This relationship was a mistake. I feel awful.

Relationship. He kept scrolling until he reached the day of his mom's death. There was a text from his dad:

Yasmeen will be home all day, but I can come to your house for a couple hours. 1:00?

She replied, Sounds good.

Not exactly sexts, but definitely incriminating. He kept scrolling, reading text after text, seeing plans to meet up at least once a week, sometimes twice. And then evidence that this wasn't a casual affair. There were feelings. They both used the word "love."

I love my wife but not the way I love u. I just don't want to hurt Yasmeen.

Zain couldn't breathe. Maybe it was better not to know. He pushed the palm of his hand against his head, which was greasy with his own sweat. How long had he been cheating on her? Zain was deep into two months of texts when he heard the toilet flush, the sink turn on. He quickly placed the phone face down on the table again, bile rising up in his throat.

"I have to go," Zain said when his dad came back in. "Work called." He rushed past his dad toward the front door.

"Zain, wait," he said. "You have to leave this suddenly? What's it about?"

"I don't know. Just some story I need to cover—"

"Okay, but Hannah. Please tell me where she is."

"You can text her," Zain said. "When she's connected to Wi-Fi. Bye."

He walked out, shutting the door behind him, and practically sprinted toward his car. He had to get back to Philly. In the car, his legs began to shake as he struggled to keep control. He couldn't even keep a steady footing on the gas pedal, and he had to pull over. He screamed, slamming his hand against the steering wheel. Emily. Why was he thinking of Emily? She would know what to do. She would say all the right things. She could help. He called her.

"Zain, what's up?" she said.

"Em." His voice cracked, and he pushed his free palm against the steering wheel. "Can you come over in, like, an hour?"

"Yeah. Is everything okay? I thought you were seeing your dad."

"I'm on my way back."

"Are you okay?"

"No. Just come over. Please?"

"Yeah, of course. I'll go now. I'll just let myself in."

He had to breathe. In through his nose, out through his mouth. But his breathing was shaky, and with each exhale, he let out a tiny moan, as if he were in pain. He wouldn't cry. He stayed on the side of the road for a few minutes more, waiting until his leg stopped shaking, until the air didn't feel so thin—so scarce.

When he arrived back at his apartment, Emily was already there, sitting on the couch with one of her med school books. Maybe he shouldn't have asked her to come. He should have handled this on his own.

"My dad was cheating on my mom," he blurted out.

Zain sat down next to her and began to tell her about the voicemail, about the texts on his dad's phone. He kept his head down for most of the explanation, but every once in a while he would look back up at Emily and see the concern on her face. The shock and pity. This conversation would be impossible with Rachel. She'd probably tell him to get over it, that that wasn't what she was there for. Emily had always been there for him.

"*My* dad was cheating on my mom, Em," he said. "Mr. I'm-so-religious-I-pray-five-times-a-day. Like, what the fuck? Who even is this guy?"

"Zain, I'm sorry." Emily reached out and touched his arm, but her show of sympathy didn't stop him from wanting to punch the wall.

That was the proper response, wasn't it? The proper masculine response. Punch something to let out the rage. When he was a kid, some of his friends' homes had had holes in the walls because at one point or another, as teenagers, someone had punched a hole through there. Zain had never had the urge. Or maybe he had, but his mom would have killed him. No one was about to punch holes in her walls. But now, in his own apartment, he wanted to punch a hole. It would bring some kind of release, but more than anything, it would leave physical evidence. It would mean the pain and anger was real. The landlord would take it out of the security deposit, though. Not worth it. Punching the wall wasn't supposed to take that much thought. It was supposed to be impulsive.

"Should I tell Hannah?"

Emily didn't answer right away. She just stared with a look of concern, eyebrows down, lips pouting. It made her look like a child. She turned her body to face him, sitting with her legs curled underneath.

"I would want to know," she said. "If it were *my* dad, I mean. She's not a kid."

But she was his kid sister. He was supposed to protect her. Emily was right, though. Hannah had a right to know.

He nodded and began to type a text:

Face?

She'd know that meant FaceTime. Three gray dots appeared underneath.

Yes! Give me two minutes

"I'm gonna—" He pointed in the direction of his room. "You don't have to stay if you don't want to."

"Are you kidding? Of course I'll stay. You go talk to Hannah."

He'd never had to break news like this to anyone before, and his stomach felt like someone had dropped a pile of rocks inside him.

His phone began to ring as he sat down at the edge of his bed. Hannah was smiling when he answered.

"Hey, how's Egypt?" he asked.

"Good. Really good. Hectic getting settled in. But other than that, good. Anyway, what did Dad say to you? I just told him I was okay and I couldn't talk yet."

Zain's stomach was in knots, but Hannah was smiling. He hated that he had to do this—that they had to deal with this on top of the grief over their mom.

"Yeah, he's worried. But listen, I need to talk to you about something. I was at the house today."

He started to tell her, slowly, about what happened, about the voicemail, the text messages, as his eyes shifted around the room. When he glanced back at the phone, he saw Hannah's face change shape. Her smile faded, and she took a deep breath in. The sound became fuzzy when she exhaled.

"Why would he do that to Mom?" she said.

"He's an asshole. I don't want to see him. He doesn't know I know."

"You didn't say anything to him?"

"No, I couldn't. I just left."

Hannah nodded. The image of her face became blurry, pixilated.

"Hannah? Can you hear me?" Sound came through in pieces, nothing coherent, then movement again.

"Zain," she said.

"Hannah, I can't really hear you." The sound cut out completely, and the call ended. She texted him.

Sorry bad wifi here

Then another text: We have to tell him we know

Hannah

The shock hit her body first, like a thousand pins pricking her skin. This couldn't be real. Her dad, of all people. The hypocrisy didn't make sense. She should call Zain back, but there was nothing else to say.

She'd only been in Egypt on her own about a week, and those days were spent getting acquainted with the apartment, buying groceries, and wandering around her own neighborhood, not going more than a couple of blocks in any direction. She was grieving and panicking about her choices. Sitting inside and crying, wishing her mom were still alive, wondering if she'd made a mistake, not sure how long she'd last, especially given this self-invoked isolation she was taking part in.

Now, from across the world, her dad's religiosity seemed like a farce.

Hannah lay down. Her body was heavy, the weight of the news pulling her deeper into the bed, into the rough sheets balled between her fists. Had her mom had any idea? While she was *dying*, he was with *Vivian*. Hannah balled her fists even tighter, until her nails dug into her skin between the sheets. She bolted up. She had to tell her dad she knew.

She grabbed her phone and made a FaceTime call. Almost instantly, he picked up.

"Hannah, are you okay? Where are you?"

"I'm in Egypt."

She saw her own face in the corner of the screen. She'd stay serious, expressionless. Her hair was unkempt, her natural curls frizzy and tangled, bent in odd places where she had been lying down.

"Have you lost your mind?" her dad said, his eyebrows furrowed, the screen moving closer and closer to his face. "Tell me exactly where you are. I'm bringing you home."

His hair was white at the temples, his face wrinkled, especially around the eyes. He was too old for affairs.

"Were you cheating on Mom?" Her heart beat fast as she sat upright on the bed.

"W-what?" He pulled the phone back slightly, so that she could now see his whole face. His eyes moved frantically across the screen.

"Don't lie to me. Were you cheating on Mom?"

"Why would you ask me this?"

"Yes or no?"

"No, of course not."

She gritted her teeth, and his face feigned ignorance. "You're lying to me," she said. "Who is Vivian?"

"Vivian? Why would you—did you talk to Zain? She's just a crazy secretary."

Hannah didn't move and kept her face stoic. "Zain looked through your texts while you were in the bathroom."

His eyes widened. "Why would he do that?"

"Because he was suspicious, rightfully so."

"Hannah—"

"Do you even care that Mom died? Or are you just like, 'Oh, what a relief, now *Vivian* and I can have sex whenever we want'?" The words left her mouth like someone else was controlling her speech, fueled only by anger and betrayal.

"Vivian and I are not—"

"Don't lie to me."

"Hannah, I can explain." His voice cracked.

"What happened the day Mom died?"

"I—nothing happened," he fumbled.

Hannah paused before speaking again, afraid that her own voice would crack, showing that the stoicism was all an act. "Zain said on the answering machine—that woman—Vivian—she blamed herself. Said something about you getting calls from Mom."

"It doesn't matter." Her dad shook his head.

"I want to know what happened."

He paused for a moment, his face blurring a little on the screen, and Hannah watched as he looked down and wiped the tears from his eyes.

He'd been with Vivian, he said, when the heart attack happened. He got a series of phone calls but didn't notice until later. Her mom didn't call an ambulance when the pain started, and instead she just called him, over and over and over again. By the time he saw the calls, she wasn't picking up anymore, so he called the ambulance for her, and when he got to the house, she was being put on a stretcher. She died hours later in the hospital.

"If I'd seen the calls sooner, or if she'd just called 911 right away," he said, "I don't know. I don't know what would have happened. Only God knows."

Hannah felt like her lungs were filling with water and she could hardly breathe. As her dad said those words, she pictured her mom lying on the stretcher, moments away from death, all because he hadn't picked up the phone. She knew that even if he wasn't with Vivian, he might have been at work, unable to answer, but he wasn't working. Her mom was dying, and he was with another woman.

Hannah's vision was blurring now from the tears that were beginning to pool, and each breath in felt more suffocating than the last, like the air in the room had disappeared and she was sinking into an abyss.

"I have to go," she mumbled, barely getting the words out.

"Hannah, wait—"

She shook her head. "No, I don't want to hear anything else you have to say."

"Hannah, please, just come home. I can explain everything."

"You don't get to ask me that." She could hear the stifled tears in her own voice now, and she looked away from the camera.

"Please, I love you."

It was insulting, really, that he thought that would sway her. She certainly wouldn't say she loved him back.

"I have to go," she said.

She hung up and threw her phone across the bed, her hands shaking as she took deep breaths in and out. Her brain felt like a thousand electric shocks zooming through a padded cell, and she just wanted it to stop—to slow down. A few times in college, she'd taken Adderall to study, and the high was such that her mind was racing, bouncing from one thought to another in a way that made her feel like she was on top of the world and could do anything. This was like that, but the opposite. Her mind wouldn't slow down, only this time she was sinking instead of floating—drowning in an ocean of grief that filled her lungs, making her gasp for air as she sat up in bed. And then, the moment passed.

She caught her breath, told herself she could control her emotions, and eventually drifted off into sleep.

By midmorning, she felt ready to get out of the apartment to try to distract herself. She got dressed and looked herself over in the dresser mirror. She had on skinny jeans and a loose gray T-shirt, but it didn't matter what she wore, because the men here even harassed the women in hijab. She grabbed her pepper spray and a small black purse off the nightstand.

Hannah stepped out into the building's windowless hallway, into the stale, dry heat. The lights were off, the pitch black eliciting a sense of doom—a reminder that all was not well. She brushed her hand against the wall to find a light switch. She'd have to get used to turning the hallway light on before shutting her door.

With the lights on now, she got into the elevator, which was different from any in America. Instead of automatic doors, each floor had a red door you had to pull open with a handle, and so she stepped into the rickety vestibule, hitting the lobby button, but something wasn't right. It wasn't moving. She pressed again. Nothing still. But then she grabbed the door handle, which felt loose, and she pulled inward. The door clicked, and the elevator began to move, loud and shaky. In the lobby, the man from the other day sat at his little desk and smiled up at her. Suddenly, the lights shut off and the man exclaimed, "Ya Allah." Power outage.

Since she'd been in Egypt, the power had gone out every day for exactly one hour, always at different times of the day. People thought it was some kind of ploy by the government or the army to show that the Muslim Brotherhood wasn't doing a good job. There was no doubt about it being purposeful, that was for sure. It was something Hannah hadn't heard about in America. Something that hadn't happened prerevolution.

Outside, the shop lights were out as well, and there was no music playing from the stores nearby. The sidewalks were still crowded, though, so there was a sense of movement despite the eerie silence. Hannah had gotten a little bit of a feel for the neighborhood over the past week, but she hadn't done much else other than wander around and get food. As she walked down the street, men leered in her direction. Some smiled, while others made a comment or two. Things like "Oh my" and "So pretty." They all spoke to her in English, like they knew she was American somehow. Sure, she didn't cover her hair, but hijab was about fifty-fifty in Egypt anyway. At least she knew to wear pants, despite the August heat. Sometimes, the tourists—white women, mostly—walked around in shorts, standing out among the Egyptian women whose legs were always covered. But shorts weren't okay in the Arab world. Anyone with common sense knew that. It hadn't always been this way in Egypt—a country once secular and liberal—but like her own father, Egypt had grown more conservative with age, and that conservatism naturally affected the women more so than the men.

As she walked, her dad's voice rang in her head, telling her to be wary of pickpockets. His was the last voice she wanted in her head, though, the thought of him now sending an anxious jolt through her body.

A few people on the corner complained about the power outage. Someone said the words "Morsi" and "al-Ikhwan." There was an unnerving energy on the streets—the power outage and political talk all around creating a sense of doom, like something apocalyptic was on its way. But as she continued down another block, music began to play again, the outages usually localized to one area at a time. The street was filled with bright lights and music, mostly American but some Egyptian as well. The creepy calm from before faded, and she took a breath, inhaling the dust and car exhaust in the air. She stopped in front of a clothing store that had balloons out front and Grand Opening signs all along the windows. A Rihanna song blared from inside the shop, which looked like the set of a Disney Channel show, with little multicolored balls hanging from the ceiling and a blue-and-orange tile floor.

"Yallah," an employee shouted, smiling and waving her in. She smiled back and kept walking. Up ahead, a red-and-white sign read "Vodafone," reminding Hannah that she still needed an Egyptian phone, so she went in.

Once she left the store, phone in hand, she hoped to find a café or someplace to sit for a bit. In her purse, she had Zakaria's phone number. He was the only person she knew here outside of her parents' family, and they didn't even know she was still in Egypt—unless her dad had told them already. She wouldn't contact them. Not yet, at least. But she couldn't keep isolating herself like this. She needed a friend.

A man with cloudy white eyes, irises like milk, walked toward her, clutching a cane to guide him. He was chanting Quranic prayers and holding his hand out for money. She pulled a pound out of her pocket and placed it in his hand. In another store window, mannequins stood on display, all wearing shorts, short skirts, and T-shirts, as if anyone in Egypt actually wore those things. One mannequin was blond and wearing an orange-and-gray-striped crop top. On the front, in English, were the words "This T-shirt is design for your buy." Hannah chuckled to herself. A block later, she spotted what looked like a small café with air-conditioning. She could sit and think for a minute—cool down from this summer heat and come up with some kind of plan. Inside, the cool air immediately sent a wave of shivers through her body.

"Salam." A young woman in a black T-shirt and ripped jeans approached. Her hair and skin were lighter than Hannah's, with loose, flowing waves, unlike Hannah's curls, which got frizzy at even the slightest hint of humidity. But her eyes, large and dark, were distinctly Egyptian, like so many of those big Egyptian eyes that have existed since the time of the pharaohs.

"Salam," Hannah said. "Um, do you speak English?"

"Oh, yeah, I assumed you were Egyptian. Sorry."

"Well, I am Egyptian," Hannah said. "But yeah, American."

The girl then said she was half Egyptian but had grown up in America, and in fact, it seemed there were a few other Americans in the café as well, chatting around small round tables with cups of coffee or plates of food. She directed Hannah to sit anywhere.

Hannah grabbed a table in the corner. On the wall to the left was a world map covered in pins with a small sign that read, "Where are you from?" This seemed to be a tourist café.

Hannah logged on to the Wi-Fi with her American phone and immediately got a series of texts from her dad, begging her to talk to him, as though he had any right to ask anything of her anymore. Flames erupted in her chest, but she ignored them, letting the fire fill her until it fizzled out. She would build a wall around her heart starting now. She didn't know him. He was a stranger.

"Hey, can I take your order?"

The same girl as before approached Hannah, who was clutching the menu and staring in front of her. Not having even really looked at the options, Hannah glanced down quickly, her eyes resting on the milkshakes.

"I'll do the Oreo milkshake," she said. "Hey, what is this place exactly? You're all American?"

"Some of us. We're all kind of in and out. I've been here for a few months, though." She explained that the owner usually hired people that were passing through Egypt and needed a job. The place was set up for tourists, so the employees all spoke English. "I'm Vanessa, by the way."

Hannah introduced herself, and when Vanessa walked away, she texted Zakaria:

Hey, it's Hannah! Here's my new number! Thanks so much for helping me the other day!

She had to forget about her dad, meet new people, and start her life here in Cairo. A life in which both her parents were gone.

She opened up Facebook and clicked on her mom's page, scrolling through picture after picture. In one, from her college graduation, she and her mom stood smiling in a garden of flowers, their eyes glimmering in the sunlight. Hannah shook her leg up and down and closed the image. The page already had condolences from people. So stupid. Why would you write on a dead person's Facebook? So fucking morbid and fake. She gritted her teeth and felt them scratching against one another in her mouth.

She suddenly remembered the man and woman from the funeral—the ones her dad hadn't wanted there. What were their names? Noha. Noha and Hamada. She clicked on her mom's friends and typed in "Noha." One person showed up. Hannah clicked on the name and zoomed in on a picture of the woman she'd seen at the funeral, standing next to three kids. The rest of her page was private. Hannah's hand hovered over "Add friend" before she clicked. She typed in "Hamada" next, and nothing came up.

Vanessa returned with the milkshake. A moment later, the lights went out, along with the gentle humming of the AC, bringing a dark, eerie silence to the room. She'd left one power outage just to walk over to another.

"Shit," said Vanessa.

"Is it really the government that's doing this?" Hannah looked up as Vanessa placed her milkshake down on the table.

"Oh, it has to be," Vanessa said. "Or the army. They're trying to show that Morsi is a shitty president, and, like, power outages happen with him in power."

"It's wild we don't hear about that in America."

"No, of course not. They don't give a shit."

As Vanessa walked away, there was one new notification on Hannah's phone that must have come in just before she'd lost Wi-Fi. Noha had accepted her friend request.

Zain

Zain typed his dad's name into the Facebook search bar. In the friends list, he typed "Vivian." One name popped up. There was nothing remarkable about her. Light brown hair, pale skin, average weight. Her profile picture was just her face, a cropped photograph someone had taken. Parts of her timeline were visible—links she'd posted, quizzes she'd taken and shared. "What color is your soul?" She'd gotten "sky blue," whatever that meant. She seemed like a typical old person on Facebook, only she didn't look terribly old. Forty, maybe.

Zain continued to scroll, knowing he wouldn't find anything, not sure exactly what he was looking for in the first place. But his thumb moved as though on a mission, gliding down the page in search of something. He couldn't believe that his dad, who constantly spewed religious rhetoric at his kids, would cheat on his wife. But maybe he'd never known his dad, not really. Their mom had been the one who'd made the important decisions in their lives. She'd been the one they'd called and talked to when they needed advice.

Zain typed her name into the search bar next. "Yasmeen Kamal." Her profile picture was from her birthday a few years back, with him and Hannah. She'd always been so happy to have the whole family around. When Hannah left for college and his parents were suddenly without kids in the house, his mom had always tried to guilt them into coming home on the weekends. Hannah went much more often than he ever did, but that's because she was supposed to be the good daughter who would check up on their parents and visit so that he didn't have to. Now he wished he'd made those extra visits.

Zain scrolled down his mom's Facebook page, where a few old friends and relatives had written that she'd be missed. His nostrils flared in frustration at every person who posted. They didn't know her—not really, and yet here they were publicly declaring their fake grief.

He threw his phone down next to him on the bed and pulled the covers over his face, blocking the sunlight. He wished it were night again so he could shut his eyes and press pause on the world, sinking instead into his dreams, where maybe his mom could be alive still.

It was nice the night before, when Emily was here, her head resting perfectly in his neck as they slept. But she'd left early, as she always did, off to do her morning hospital rounds. If she were still here, though, she'd try to get him to talk about *everything*, when he just wanted it all to go away. Rachel helped him forget, so he grabbed his phone and sent her a text.

Hey, do you want to come over tonight?

The gaping weight in his stomach returned, guilt mixing in now with anger—at himself, at the world, at his dad most of all.

His phone buzzed.

Sure

They made a plan to meet later, but in the meantime, Zain was supposed to meet his childhood friend Hasan for lunch—or really, for him it was breakfast, seeing as he'd just woken up. Maybe he could cancel. The idea of going out to lunch, of pretending to be okay—it was too much.

At this point, though, it was too late to cancel on Hasan. It would be rude, especially given they weren't particularly close and only saw each other once in a while. Plus, after Zain's mom died, Hasan had reached out immediately and it seemed that he actually cared.

Zain picked a café near his apartment so he wouldn't have to travel far. Outside, couples gathered around the fountain in Passyunk Square. Two old men sat at the chess table, one carefully moving his white knight, the other seemingly deep in thought. Some Maroon 5 hit was playing out of a bush with a speaker inside.

Zain arrived before Hasan, so he grabbed a seat and checked Facebook on his phone. He typed Vivian's name again. There she was, smiling. He'd have to confront his dad at some point, but when? Hannah probably wouldn't have said something already. Not from Egypt. Not yet.

"Zain," a voice said.

He looked up. Hasan walked in, a smile on his face, arms open for a hug.

"Listen, man, I'm so sorry about what happened," Hasan said when he sat down. "Your mom was awesome. I still can't believe it. I remember every time we used to come over, she would give us snacks, and your house always had the best snacks, man."

Zain laughed. His house did always have the best snacks. It was before health became a big issue, when parents would buy Gushers and think all that sugar was no big deal for kids.

As they looked over the menu, Hasan asked about Hannah, and Zain gave him the quick update. They got up and ordered at the counter, making small talk as they waited in line.

Seeing Hasan felt like coming face-to-face with the past. There was something comforting—or familiar maybe, like Hasan reminded him of what home used to be. Family barbecues, the smell of burgers and chicken in the backyard, mixed with freshly mowed grass—a smell you really only got in the suburbs. And that innocence of youth, before they'd kept secrets and become people their parents wouldn't understand. Zain untensed his shoulders and smiled.

"So, are you still with Emily?" Hasan asked once they returned to their seats.

And just like that, the sense of home lifted off him and he clenched his jaw. That feeling in his stomach came back—the one that wasn't quite nausea, but if guilt were a physical sensation, this would be it.

"Yeah, sort of."

"Sort of?" Hasan repeated, smiling. "What does that mean?"

Zain shifted his body, leaning forward, then back. He didn't want to talk about Emily because then he'd think about Rachel.

"I mean, yeah, we are. It's just—you know it's always complicated with me and Em. But what about you? Still with your girlfriend? What's her name? Farah?"

"Yeah, I am," Hasan said. "We're actually reading the Fatiha tomorrow night with our families. First step, you know. I picked out a ring and everything."

"Dude, you're kidding!"

"No, man. It's happening. My family loves her. They're just glad I found a Muslim girl. I think they got a little worried back in college when I was seeing Ashley. But you get it."

Hasan had been so different in college. They were a lot alike, living one life around friends and another around family. But here Hasan was, with a nice Muslim girl to bring home. They were practically strangers now. Something had changed after college—a shift in social media etiquette. Part of that, of course, could be the fact that his parents had joined Facebook and anything incriminating had to be deleted fast. But had Hasan really changed since then? Maybe he'd found a Muslim girl with the same secrets. Muslims like him and Hannah.

As they chatted some more about Hasan's soon-to-be fiancée, the woman behind the counter walked up with their sandwiches.

"Are your parents cool with Emily?" Hasan asked. "Like, was your mom?"

"Eh, you know. As cool as they can be."

He'd never actually talked to anyone about this, surrounding himself, normally, with other Americans who'd only vaguely understand the religious and cultural divide.

"But they liked her?"

"I mean, they'd prefer me to be with someone from our own background. I don't know that they'd want Emily and me to get married or anything."

Zain took a bite of his sandwich. After college, the topic of marriage had begun to come up more frequently. By the time he turned twenty-five, his parents stopped being subtle—or at least what they thought of as subtle—and flat-out asked him when he would get his shit together and find a wife. Not in those exact words, of course. But they were direct.

As they ate, Hasan probed a bit more into how Zain was really doing.

"Do you need anything? Is there anything I can do?" Hasan asked.

"No, man, I'm okay," Zain said.

"How's your dad been?"

Zain's eyes drifted around the café, avoiding Hasan's glance. "He's, uh, you know . . . I don't know."

"It must be really hard for him."

Zain looked down at what was left of his sandwich, suddenly losing any appetite he'd previously had. He leaned back in his chair and nodded slowly at Hasan. But then the words flowed out of him like lava.

"Honestly, he deserves what he gets," Zain said. "He cheated on my mom."

Hasan had just taken a bite of his sandwich and stopped midchew. His eyes widened, and he paused for a moment before swallowing.

"Zain, I'm sorry. What—how did you—when did this happen?"

Zain started to tell Hasan the story, as much as he knew at least, and Hasan listened, his mouth open the whole time.

"I'm really sorry, man," Hasan said once Zain finished talking. "I can't even imagine finding something like that out, right after everything." Zain nodded and didn't say anything, so Hasan continued. "Do you think they were ever happy together?"

Zain, taken aback by the question, didn't know what to say. He thought back on their marriage. *Were* they ever happy? To him, his parents were always just that—parents. They'd fought sometimes and gotten along other times, but Zain had never once considered their happiness. They'd never really seemed to be in love, but he'd always just assumed that's how things got when you were married for that many years.

"I honestly don't know," Zain answered. "I never really thought about it."

Hasan opened and closed his mouth, like he was about to say something but changed his mind.

"What?" Zain asked.

"I just, I mean, you might already know this . . ."

"Know what?"

"Well, you know how our parents knew each other in Egypt, before they moved here?" Zain nodded, and Hasan continued. "Well, I don't know, my mom has just told me stories about the old days before they left."

"What did she tell you?"

"Maybe you know this already. And, like, it's not even that big a deal."

Zain waved his hand in front of him, gesturing for Hasan to get to the point.

"Well, you know your mom was engaged to someone else before your dad, right?"

Zain leaned back. "I did not know that."

"Shit, sorry."

"What's your point with this?"

"No, no point, really. It's just, I heard that part of the reason they left Egypt was because of that other guy." Hasan put his hands up in defense. "Now, I don't know what that means. Like, if she was still seeing him, or if your dad was just jealous for no reason, I don't know. I don't even know why I'm telling you this. I assumed you already knew."

Zain had always been told they'd moved to America for him and Hannah to have more opportunities. He'd never even heard of this other guy, and he didn't really know what to do with the information. Had his mom cheated on his dad before they'd even left Egypt? Or had something happened to indicate that she might? Or was his dad just so jealous that he'd upended their lives and moved them out of the country for nothing? Maybe his mom's life here was one she'd never wanted. Maybe their marriage had been more complicated than he'd imagined.

2010

Zain

"When are you getting married, Zain?" his mom said over dinner.

"What?" His mouth was full of pasta.

"Zain can't get married," Hannah said, rolling her eyes as she spun spaghetti around her fork.

"What do you mean?" his mom asked.

"He's, like, a kid," Hannah said, pointing toward the spaghetti dangling out of his mouth. "And anyway, I don't want a new person in the family."

Their dad laughed at that. "Neither do I," he said.

"Yousef, come on." His mom picked up a piece of garlic bread from the center of the table and dropped it on Zain's plate. "He has to start thinking about this. Do we know anyone we can introduce him to?"

"Mom," Zain said. "No."

"What about Zeina?" his dad asked. Zeina was Hasan's sister, closer in age to Hannah.

"Ew, *Zeina*?" Hannah said. "I refuse to accept her as a member of our family."

"You guys, I'm right here," Zain said, irritated now. "Can we stop talking like I'm not in the room?"

"What's wrong with Zeina?" asked his mom.

"She's so *blah*," Hannah said. "Her interests probably include, like, filing taxes. I've literally never met anyone so boring."

Zain laughed. It was true. He'd never had an interesting conversation with Zeina, but she was quiet, and he'd always just attributed that to some measure of social anxiety.

"Yeah, I'm not interested in Zeina." He took a bite of the garlic bread his mom had put on his plate. "Besides, we have almost the same name."

"Yeah, they'd sound ridiculous introducing themselves," Hannah said.

"Okay, fine, no Zeina," his mom said. "But you need to think seriously about this."

"He's only twenty-five," said his dad. "We were older than that when we married."

"Yes, but we weren't like Zain either."

He wasn't sure what that meant and didn't bother asking, hoping only that the conversation would end.

"Are you still seeing Emily?" his dad asked.

"No," he said. "We're just friends." That was true. They had broken up and agreed to stay platonic.

His mom was looking down at her plate.

"Emily is a nice girl," his dad said. "But you should be careful. You don't want to give her the wrong idea."

"Emily's cool," Hannah said. "I could maybe, eventually, accept her as one of us."

"Be serious, he's not marrying Emily." His mom looked up from her plate. "She's not Muslim."

SUMMER 2012

Zain

On his walk back home, his dad called, and Zain picked up and sat at a bench in front of the Passyunk Square fountain. He'd play it cool and pretend nothing was wrong.

"Hey, Dad," he said.

The fountain water, as usual, splashed onto the ground around the borders, and a little boy stood in front of it, jumping up and down as he got his feet wet. The woman who appeared to be his mother sat on the bench a few feet back and scrolled through her phone. It was amazing that the world just continued—kids playing in fountains, everyone living their own separate lives—while his own life was in turmoil.

"Zain, we have to talk," his dad said on the other end of the line. "I have to explain."

He was going to be sick. Hannah couldn't have said something already.

"What are you talking about?" Zain's body tensed up.

"I talked to Hannah."

He felt his lunch slowly creeping back up into his throat. He wasn't ready for this. Not now on this bench in front of a fountain while a Jason Mraz tune played from a bush. He leaned forward.

"I didn't mean for any of this to happen," his dad said. "I love your mother very much."

"I don't want to talk."

"Please, I know I can't defend myself. It was wrong, but—"

"You cheated on Mom."

The woman on the nearby bench looked up from her phone. Zain stood and began to walk toward his apartment.

"Can we talk in person?" his dad said.

"I don't think so, Dad. I have to go."

He hung up without saying goodbye, and once in his apartment, a sense of panic began to build from somewhere deep within. He couldn't call Emily again, not with Rachel coming over in a few hours. He sat down and pulled his weed out of a drawer—something to calm him down. He wished he had something stronger, to make him forget entirely, to take him someplace else, but the weed would have to do.

2002

Zain

Zain was always closer to his mom than his dad, but now he'd have to spend a whole weekend alone with him while visiting colleges.

"This is the first time you'll be on your own," his dad said on the drive.

"Yeah," Zain said, looking out the window at the passing cars on the highway. He wasn't really sure how to talk to his dad—or what to talk about.

"When you live on your own, you're going to be around a lot of things you weren't exposed to at home," his dad said. "People drinking, doing drugs . . . and girls."

"Oh my God, Dad." Zain slouched down in his seat and rolled his eyes. He'd already been drinking and smoking weed for a few years at that point, unbeknownst to his parents. And he'd had a few girlfriends too. But his parents somehow thought he was innocent, sheltered from the world at large.

"I'm just saying, Zain, you have to be careful, and remember Allah."

He went on to tell Zain that he couldn't give in to temptation—that he had to stay close to God and focus on school.

"You should join the MSA," his dad said. "Muslim Students Association. And then you can be involved with them and have a group of friends like you."

Zain nodded, knowing full well he wouldn't join. It's not that he had anything against them. He just didn't think he'd fit in with that crowd—not with his own severely lapsed Islam.

SUMMER 2012

Hannah

A few weeks had passed, and Hannah was waiting tables at the café. She'd gotten the job almost too easily. The day after ordering her milkshake, she'd gone back and asked Vanessa for a job application, but Vanessa had introduced her to the owner instead. After a few basic questions, he'd hired her.

Today, a familiar face walked in, one she was expecting but hadn't seen since her first day alone in Egypt.

"Zakaria." She approached the entrance where he was standing with a friend. "It's good to see you again."

She hadn't made any Egyptian friends in the time she'd been in Cairo. Not *Egyptian* Egyptian, at least. There were Egyptian Americans in the café, one Egyptian Australian, but that was it. She and Zakaria had been trying to coordinate a day to meet up for some time now, but he had been traveling again. Still, he seemed eager to see Hannah, and she needed more friends here.

"How are you?" Zakaria said. He spoke to her in English again.

He'd texted her that he would stop by at some point that day. Hannah looked from Zakaria to his friend, who he introduced as Ahmed, and she quickly seated them both.

"Who are they?" Vanessa asked as Hannah went back to grab some menus for them. "The one with curly hair is cute." She pointed her chin at Zakaria, and Hannah quickly explained how they'd met.

Vanessa wasn't wrong. He was cute and nice too, but that's not what she was here for. She needed friends here, and Zakaria could be just that, maybe. Plus, he was Muslim, probably a good Muslim. Not that there was anything wrong with that, but it wouldn't work—their two vastly different levels of religiosity. Being around Zakaria was almost like being around her parents, like she had to hide who she really was in case he judged her for not being Muslim enough. Hannah tucked her pen and notepad into her apron and walked over to their table.

"Hannah," Zakaria said. "Ahmed and I are wondering. Why your name is Hannah? You are Egyptian, no? Hannah—this is an American name."

"Yes, true," Hannah said. She enunciated her words. They understood English well enough, but with their accents, they stressed every *T* and didn't slur syllables together the way Americans did. Hannah mirrored them, in case they missed something with her dropped letters and quickly strung-together words. "I guess the Arab version would be Hanan."

"Yes," Zakaria said. He smiled, like he was excited she knew. "So your name is Hanan?"

"No, I think my parents wanted to name me Hanan, but they thought I needed to be assimilated." Hannah shifted her weight from one leg to the other, then tucked her hands into her apron.

"What is assimilated?"

"Oh, it just means to fit in. With American culture. They didn't want me to be the girl with the weird name—for Americans, I mean. It's stupid. They should've just named me Hanan. My brother's name is Zain. More Arab, I guess."

"Yes, Zain is Arab. Not common *too* much in Egypt, though."

As a kid, having an American name had been nice. While her brown skin had made her different from the other girls in her grade, her name at least tied her to them in some way. It was only in college that she'd recognized the whitewashing her parents had participated in through naming her. "Hannah" stripped her of her cultural identity to some degree.

"In America you'd be Zach," Hannah said. "Or Zachary." She faced his friend. "Not sure about Ahmed, though. Can't really Americanize that."

She took their orders, and they both got cheeseburgers and fries. Two Egyptians ordering the most American item on the menu. Before they left, she made plans to get lunch with Zakaria the next day, hoping he didn't think it was a date. She wasn't sure if men and women hung out casually like that in Egypt. Her parents had always made it seem like they didn't, but they were from a different generation.

"I can meet you outside your apartment after prayer?" he said. Friday prayer. So he was definitely religious. "Are you Muslim?"

"Uhh, yeah," Hannah said as she ran her hand through her hair.

Suddenly she was the good Muslim girl. Now that the assumption was there, she couldn't have them think otherwise. She couldn't let them view her as a heathen.

"You want to come to prayer?" he said, his face lighting up. "My sister will be there."

"Oh," Hannah said, tugging at a loose string on her apron. "Um, maybe." Her first instinct was to lie, to find some way out like she would when her parents asked her to pray, but she was here in this country, so she might as well go and learn more about life in Cairo. She'd never been to prayer in Egypt—just funeral prayer. "You know, yeah. I can come."

Zakaria smiled. "Okay. You can meet my sister, Layla. You'll like her. We can pick you up at your apartment."

Well, one thing was for sure, if his sister was coming, this certainly wasn't a date.

Meanwhile, Hannah had plans to go out with some of her new coworkers, but before that, she was meeting Noha, the mystery woman from the funeral. Noha had agreed to dinner—was eager to meet, even—quickly responding to Hannah's Facebook message that she'd waited a few weeks to actually send. They set up a time to eat at some restaurant downtown—a place by the Nile.

When Hannah arrived, Noha was standing outside in a long white flowing dress that hugged her body at the top, so different from some of the more conservative styles in Egypt. Her dress was paired with her oversized sunglasses, and with the sun and Nile River in the background, she looked almost like a 1930s movie star.

"Izayik?" Noha smiled and reached in for a two-cheek kiss. "We can sit outside. It's beautiful today."

The host led them through the restaurant—a fancy place that her parents would probably approve of—and out the back door to a patio overlooking the Nile. The water glistened with Cairo's reflection as the sun beat down on the river. They sat at a table alongside the water, with an umbrella overhead to shield them from the sun, and Noha smiled.

"So you are Yasmeen's daughter," she said. "I can't believe it."

"How did you know my mom?" Hannah squinted slightly in

the sunlight. She should have brought sunglasses, like Noha.

"We were friends in university," Noha said. "Me, Hamada, and Yasmeen. Very close friends."

Her mom had never mentioned them. Hannah, in fact, didn't know anything about her mom's life in college.

"Did you not keep in touch after that?"

"No, not really," said Noha. "Yousef—and then Hamada—well, it doesn't matter." She waved her hand in the air dismissively.

"Wait, what doesn't matter?"

"We just—Yousef, your father, he didn't like us." Noha forced a small smile.

"Why not?" Hannah leaned forward now.

Noha hesitated. "It was so long ago," she said. "Why don't we just order our food?"

When the waiter arrived, Noha ordered for them both, telling Hannah that the kebab was their specialty and they had to have it. The whole restaurant, in fact, smelled of grilled meats, like when she walked past a barbecue in Brooklyn, hunger suddenly hitting her as she took the flavors and spices in through her nose.

There was something glamorous about Noha—her chunky jewelry glimmering in the sunlight as she gave the waiter their order, the bracelets on her wrist clanging together when she handed back the menu. When the waiter walked away, she picked up her water glass and took a sip, leaving behind a red lipstick stain as she looked at Hannah and smiled. Hannah, in her blue jeans and white T-shirt, felt like a kid, suddenly unsure of herself and the space her body inhabited. She crossed her legs and tucked them under her chair, making herself small next to Noha, who inhabited the space like it was her home.

"Were you in AWSA with her?" Hannah asked.

"What?" Noha said, seemingly caught off guard.

"AWSA. I saw some pictures. My mom was in this group for women." Hannah placed her hand on the stem of her glass and spun it slowly in place on the table. She was finally digging into her mom's past like she wanted, but now that the moment had come, she felt nervous.

Noha smiled. "Those were different days," she said. "But yes, your mom was very involved in activism—women's rights and things like that. We went to protests together all the time."

Hannah smiled. "Wow, she never told me."

She tried to imagine her mom at protests, and somehow, it made sense. Her mom had been so happy when the revolution started in Egypt—thrilled for Egypt's potential liberation from an oppressive president.

"That's a shame," said Noha. "It was a big part of our lives."

Noha started to describe their days in AWSA, regaling Hannah with stories of her mom in college. Noha knew her mom in a way Hannah never had—never would. She knew parts of her mom that were hidden and that Hannah would never have the opportunity to uncover.

"What did my dad think?" Hannah asked after Noha described their AWSA days.

Perhaps that was the reason for his disapproval of Noha and Hamada. Her dad had been happy too, when the revolution started—proud of Egypt—but maybe he saw getting involved as a step too far.

"Well, when she started seeing your dad, she stopped going to AWSA events as much. But eventually, we all stopped."

Noha wasn't telling her something. Hannah could tell that there was more to this story, but the waiter arrived suddenly with their kebab, the service here faster than any restaurant she'd been to in Egypt. The smell of freshly grilled meat overwhelmed her senses, and for a moment, she forgot what they were even talking about, hunger taking over. As they each filled their plates and began to eat, Hannah remembered the situation at hand.

"You don't like my dad," she said, taking a bite from her kebab, which was somehow juicier and tastier than any she'd ever had in America.

Noha smiled slightly. "I won't speak badly about your father."

"It's fine," Hannah said. "I don't like him very much either right now."

The words came out of her mouth before she even knew what she was saying, but there was no point in keeping anything secret anymore.

"Oh, you shouldn't say that," Noha said.

"He had an affair." Hannah stopped eating and looked down at her plate. "I just found out."

Noha dropped her fork. "Oh my God. Yousef?"

Hannah nodded.

"I'm sorry. Did Yasmeen know?"

Hannah shook her head.

"I'm so sorry."

Noha spoke in the same cadence as her mom—a quiet, gentle tone that had the potential to be loud and strong too.

"Why didn't you and my mom stay friends?" Hannah asked. "And Hamada too."

Noha hesitated, as though unsure of what to say next. "Your mom and Hamada were engaged."

Hannah looked up from her plate, a piece of meat hanging tenuously off her fork.

"For a short time," Noha added.

"So that's why my dad didn't like him." Hannah leaned back in her seat. "What about you, though?"

Noha smiled and said nothing, but she looked uncomfortable suddenly, moving a piece of kebab back and forth on her plate. "After they moved to America, Hamada and I got married."

"Oh." Hannah held her fork still, the meat left suspended in the air.

The smell of kebab wafted through the patio, the barbecue leaving smoky clouds in its wake as the drama of Noha's story picked up.

"It was . . . complicated," Noha said.

She told Hannah that she and Hamada had three kids.

"Wow." Hannah put her fork down, finally. "I mean—wow."

She didn't know what to say. She wanted to ask Noha how her mom had felt about it, if they'd talked again after, if this was something that had started while her mom and Hamada were together, but all those questions seemed too invasive.

"You want to know if we did this behind Yasmeen's back," Noha said.

"I mean—"

"Nothing happened until after Yasmeen and Yousef went to America, and I told her right away. I just think she never really was okay with it, and we stopped talking."

Hannah nodded, pausing before she asked her next question. "Why did she and Hamada break up?"

She desperately wanted to know more—to know everything about their past and the drama it entailed.

Noha told her that her dad met her mom when she was still with Hamada. He liked her, and they became friends, but Hamada got jealous—so jealous that it created tension in their relationship and her mom broke off the engagement.

"She never cheated on Hamada," Noha said, "but it wasn't that long after they broke up that she got engaged to Yousef."

Hamada was Noha's close friend at the time, Noha said, so of course she was on his side in the Yousef and Hamada rift. But it created issues between all three of them, and soon, their little friend group had fully dissolved, leaving space for Noha and Hamada to grow closer.

"Hamada actually said I shouldn't meet with you today," Noha continued. "But I really wanted to. Yasmeen was my best friend, and you're her daughter. I will always love Yasmeen. But things weren't the same after she met Yousef."

According to Noha, Hannah's mom stopped going to AWSA meetings, stopped involving herself in politics and women's rights. They both got their law degrees, but her mom moved to America and gave up her mission to liberate Egypt. Noha and Hamada, on the other hand, were still involved in politics, and they were at the forefront of the original protests.

"Did Yasmeen work as a lawyer in America?" Noha asked.

"Oh, no, she didn't," said Hannah. "She worked in law offices—like as a paralegal and stuff, but she never took the bar exam."

Noha looked out at the Nile. "That's so strange. She was very ambitious in school. I wonder what happened."

Hannah didn't know what to say. She wished she could have known that version of her mom. She'd talked about studying law in Egypt but then never really explained what had happened after that.

Noha smiled. "You look like Yasmeen, you know."

As they ate, Noha told Hannah more stories of her mom in college, of the protests they went to, and Hannah told Noha about her life in America, her family, and how all their lives had turned out.

"You remind me of her," Hannah said. "Something about the two of you is similar, somehow."

"Well, we were best friends," said Noha. "I miss her."

They finished their meals and parted ways, with the promise to stay in touch and get dinner together again soon.

Once Hannah was back at her place and connected to Wi-Fi, a series of texts from her dad came through on her American phone.

Need to talk to u

Have to know if ur ok

Hannah answer me

Tell me if ur alive

Coming to Egypt if u don't answer

It had been weeks of this. She typed a quick response:

I'm fine. Stop texting me.

Her chest flared with rage again, little fires lighting like matches. He didn't deserve her sympathy. Her phone began to ring a moment later, the high-pitched FaceTime ring. She would pick up this one time and put an end to things. The screen began to shift into focus as she sat down on the couch.

"Hannah?" he said. "Hannah, are you there?"

"What do you want?"

She forced a solemn expression again, looking only at her own face in the corner of the screen.

"Hannah, I'm sorry. I didn't mean to—"

"You didn't mean to sleep with another woman?" she interrupted, her voice coming out louder than intended. "What, was it an accident?"

"I was going to say I didn't mean to hurt anyone."

Hannah rolled her eyes. "Right. You thought cheating on Mom wouldn't hurt anyone."

He didn't say anything for a few seconds, and Hannah was tempted to just hang up, when he spoke again. "I don't know how I can fix this."

"You can't," Hannah said, leaning back on the couch.

"So what does that mean? You're just not talking to me anymore? I'm your father. I can't lose you and Zain."

The fires continued to light inside her, flames growing more and more out of control by the second.

"You don't get to make me feel bad for you." She turned her head to look out the window for a moment before looking back at the screen. "You did this to yourself."

"I know. I'm not trying to make you feel bad."

"I thought you were religious. All the praying and shit." That was something Zain would say. She never cursed around her parents. "Was that all an act?"

He shook his head and looked down solemnly. "No, I believe in God. I pray. I've been praying for months to let God help me end this. To stop this behavior. It's been killing me. I've felt terrible, completely sick about this, and then Zain found out, and I swear to you, it's over now. I ended everything."

Hannah took a deep breath before speaking again. "You only ended it because you were caught."

"No, before that."

"Yeah, because Mom died." Hannah scrunched her eyebrows together and made a face of disbelief. "Also, what do you mean praying to have God help you? You could have ended it whenever you wanted."

"Zain finding out, maybe that was a sign from God," he said. "So I could see how wrong a path I was on. Everything is a part of God's plan, Hannah. You just have to pray."

That was enough. All this talk of God and God's plan and

the conversation suddenly turning into a lecture about prayer—it was bullshit. He was a hypocrite.

"I'm done," she said. "Don't call me again."

"Hannah, no, wait—"

"I'm hanging up, Dad."

She clicked End. The fact that he had the audacity to speak to her about religion was laughable. So laughable that she felt nothing.

2003

Hannah

Her parents weren't in love—at least not in any of her memories of them. In fact, Hannah wasn't even sure what a marriage looked like when two people were actually in love. Instead, her parents acted like very close coworkers, in charge of the children and the house. They went to work, they came home, they ate dinner, they watched TV—every day the same. She'd never even heard them say "I love you."

But to Hannah, that was normal. That was all she knew.

Of course they fought. Over small things. Sometimes, it seemed like her mom couldn't even stand her dad.

Her dad was supposed to come home with groceries after work. They needed cereal for the morning—for her and Zain before school. But he forgot, and he came home empty-handed.

"We need it now," her mom said when he offered to get some the next day instead.

They were all in the kitchen, getting ready to eat dinner.

Hannah sat at the table as her parents stood face-to-face at opposite ends of the room.

"It's not a big deal," her dad said. "The kids can eat something else for breakfast tomorrow. We'll make them eggs or something."

"No, it's a very big deal," her mom said, raising her voice now.

Hannah rolled her eyes, knowing this would be a whole thing, so she stood up and left the kitchen, letting her parents argue like that until her mom eventually won, like she always did, and her dad went out to get the groceries. But every day it was something new—something stupid they'd find to butt heads about.

SUMMER 2012

Hannah

In front of the café, Hannah met up with Vanessa and a few others, trying to push her dad out of her mind entirely.

"Hannah, hey." Vanessa waved her down. "I don't think you've met Rami."

Hannah smiled and shook his hand. He looked Egyptian, but his accent was American. He was from Delaware, he said, but Egyptian like her. He was in Egypt working at a nonprofit to provide teachers for kids in underprivileged areas.

The rest of the group seemed to know each other well, recalling some memory of the last time they'd gone out together. As they walked, it was clear they stood out as loud Americans, laughing and joking in English.

Egyptians were loud too, but in a different way. Less obnoxious, maybe—or just less entitled. The people she was with now laughed and talked like they owned the street. They exuded a sense of confidence—arrogance even—that Egyptians didn't have. No one in the street harassed them, a group of five, but there were stares. The others didn't seem to notice, but men and women glared at them, the men with a sense of hunger, the women with disdain. One woman pulled her little boy away, the boy staring up at them.

"Yallah," Hannah heard her say.

Cairo's streets were different at night, brighter somehow. All the stores and cafés remained open, the streets just as packed as in the daytime, with lights and music—mostly Arab music—everywhere. This was different from the music her parents listened to—more modern, no Amr Diab.

A group of boys stood on a street corner singing and dancing to an upbeat tune. There was a sense of both momentum and stagnation here. New York was supposed to be the city that never sleeps, but that name seemed more suitable to Cairo, from what Hannah could tell. People were always out and moving, giving the illusion of forward motion, like the city was alive and thriving. Kids sat on car roofs and laughed. People blasted music with their windows down. Once, a few years ago, while out visiting some family member with her parents late into the night, they'd walked into a bakery at two a.m. to find it bustling. At the same time, though, there was a sense of being stuck inside a music video that was playing on a loop. Like everyone was trapped, somehow, making the best of a bad situation. Cairo was different this time around. As they walked, there were rumblings of Morsi and the Muslim Brotherhood—al Ikhwan. Beneath all the charm and lightheartedness in the streets, there was fear. Men stood in front of stores, solemn expressions on their faces, shaking their heads and grumbling about the revolution and what was to come. She only heard men talking about it, though, as women on the street all moved with a sense of purpose, not standing around to chat, but rather maneuvering past catcallers to get where they needed to be.

After the initial protests in 2011, and the ousting of Mubarak, they'd elected Morsi—the Muslim Brotherhood—but now, people seemed restless and unhappy. Nothing was really happening, but these power outages, those mini-protests in Tahrir, the uptick in street harassment unlike any she'd experienced in Egypt before—it was leading up to something more.

And here she was, in the middle of it all, with a group of Americans headed to a bar. The last time she'd visited with her whole family, her dad had taken them to restaurants at the Hilton or Sofitel. He insisted that all the good places to eat were in hotels, but she knew now that he was wrong, given the nice restaurant Noha had taken her to. Hannah resolved that this night would be different from all those family trips. Maybe not an authentic Egyptian experience, but definitely more of an experience, at least. They stopped in front of a place playing TLC's "No Scrubs," and for a second, it seemed like they weren't even in Egypt anymore.

"We're here," Vanessa said.

Inside, there were mostly Egyptians, which seemed odd, given the fact that alcohol was frowned upon here. Immediately, the group walked toward the bar, and Vanessa ordered a round of shots for everyone, plus a few appetizers for the group. A couple next to her was speaking in Arabic, but with a different dialect than what she knew. It seemed, now, that the bar wasn't filled with Egyptians after all, but rather Arabs from all over coming to escape. Hannah looked at Rami. Was he Muslim too? He downed his shot in an instant, and she quickly followed his lead. Maybe he was a Muslim like her—or maybe he wasn't even Muslim at all. The group ordered another round of drinks and moved to an empty booth in the corner. Hannah sat between Rami and Vanessa.

"So does your family live here?" she shouted over the music.

"Not my parents or siblings," he said, "but my grandparents."

"Are you staying with them?"

"No, I've got my own place. What about you? What brings you to your homeland?"

She told the group about her family in America, and about the family in Egypt that didn't know she was here.

"I was supposed to start law school this year," she said, "but I changed my mind." She looked down at her drink, hoping they wouldn't press her for more.

"Are you kidding?" Rami said.

"No. Columbia."

"You turned down Columbia?" Vanessa said. "Come on, there has to be more of a story there."

Hannah took another sip of her drink and shifted in her seat. They were crammed together in the corner booth at a sticky table, her arms touching both Rami's and Vanessa's, and she was starting to sweat. The place had AC, but it was still too hot. She reached her hand up to her forehead, wiping away beads of sweat.

"My mom died this summer."

"Oh God," Vanessa said. "I'm sorry." Everyone echoed her sentiments.

"Thanks."

No one spoke, the atmosphere suddenly somber. She had to say something. "It was just a lot, obviously. But, like, I guess it kind of got me thinking about my life. I don't know anything about Egypt, and every time I've been here it's been with family. Plus, I'm interested in what's going on politically."

Hannah sipped at the last of her drink until there was only ice left. She desperately wished someone would change the subject.

"Do you want another drink?" Rami asked. "I'm going up."

"Yeah, I'll go with you." She was grateful for the chance to step away for a minute and followed Rami to the bar.

"Sorry, I feel like I made things awkward over there," Hannah said.

"What? No, of course not. I'm really sorry about your mom, though. I can't imagine."

When they got back to the table, it felt like everyone was still looking at her, so she started to crack her knuckles, giving herself something to do with her hands—an anxiety tic she'd had since childhood.

"Hey," Vanessa said, "if you're trying to get involved with politics, I can probably connect you with people."

"Really?"

"Yeah, I've met a bunch of people while doing research."

Vanessa told her that she was doing some postgrad research, writing about the Egyptian revolution as it was happening, interviewing protesters and activists. Hannah was surprised to learn that she knew Arabic well enough to do her research, given that she had more of an American accent when speaking Arabic than Hannah herself. Although Vanessa had grown up living with her mom, she'd seen her Egyptian dad every other weekend, and he'd tried to speak to her in Arabic whenever he could. On Hannah's first day of work, Vanessa had mentioned that her minor in college was Arabic and in her senior year, she'd taken Egyptian Arabic and had been practicing the dialect ever since.

"So have you been to Tahrir?" Hannah asked.

"I have once, but I brought people with me, like bodyguards, almost. It's sort of dangerous, so you have to be careful. But something is happening right now. You can feel it, and this is only the beginning. They're not happy with Morsi."

Hannah wanted to know more—more about Vanessa, about

her time in the square, about what was going on in Egypt, information she couldn't garner from the news alone.

"We'll talk more about this later," Vanessa offered, though Hannah was slightly disappointed, wanting to delve into the topic even further, especially given what she'd recently learned about her mom's activist work.

"Yeah, that'd be awesome," Hannah said, resolving to remind Vanessa the next time they spoke.

They continued drinking, and another girl from the group suggested going to a place by the Nile after this. Around them, Arabs with drinks in their hands danced to Destiny's Child, and there was something surreal about it.

Before, Egypt was always boring. Did this make it more fun? After all, she could have done this in America. Somehow tonight just felt like she was back in college, meeting new friends and going out with them on some kind of study-abroad trip. Maybe she was just a typical American trying to immerse herself in what other Americans deemed exotic, despite knowing that she would never be a true part of the culture. The bar might be filled with Arabs, for the most part, but this place wasn't Egyptian. This wasn't a place her mom would have gone when she lived here.

A wave of sadness began to build, rising and rising, but no one else seemed to notice. She leaned her head back, her chin raised, trying to breathe through the growing grief threatening to drown only her. Everyone was talking, but she couldn't focus on what they were saying. She took another sip of her drink and hoped now that the alcohol would drown her instead, soaking up her sadness until there was no life left. She needed to go home. Or back to her apartment. Home didn't really mean anything anymore.

"Hey, can I get out to use the bathroom?" she said, touching Rami's shoulder.

"Yeah, sure."

She pushed through the groups of people dancing now to Outkast, like she was swimming out of the grief. This place was her middle school dream, and under any other circumstance, she would have been having fun, experiencing this rowdier version of Egypt.

Unsurprisingly, the bathroom was dirty, pee on the toilet seats, ambiguous liquids on the floor, the stench of piss bringing her back to late nights on the subway terminal, urine wafting through the air as a train whizzed by.

"Gross," she mumbled to herself.

She didn't even really have to go—just needed a break from the group, some air and space to keep from sinking, but not this air, so she washed her hands and went back out. Maybe she should just go home, but she wasn't sure how safe it was to walk alone at night. The path back was simple enough. They'd only turned down two streets. Still, her parents' voices echoed in her head. *Egypt is dangerous. Women shouldn't be alone at night.* And then there was the man from that first day. What if something like that happened again? She didn't know the group well enough to ask anyone to walk her back. It would be too much of an inconvenience. Maybe the next bar they wanted to go to was closer to home and she could dip out then.

Rami stood to let Hannah back into the booth as he saw her approaching.

"Hey, got you another drink," he said. "Yours was low."

"Thanks. Let me pay you back."

"Don't worry about it," he said as she sat back down. "You're new, my treat."

This had to be because she'd told them her mom died. Great—everyone would act like she was fragile now. Hannah sipped on her third drink, which she didn't even need, and stayed quiet, listening to the conversation unfolding around her. They were discussing what had brought them to Egypt. Despite what it seemed like before, no one knew each other particularly well, and most of them hadn't been there long.

"I just wanted to take a gap year," one girl said. "My parents weren't too psyched about Egypt, given everything that's been going on, but I'm headed to Israel next, and I figured this would be a cool stop for a month."

A cool stop, like this was just a place in a brochure. Hannah almost corrected the girl and said "You mean Palestine," but she couldn't muster up the energy for that conversation. An Arab couple near their table was swaying to the music, their bodies pressed up against one another.

The conversation shifted to Rami's job, and Hannah was more than a little drunk now—definitely too drunk to walk home alone. She couldn't remember anymore if they'd made a left or a right to get there, but at this point, it was better to stay with the group. At the next bar, she'd make sure to drink water.

Hannah was relieved, though, when the next bar turned out not to be a bar at all, but a hookah place, or sheesha, overlooking the Nile. They all sat around a small table near a window, and Hannah glanced out at the expanse of dark water beyond them. People around them were speaking Arabic—the Egyptian dialect this time—and R&B wasn't blasting through the speakers. Instead, an Egyptian song played softly overhead. The tables were small, able to fit one sheesha and a few cups of coffee. The men around them were smoking and drinking coffee out of tiny teacups. Turkish coffee, probably. Thick and strong, a taste that Hannah had never managed to acquire. The men stared, possibly because they were a group of loud Americans speaking English. They didn't belong in a place like this.

Her parents had always made it seem like public drunkenness in Egypt was the arena of alcoholics or drug addicts. Yet here they were, proudly on display for all. The others didn't seem bothered, or at least they weren't letting on that they were. Hannah looked down, trying to keep her gaze away from the staring men, but she felt their eyes on her all the same. Rami took a puff from the sheesha and handed it to Hannah. She looked back up at the men. They were still staring. Was it wrong for a woman to smoke in Egypt? No, that wasn't it. Plenty of women around Egypt smoked sheesha. She took a puff and glanced quickly into the brown eyes of the man at the table across from her.

Mixed with alcohol, the sheesha made her more lightheaded than it would have otherwise, and she leaned her head back and let the dizzying feeling take over for just a moment. Hannah lifted her head and watched through the haze as another group of men sat down nearby. Younger and louder than the other patrons, they didn't stare at her group like the others. Eventually, one of the men turned to face them.

"You are Americans?" he said in an accent that reminded her of Zakaria's. They were around the same age too. The image of Zakaria smoking sheesha with a group of drunk Americans seemed strange to her. This wouldn't be his scene. She'd created a narrative of Zakaria as the good Muslim, not like Rami, who might not even be Muslim, as far as she knew.

Vanessa answered. "Yeah, we are."

The group of young men turned their chairs toward them and pushed their table closer to join in their conversation. They were loud and funny, making joke after joke in the way only Egyptians could. In visits with her family, she'd caught glimpses of that Egyptian humor, the uproarious laughter and the quick, silly jokes. As they left, one of the girls in their group exchanged numbers with the guy that had held her attention.

Outside, the group of them huddled together, as everyone discussed how they were getting home.

"I'm not really sure how to get back from here," Hannah said.

"What's your address?" asked Rami.

She told him, and he pulled it up on his phone, which had internet access, unlike hers.

"It's not too far from my place," he said. "I can walk you there if you want."

"Oh, yeah, if you don't mind," Hannah said, relieved at the offer, as she was too nervous to walk back this late alone.

"Yeah, of course."

Hannah and Vanessa hugged goodbye, and they split off in different directions, Hannah going with Rami, and the others going with whoever lived closest to them. No one wanted to travel far on their own.

As they walked, Rami made small talk with Hannah, and she felt safe in his company.

"This is my place up ahead," he said, pointing to a building down the street. "But I'll walk you to yours first."

"Thank you," Hannah said.

"Hey, actually, I got some hashish from my friend this morning," he said. "Do you want to come up and smoke?"

Hannah hesitated. The alcohol in her system was wearing off now, as they'd stayed at the hookah place for nearly an hour and a half, long after their sheesha ran out. It was two a.m., but the streets were still busy. Not quite as crowded as before, but outdoor cafés remained lively and lights and music still filled the air.

"You don't have to," Rami said. "Like, no pressure whatsoever."

"Yeah, I guess, why not?" Hannah said. "As long as you still get me home later."

"Absolutely."

As they approached his building, Hannah told Rami about her and Zain smoking on their grandmother's balcony. How she felt guilty for doing that during her mom's funeral. Sure, hashish was popular in Egypt, in the Arab world as a whole. Certain Muslims rationalized to themselves that only alcohol was a sin. Cannabis—not so much.

"Anyone in our family would kill us if they knew."

"I mean, it's a different generation," Rami said. "My parents are like that too, but they raised us in America. Of course we have different values."

"Is your family Muslim?"

"Yeah. Amr is my uncle."

Amr was the café owner, and he was religious, but not in the same way her dad was. Amr was so open, so accepting. It seemed to Hannah that he understood there were different levels of religiosity, and there was no judgment from him when the Americans at the café talked about drinking or whatever else. He just smiled and treated everyone equally. He had a prayer room in the back of the café, and five times a day he could be found back there with his wife, focused on God and God alone. Rami didn't seem like he'd be in the same family. Amr had kids, but they were younger. He'd brought them into the café once while she was there, and they'd gone in the back and prayed with him. She'd have assumed any nephew of his, especially one close enough to make frequent visits, would be just as spiritual and religious, but Rami was so Americanized. He definitely didn't leave the room to pray, and his uncle couldn't have known about the drinking and smoking. She shouldn't have been surprised, though. She came from a religious family too, after all.

Rami's place was bigger than hers, his living room area open and spacious with only one couch, a chair, and a television. His hardwood floors and white walls were bare, so it was impossible to tell anything about him just from entering the space, but on the TV stand was one framed picture. It was him, two other boys, and two girls with their arms around one another. They all looked vaguely alike.

"Those are my sibs." He stood next to Hannah as she looked down at the picture.

"Five kids," she said. "Big family."

"Yeah. I'm right in the middle."

Rami grabbed the hashish from his room and sat next to Hannah on the couch. He opened the bag, and the smell, again, was different than American weed—weaker, less skunky. After Rami took a hit, he passed the joint to Hannah, who let the smoke fill her lungs and then leaned back to breathe out.

They didn't finish the joint, Hannah shaking her head when Rami passed it to her after two hits. They chatted for a while about what Rami's time here had been like, until eventually, after what seemed like forever, they hit a lull in the conversation. They sat on the couch in silence for a minute. She didn't know what time it was and didn't feel that drunk anymore. Instead, the hash coursed through her body, creating a sense of euphoria.

"I'm getting tired," Hannah said.

"You could crash here if you want and sleep on the couch."

Hannah didn't respond right away, her focus centered on the wall in front of her. Where was she in relation to anything? How far was her apartment? This was a mistake, coming to Rami's, forcing herself to be reliant on this man she'd just met.

"Or I could walk you back," he said, as though he knew her concerns.

"What time is it?"

He picked up his phone. "Almost four, but it's not a big deal." He paused. "But really, if you want to crash on my couch, that's totally cool."

Crashing here would be easier, but then morning would come, and she'd be tired and hungover, having to deal with getting home.

"So . . . what do you want to do?"

Hannah turned her head and looked up at him. They were sitting close, their legs and shoulders touching. Rami had nice hair, curly but not frizzy. Soft curls too, kind of like Zakaria's but lighter in color—a light brown, different from the usually dark Egyptian hair. She reached her hand up and ran it through his locks. This wasn't like her, but his hair just looked so soft, and she was floating, peaceful, and he probably didn't mind anyway.

"Your hair is really soft."

He laughed. "Thanks."

She turned her body slightly to face him, her knee leaning over his leg. "Yeah, I could just go home in the morning."

Their faces were close. He leaned forward, and she did the same, their lips touching. Soon, his tongue was in her mouth, and after a few minutes, he pulled back.

"Do you want to go to my room?"

"What, I don't have to sleep on the couch?"

"I mean, not unless you want to." He laughed.

He grabbed her hand and led her toward his bedroom, when a rush of electricity turned on inside her. She couldn't be here with Rami, enjoying herself, when her mom was dead in the ground and her dad dead to her.

"Can I get some water?" she asked. "I just—my mouth is really dry."

"Yeah, sure." He turned around to head into the kitchen.

"Thanks. Can I also use your bathroom?"

Rami directed her to a door on the right, which she quickly stepped into. She turned on the bright fluorescent bathroom light while her mind raced. A few hours earlier, she'd wanted to collapse into bed, alone, and now here she was, ready to collapse into Rami's bed instead. She was supposed to be grieving, not drinking and smoking, hooking up with random boys. Or maybe that was the grief. She couldn't tell anymore if this was fun or just a way of coping—a cliché like in the movies. And what if her mom was watching and judging?

Hannah shook her doubts away, left the bathroom, and headed toward Rami's room, where he waited, sitting up on the bed. He handed her a bottle of water, which she drank most of almost immediately, not even realizing how thirsty she was.

"You okay?" Rami asked.

"Yeah, I'm fine."

"We don't have to do anything," he said.

He must have noticed her anxiety—unconnected to him, really, but more the state of her life at the moment.

"No, I want to." Hannah slipped her hand into his nest of curls, pushing him back onto the sheets.

"You sure?"

"Yes."

She kissed him again to show that she was fine. Then she let him reach his hand up her shirt, but she didn't want to be too passive, so she began to pull him forward as well. She needed to get out of her head, shut off her brain, allow the moment to happen, allow herself to enjoy it—and she did, forgetting, even, that she was in Egypt.

They were lying in bed without clothes, still awake, when the call to prayer began, and from a loudspeaker outside, a booming, melodic voice rang out, *"Allahu-akbar Allah."* The light began to shine in through the blinds.

"La illahah illah Allah."

She usually slept through the call to prayer, or fell right back asleep after. Occasionally, in past visits with the family, she and Zain would still be awake playing cards or watching a movie because of their jet lag. Now she was awake for a different reason.

Rami didn't seem to mind, reaching his hand over her stomach, resting his face above her shoulder and against her neck.

"What am I doing?" she asked, staring up at the ceiling.

"Huh?" His head was still buried in her neck, words muffled on her skin.

"I just—do you not have this weird guilt all the time? Like you're disappointing your family or doing something . . . bad? I mean, it sucks that I have to lie all the time."

"Not . . . really." He looked up at her. "I mean, I'm used to it. I think I struggled with that more in high school."

"Yeah, me too." Hannah reached her hand up and around Rami's head, running her fingers through his soft curls again. "Well, not as much in high school, but the first couple years of college. It's just lately, I've been thinking about this more, I think because of my mom, and how she'd be disappointed in me."

Why was she telling him all of this? She had to stop talking—to calm down.

"That makes sense." He turned his body so that he was lying on his back next to her. "Your mom died, and you're thinking about her values and whatever. Was she really religious?"

"I don't know." Hannah looked at Rami. "I mean, yeah, to a certain extent. She wasn't militant about it or anything. But she cared about stuff like this. Drinking and drugs and sex."

"I just rationalize, like, you're not doing anything inherently wrong. You're not hurting anyone. It's all just fun, and you can believe a certain thing—I mean, I don't know what you believe—but you can believe in God and spirituality and still do this kind of thing. I don't think the two are necessarily in opposition."

Hannah laughed. "I mean, that's a nice way of looking at it, but it's definitely a less common interpretation of Islam." She paused. "I agree with you, though. I don't believe anything we're doing is wrong, and it's not like I feel guilty for having sex. It's more—I don't know."

"No, I get it." Rami turned his body toward Hannah. "Your mom died. You're thinking about what she'd think of you."

"Yeah. Also . . ." Hannah paused, turning onto her side as well. She stared into Rami's dark brown eyes for a moment, then quickly averted her gaze.

"Also what?" He reached to brush some hair from her forehead.

"I also found out that my dad was cheating on my mom."

"Shit," he said, dropping his hand to her shoulder. "Are you serious?"

"Yeah." She couldn't help but laugh at the absurdity of it all and the expression on Rami's face.

"You're having a rough month."

She laughed again, then shook her head. "I don't even know why I'm here. Like, last night, I could have done that in America. I didn't need to drop law school to do this."

"It makes sense. You just need time to figure out what you want."

"I'm sorry I just unloaded this all on you. You barely know me." She turned to lie on her back again, looking up at the ceiling.

"It's cool." He closed his eyes and moved closer to Hannah, burying his head in her neck as his arm stretched across her body.

"Would it be a huge burden to ask you to walk me home?" She reached her hand up and ran it through his hair again. "I just have no idea where we are."

"Right now?" He looked back up at her.

"I mean . . ."

"Do you want to just sleep for a little bit first? I can take you home when we get up." She didn't say anything. "Or we can go now," he said with minor irritation in his voice.

"No, it's fine," she said. "I just have to meet a friend around noon. We're supposed to go to Friday prayer."

Rami laughed. "You're kidding."

"I wish I was."

"Cool, love the irony. You're a complex person." Rami smiled and stretched his arms before placing them back around Hannah. "Okay, I'm gonna sleep now, but I'll set my alarm for eleven, and I can take you home."

"Thanks," Hannah said. She'd try to sleep. It was nice, at least, having another body next to hers. She moved closer to Rami, letting him keep his arm around her, their legs intertwined. Normally, she'd want her own space, but something about sleeping next to him made her feel safe—like she wasn't by herself here in Egypt, instead enveloped in his warm body.

Zain

Zain sat at his desk on Friday morning waiting for a call about some church's fundraiser. Other than that, he had no assignments, and simply scrolled through the news at his desk, clicking on an article about Egypt. Protests were still happening in Tahrir. Something big would happen soon, it was clear. Egyptians were unhappy. He could hardly imagine working for a real newspaper, one that would let him write about this. Hannah was right there—part of the action. She'd told him about all the power outages too. If he could just write about that—if Rachel would give him the opportunity—then he could maybe be someone his mom would've been proud of. The pang of grief returned, a sickness in his gut, eating away at his soul.

"What are you doing?" Rachel walked up behind him.

"Huh?" Zain turned around. "Oh, I'm waiting for a phone call."

"And you have no other work to do in the meantime?"

He looked up at her, towering over him as he sat in his desk chair. "Nope. You didn't assign me anything." At that, his desk phone rang. "Oh, that's probably the call."

He picked up. He liked Rachel now, sure, but she still wasn't giving him meaningful work. He smiled up at her, and she rolled her eyes and walked away. A little while later, he popped into Rachel's office.

"Hey," he said. "Headed to this church in West Philly. I'll let you know what I dig up in my investigation."

Rachel stared at him from behind her desk. "Zain, I'm over your snark. Just do your job, okay?"

Zain smiled and stepped farther into her office, shutting the door behind him.

"You love my snark." He smiled.

"Zain, we talked about this," she said. "You can't just come in here and shut the door. People will get suspicious."

"Come on, lighten up," he said, approaching the side of her desk and leaning down to kiss her where she sat.

When she didn't pull away, Zain knew he had her under his spell and pulled her chair closer to him, running his hands alongside her thighs, then up her shirt. With one hand, he grabbed hers and guided it down toward the front of his pants, when suddenly, they heard a knock at the door and Rachel shoved him away.

He stepped back, surprised by her aggression, and began to adjust his pants before anyone walked in. Rachel, meanwhile, straightened her shirt.

Slightly more composed, Zain walked toward the door and opened it.

"Oh, sorry to interrupt," his coworker said, seemingly surprised to see Zain.

"No worries," Rachel said from her desk. "We were just finishing up." She looked at Zain, a fake smile plastered onto her face. "See you when you get back from your assignment."

"Sure thing, boss," he said, giving a quick salute as he walked out.

The interview, unsurprising to Zain, was boring and meaningless, but his little chat with the overly enthusiastic pastor gave him enough for a quick fluff piece on the event. The whole time, though, he found his mind wandering over to Rachel, and he was eager to get back to the office and finish what they'd started—if she'd even let him. This thing with Rachel, as guilty as he felt, did at least make his job more interesting. Sure, he was writing the same stories the interns wrote, as if he couldn't handle something more substantive, but at least now there was some excitement on the side.

When he returned to the office, Rachel was out at lunch, so he sat at his desk and stared at an empty Word doc, his body sinking deeper and deeper into his chair, the chair itself becoming a part of him—a replaceable object in this office. He had to talk to Rachel. Tell her this was ridiculous. She'd have to listen. Maybe he could just continue where they'd left off earlier, then bring up the work frustration right after.

A little after she returned from lunch, he walked over to her office again, gently tapping on the door until he heard her call for him to enter. He walked in and shut the door behind him.

"Zain, we can't do that again," she said. "We almost got caught."

"Oh, come on, wasn't that kind of fun, though?"

She rolled her eyes and smiled, and he knew then that she could be persuaded.

"You need to get back to work," she said. "How did the interview go?"

"Oh, it was okay," he said, still standing.

"Okay, well, I'm kind of busy," she said. "Is there something you need?"

Maybe he'd just launch right into the work frustration, saving the sex for later.

"Uhh, yeah, actually." She didn't look up from her computer, but Zain sat at the chair in front of her desk anyway.

"Listen, I can't fucking do this anymore," he said.

"Do what?" She was still typing, not looking up at him.

"These bullshit stories you have me writing."

She looked up and stared at him for a moment, not saying anything as he fidgeted in his seat and wondered if he should've taken a more subtle approach.

"Zain, just do your job."

"I'm not a fucking intern, Rachel."

"You can't talk to me like that," she said, her tone irritated now. "I could fire you."

"Yeah, okay." He leaned back in the chair and rolled his eyes, and before he knew it Rachel spun into a tirade, bombarding him with accusations of unprofessional behavior and wholeheartedly lazy work. Zain said nothing, his plan backfiring entirely.

"Your behavior lately has been completely unprofessional, and I've just been letting it slide," she continued. "And then today, in the office, with people right outside . . ."

"You can't be serious," Zain interrupted. "*My* behavior?"

"Zain, my relationship with you outside of work is just that—outside of work. And it should stay outside of work."

"You seemed just as into it as I was," Zain said. "You weren't stopping me."

"Okay, even so, you can't talk to me the way you do at work. You've been rude and entitled, and you slack off every day. You miss work randomly. I go to your desk and find you reading something not at all related to work, and you're so *casual* about it, like there are no consequences for you. I get that your mom just died, but you need to get it together."

"You *get* that my mom just died?"

"That's not what I meant," Rachel said, her desk seeming to grow in size, creating a separation between the two of them that

Zain had no way of breaching. She seemed miles away now, and Zain could feel that gap growing.

"You know, I was reading the news when you came up to my desk earlier," Zain said. "Had to remind myself what that is, since I don't actually get to write any."

"I can't assign you real news if you don't take your current assignments seriously."

He shook his head. "This is so unfair. I've *been* doing my job. It's been two years, and you still have me on these local bullshit stories. I had to interview an eighty-year-old man about his church's fundraiser today. Who the fuck reads those stories? Get some interns to write that. I'm literally doing the job of an unpaid intern."

"Then be thankful you're getting paid," she said with a tone of finality, her desk again seeming to create an impossible distance between them.

"Why are you doing this?" He started to shake his leg up and down.

"Doing what?"

"Why haven't you promoted me?"

"You're a good writer, but I don't trust you to take anything seriously. Even before your mom died, you missed deadlines all the time."

"Not when it mattered," Zain said, looking up at the ceiling for a moment in despair. "Just with the bullshit stories."

"You shouldn't miss deadlines at all," Rachel said, her voice flat and emotionless.

"It's like you're purposely trying to keep me down." Zain could hear the petulance in his own voice, but he couldn't stop it.

"Don't blame me for your problems, Zain."

He was looking up at her, wishing he could make her pay

somehow—for making his life miserable all these years. "Maybe I should tell your supervisor that you took advantage of an employee. Bring a sexual harassment charge your way."

He knew even as the words were leaving his mouth that they were a mistake.

Rachel raised her eyebrows. "Are you threatening me?"

"Sorry, no." He edged backward a little in his seat. "I shouldn't have said that."

"You think because I'm sleeping with you, I'll give you a promotion, let you write the big stories? Is that what this is about? Sleep with the boss to move up in the ranks?"

Her desk seemed to be growing and growing, pushing them even farther apart.

"Wait, first of all, *you* came on to *me*," he said.

She didn't say anything and instead took a deep breath in and out, keeping her face and body composed. Her hands rested flat on the notepad in front of her. Zain would have preferred her to fight back, but instead, her silent stare and deep breathing pierced him like an arrow.

"I just think I deserve better work than I'm getting," he finally said.

She was looking directly at him. "If that's what you think, then go find better work." She pointed toward the door. Zain said nothing. "I'm firing you. You're fired."

"You can't be serious." He leaned back.

"I am. You're rude and insubordinate, and you slack off at work. If anyone else treated me the way you do, they would have been fired immediately."

"No fucking way." He shook his head.

"I'll give you fifteen minutes to clear your desk." She kept her eyes on him, staring him down. Her desktop pinged with a new email notification, but her gaze didn't shift.

"You can't fire me." He stayed planted in the chair across from her. "You're fucking me. It's sexual harassment. For real this time."

"Go ahead, tell them. No one will believe you."

His hands were shaking now.

"Our texts."

He'd been deleting the texts, just in case Emily should ever see his phone, but Rachel didn't know that.

"Really?" She tilted her chin up slightly. "You've kept our texts?"

"Yes."

"I saw you delete our texts, Zain. I know you don't want that girl you're dating to see them."

"I have the texts." Zain continued to plant his hands firmly on the arms of the chair. "Plus, I'm sure people in this office have noticed an increase in our private meetings lately."

"Let me see the texts," Rachel said. "If you've actually kept them, I mean."

"I'm not giving you my phone."

"Okay then. Good luck with everything. I'm sure the office rumor mill will be enough evidence for you. In the meantime, you have fifteen minutes before I call security." She looked back down at her desk, where she riffled through her planner as though Zain wasn't even there.

"Rachel, please, I'm sorry." He leaned forward in his chair, this time pleading, begging her to look back up at him. But she didn't, instead turning her head to face her computer screen.

"Please leave, Zain."

"This is bullshit—I'm not leaving."

She looked back at him. "Then I'll call security."

He stayed in his seat, hands pressed against the arms of the chair again. "Call them." His heart was pounding, like something inside was banging on his chest, telling him to stop, to apologize, to go back in time—back, back, back before any of this, before his mom died.

"Zain, listen to me very carefully," Rachel said, leaning forward now, as though trying to bridge the gap that the desk was creating. She spoke slowly. "I'm firing you. You've become a problem. Now, I think that you've been through a lot recently, so I don't want you to make this any harder on yourself than it needs to be. Being escorted out of the office by security is embarrassing. The people in this office like you. They're your friends, and you don't want to make a scene in front of them. It'll just make all of this worse. So stop being irrational, and discreetly clear your desk."

"No." He didn't move. He wouldn't. Not until she backed down. But instead, she picked up her phone and started dialing.

"Rachel." He leaned forward, his elbows on her desk now, his arms stretched out.

"Hi, this is Rachel Harris. I'm having an issue with an employee I just let go. He's refusing to leave my office, and I need security up on the third floor." A pause. "Thank you." She hung up.

"Rachel, are you serious? You didn't have to do that."

"You weren't moving." Her octave rose, so that the words came out in a high-pitched screech.

"I'm not just some random employee. I'm trying to have a conversation, and you call security on me?" He leaned his forehead into the palms of his hands, then looked back up at her.

"You're not trying to have a conversation. You're threatening me." Her voice was flat again—controlled.

"Because you didn't give me a choice," Zain said. "You can't treat me like this."

"I didn't give you a choice? You said you would report me for sexual harassment if I didn't promote you."

She was right. He had to fix this.

"Look, I'm sorry. I was angry. Frustrated. Can we talk about this?"

There was a knock at the door, and two security guards came in and attempted to pull him out of the room.

"Don't touch me." He ripped his arms out of their grip. "Rachel, say something."

She said nothing and just looked down at her desk, avoiding his eyes.

"All right, let's go," one of the security guards said, grabbing his arm again.

"I can walk myself." Zain pulled away.

He turned in the doorway to face Rachel. "Fuck you," he said, just before exiting her office.

Security walked him to his desk as his coworkers stared. One person asked what happened.

"I was fired."

Off his desk, he grabbed the card of condolences, his notepad, a wad of Post-it notes, and a stapler that didn't belong to him and placed it all in the box they provided. There were no pictures on his desk, no whimsical stickers like some of the other writers had, so he didn't have a hard time cleaning up. The two security guards walked him to the elevators and then out of the building, as though afraid he'd hide out in the lobby, stapler in hand to use as a weapon.

Once outside, they left him to fend for himself on a street corner, and he could feel his heartbeat, pounding, pounding,

pounding, like his heart was trying to escape his body and end it all on these dirty Philly streets. He had to clear his mind. Maybe he'd take the subway to Emily's. She probably wouldn't be home, though. It was impossible to keep track of her schedule. Her place was close, only two stops away. He could walk there, even. But then there was this cardboard box of desk belongings to carry around Philly. It was all garbage, anyway—nothing important. He spotted a trash can on the corner and dropped the entire box into it.

Again, it was like he was in a movie about his life. None of this was real. It couldn't be. He exited his body in that moment, watched himself from the outside. Rachel had fired him. He was unemployed. Normally, he would have called his mom, maybe even cried to her about getting fired unfairly. He wouldn't have told her the truth, of course—that he'd brought it upon himself—but her voice would have been a comfort. Now he had no one.

2006

Zain

Zain was in DC, in the final weeks of his internship with *The Washington Post*. Today, he was shadowing one of their lead reporters, following her into the White House briefing room for a press conference. Zain could hardly believe it, sitting on one of the black folding chairs to the left of the podium. He was in one of the coveted seats saved for top press officials only, and camera crews were setting up all around him.

He wanted to take it all in. The lights, the mics, the White House seal in the background. The president wasn't scheduled to be at this conference—just the press secretary—but this was only the beginning. He knew he'd be back here before long, and maybe one day, he'd be sitting front row, asking the next president a question.

Zain was the politics editor for his college newspaper, and now, with this *Washington Post* internship, he had enough clips to land him a real job when he graduated. He imagined traveling the world, reporting on humanitarian issues around the globe. He would go to the Middle East—to Egypt, to Palestine.

"This is exciting, huh?" said Kristen, the reporter Zain was shadowing. She smiled in his direction, and he smiled back.

"So cool," Zain responded.

The chatter of the crowd began to die down, as Press Secretary McClellan approached the podium. Zain, on cue, pulled his little notebook out of his backpack, ready to take notes on anything and everything, as camera lights flashed in all directions.

When he got back to his apartment that night, he immediately called home.

"Mom, you would not believe what I got to do today."

He could hear her beaming on the other end as he described every detail.

SUMMER 2012

Hannah

Hannah paid attention to the route back as Rami walked her home. She needed to figure out the area—not be dependent on others. The streets were lively, small shops not unlike bodegas back home, selling water and snacks at every corner. Groups of teenagers stood outside laughing and shouting. Hannah and Rami didn't speak, and amid all the noise outside, she could hear the loud silence between them, piercing and tense. Last night, though, everything had felt right, like she'd briefly turned off her brain, but now, slightly hungover and having to get ready for prayer, her mind turned on again, slowly filling with anxious thoughts, funneling into whirlpools of sadness. She was alone here, and while sleeping with Rami had brought some temporary relief, this silent walk the next morning only heightened the reality of her loneliness.

She needed to get these jeans off her—tight and constricting under the Cairo sun. She needed to shower, to wash away the sweat, smoke, and sex. When they arrived outside her apartment, she thanked Rami for walking her back.

"I guess I'll see you around," she added.

They didn't exchange numbers or contact info. Instead, they quickly hugged, awkwardly saying goodbye. Maybe she shouldn't have told him so much personal shit. They barely knew each other. The goodbye without an exchange of info felt final, like a rejection—an indication that he had no interest in seeing her again. It was fine. There was no use dwelling on what Rami thought of her. She had to get ready for prayer.

Growing up, every year at the end of Ramadan, her family would go to the local mosque for Eid prayer. They were a twice-a-year kind of family—just for the holidays. Her dad would occasionally go to Friday prayer alone, giving himself a long lunch break during work—or at least they thought—but not her mom. It wasn't that her mom didn't pray. She did, but not in the mosque, just alone in her bedroom.

Hannah remembered her mom standing, arms folded across her stomach, long white scarf over her head. She would focus on nothing besides the prayer in those moments, ignoring everything else—ignoring Hannah, who would be shouting "Mom" from another room. It was like she was in a trance, in conversation with God.

"Mom, I've been calling you from downstairs," Hannah would say, barging into the bedroom.

But there she was, bent over in prayer as Hannah groaned, irritated that this took precedence over her own problems—problems that at the time consisted of Zain hiding one of her toys or ripping the heads off her Barbie dolls. Pressing matters.

This wasn't right. Having sex and then going to prayer. It almost seemed worse than not praying at all. She peeled her clothes off, the sweat on her body dry now—hers and Rami's. Zakaria would be here any minute. Standing in her bra and underwear, she grabbed a chunk of her hair and sniffed. It smelled like sheesha. Maybe no one would notice if she tied it in a bun. She headed to the bathroom to do wudu. Her dad had taught her how when she was a kid, and as she turned on the water, washing her hands and arms three times each, moving up to her face, nose, ears, and head, it was like he was standing next to her, explaining each step, talking about how important it was to be clean before God.

"In the desert," he had said, "if people didn't have access to water, they'd use sand."

Seven-year-old Hannah couldn't help but point out then that sand does not, in fact, get one clean, and that whenever they'd return home from the beach, covered in sand and salt, her parents would insist on a shower immediately. But apparently, in certain instances, God had okayed sand.

She finished the wudu and dried herself, quickly changing her clothes. She needed food—something to quell this hangover and stop the heavy, churning feeling in her stomach. But the kitchen cabinets were mostly empty, as she had been eating out or at work. There were some crackers on a shelf. That would have to be enough.

A minute later, Zakaria texted that he was downstairs, and she stuffed a few more crackers in her mouth just before heading out the door. Outside, he introduced her to his sister, Layla, a pretty girl a few years younger. Hannah noticed that her dark blue head scarf was pinned up and wrapped around her head in a way that made it look more like a fashion piece than a religious statement.

"Salamu alaikum." Layla reached forward and gave Hannah a kiss on each cheek.

Hannah could taste the alcohol still on her own breath as she reciprocated the greeting. Hopefully, they couldn't smell it.

"You have something for your hair?" Zakaria motioned to his own head. Hannah looked at him for a few seconds, mouth open, before understanding.

"Oh, yeah, it's in my bag. I figured I'd put it on when we got there."

The mosque was close, Zakaria said, so they would walk. This gave Layla ample time to grill Hannah about her life in America, about her studies and her plans. She wanted to know if in America, life was the way it seemed in movies.

"What do you mean?"

"Everyone is always doing parties and going to dates."

Hannah laughed. "I mean, people have parties and go on dates but not all the time. Egyptians have parties too."

Layla shook her head. "Not the same."

As they walked, the adhan began, and Hannah was brought back to Rami's bed, hours earlier, listening to this same call to prayer. A feeling of not belonging deepened within her.

"Are we late?" she asked, as the adhan ended.

"No, we can go at any time," Zakaria said. "Do you go to prayer in America?"

"Not really." Hannah avoided Zakaria's eyes as she said this, not too keen to see the likely look of judgment on his face, and instead studied the building before them. This mosque wasn't off in its own area separate from other buildings, like the one her mother's funeral was held in. Instead, it was enclosed between two small shops and didn't have the look of a mosque from the outside, save for the rounded minaret at the top.

Hannah took her scarf out of her purse and wrapped it around her head, not with any flourish like Layla's, but just around, with the ends draped over her shoulders. She wore it loosely, her hair visible through the sides, her bun creating an odd bump in the back.

The inside of the building didn't match the plain facade outside. Instead, the place was decorated ornately, with blue-and-gold carpet, the walls covered in flowery tile patterns and matching blue-and-gold Quranic writing along the trim. This mosque was smaller, the women's section not upstairs but in the back. They took off their shoes, and Hannah and Layla went one way, Zakaria another.

"Do you need to do wudu?" Layla asked.

"No, I did it at home." Hannah readjusted the scarf on her head.

She didn't even know if the wudu counted, having had sex the night before. She probably should have showered, but there just wasn't time.

They made their way past rows of women, their section less crowded than the men's. Layla found a spot near the back where the two of them stood side by side. Everyone was praying, or just arriving and praying, not waiting for anything too formal. It wasn't as ceremonial as she'd thought it would be. People just came and went as they pleased. Layla stood in place, raising her hand above her head to begin prayer, and Hannah followed suit, mumbling the words under her breath.

She thought about Rami again—about being in his bed, about kissing him, about . . .

"Allahu-akbar . . ."

This wasn't what she was supposed to be thinking about during prayer. Her eyes darted across the room as she bent down—losing focus of the spot on the rug that she should have been looking at.

"La illaha illah allah . . ."

So many women were in here, probably focused on their prayer, not on a hookup from the night before. Still, something about that knowledge—that she had come back from a guy's house just that morning—was sort of thrilling, in its own way. She didn't belong here, didn't have any right to be here praying, but the incongruity of it all gave her a little bit of a rush.

The place wasn't air-conditioned, and beads of sweat trickled down her forehead, down her chest. Hannah said the words, knelt, stood back up again. She went through all the motions, but still, all she could see, all she could feel, was Rami's skin on hers.

They finished and stood, and she wiped the sweat from her brow as Layla guided her back to the entrance of the mosque, where Zakaria waited. Outside, Hannah immediately took her scarf off and shoved it back in her bag, relieved at the burst of fresh air and eager to go for a meal at Zakaria's suggestion.

At the café he chose, two men at a nearby table were conversing about Morsi. Hannah momentarily forgot her hunger as she listened in.

"Morsi is no good," said one of the men. *"But there's movement now. Things are going to change."*

"I know, I've got friends over in Tahrir every day. It's starting. We'll see very soon."

Since Hannah had been in Egypt, the movement had been confusing and the protests disjointed and misplaced. She'd been reading the news, but it was hard to tell what people were even protesting anymore, and every week, there was some new issue, seemingly unrelated to the government. For instance, earlier in the month, people were protesting a movie—something about the depiction of the Prophet Muhammad, which, sure, wasn't allowed in Islam, but definitely wasn't worthy of all that anger.

That protest had started to get violent too, and of course, the media latched on to that as proof that Muslims were violent and extremist. Those people made Muslims look bad and distracted from what was really important, but they weren't nearly as bad as the Christian fundamentalists shooting up abortion clinics or the Zionists murdering Palestinians. But when it came to Muslims, the media treated every act of fundamentalism like a representation of the religion as a whole. Meanwhile, all the women who had been protesting for real change and freedom when the revolution first started seemed to have been silenced, Tahrir now occupied by angry men with no clear purpose or message.

The two men sitting nearby whispered their vague grievances to one another, neither of them really talking about what change, exactly, they were hoping for. Hannah hoped they'd go into more detail about their friends in Tahrir, or what they hoped to accomplish. Was this something the college version of her mom would have been a part of? She wanted to understand more, but ever since Morsi was elected, nothing was clear. The country seemed just as lost as she was, and on top of it all, women were no longer at the forefront.

"What did you think of prayer?" Zakaria asked as they scanned their menus.

Hannah was jolted back to reality, back to the memory of the mosque, when all she could think about was Rami's body against hers. "It was good." She took a sip from her water bottle. "Really cool."

"Really?" Layla said, leaning forward in her seat.

Hannah nodded. "Yeah, totally."

"Next time, we can stay until the Imam speaks," Zakaria said. "I was just very hungry today." He leaned back and patted his stomach.

Hannah was only half listening to Zakaria, still keyed into the conversation of the men next to them quietly but fervently discussing the protests.

"Hey, what was it like in Tahrir?" Hannah looked from Layla to Zakaria. "The protests, I mean."

"Mama and Baba wouldn't let me go." Layla rolled her eyes.

Zakaria's face turned solemn.

"I only went at the beginning." He looked down at his hands, which were folded together on the tabletop. "Last year, when everything was different."

"How was it?"

"Amazing . . . at first."

He leaned back again and looked up at Hannah, then began to describe the sense of community in the square—how they were all there for a purpose, and how it meant something. They wanted liberation, Zakaria told her. In Egypt, the rich were getting richer, and the poor were getting poorer. Women had no voice. Everyone was out there with a common goal—or so they thought.

"We used to organize on Facebook," Zakaria said. "It was peaceful, and then it wasn't anymore. I stopped going because it started to get dangerous. The government, the people—the message wasn't clear anymore, and the Muslim Brotherhood took over the protests, but they didn't want the same things. They just wanted power."

Although Zakaria had only gone a few times, at the very beginning, he told Hannah about friends of his that kept going, even after the situation became less safe. They were attacked by the army, he said. His parents made him promise he wouldn't go back—that he would stay out of it.

"My friend Ali," Zakaria said, looking down again as he folded and unfolded his hands, "he was killed at one of the protests."

"Oh my God, I'm so sorry."

Zakaria wouldn't look back up at her, his eyes down on the table. "The army—they beat him, and . . ." He shook his head. "Masr—it's a disaster."

Talking to Zakaria and Layla was so different than talking to the Americans the night before, none of whom really got what was at stake. She didn't fully get it herself, but hearing Zakaria speak about what he'd lost made this all the more tangible.

"When I first got here, we passed by Tahrir," Hannah said. "I heard people protesting about lights or something."

"The power outages," Zakaria said. "It's the army, trying to show that Morsi is no good. Like this is what happens under the Muslim Brotherhood. And the garbage collection too—they don't come sometimes, to show what happens with Morsi in charge, so there's garbage everywhere."

"Wait, the army prevents them?"

Zakaria nodded, looking up at Hannah again. "It's a shame. The army wants to take over and have another revolution to get rid of Morsi."

"No one is talking about that in the news. We just heard about the protests around that movie." Hannah looked from Zakaria to Layla, two people who were clearly in mourning.

"So stupid," Zakaria said. He raised his hand as the server walked by, and the man nodded in their direction but didn't come over to the table. "The Americans don't care," Zakaria continued. "They like this story about the film because it makes us look bad. Most Egyptians, we don't even care about this." He waved his hands in the air dismissively.

"We have no good choices," said Layla, who had stayed quiet for most of the conversation. "When Egyptians go to vote, they have to choose between two bad regimes."

Finally, the server approached their table and pulled out his notebook without saying a word. They placed their orders; the server jotted them down and then walked away briskly.

Hannah looked back at Layla and Zakaria. "And the protests in Tahrir now? What are they trying to accomplish?"

Layla shook her head. "It's a disaster, like Zakaria said. And more dangerous, especially for women."

Hannah paused and remembered her mom's work in her youth. "Have you guys heard of AWSA? Arab Women's Solidarity Association?"

Layla furrowed her eyebrows and looked up for a moment, as though trying to recall some lost memory. "This is old, right? In the '80s?"

"Yeah." Hannah sat up straighter now, excited that they'd heard of the group. "My mom was a part of it. I just found out."

Layla said she had learned about AWSA in school and knew they did work to help women in need, but she didn't know much more than that.

"What is your mom doing now?" Zakaria asked.

"Oh my God." Hannah lurched back in her seat. "Sorry, I thought I told you."

Her stomach sank yet again, as she knew she'd have to repeat the same story she'd told the group the night before. That she'd have to endure the same pity and awkwardness. How many people would she meet here in Egypt? And when would she just stop telling her story and instead make up some lie about what she was doing here? For now, she would tell the truth, though, about her mom and about giving up law school.

"I'm sorry," Layla said when Hannah finished speaking.

"This is unbelievable," Zakaria said. "You just changed your whole life."

Hannah nodded.

Zakaria and Layla stared at her with that familiar look of pity. It was clear they didn't know what to say. Once again, she was sharing too much with people she barely knew.

"Anyway, let's talk about something else." Hannah shifted in her seat, desperate now to change the subject. "I don't really know much about you guys. Are you two in school? Or working?" She looked at Zakaria. "How old are you?"

Zakaria was twenty-four, Layla only seventeen. He explained that he was in grad school, getting his master's degree in biology, and didn't yet have a plan for after.

"Maybe I will try to go to America," he said. "I don't know yet."

Layla was in her first year of college, hoping to become a pediatrician. They both lived at home with their parents, as was the norm in Egypt, but they were so much like Hannah and her peers back home in their interests and indecisions. They seemed religious, and normally, that meant more conservative, and to a certain degree it did, but they watched all the same shows, knew all the same movies, even listened to some of the same music. Layla was a typical seventeen-year-old girl. She was good in school, really smart it seemed, but also somewhat boy crazy, as evidenced by her obsession with Justin Bieber, who she managed to bring up in the conversation.

Zakaria shook his head, as though exhausted by this topic, and Layla held up her phone to show Hannah her screen: a picture of Bieber doing some sort of pouty lip thing as he looked into the camera.

Their food—a rich, smoky kofta, unlike any she'd ever had in America—finally arrived after about forty-five minutes of waiting, but the wait didn't seem to bother anyone, as it was a thing of normalcy here. Hannah had never been to a small local restaurant like this one in Egypt. When she'd visited in the past, some relative or other would occasionally suggest an eatery, but her mom would shoot the idea down, saying she didn't want to get sick, as if all Cairo food would make her sick. It was like she hadn't grown up there.

2003

Hannah

Her dad always gave her and Zain a hard time for not being more religious. Her parents would often try to get her and Zain to pray, but five prayers a day was a tough commitment. Hannah was too lazy to clean her room, let alone get up to do wudu and prayer. God had too many demands. But fasting during Ramadan was a whole other story. Starting at age fourteen, there were no exceptions. There was no reason for fourteen—just an arbitrary age her parents had decided on, perhaps assuming fourteen meant some newfound maturity, some strength to abstain from food for the day. Maybe they figured Jews had Bar and Bat Mitzvahs at thirteen, so that was a good age range to officially grow up. So at age fourteen, they told her she would have to start fasting. She'd known it was coming. Zain had been fasting for a few years already, but she'd hoped maybe this would be another double standard. Maybe they'd think girls couldn't handle it. It was the only time in her life she wanted sexism to save the day. It didn't. Of course, she protested at first.

"I can't. I have school and soccer," she pleaded from her spot on the couch.

"Zain fasts, even with sports," her mom said, not bothering to look away from the TV.

"Yeah, but Zain is older. He's more—fit."

She knew that her argument was falling apart.

Her mom looked at her and sighed. "Just try. If you can't do it, we'll talk about it."

On the first day, all her friends sat in the cafeteria with their bag lunch or waited in line for school lunch. When she reached the cafeteria, she didn't know what to do exactly. Everyone would ask why she wasn't eating. She could just say she wasn't hungry, but no one would buy that. She always spent the period before lunch complaining about how starving she was. She could tell them the truth: "I'm fasting for Ramadan." But they wouldn't understand. None of her friends at school were Muslim, and she didn't want to be the one that was different—the freak. The Muslim girl who didn't eat. So she stood in line for lunch that day, eating with everyone else in the cafeteria, and she did the same every day after.

"How was it fasting this year?" her dad asked at the end of that month, just as they sat down for their last Ramadan dinner.

"It wasn't that hard," she lied, looking him right in the eye.

He smiled. "Next year," he said, "you need to make sure you pray five times a day too. I know it's hard with school, but you can pray when you come home."

SUMMER 2012

Zain

After wandering the streets of Philly, Zain ended up outside Emily's apartment in Old City, ringing the doorbell. He didn't even realize, really, that he was walking there. No answer. She must have been in class, so he walked away and texted her that he was in the area and wanted to meet. She definitely knew he'd been avoiding her. But Rachel was out of his life now, and he could be a better person.

He was walking fast, like he couldn't stop moving, didn't know where to go as his thoughts bounced from one corner of his mind to another, a million little balls being thrown around his brain. Rent was due soon, and he could afford it, but beyond that he'd be out of money. He debated whether to just walk around for a couple of hours until Emily got home, but that was stupid. He should just find a coffee shop that was open and collect his thoughts. Although what would he even do in a coffee shop with no laptop to keep him busy? He could go into a bar. No need for a computer to kill time there. But it was only a little after eleven thirty in the morning. Race Street Cafe seemed to be open, though—he'd been to that bar a few times before. He checked his phone. No response from Emily yet. Since he was just fired, he owed it to himself to get one drink, at least.

The place was nearly empty, save for one person eating a sandwich. Zain sat down a few seats away, and the bartender handed him a menu.

"Actually, I'm just gonna have a drink for now," Zain said, ordering a whiskey sour.

When Emily finally responded an hour and a half later, he was four and a half drinks in and venting to the bartender about Rachel. How she had no right to fire him, how he could sue her for sexual harassment. He'd talked himself into even more anger, more frustration, and Rachel was the source of it all—the cause of his pain, the villain in the movie that was his life. None of this was his fault.

"Sleeping with the boss," the bartender said. "Big mistake, buddy."

"Whatever. Fuck her. I'll find a new job. I can write. I'm good at it. She just never gave me a chance." He took one last sip of whiskey. "Anyway, I gotta go meet my girlfriend."

"You have a girlfriend?"

Zain looked up. "What? No. Did I say 'girlfriend'?"

"Are you telling me you have a girlfriend and you're sleeping with your boss? Man, I don't feel bad for you anymore."

The bartender smiled as he said this, but Zain felt like he'd been slapped in the face, waking him up to the fact that maybe *he* was the villain in his movie—the cheating boyfriend that no one roots for.

"She's not—I don't have a girlfriend," Zain said. "She's just—it's complicated. We've known each other for a while, and we used to date, and now it's—I don't know what it is."

He began to sweat, little beads of shame forming on his forehead.

"All right, I'll get you your check."

He'd lost the man's respect, or his camaraderie, at any rate. Before, he was just some jackass who'd slept with the boss and gotten fired. Now he was the drunk guy going to a bar in the morning, going to meet his girlfriend while drunk. The guy who would cheat on his girlfriend.

Zain paid his bill, quiet now, no longer chatting with the bartender. He left him a good tip, at least. There was a gnawing sensation in his gut. He was drunk on an empty stomach, feeling guilty and angry all at once. He had to see Emily. He had to fix everything.

Emily answered the door still in her blue scrubs, and Zain stumbled inside before she could say anything.

"I got fired this morning." He looked down at the square pattern on her blue rug.

"Oh my God, what?"

He plopped himself onto the couch as she stood over him.

"Are you drunk?" she asked.

"A little." He leaned forward and pushed his forehead into the palms of his hands. "You weren't here, so I went to that bar down the street."

His mind was going in circles, and he knew then that he would tell her everything. He sat up but couldn't look at her, instead keeping his eyes locked in front of him on the black emptiness of the television screen. If he didn't tell her, he would puke, and not from the alcohol, but just from the need to get it all out. He was so disgusted with who he'd become—a dark shadow of his former self. He'd never seen himself as a cheater, or as someone who would hurt another person, especially not Emily. Maybe his dad also felt that way. They were the same, the two of them.

"Zain, you can't keep doing this." She sat down and placed her hand on his shoulder. Her flowery perfume wafted into his nostrils. "I can't take care of you."

He hadn't wanted to be around her lately. It was irritating how nice she was and how much she cared, and right then, he hated himself all over again—this time for being irritated by her goodness.

"I slept with my boss," he said.

Emily took her hand off his shoulder. He still didn't look at her, but he could see her looking at him out of his periphery.

"Can you please repeat that?"

He lifted his head slightly. She looked serious, concerned almost, but surely not concerned for him anymore.

"Emily," he said.

"Repeat what you said, because I'm just really hoping I heard wrong." Her tone was angry now.

"I'm sorry."

"When? When did this happen?"

"When I came back from Egypt, at the work party you couldn't come to." He heard her breathe out through her nose, a heavy breathing like she was trying to steady herself. "And it's been going on since then," he continued.

"You're an asshole."

She was right. She stood and began to pace back and forth in her living room.

"I want to tell you to leave," Emily said, "but I feel like that would be letting you off the hook. I've been so *nice* to you since your mom died, and do you know how much of an effort that's been? I was really, truly sad for you. And this entire time, you've been treating me like shit, but I wasn't gonna say anything about that because your mom *just* died. And then you find out that your dad is having an affair, and I'm like, okay, I need to be supportive. I need to *be there* for Zain."

Zain had never seen her like this before. They'd had spats as a couple in the past, but he was unaccustomed to seeing Emily's soft features twisted by anger.

"I'm sorry," he said, his body at the edge of the couch, facing her as she continued pacing.

"Which boss? Is it Rachel?" She stopped walking and looked at him, her arms on her hips.

"Does it matter?" He averted his eyes from her gaze.

"It's Rachel, isn't it? You complain about her so fucking much, and then you went and fucked her?"

"Emily, you and me, we weren't really together." He looked back up at her.

Again, he knew as soon as he said those words that he'd made a mistake. That was the worst possible thing he could have said. The gnawing in his stomach grew.

"What?" She laughed humorlessly. "You're fucking with me, right?"

"I just meant we weren't exclusive." He shifted his body, moving back a little on the couch. "We never had a conversation about a relationship."

Emily moved toward him. He thought she would hit him, the way she walked forward, and he leaned back slightly as she yelled in his face.

"Don't talk to me like I'm some girl you barely know."

He stood and faced her, holding her shoulders in his arms.

"I shouldn't have said that," he said. "I don't think of you as some girl that I'm casually seeing."

"Why would you do this?" She looked up at him, her eyes

begging for some kind of explanation he didn't have, and he didn't know what to say. He stared at her for a moment, his mouth open, hoping the right words would come flowing out, but instead, there was silence.

She twisted her body and pulled her shoulders out of his grip, looking down at the ground.

"I think you need to leave."

Zain sat alone on the subway. His life had fallen apart, and he was entirely to blame. He wanted to crawl into bed and never wake up. He didn't understand how he could have let everything come to this. He thought back to that day in college, during his summer internship, when he'd gotten to go to the White House pressroom. He was sure then that he'd be back before long, that he'd be traveling, reporting on all the injustices of the world. But somewhere along the way, he'd lost that idealism—that motivation. He'd never gotten past Philly, where he wrote fluff stories by day and partied with his friends by night. He had his fun, sure, but now it had all gone to shit.

He'd blamed everything and everyone else for how his life had collapsed, but maybe all of this was his own fault. He'd never really tried that hard after college. And then he'd chosen to sleep with Rachel, and he'd slept with her over and over. He'd screwed everything up for himself. He was a disease, like his dad, creeping around until he infected those he loved and destroyed what he had. He rode home silently, the harsh hum of the subway car grating into his brain like a chainsaw.

FALL 2012

Hannah

Hannah's life began to fall into a sort of routine as the days passed. The owner of the apartment she was staying in had agreed to let her rent the place month to month, so she could leave at any time and stay as long as she wanted. She'd go to work, hang out with her American friends, spend time with Layla and Zakaria, and repeat. Egypt was starting to feel like home, but she still didn't know what she was doing there.

On her free days, she sometimes volunteered with Noha at women's shelters around Cairo, hoping the work would at least bring some meaning to her life here. They collected blankets, food, and other supplies, handing them out to women and children. It was something to do—some way to help out. Her mom, at least, would be proud.

All the while, Cairo grew restless, and people seemed tense. It was November now, and often, she'd overhear political discussions in the café and read about the growing hostility in Tahrir Square, a place she had yet to visit. All throughout October, protests had picked up, this time with more clear criticism of the government. People were accusing the Muslim Brotherhood of trying to take over the country, which, yeah—they were kind of elected to do just that. But the country was becoming more and more divided. There were shifts in government positions and changes to laws, but all in all, that seemed normal for a new government.

"I'm interviewing some protesters," Vanessa said one day at work. "For this piece I'm working on."

"That's awesome." Hannah handed an order to the kitchen staff. "How'd you get in touch with them?"

"Facebook," she said. "There's groups and stuff."

After their first night out with friends, Hannah couldn't stop thinking about Vanessa's time in Tahrir. She'd asked her questions about what she was doing here and what her time had been like so far. Vanessa had come to Egypt with lofty academic goals—writing about a revolution in real time, talking about the theory of it all—but somehow, her focus had shifted more into journalistic work, not reporting, necessarily, but longer think pieces that would get picked up at different publications. She found herself getting in touch with protesters and going out with them to Tahrir, with a few other folks there for protection. Vanessa said she couldn't accurately write about the movement without immersing herself in it. To a certain degree, Hannah was jealous. Vanessa seemed to have some purpose here—she was doing something, getting involved.

"Hey, do you think I could come with you?" Hannah tucked her notepad back into her apron. "Unless that's weird. I don't know. I just want to sit in."

"Oh, yeah, sure. Why, though?"

She didn't know how to explain that she wanted to be a part

of what was going on—to be immersed in Egypt as much as she could. That she needed some reason to be here. There was some existential tug on her body, asking, *What is the point of all this?* Going with Vanessa wouldn't exactly answer that question, but it was *something.*

"I'm just interested," Hannah said. "I kind of want to hear what they have to say."

Perhaps hearing from someone involved would clarify the whole goal of the movement—because the news was just so unclear, like no one knew, really, what anyone wanted. Vanessa was meeting with the protester right after work, so Hannah left with her, the two of them headed to someone's home downtown.

"Is it dangerous for them to talk to you?" Hannah asked.

They were in a taxi, Vanessa riffling through the notes in her backpack.

"It can be. I mean, we don't know what will happen, so even if it's safe now, this could affect them a year from now." She paused, then looked at Hannah. "And all that shit that's happening to journalists—I'm not, like, live reporting or anything, but it's still risky."

They pulled up in front of a nondescript building, one that looked a lot like her grandmother's but newer, as it had an intercom at the front. She couldn't think of her grandmother now, though. She didn't need that nagging guilt in the pit of her stomach—four months here and not a single call to anyone in the family.

Vanessa hit the buzzer for apartment 1C. A muffled voice over the intercom said something unintelligible.

"Uhh, it's Vanessa. Here to meet with Hamid."

"You have to leave," a woman's voice said.

"What?" said Vanessa into the intercom. "No, I'm meeting with Hamid. We have an appointment."

At that, the door opened, and a man in a white T-shirt, shorts, and flip-flops stood in front of them. He was out of breath.

"Hamid," Vanessa said, stepping back. "I was just buzzing."

"I'm sorry." He shook his head. "You have to go."

"What, why?"

"Someone from the government found out you were coming. We can't have the interview anymore." He appeared frantic, his eyes darting all around them.

"What happened?"

"A man came to my wife's office, and he said if we talk to you, there will be trouble."

"Jesus." Vanessa pressed her hand to her forehead.

"Vanessa, we should go." Hannah pulled lightly at her arm. She didn't want this man to get into even more trouble, especially since anyone could be watching them at this very moment.

"I'm sorry," Vanessa said. "I didn't intend for any of this to happen."

"I know." Hamid nodded. "I'm sorry too."

When they got back to Vanessa's apartment, she immediately emailed her editor, asking if they had any advice.

"This is ridiculous." She looked up from her computer. "The government can't really do anything. They're just scaring this poor family."

"I don't know," Hannah said. "This is Egypt. The government can do whatever they want, and they know it."

She was sitting on Vanessa's couch with a glass of wine. They were getting ready to go to a friend's party, but Vanessa was angry, unable to believe that her interview had gotten canceled in the way that it had. Though it wasn't at all surprising. This kind of stuff happened in America too.

"No," Vanessa said. "Not after the revolution. Not when they know the power of the people."

"I just think it'll be a while before Egypt becomes not corrupt," Hannah said, surprised at Vanessa's naivete. She'd been studying Egypt long enough that this shouldn't have been a shock to her, though her optimism was nice.

"But hey, here's your story," Hannah added, her voice rising in pitch as she tried to quell Vanessa's disappointment. "Intimidation of protesters—threatening their families. Follow that lead."

"Yeah." Vanessa took a sip of wine. "I just don't even know where to begin, especially if Hamid won't talk to me. Anyway, we should go soon."

Vanessa shut her computer and headed to her room to get changed. Hannah noticed she'd missed a bunch of texts from Zain.

I can't fucking take this anymore

Dad is driving me insane

Think I'm gonna use the rest of my money to visit you

Living with dad is killing me

Zain was unraveling. That much had been clear since he was fired from his job. Hannah had told him to visit back when he had to move out of his apartment, but he'd said he had to save money, which made sense. He'd been talking to her more, almost as though he had no one else. Hannah didn't reply to the texts but instead put the phone back in her pocket and followed Vanessa into her room.

"My brother is having a meltdown."

"Why? What happened?" Vanessa riffled through her clothes without looking back at Hannah.

"I don't think anything new." Hannah sat down in a chair in the corner of the room. "He moved in with our dad, and he doesn't have a job."

Vanessa paused and turned around. "I thought he was working at, like, a coffee shop or something now."

"Well, yeah, but you know what I mean." Hannah lifted her legs up on the chair so that her knees were at chin level, compressing herself as she spoke.

Zain had never told Hannah why he'd gotten fired. When she'd asked, he'd just said his boss was an asshole, that she was trying to hold him back from success. But that obviously wasn't the real story—or even close to the truth, probably.

"He's looking for journalism jobs, right?" Vanessa said, finally deciding on a flower-patterned blouse from her closet.

"Yeah."

"Why doesn't he freelance and, like, pitch stories for now?" She sat down on her bed.

"I think Zain has a tendency to feel sorry for himself." Hannah contorted her body so that her legs fit fully between the arms of the chair. "And it prevents him from moving forward."

He'd been that way since they were kids. When he'd do poorly on a test, he'd come home and tell his parents it was the teacher's fault.

"Mrs. Roberts just doesn't like me," he'd said one year in high school, after coming home with a C– on a math test.

"Mrs. Roberts gave you a bad grade on this math test because she doesn't like you?" Their mom was standing over him at the kitchen table.

"Yes."

Hannah was in middle school at the time, and she remembered smirking to herself as she watched this exchange.

"Zain, this is a *math* test," their mom said. "There's a right and wrong answer. This isn't subjective at all."

"Mom, it's not my fault. Roberts has it out for me."

"Zain just, like, needs more drive maybe," Hannah said to Vanessa. "He never admits things are his fault, and he expects opportunities to fall into his lap."

"Zain is older than you, right?" Vanessa asked. She started to change her shirt as Hannah spoke.

"Yeah, why?"

"I don't know. Boys are stupid, I guess. They all expect things to just happen for them, I think because they're so used to being coddled."

"Maybe," Hannah said. "Definitely Arab boys. Parents view them as, like, God's gift."

"You don't need to tell me." Vanessa looked at herself in the mirror now.

Hannah forgot sometimes that Vanessa was half Egyptian, though her family was Christian, so things were a little different for her. Vanessa had been around her Egyptian dad's family plenty, but in the end, they were much more American than Hannah's. Plus, they weren't religious, which automatically gave Vanessa more freedom and fewer hang-ups. And she hadn't lived with her dad, her parents having divorced when she was only five, so she'd grown up with her Midwestern mom, outside the culture. Some things, though, Vanessa could understand.

"My dad was the youngest of six kids, and the only boy," Vanessa said, taking her shirt off again, seemingly unsatisfied with the look. "My grandma treated him like the little prince. And, like, I love my dad, but he was coddled too much."

"I think Zain and I were both coddled, though." Hannah

crossed her legs and slouched down in the chair. “It’s not like I’m doing anything with my life either. I gave up law school.”

Vanessa, now in her bra, riffled through her closet again.

“Why did you come here?” Hannah looked up at her. “Like, I know why. You know, your research, but . . . why?”

“You’re asking what I’m running away from.” Vanessa stopped flipping through her shirts now and looked at Hannah.

“No, I mean . . .” Hannah sat up a little.

“It’s cool, I get it,” Vanessa said.

“I didn’t mean to imply . . .”

“It’s okay,” Vanessa said as she grabbed another shirt, this time black with lace trim, from out of the closet and put it on over her head. “I *am* running away. My dad—he has early onset dementia. I spent six months living with him right before I decided to come here, and I just couldn’t handle it. I had to leave, and, I don’t know, Egypt made sense.”

“I’m so sorry.” Hannah sat up fully now. “I didn’t know.”

“No one does.” Vanessa ran her hand over her shirt to smooth out the creases. “You’re the only person I’ve told since coming here.” She paused. “I think I just always feel like I’m being selfish. I left my dad, and when I get back, I don’t even know if he’ll recognize me. But I couldn’t do it anymore.”

Hannah didn’t know what to say, or how to be a comfort. Her own mom was dead, but she couldn’t imagine what it would be like if she were alive and just didn’t remember her kids anymore. In some ways, her mom dying with her memories intact seemed better.

“I’m really sorry,” Hannah said.

“Anyway, it doesn’t matter,” Vanessa shook her head, then looked toward Hannah. “How are *you* doing? You know, life here—your mom and everything?”

"I'm fine." Hannah lifted her legs onto the chair again.

"Are you?"

"Yeah, why? Do I not seem fine?" She pulled her legs into her chest, compressing herself even more.

The night before, she'd cried herself to sleep. The grief was too much to handle sometimes, consuming her entire body like a sickness, tugging at her insides so that all she could do was sit in the dark and cry. But here, with Vanessa—with anyone, really—she tried to compartmentalize, forgetting the grief for the sake of survival.

"I'm gonna get more wine." Hannah stood.

In the kitchen, she poured another glass, hoping to drown her feelings into oblivion. A little while later, she and Vanessa headed out to the party.

"Beautiful," a man around their age said shortly after they stepped outside.

Hannah and Vanessa ignored him, not even making eye contact. This was normal now—the stares, the catcalls. They just kept their heads down. Hannah had kept her pepper spray always within reach since that first week. There hadn't been a reason to use it again, but things had seemed more tense in recent days as the protests in Tahrir picked up. Though she had become an expert at navigating the crowded streets, revolution made the catcallers more belligerent, more demanding. Usually, they'd make a comment and walk by, like the man who'd called them beautiful, but in the past week, some would grow angry when she didn't respond, as though she were the one being rude. That first day here was a warning, a reminder that they were never safe.

Zain

Zain had been living at home for almost a month now, working at a local coffee shop. He and his dad barely talked, but they were civil with one another, behaving like roommates who weren't friends but weren't enemies either. In each of their interactions, Zain could feel his stomach doing flips. He couldn't quell his fury about the affair, the lies, the hypocrisy. But his dad was going out of his way to be nice, and Zain was just living in his house, eating his food, and accepting his help, all the while shutting out the man who'd helped raise him, when they were both grieving. For that reason, each interaction also served as a trigger for guilt, manifesting again in his churning stomach. The anger and guilt swirled inside him in a constant battle that would bring nothing but pain in the end.

He'd been searching for journalism jobs, but many of them asked for references, and since Rachel fired him, he had zero. When he'd applied for his last job, he'd used references from college, from internships, but that was so long ago. Maybe it was time to contact Rachel—if she'd even agree to talk. He couldn't blame her if she wouldn't. The way things had ended were shitty enough, and he had no right to call or ask for anything, but he also couldn't think of any other options.

It was early morning, and Zain sat on his bed and stared down at his phone. He clicked on Rachel's name and began to draft a text.

Hey, I know you don't want to hear from me, but it's important. Can we meet?

His hand hovered over the send button. This was a bad idea. But he hit send anyway.

On his drive to the coffee shop, he kept his phone in his lap, looking down every few minutes, feeling the phantom buzz of an incoming text, but there was nothing. If he could at least engage her in some way, he had a shot of convincing her, or apologizing. But Rachel would never accept an apology. His best bet was pity. Maybe she'd feel bad enough for him to agree to be a reference.

A few hours later, after the morning crowd died down, Zain stood in the corner by the espresso machine and drafted another text.

Rachel please. I need to talk to you. This will be professional. Not a repeat of our last meeting. I'm very sorry to bother you.

He waited, staring at his phone until the three typing dots appeared. He straightened his back. This was it. This was his one shot.

What do you want?

He told her it was work related, and she agreed to meet that evening.

When his shift ended in the afternoon, he rushed home and chose an outfit. He'd dress nicely to look like he was serious: a button-down shirt, work pants. He got back in his car and sped toward Philly. It had been a while since he'd been in the city, and as soon as he crossed the bridge from Jersey, his past life came flooding back—friends, parties, fun. He wanted nothing more than to be here, to go back in time to before his mom died, when he still had Emily, when he had his shitty old job. It was easy, that life. Philly now, though, was more like a museum of his recent past, sending pangs of grief and nostalgia all at once—it was a past that had died along with his mom.

There was time to kill before meeting Rachel, maybe enough to drive down to South Philly, check out the old hood, but it was better not to be late. Plus, he wasn't sure he could take it—driving through his old neighborhood. It would only serve as another reminder of how much he'd fucked up. So instead, he searched for a parking spot near Rittenhouse. He would meet Rachel at Parc, the nice Ameri-French restaurant that seemed like a good place for a business meeting. He wiped his sweaty palms on his pants and went inside early to order a drink—something to ease his nerves.

There were two open spots at the bar, so he put his coat on one seat to save it for Rachel and ordered himself a beer as his stomach bubbled in anticipation. When Rachel arrived, he was already on his second beer. It felt as though the temperature in the room had suddenly risen, and beads of sweat formed on his forehead, which he promptly wiped with his sleeve. She approached the bar, serious and unsmiling.

"Hi, Zain," she said. "I don't have a ton of time, so let's not drag this out too long."

She took her coat off to reveal a tight black professional dress. She'd worn that to his apartment one night, and as he'd tried to take it off her, the zipper had gotten stuck, caught on some of the dress fabric. They'd laughed as he struggled to unzip her, and Rachel had asked, jokingly, if this was his first time. As shitty as it was, he missed having her in his bed, tracing the curves of her body with his fingertips, feeling her nails on his back. But then right after, he'd think of Emily, or his dad, or the fact that he'd hated Rachel for his entire time at that job.

"So, what is it?" she said, sitting down on the barstool. "What's so important?"

He took a sip of his beer, cold in his mouth. "Can I get you a drink?"

"You can tell me why I'm here, and I'll order my own drink." She looked him up and down, as though aware he was stalling.

The bartender came over just then, and Rachel ordered a gin and tonic.

He had to speak—to apologize and make his case.

"I need to say I'm sorry." His hand still gripped his glass in front of him. "I should have never behaved the way I did. It was childish and entitled and just completely unprofessional—although I guess we were both a little unprofessional."

Rachel said nothing as the bartender brought over her drink. Zain let go of his own drink then. He wasn't sure if his hand was wet from the glass, or if he was sweating, but he wiped it on his pants.

"I know I messed things up for myself," Zain continued. "And I unfairly blamed you and put you in a difficult situation, and I completely understand why you fired me. I deserved it." She slowly sipped her drink as he spoke, his words coming out fast and frantic.

"Are you here to ask for my forgiveness or something? Ask me to absolve you of your sins?"

"No," he said. "I'm not—no. I just needed to let you know that I'm sorry."

"Yeah, okay," she said, taking another sip of her gin and tonic. "I know there's something else coming, though. You're working up to ask me for something."

He took another gulp of his beer. There was a couple sitting next to them at the bar. The man spoke, and the woman laughed, leaning into him. Zain looked back at Rachel. He began to crack his knuckles, and when he'd done that once, he tried again, pressing down on his fingers one at a time, but there was just pain.

"So . . ." She was still looking at him. "Do you have something else to say to me?"

"You know what? No," he said. "This was a mistake. I shouldn't have texted you. I'm sorry."

Zain gestured for the check.

"Hold on, no." She put her hand on his arm. "You can't ask me to come meet you and then bail like this. What did I come here for?"

He hesitated. "I need a reference."

She removed her hand and said nothing.

He faced her. "I know I shouldn't be asking, but I'm desperate."

"So that apology was bullshit, then?"

"No, I meant every word." Both his hands were sweating now, and he wiped his palms on his pants.

"Well, you know you can't use me as a reference," she said. "I fired you."

"I know," he said, "but I need to get my life together."

"I'm sorry, Zain." She shook her head. "It's just not going to happen."

She finished what was left of her drink, then paid and left. He sat alone at the bar, his heart heavy with past mistakes. He wanted another drink, but not here. Not in this fucking expensive place. So he sent a group text to his friends—friends that he hadn't seen since moving out of Philly—and asked who was free that night.

Zain finished his beer and coordinated plans to meet up with people at Dirty Frank's. His excitement felt muffled, though, given that they were Emily's friends too, but outside of family, they were all that he had left, and his stomach twisted at the prospect of sinking even deeper into loneliness. He wondered, though, if they would ask him about Emily—about why they broke up. He wasn't even sure what Emily had told them. As he walked over to the familiar haunt, Zain pushed the thought out of his mind, determined to have the dive bar whisk his problems away.

Hannah

With Vanessa's interview not happening, she and Hannah made their way to their friend's party, where groups of people Hannah knew from the café sat in circles and discussed the changes happening in Egypt. Vanessa told them about that afternoon and being unable to conduct her interview. In general, people agreed that Morsi was bad for Egypt, but no one in the room was *from* Egypt, so they couldn't *really* understand what the people here were dealing with. They were just a group of Americans discussing the state of a country that wasn't theirs—interjecting their opinions where they didn't belong. Hannah wished she could be with the actual people of Egypt instead, hearing their thoughts, but she knew in reality, this was the room she belonged in. These were her people more so than the ones born and raised in Cairo.

"If things get too heated," one girl cut in, "I'm just going back to the States. I didn't come here to get myself killed."

"I mean, you're lucky you've got that privilege," Hannah said, her tone purposely demeaning. "But what about everyone who can't leave? What are the Egyptian people supposed to do?"

Everyone got silent.

"Guys," someone said. "Could we chill for a minute? This is a party."

As the conversation shifted to lighter topics, Hannah got up to get another drink. This was her country, sort of, but she would leave too if the situation became too rough. She was no different than all the other privileged Americans at this party, and what was worse, she wasn't even using that privilege to do any good, instead wallowing in grief as she tried to escape her own life. Her chest panged as she walked into the kitchen, a sharp pain through her heart that she wished she could numb. She wanted to leave, but she knew if she did, she'd just go home and continue to feel jaded and useless—like she was wasting her time, her life. At least here at this party, she could distract herself.

As she grabbed a beer out of the fridge, she heard footsteps behind her and looked up.

"Oh, hey," Rami said, seemingly taken aback.

She hadn't seen him since that morning he'd walked her home. Hannah shut the fridge, shifting her weight awkwardly from one foot to the other.

"Hey! I didn't know you'd be here." She winced at the fake enthusiasm in her voice.

"How've you been?"

"Good," she lied. "Just busy. You?"

He nodded. "Good."

They made some more small talk in the kitchen, until they finished their drinks and had another. Eventually, he leaned in to kiss her, and at the end of the night, it just seemed so easy to go home with him. It was almost two a.m. when she was lying awake with no clothes in his bed again.

"I have to leave." She started to sit up.

“What?” He looked at her.

“I don’t want to spend the night.”

She could easily stay over. She wanted to, even, as she pictured falling asleep with their bodies touching again, his warmth a salve that would ease the bruising of the past few months. But she knew that the longer she stayed, the more difficult it would be to peel herself away, and she’d start to crave his body next to hers, when this was nothing more than a hookup. She began to get up and put her clothes back on.

“You shouldn’t walk back alone.” He sat up now. “It’s late.”

“I’ll be fine.” She pulled her pants up and buttoned them. “I know how to get back.”

“I can walk you.” He was still in the bed.

“No, it’s fine.”

She couldn’t handle another awkward post-sex walk home, so he told her to text him when she got back, and they quickly exchanged numbers.

“I’ll stay up,” he said. “Just wanna make sure you get back okay.”

He put a pair of sweatpants on and walked her to the door. They hugged goodbye, and Hannah began the walk home, drunk and tired, pepper spray gripped tightly in hand. There were still people out in the streets, but they were mostly men, the few women outside accompanied by fathers, husbands, boyfriends, brothers. She kept her head down, ignoring any catcalls. The sidewalk blurred, and she focused on keeping her feet in line, not swerving off to the side in a drunken mess.

“Hannah?”

There was a familiar voice. Zakaria? He wouldn’t be out this late. She turned around and saw him sitting outside a café with a group of men around their age, smoking sheesha. This didn’t seem like Zakaria. He wouldn't be out at two a.m. smoking sheesha. Or maybe he would. Perhaps she'd simply constructed a version of him that was wholesome, religious, home in bed by nine. But then again, everyone in Egypt smoked sheesha, and men were always out late into the night, religious or not. He was just doing what Egyptians did.

"Hannah, what are you doing here?" he said from the table where he sat.

"Hey, oh my God," she said. "I didn't expect to see you."

"Where are you going?"

"Home. I was at my friend's party."

It was good that Rami hadn't walked her home. How would she explain that to Zakaria? Not that she needed to, but how would it look for her, a Muslim girl, to be out alone with another man this late at night? Zakaria would realize she wasn't a real Muslim. She'd feel almost as bad as she would if anyone from her family caught her out late with a boy. If they knew what she'd been up to that night, they'd view her as destined for hell.

He stood and approached her, standing close enough to smell the alcohol on her breath.

"It's dangerous to walk by yourself at night."

"I know, but I'm being careful." She loosened her grip on the pepper spray to show him, and he laughed. He motioned for her to sit at the table.

"Come, sit with us."

"I should really get home."

"No, just stay for a little bit. I'll take you home after. Meet my friends."

"Okay." She nodded. "Okay, just a little bit."

He grabbed her hand to pull her to the table. When he didn't immediately let go, she yanked her hand away and motioned as if to wave to his friends. Zakaria introduced them, listing off a set of names she wouldn't remember. They passed her the pipe. She should say no. It would make the drunkenness worse, but she took a small puff anyway and felt Zakaria's eyes on her as she inhaled. Would he allow his sister to be here, smoking with this group of men?

His friends were funny, and Hannah laughed at their jokes, noticing out of the corner of her eye how Zakaria kept looking at her, like he knew something was off. Could they tell she was drunk? Rami texted her, asking if she made it home okay, and she lied, telling him that she was back.

Eventually, everyone else was ready to head home, and Zakaria, keeping his promise, walked Hannah back to her apartment.

"So you were at a party tonight?"

"Yeah." Hannah looked down at the sidewalk, at her white sneakers now streaked with dust.

"You drank a lot?"

She looked up at him. "Fuck," she said, "is it that obvious?"

"No," he said, "but when I stand next to you before, I can smell it."

The streets were darker now, Cairo seeming quieter than usual that night.

"I don't—I mean, I don't drink that often. I know it's, like, haram . . ."

If she were with her family, she would come up with any excuse, any denial, anything so that they wouldn't know the truth. But Zakaria wasn't family, and he was her age, making him less likely to believe some loosely crafted lie, anyway.

He smiled, as though amused by the revelation. "I just never knew before. It's interesting, I think."

"Interesting?" She raised her eyebrows at him.

"Yes. A different Hannah."

They arrived outside her apartment, a short walk from the sheesha place, and they stopped and faced one another.

"If you knew," she said, "why did you invite me to hang out with you and your friends?"

"What do you mean?"

"Well, don't you have a problem with this? You don't want a drunk girl hanging around."

Zakaria smiled again. "Hannah, I'm not a perfect Muslim either."

She paused to think. "What does that mean?"

"Just, I'm not perfect. I break the same rules sometimes. It's okay."

She'd never considered that Zakaria could be like her, that he also broke the rules from time to time. Still, he was a better Muslim than her. He went to Friday prayer, after all. He wasn't like her, living life with no regard for the rules of Islam. She didn't even feel guilty for it anymore, not like when she was younger. But she didn't want others to judge her—for the real Muslims to know she wasn't like them.

"I have to go to bed," she said and gave him a small smile back. "Thank you for walking me home."

Zain

When Zain arrived at Dirty Frank's, a sticky beer smell wafted through the air, taking him back to summer nights in this very bar and filling him with a warmth he hadn't felt in weeks, a sense of comfort he'd gotten from nights out with good friends, when life was less complicated. Someone sat in a booth with a dog in his lap. Zain grabbed a seat at the bar and ordered himself the beer-and-shot special. He was halfway through his beer when his friend James walked in.

"Dude, where have you been?" James said, reaching in for a hug.

"Hey, man," Zain said. "Just, around. Had to move back home for a bit."

James, one of Zain's oldest friends, had heard about the breakup, about Zain getting fired, but he had a ton of questions, and Zain tried to fill in the gaps as best he could, leaving out the affair with his boss and his dad's affair with Vivian. He hadn't spoken to any of his friends since he'd moved home, mainly because he was ashamed, the memory of what he'd done building first in his chest, spreading to his lungs like a cancer so that he couldn't breathe, his own sense of panic threatening to suffocate him entirely. If he said the words out loud, letting others hear what he'd done, he'd surely die, the shame consuming his body entirely until no part of him could function.

More friends began to flow in, and before long, it was like he'd never left. The night began to feel like so many Philly nights before that, only it wasn't. He wouldn't be stumbling back to his South Philly apartment later, for starters. Or actually—Dirty Frank's nights usually ended up back at Emily's, since they were closer to her apartment than his. This night wouldn't end at Emily's because Emily wasn't here.

"So what's next?" James said. His other friends were out of earshot.

"I don't know, gonna order another drink probably." They

were sitting at the corner of the bar, Zain's drink nearly empty.

"No, I mean, in life. Are you and Emily trying to work things out?"

Zain shook his head.

He didn't want to talk about Emily, so he changed the subject and asked James about his own life instead, listening as James recounted his issues with a new girlfriend Zain had never met. Soon, it was past midnight, and his phone buzzed on the table, "Dad" flashing across the screen. The drinks in his system made everything fuzzy, and he stared down at his phone, the screen blurring before his eyes.

"Hello?"

"Yo, you sure you want to answer that?" James said.

"Zain, where are you?" his dad asked. "Are you coming home tonight?"

It was like high school all over again, when his parents would call to check in if he was out too late. Maybe he needed to end the secrets.

"Yeah, no, I'm honestly too drunk to come home tonight." He hobbled off the barstool.

"Shit, Zain, hang up." James stood too, making a grab for the phone.

Zain swatted his hand away. The words came out of his mouth before he could even think about them, but this was it. He'd stop living a double life and tell his dad everything.

"Zain, what's going on?"

"I'm very drunk right now, so I will most definitely be staying with a friend." He was walking away from James, toward the door.

"Where are you?" his dad asked. "I'm picking you up."

"Dad, I'm fine," Zain shouted over the sounds of everyone at the bar. "It's no big deal. I drink. Maybe you should know that."

"Dude, hang up," James continued, trying to grab the phone, but Zain swerved out of reach.

"Dad, I need to tell you everything," he shouted.

"You're gonna regret this," James said.

Zain waved him away.

"I drink, like, all the time. I also smoke. Not cigarettes. I smoke weed—like, a lot of it. There's some in my room now. Surprised you haven't smelled it since I moved back in, actually, 'cause I've been smoking every day. Also, I slept with my boss, and then I got fired. So I'm no better than you."

"Dude." James threw his hands over his head in dismay.

Zain looked over at him. Now *he* knew too. His friends would take Emily's side, and they should. He didn't deserve them.

"Zain, come home," his dad said. "Let me pick you up."

"I don't think so," Zain said. "We'll talk later."

He hung up. James stared at him, open mouthed, the two of them standing near the doorway, away from their other friends.

James shook his head. "Was that true? About your boss? Is that why you and Emily broke up?"

Zain nodded. "I'm not a good person," he said. "I think I need to go see her."

The bar was spinning, and somehow, it seemed that Emily was the only one who could make it stop—who could bring stability.

"Wait, right now?"

"Yeah, I have to talk to her."

He started to walk out the door and felt a tug at his shoulder as James attempted to convince him that Emily wouldn't want to see him, especially in his current drunken state. But Zain just shook his head and headed out the door, determined.

"Zain, don't do this," James shouted out behind him, but Zain ignored him.

The air hit like ice on his face when he stepped outside. He swallowed, his mouth dry from all the alcohol. If he had just one more drink, he'd be sick, but the cold might at least sober him up.

A group of women in short, tight skirts walked past. They must have been freezing. He put his hood up. It was late, but the streets were still busy as he walked past bar after bar. Emily would talk to him. She'd hear what he had to say. And he'd know what to say when he saw her. Something about how he still loved her, how they were meant to be together, maybe—because they'd always been together. They were best friends. She'd take him in, let him sleep in her bed, and things would be okay. With Emily, it was always okay.

As he walked, the city lights and sounds began to die down. It grew quieter, more residential, once he got farther into Old City. What would it be like to own a home there, have a family? Emily was the only person he'd want to do that with. He was two blocks from her apartment. He had no plan, nothing to say, but it was like the night air propelled him toward her. He wasn't even nauseous anymore, the cold cleansing his body and soul. He needed water, but he could ask Emily for some.

He stood in front of her door and knocked. He knocked and knocked to no answer. Maybe she was out. Or asleep. He would have to call her. He pulled out his phone and searched for her name in his contacts. Everything was spinning again, and the phone slipped out of his hand, falling face down on the concrete.

"Shit." He bent over to pick it up, almost losing his balance in the process. The screen had cracked, little bits of smashed glass in the lower right corner. "Fuck," he mumbled to himself.

"Zain?" a voice to his right said.

He looked up. Emily.

"What are you doing here?" she said.

"Em—hey."

She was just arriving home and approached him, her face close to his now. He wanted to kiss her, but even this drunk, he knew that was clearly a bad idea.

"Are you drunk?" she said.

"No." He shook his head adamantly, his body wavering in place. "I mean, yes. A little. Are you?"

"Not as drunk as you, clearly."

"Can I come in?" Everything was spinning now, as Emily asked again what he was doing outside her apartment.

"I needed to see you."

"You can't come in." She was shaking her head, or was the world shaking and her head just following along? Zain couldn't be sure.

"Em, please."

That's when it happened—the nausea. Maybe he could swallow it. He shouldn't have had so much to drink. Before he could stop himself, he was bent over on the sidewalk, yellow chunks projecting from his throat, Emily looking on.

"God damn it, Zain," she said as he wiped his mouth on his sleeve. He spit out whatever was left. "Right outside my door? Really?"

"I'm sorry." He looked down at the chunks of yellow vomit on the sidewalk.

"Fine, come inside."

She opened the door and let him in, pointing to the bathroom.

"Go," she said. "Clean yourself up. You can crash on my couch."

2010

Zain

Hannah was in college, and the family was visiting her in New York. Zain was taking the train from Philly early that morning and meeting them in the city. But the night before, he'd gone out for a friend's birthday and couldn't even remember how he'd made it home.

He woke up at six a.m. feeling like his insides were throbbing, struggling to function, and he was in the throes of death. But he managed to stumble out of bed and into his living room, where he discovered that he'd thrown up the night before and shoddily cleaned it up with some paper towels sitting at the top of his trash bin. The sight alone made him sick again, and he ran to the bathroom, this time making it to the toilet. Somehow, he also showered and made it to the train, where he threw up again in a plastic bag that he'd brought just in case. When he arrived in New York and met up with his family at Penn Station, he just knew there was more coming.

"Zain, you look terrible," his mom said as they stood outside on Thirty-Fourth Street, crowds of tourists and travelers rushing by.

"I think I have food poisoning," Zain lied. "Bad sushi or something."

For the rest of the day, as he struggled to keep even water down, his mom took care of him, buying antinausea medication and making sure they didn't walk too much, having him sit down whenever possible. She wiped his sweating face with tissues and asked if he didn't just want to go back to their hotel and rest. He wasn't sure if Hannah suspected anything at the time, but his parents fully bought the food poisoning lie.

He felt awful—not just physically, but also for making his mom so worried, when he'd done this to himself. They even canceled their reservations at the Japanese restaurant Hannah had picked out and instead went somewhere with more mild food—bland soup and chicken that Zain could hopefully keep down.

"I really wanted to take you to this restaurant," Hannah said. "It's so good."

"Next time," his mom said.

When they got back to the hotel later that night, Zain was feeling somewhat better. He wasn't nauseous anymore, at least, but his mom set up the sofa bed for him as he watched, and then she literally tucked him in, handing him a bottle of water as she said good night.

"Inshallah tomorrow you'll feel better," she said.

FALL 2012

Zain

Zain woke up with a blanket over him, his body shaking, mouth dry. The taste of vomit lingered on his breath, and he still had his coat on. What time was it? He was sweating. Emily had let him in, but what happened after? Did he just pass out? Did they argue? His head was pounding. Last night was a mistake. He shouldn't have come here. James had tried to stop him, and he should have listened.

And then he remembered the conversation with his dad. Where was his phone? He lifted his head and found it on the ground next to him, the screen cracked, the battery at 14 percent. His dad had texted him.

Zain let me come get u.

Please be safe.

We need to talk tomorrow.

He pulled himself off the couch and walked to Emily's kitchen. He needed to focus on getting water. He reached into the cabinets, knowing right away which one held the glasses. As he opened the fridge, a wave of nausea rose in his throat, and he stood still until it subsided. Zain grabbed the pitcher of water and poured himself a glass. He drank it all and poured another.

As he put the pitcher back, he noticed a photo on the refrigerator. It was of him and Emily in his college dorm room. They were sitting on his bed, big goofy smiles on their faces. Emily had shorter hair back then, reaching only her shoulders, and she was wearing flared jeans and a sweatshirt. Very early 2000s, his own pants and shirt too loose and ill fitting.

He should apologize for showing up here the way he did. Or maybe just leave. There was no way she wanted to see or talk to him after last night. Not just last night, but everything. Maybe a note.

Zain found a pen and paper and began to write. He apologized for being there, for showing up at her door the night before. He apologized for everything and told her he would leave her alone, that she wouldn't have to see him anymore if she didn't want to.

It felt shitty—leaving before she woke up—but there wasn't really a better option. He'd already fucked up. Zain left the note on her coffee table and walked out the door. He would go home. Another wave of nausea hit, and he wasn't even sure if it was the alcohol or the grief over truly losing Emily. As badly as he'd treated her, he'd always thought they'd end up together—that he'd eventually get his shit together and one day they'd get married. But it was over now, for good.

He walked back to his car, and a parking ticket sat underneath his windshield wipers. Of course he'd get a ticket in Rittenhouse. The feeling of nausea kept coming and going, but he had to get home. If he just focused on driving, not on Emily, not on the nausea, then everything would be okay.

On the drive home, though, he racked his brain over what he'd say to his dad. He wanted to say that wasn't him—that someone had taken over his body and forced those words out of his mouth. He wanted to come up with any excuse, any denial, but there was none. The secrets had ended between him and Hannah. Maybe it was time for the secrets to end between him and his dad as well. Nothing mattered anymore anyway. His dad had no right to pass judgment, not after everything.

Still, that unsettled feeling in his gut—the one underneath the hangover—wouldn't go away. His parents were never supposed to find any of this out, especially not his mom. She wouldn't want this. This would have hurt her more than anything. He was a disappointment.

Back at the house, his dad was awake and making coffee when Zain walked in.

"Dad." Zain stood in the kitchen entryway. His dad turned to face him. "Um, about last night—" He leaned against the wall, stabilizing himself, his hangover making him dizzy as his stomach did flips.

"I'm just glad you're okay," his dad said, still standing by the coffee maker.

"Yeah, I'm fine. I should explain, though." He was looking down at the floor.

"I'm not oblivious, Zain," his dad said. "I know you do those things."

"You—what?" He looked up at his dad. "How—what do you know?"

His dad pointed to a chair at the kitchen table, motioning for Zain to sit as he poured himself a cup of coffee and offered Zain one as well.

"The first time I figured something out," his dad said, handing Zain the hot mug, "you were in high school."

"High school?"

His dad sat across from him and told him about the time he'd found an empty bottle of liquor in Zain's nightstand, then about the time he'd found a box of condoms in Zain's glove compartment.

"Why didn't you say anything?" Zain's fingers tightly gripped the mug that was warming his hands now.

"I didn't know what to say."

"Did Mom know?"

His dad shook his head. "It would have upset her. And besides, I made mistakes when I was younger too. I just thought you would grow out of it by now."

"What kind of mistakes?"

"It's not important."

"You can't just say that and not tell me."

His dad sighed and looked at the ceiling. "In college, you know, we used to go to parties, and people would be drinking . . ."

Zain sat up straight. "In Egypt? Were *you* drinking?"

"Sometimes."

"Was it a lot?"

Zain needed to know more. His whole life, he'd had one idea about his parents. They were strict and wholesome, but that image—when it came to his dad, at least—was shattering more and more with each passing day.

"It was a long time ago," his dad said. "It doesn't matter anymore. It's haram, and I've asked God for forgiveness."

Zain shook his head and slouched down again.

"I want you to ask for forgiveness too," his dad continued. "And to stop this behavior."

Zain didn't say anything as he processed the latest revelation. There were so many secrets. Maybe everything Zain knew about hiding things, he'd just inherited from his dad. He didn't agree with his dad that he needed to ask forgiveness, but even though he wouldn't admit it out loud, he knew his drinking had gotten out of control. He couldn't continue like this.

At the same time, Zain felt lighter, almost, like the weight of the secrets—a weight he didn't even know he was carrying—had been lifted, but it was quickly replaced with a new weight, one that again tore him further and further from his dad, a man he couldn't really recognize anymore. He was a hypocrite, again. Zain understood, in some ways. And a part of him even wanted to be able to relate, to commiserate, but all he could feel was anger. His dad was trying to show that they were alike, but Zain didn't want to be like him. His hands were shaking slightly, and he didn't know if he was anxious, angry, or just weak from dehydration.

"When did you stop drinking?" Zain asked, ignoring his dad's pleas about asking for forgiveness,

"What does it matter?"

"It matters. And don't lie to me."

"Well, when I got together with your mom," he said. "She didn't like it. She told me to stop, so I did."

"And that's it? You just never drank again?"

His dad looked down at his coffee, and Zain knew there was more to the story.

"Not exactly." He began to describe the stress of moving to America. "It was just a big decision, and your mom was pregnant with you, so we didn't even know if it was the right thing. And then . . ."

"And then what?"

"I don't know if I should be telling you this." He paused again. "There was this man that your mom was with before me."

Zain recalled the conversation with Hasan. Was he right? Did they leave Egypt because she was still seeing that guy?

"I just—I was jealous all the time," his dad said. "They were still friends, and I was angry and stressed."

"Did anything happen between them?"

"No, no, of course not. She wouldn't do that. I know she wouldn't."

Zain wondered still. Maybe something had happened that his dad didn't want to say—or that he didn't even know. "So you started drinking again?"

His dad nodded. "And for the first few months after we came to America. But we had you, and your mom didn't want you around that, and she was right. She said she would leave and take you back to Egypt with her if I didn't stop, so that was it. That was the end."

The two sat in silence for a moment, as Zain didn't know what to say. He hated finding out he was more like his dad than he'd thought. His mom would hate him.

"I have to go to sleep," Zain said, standing up.

His dad, passive as ever, just nodded and stayed seated as Zain went upstairs to lie down.

In his room, Zain grabbed his bag of weed out of his nightstand and held it in his hands for a minute, but then he put it back in the drawer. He needed to clear his head. He'd stop drinking too. For now, at least.

The house was so different without his mom in it. Quieter. Sadder. He shut his eyes and covered his face with his hands. He needed her. He lifted the covers over his head.

"Please," he whispered. "If anyone is listening, help me."

He couldn't feel like this anymore. Sometimes, he wished a car would just hit him, or he imagined himself jumping in front of a subway train and ending it all. He wasn't actually suicidal, but he didn't want to live like this. Death seemed a happy fantasy.

"Please, God."

He didn't know if anyone actually heard his pleas. But there was nothing else he could think to do, so he prayed for his life to get better, to find what he was looking for. He prayed for Hannah, for Emily.

"Mom, if you can hear me," he said, tears streaming down his face as he lay in bed, "I'm sorry."

He didn't care about apologizing to God like his dad wanted. He only wanted his mom to hear him. He would fix this. He would fix his life.

Hannah

Hannah and Noha were driving to drop supplies off at a women's shelter. They were armed with blankets, canned food, shampoos, and soap. Being around Noha, somehow, made it feel like her mom was there with them, watching as the different parts of her life converged. Noha's life was one her mom might have had if she'd stayed in Egypt—right down to the husband.

"These women," Noha said, telling Hannah about the shelter they were going to, "many of them are here because they faced domestic violence, and now they have nothing, not even their children. The Egyptian government doesn't help them, and the men—they have all the money, so they take the kids. The same problems Yasmeen and I were fighting against are still here today."

"My mom never talked about that." Hannah looked out the passenger-side window at the street carts selling fruit and snacks next to them.

"I think when she went to America, she wanted to forget," said Noha.

Hannah felt the blood rush to her cheeks, the sentiment all too familiar. Slipping into a new life in a new country made the old one disappear.

Noha turned left, down the street where the shelter was, but stopped in front of a line of police blocking the road. The police in Egypt were always armed with rifles and military equipment but wearing little berets that somehow made them look less threatening.

Noha rolled down her window. *"What's going on?"* she asked one of the officers in Arabic. *"I need to get through."*

"The street is closed," the officer said, standing with his legs apart, hand gripping his rifle.

Noha told him she was trying to get to the shelter.

"No one is allowed in or out."

"Why not?"

"That's the way it is," said the officer.

A woman in a pink galabiya approached the car.

"There was an incident today," she said to Noha in Arabic.

She explained that a man was looking for his wife and showed up at the shelter with the police. They raided the place and destroyed the supplies until they found her.

"Lady, you have to step back." The officer reached his arm out as if to push her away.

"I'm just telling them what happened!" she shouted back.

"Shukran." Noha put the car in reverse, but as the distance between them and the shelter grew, Hannah became angry.

"They can just raid the shelter? Because some guy is looking for his wife?"

"Typical," Noha said.

They spoke little for the remainder of the ride as a sense of fury continued to fill Hannah's mind. Here they were, doing the bare minimum—simply bringing blankets and clothes to women in need—and even that was thwarted. If they couldn't even do that, then what hope was there for Egypt?

"There has to be something we can do," Hannah said, finally breaking the silence as they sat in traffic, the smell of car exhaust seeping in through the vents of Noha's car.

"There's nothing," Noha said, her voice flat, staring at the congested road in front of her.

"What did people protest for if the police can just do this to women whenever they want?"

"The protests were not for us," Noha said. "We thought they were, but nothing changes."

Maybe that was why her mom had left. Why she'd chosen to forget. She'd seen for herself that no matter how much work they put in, Egypt stayed the same. America was only slightly better, though, with people struggling to make ends meet, dying because they couldn't afford their prescriptions or medical bills, while the government did nothing. The police, too, weren't protecting anyone, in either Egypt or America, and for marginalized groups—or in Egypt's case, the poor—the police posed more of a threat than anything else. It dawned on Hannah then that she was just running away to the same kind of problems they had back home.

At the café later, Hannah couldn't get the incident at the

shelter out of her mind. She didn't know what she was doing here in Egypt, since she certainly wasn't helping anyone. Everything she did seemed meaningless, like there was no reason for her to be here, but also no reason to be back in America, not since she'd given up law school. What would she even do back home now? She had no place and no purpose.

As she handed a menu to a couple that had just sat down, Rami walked in with two men she didn't recognize. One week earlier, she was drunkenly leaving his apartment, just before bumping into Zakaria at the sheesha place. Rami crossed her mind often, when she wasn't distracted with other things—and she did try to stay distracted. But there was something about him, some element of charm and standoffishness that drew her to him. And even though she didn't really want to date him—or date anyone at the moment—she wanted him to want her. She wanted to cross his mind as often as he crossed hers.

"Rami, izayak?" Amr said, making his way to the front of the café.

"How are you, Uncle?"

Rami had a job here in Egypt—a real one—whereas she was still working at this café, trying to get more involved with Egyptian life and politics but hitting a roadblock. It was December, and her life in Egypt had become a repetitive, stuffy cycle, and now here Rami was, his mere presence making her heart beat faster with anxiety. She wanted him gone so she could breathe freely. But now, she had to be *on*—his presence turning her into a cliché, trying to impress a guy who didn't care, and she couldn't even understand or explain why.

"Hi, can I take your order?" she said with a cheerfulness that went no deeper than her plastered-on smile as she approached his table.

Rami glanced up. "Hey, I forgot you worked here."

She was pulled back to the same sense of insecurity she'd felt in high school, in those tumultuous, hormonal teenage years. "How are you?" She smiled wider.

"Good."

Maybe he would just order and they could get this over with. Instead, he introduced her to his friends, two men he knew from work, an American and an Egyptian. It wasn't even a big deal, but "I forgot you worked here" echoed in her head as she quickly jotted down their orders. She was nothing to him. Just a waitress. She couldn't focus after that, irritated at Rami's comment and wishing she could just leave. At the counter where she picked up the orders, Hannah stared into space, wondering again what she was even doing here.

"Hannah . . . Hannah . . ."

She looked up. The line cook was handing her plates of food, pulling Hannah out of her trance.

As she brought Rami and his friends their orders, she overheard snippets of conversation about the assaults in Tahrir.

"It's insane," the American said, "how many women are getting attacked."

"It's their own fault." Rami leaned back in his chair. "It's dangerous there. Those women are idiots. They deserve it."

Hannah placed Rami's sandwich in front of him.

"They deserve to be sexually assaulted?" The words raced out of her mouth before she could even think.

Rami looked up at her and smiled. "That's not what I meant."

"What did you mean?" She was looking down at him, at the smug smirk plastered across his face.

"I just mean it's stupid to go," he said. "Like, obviously it's not their fault, but they should also know better than showing up there. Assaults have been happening since the beginning."

"So the solution is just that women shouldn't go?" Hannah said. "'Men only' kind of thing?" She couldn't understand why, but inside her was some urge to fight—to pick up his plate and throw it across the room in a fit of rage. Instead, she just stood there, waiting for Rami to respond.

"Come on." He tilted his head and smiled again.

"Sorry, forget I said anything. Enjoy your meals." She smiled back stiffly and walked away.

Her hands were shaking now, her heart ready to jump out of her chest. She shouldn't have engaged. They were customers. Plus, he was Amr's nephew. She wouldn't get herself fired over this.

"You're right," she heard Rami's friend say after she walked away. "I don't know what she's getting upset about."

"Women get upset over these things," his other friend said. He had a slight Egyptian accent, like someone fluent in English but still born and raised in Egypt. "They don't like being told they can't do things."

Hannah could still see them out of the corner of her eye. Rami didn't say anything, but he was watching her, that slight smirk still visible on his face. She slammed her tray down on the counter so hard that the server standing in the back looked up.

"You okay?" Vanessa said, approaching her.

She desperately wanted to go home—whatever that meant. She wasn't even sure where home was anymore.

"Yeah." Hannah began anxiously fidgeting with the tray on the counter. "Did you hear that conversation?"

"Yep," Vanessa said. "Bunch of fucking misogynists."

"I don't know why I got so angry. People say shit like that all the time. I think I'm just a little oversensitive today."

"Dude, no, you should be angry. But what's going on today?"

"I don't know." Hannah looked around the restaurant and avoided Vanessa's eyes. She saw Rami at his table, laughing with his friends.

Vanessa looked at her but said nothing. Hannah didn't want to talk, but she could tell that Vanessa, with her astute way of reading people, knew she was not okay.

"I should get back to my tables," Hannah said, quickly looking away so that Vanessa couldn't read any more into her eyes.

But as she walked off, Vanessa suggested they talk later, and Hannah nodded at her invitation, knowing that as soon as her shift ended she'd just head straight back to her apartment. She didn't say much to Rami and his friends after that. Just brought them their food, their drinks, played nice until they left.

"It was good seeing you," he said as he was leaving, reaching in for a hug.

She was caught off guard but hugged him back, his body's warmth coursing through hers.

"We should hang out soon," he said.

"Yeah, totally."

"And sorry about what I said earlier." His hand reached out and touched her arm. "I didn't mean it like that. I shouldn't have said it."

"No worries." She shook her head and smiled.

The group left, leaving behind a nice tip that did nothing to quell Hannah's unsettled mood. In the hour that followed, she got three people's orders wrong and dropped a plate, which shattered on the floor. Grateful as she was that Amr swooped in quickly to sweep up the pieces, Hannah couldn't help but feel even more defeated.

"I'm so sorry, Amr." She stared down at the mess. "I'm just having a bad day."

She reached her hands over her forehead, trying not to cry.

"Take a break, Hannah," he said. "Or go home if you need."

She shook her head. "No, I'm okay."

"Are you sure?"

She nodded. But she wanted her mom. She was alone here in Egypt. She had friends, sure, but they didn't know her. Not really. It had only been a few months, and how well could you really know anyone in that time? She bent over to pick up the large pieces of broken glass as Amr tried to shoo her away, promising to clean it up himself.

"No, I can do it," Hannah said.

She was on the floor now, and her vision started to blur, tears forming a gloss over her eyes. She wouldn't cry. Not here. Not in front of everyone.

"Hannah." Amr bent down to her level. "I can clean this."

She shook her head again. Vanessa must have noticed what was going on because she was suddenly crouched down on the floor too, and then the tears started to stream, and was that blood on her hands?

Vanessa's arms were intertwined with hers, lifting her up, and they were both standing. She could barely see, barely move. She couldn't breathe anymore. It was like her lungs didn't have the capacity, and she was gasping for air. Maybe she was having a heart attack. Vanessa was holding her, pulling her away somewhere, but she had to clean the plate up. She looked back, and Amr was standing, holding the broom with a concerned look on his face. Why was he so concerned? Was it because of the plate?

"Hannah, Hannah, it's okay." Vanessa grabbed her shoulders now. "Just tell me what's going on."

They went into the bathroom, and Hannah stood over the sink with her hands under the faucet. Her blood mixed with the water, a light red liquid circling the drain. She didn't even feel the cut.

"I dropped the plate," Hannah said, tears silently streaming down her face. Her breath was coming in evenly again. "I have to go clean it up."

"Don't worry about it. Amr already got it." Vanessa's hand was on Hannah's back.

"But I'll get fired. I can't get fired. I've never been fired." She stared down at the faucet, the water beginning to clear up.

"You're not getting fired," Vanessa said. "Jesus, what's going on?"

Hannah removed her hands from the sink, watching silently as Vanessa grabbed a wad of paper towels and wrapped her bleeding hand. Hannah appreciated the numbness in her body for keeping the pain away at least.

"Okay," Vanessa said. "Why don't we take you home?"

"No." Hannah wiped her face with another paper towel. "No, I'm okay."

"You're not, though."

Hannah shook her head. "What's happening?" Her voice began to crack, and she couldn't stop crying now.

Vanessa talked to Amr and took Hannah home—tucked her into bed and everything, and she lay there next to her.

"You can go home." Hannah sat up. She had stopped crying ages ago and now felt bad that Vanessa had been forced to babysit her. Instead of leaving, Vanessa stayed put and sat up too.

"Hannah, what happened?"

"I don't know." She lifted her knees to her chest and stared in front of her.

"I used to have panic attacks," Vanessa said. "And I would have moments like that. Do you get panic attacks?"

She shook her head.

"Well, I think you had one today." Vanessa paused. "It wasn't because of Rami, was it?"

She looked at Vanessa and widened her eyes. "What? God, no."

It might have been because of Rami, though. Not him, exactly, but seeing him, hearing him say "I forgot you worked here"—that was what had triggered it. Rami had brought out the flood of emotions that she'd been burying for the past four months. She couldn't even remember the last time she'd cried. At the funeral, maybe. She missed her mom more than anything, but until now—until that moment in the café—she hadn't let herself feel the full force of grief. It was bound to break through at some point.

"I miss my mom." Hannah spoke into her knees.

Vanessa turned and hugged Hannah from the side, the two of them sitting on the bed as tears slowly streamed down her face.

"What if staying here was a mistake?" Hannah said, pulling herself away. "I gave up Columbia."

"Do you regret it?" Vanessa asked.

She thought for a moment before responding. "I don't know. I mean, no. I'm glad I'm not at Columbia, but I want to feel like I gave it up for a reason, you know?"

"Yeah. But isn't not wanting to go reason enough?"

Hannah tucked her knees under her arms as she pulled them even closer to her chest. "My mom was really excited when I got in, though."

"Alhamdulillah," her mom had said over the phone when she heard the news. "I was praying for you. I'm so proud."

"But if your mom knew you wouldn't be happy," Vanessa said, "would she still want you to go?"

"I don't know." Hannah stared in front of her. What would her mom say if she knew what she'd done? She would be disappointed, for sure. She'd always said she'd come to America so that her kids could have better opportunities, and here Hannah was, squandering those opportunities and going back to Egypt.

This panic attack thing—this was new. She couldn't be having panic attacks like this, not in public, especially. She was usually so good at controlling her emotions, but now they were all just pouring out.

Life didn't seem to mean anything. Columbia, Egypt, Rami. He was such a dick, saying women couldn't be in Tahrir—that it was their fault if something happened. If she could focus her thoughts on how Rami was an asshole, on Tahrir and everything going on in Egypt, she could stay distracted. She could stop crying, stop wallowing in grief. She would sleep with Rami again, probably. It was bound to happen. But in the meantime, she had to prove him wrong—prove that women were just as important to the movement.

After ensuring that Hannah would be okay for the rest of the night, Vanessa left a couple of hours later, just in time to escape the sudden darkness the apartment was plunged into when the lights suddenly went out. Another power outage. Hannah flicked the lights on and off, even though she knew it would be an hour. These scheduled outages were ridiculous. The government just thought they could play games like this and get away with it. If only she could go to Tahrir herself and actually see what was happening in the resistance. There was some article recently about groups of women with bodyguards going in and protecting other women. Maybe they just needed numbers—women to go out in groups and protect each other. That would prove Rami wrong.

It wasn't entirely clear what the Egyptian people wanted

beyond ousting Morsi, though. Just a week earlier, he'd announced that the judiciary couldn't challenge any of his actions and that he could essentially do whatever he deemed necessary to protect the country. Obviously, people were angry, as that bordered on dictatorship. Protests had picked up in recent days, but there were hardly any women going out to the square anymore because it had become so dangerous for them. Women weren't a part of this new movement at all, and it was difficult to understand what the people were demanding. The old regime to return? The army to take over? Did they have another leader in mind? The past week had seemed hopeless, like no real change would ever occur in Egypt. But she had to give it to the people, at least. They were standing up for something, however unclear that something was.

Hannah grabbed the flashlight off her dresser. She lit some candles and rummaged through the closet, looking for her most masculine clothes. If she could disguise herself as a man, maybe Tahrir would be safe. Maybe she could follow in her mom's footsteps and help finish the work she'd started with AWSA. She could finally do something that would make her mom proud and pick up where she'd left off all those years ago.

From her closet, she pulled out a pair of sweatpants and a baggy sweatshirt. She found a baseball cap that she'd packed but never worn, and a plan began to take shape.

Zain

Zain had been avoiding his dad since that hungover conversation. For a week he'd been sneaking around the house like a shadow, going from his room to the kitchen, back to his room again. That whole drunken night was just a series of bad decisions soaked in whiskey, leading him to Emily's doorstep in a haze. He tried to shake the memory from his mind as he stood in the kitchen now, making a bagel and riffling through the mail. His security deposit had finally arrived. That was something to put in his bank account, at least.

His dad wasn't home, so he took his breakfast to the living room to watch CNN's coverage of the new protests in Cairo. Morsi had announced that the judiciary couldn't challenge his decisions, and the country hadn't taken that well. These protesters seemed more violent, and now women were being assaulted. Hannah would be okay, though, as she was too smart to get herself into anything dangerous.

"Egypt has become a divided country," the reporter on TV said. There were men in the streets, yelling and marching in the square, their words just a series of incomprehensible shouts.

The reporter looked young. How had he gotten a job with CNN? Staying with that Philly paper for so long was a mistake—letting Rachel treat him the way she did. He should have applied to new jobs years ago and gotten the fuck out of there. But then, maybe he wasn't even a good enough writer. The screen switched over to two reporters in the CNN offices. Talking heads providing their analyses. He lowered the volume and opened his laptop to read about the situation instead. He could write articles like this, if someone would let him.

Rachel was right. He was lazy. The reason he wasn't writing these stories was because he never tried. He just expected it to happen. He didn't have connections like so many other writers, and so the only way to make it as a journalist would be to fight and claw his way to the top, but he never made any effort, and now here he was, unemployed and living at home. Each morning he woke up in this house was a reminder, again, of his failures—of the decisions that had led to this moment. And instead of doing anything, he just burrowed deeper into bed, wishing he could sink into the sheets and disappear.

As he stared blankly at the TV, he heard the front door open. His dad was home. Zain was finishing up his bagel and decided he would use that as his cue to leave, but his dad came in and sat down next to him, merely looking from him to the television, as though getting ready to say something. Zain kept his eyes focused on the screen, hoping his attention discouraged any ideas his dad might have around engaging in conversation.

"I'm worried about Hannah," his dad said anyway.

On TV, they were showing footage of the protests again.

"She's fine." Zain kept his gaze on the news as he spoke, his voice monotone and uninterested. "She knows to stay safe."

"I just wish she would talk to me. You know she hasn't contacted anyone in the family?"

Zain nodded, his eyes never wavering from the screen, though he wanted to say that Hannah wasn't even talking to him as much as she used to. He'd been so focused on everything going on at home that he didn't really know what was going on with her.

"We need to fix our relationship," his dad continued. Zain got up to take his plate to the kitchen, hoping he could just exit the conversation, but his dad followed. "This is killing me, my kids hating me like this."

There was nothing to say in response, really.

"I don't know what to do to fix this." His dad stood unmoving next to Zain, who was rinsing his plate in the sink. "Can we talk?"

"I have a lot to do." Zain shut off the water and placed the dish in the dishwasher. His dad was still next to him, following him through the kitchen like a sad puppy.

"Please, Zain, just sit for a minute."

Zain hesitated. He could get out of this, say he was running late for something, rush out of the house. But something inside him—the part that was desperate to have a parent again—told him to stay. He wanted to pull away, to fight, but at the same time, he wanted his dad to fight too, to earn back his place, somehow, so Zain slowly nodded and took a seat at the table.

"I want to fix things," his dad pleaded, sitting in the chair next to him. "Tell me what I need to do to make you and Hannah not hate me anymore. I'll do anything."

"I don't hate you." Zain shook his leg up and down, the kitchen table shaking along with it. "But I don't know if this can be fixed."

His dad put his hand over Zain's leg to steady the shaking, and Zain stopped.

"I've been a good father to you, haven't I?"

"That's not what this is about." Zain pulled his leg out from under his dad's hand. "You still—did what you did."

He thought back to their last conversation and the revelation about his mom's former flame. Had she been unfaithful too? Was he judging his dad too harshly?

"I've been seeing a therapist."

"Really? And how's that going?" Zain said, his tone more sarcastic than he intended.

"It's helping. But the only thing that really matters to me is you and Hannah." He paused. "So I need to explain to you how this all started with Vivian."

The words hit him over the head like a brick as he struggled to comprehend why his dad would think it was a good idea to give the backstory of him and his mistress.

"I *really* don't want to know." Zain began to move his chair back. "I don't even want you to say her name."

"My therapist says I need to be honest with you both. To just tell you everything so that we can move forward. Like a confession."

"Your therapist is full of shit." Zain stood up, perhaps too aggressively, causing his dad to wince as the legs of the chair screeched along the beige tile floor.

He bolted from the kitchen and had begun to make his way toward the stairs before remembering that he'd left his laptop in the living room. When he turned around, his dad was right behind him, eyebrows furrowed, his face serious-looking.

"I'm your father," he said, his voice slightly raised. "You can't just walk away from me."

"I can't walk away from you? Are you fucking kidding me?"

He was getting heated, the anger bubbling in his chest and ready to boil over.

"Zain, don't talk to me like that. Have some respect."

His dad was quiet now, almost small-seeming as he stood in front of him, eyes begging for some kind of mercy.

"Why?" Zain said, secretly hoping for one last reason to hear him out.

His dad opened his mouth as though to speak, then shut it again. Zain stood in place, waiting for him to say something, until finally, he practically whispered, "It would just mean a lot to me if you'd hear me out for a minute." He looked ready to cry. "Please."

Zain leaned his head back and sighed, walking into the living room toward the couch now. He couldn't help but feel guilty. "Fine. Let's hear it."

His dad followed and turned off the television. “I met Vivian at work,” he began to explain, wringing his hands together as he spoke.

She was his partner’s secretary.

“I know,” Zain said, remembering his dad’s bumbling explanation from months earlier. His dad was one of them—the old men who slept with secretaries.

Vivian was forty-two to his dad’s fifty-four, Zain learned.

“Has there been anyone else?” Zain asked. “Or was it just—this woman?” He didn’t want to say her name.

According to his dad, Vivian had been his only affair, and they were solidly friends at first. Some mixture of curiosity and rage kept Zain glued to the couch, listening to the betrayal.

His dad shook his head. “I shouldn’t have encouraged her flirtations.”

Zain cringed and arched his neck back. This was too much. It was disgusting, really—the thought of his dad flirting with a secretary. He clenched his jaw and gripped the arm of the couch.

“I just don’t know why you’re fucking telling me all this.” Zain gripped the couch even harder now. “Do you realize how sleazy this sounds?” As he said the words, he thought of his own indiscretions with Rachel—all the lies he’d told.

His dad looked at him. “Zain, I—”

Zain stood and began to shake his head. “You know what? I don’t want to hear this. I don’t know if I can forgive you.” He looked around the room, trying to decide what to do, whether to leave the house entirely, go for a drive somewhere to cool off, or just go upstairs and sob into his pillow, reliving his childhood as he cried in his room while his soccer trophies from elementary school looked on.

“I’ve been a good father to you, Zain. What happened has

nothing to do with you, and it's not for you to forgive. In the end, it was between me and your mother. I'm sorry you found out." He looked up at Zain but didn't move from his spot on the couch.

Zain stopped and looked back down at his dad. "Wait, did Mom know?"

"No, I just mean—"

Zain shook his head. "Then how can you say it's between you and Mom? You cheated on her, and now she's dead. You don't expect Hannah and me to care?"

"That's not what I meant. Just let me finish explaining."

Zain stood in place and bit down on his bottom lip. His eyes darted around the room, around the family photos his mom had framed and placed on the mantel, around the vase of dried flowers she'd kept on the coffee table, then back at his dad on the couch. He couldn't help but feel his own hypocrisy as he stood over his dad, judging him, when he himself was no different.

"Fine," said Zain, sitting back down. "Finish."

His dad sighed before beginning to speak again. He told Zain that he'd gotten to know Vivian better and they'd become good friends. He was speaking more quickly now, as though he didn't know how much time he had before Zain decided to leave again. Either that or he wanted to get this over with as quickly as possible—one of his therapist's steps. He said Vivian was having family issues at the time and he'd listened.

"What is the point of this?" Zain interrupted again. He leaned forward now and looked at his dad. "Are you trying to make her into a good person? Or make yourself into a good person?"

"No, I'm—"

"The fact that it started as friendship or that there was this emotional connection makes it worse." He could hear the volume of his voice rising. "Next you're gonna tell me that you and her are dating out in the open now that Mom's dead."

"No, absolutely not." His dad began to fervently shake his head. "I know what I did was wrong."

"Do you love her?" Zain said. He shook his leg up and down again.

"I cared about her, yes."

"But did you love her? Did you even love Mom?"

Zain thought back to his parents' marriage. Was there any love there? Or was it just obligation? Maybe his mom had only had one real love, and he was back in Egypt. His parents had been two people raising two children, and they'd just happened to be married. Their lives had been more of a routine than anything else. Maybe with Vivian, it was different. Zain cringed at the thought.

"Of course I loved your mom." His dad looked down at the floor for a moment before continuing to speak. "Things between your mom and me—well, you know, we were together for so long. Relationships change. I loved her, of course, but . . ."

His voice trailed off, as though he didn't know what to say, and Zain was afraid of what would come next.

"I regret everything with Vivian," he continued. "I knew it was haram. And your mom and I, we had our problems, but there's no excuse. I just wish, now, that there was some way to apologize to her. I want her to know how sorry I am, but it's too late."

He had tears in his eyes, and Zain looked away. He wouldn't feel bad for him. Zain began to stand. He'd heard enough, and the explanation didn't change anything. It was a stupid idea by a bad therapist, clearly, and only served to reopen wounds, though the wounds weren't really healing to begin with.

"Zain, please don't go."

"I just don't know what I'm supposed to do with this information." He stood in front of the couch, looking down at his dad, who appeared small and helpless again.

"I'd like you to consider coming to one of my therapy sessions. I want us to be able to talk."

"I don't see that happening." He paused for a moment. "I don't want to be like you, and I'm scared that I'm like you."

"What do you mean?" His dad looked over at him.

"I cheated on Emily."

"In college?"

"No, recently. After Mom died."

"I wasn't aware you and Emily were even together," his dad said.

"We were, sort of." Zain bit his fingernail, watching as his father slowly put the pieces together in his mind.

"Your boss—you were with Emily at the time?"

Zain nodded. "And it kills me that I'm like you."

"Does she know?"

"I told her."

"Then you're not like me. You're already better than me."

It was true, in some ways. For Zain, the guilt had eaten away at him until he'd drunkenly confessed in Emily's apartment, but he didn't know what his dad felt. He was guilty now, it was clear, but had he felt that same tug on his conscience before the tragedy? He obviously hadn't been guilty enough to admit his indiscretions—though admittedly, there was more at stake for his parents than for him and Emily.

"I don't need her to forgive me," Zain said, avoiding eye contact with his dad. "But you said you wish you could apologize to Mom. What would be the point? Just to make yourself feel better?"

"I don't think it would make me feel much better," his dad said. "But she deserves an apology, at the very least. And I wouldn't expect her to forgive me."

Upstairs in his childhood bedroom, Zain shut the door and felt an overwhelming urge to scream—to let out a primal shriek and release all his pain along with it—but all he could do was open his mouth and bite his own fist as he crouched down on the floor and tried not to cry, instead keeping the pain inside to burrow through his veins like a cancer. This act of confession from his dad—it didn't change anything. He didn't want to be the one who had to forgive. He couldn't forgive. But more than anything, he didn't want to be like his dad, even though he'd hurt Emily in the exact same way.

Hannah

In the morning, her mind was set. She stood in front of the mirror and began to pin her hair up and back with bobby pins. She put on the sweats and the baseball cap, loosening it slightly so that it could fit over her hair without anyone noticing. She wore a tightly fitted sports bra to flatten her chest. The only problem was her face. Her body was small, and it could pass for a teenage boy's. Her face, though, looked too feminine. She needed facial hair, messier eyebrows, something. She looked in the mirror and tried to scowl. Maybe that would make her look tougher, and in that respect, masculine. But she just looked like a kid trying to make an angry face. She rummaged through her makeup bag. Maybe she could thicken her eyebrows, make them look a little more boyish, at the very least. She tried to color them in slightly, but it only made it look like she'd drawn on eyebrows. She washed the makeup off. Keeping her head down would have to be enough.

Hannah pocketed her pepper spray and grabbed just enough cash for the taxi there and back. Just enough so that if she were robbed, it wouldn't be much of a loss. Out of instinct she grabbed her phone, but maybe it was better to leave it so as not to have it stolen. She needed to document this, though, so she stuffed it into her sports bra.

Her heart was pounding as she sat in the back of the taxi. The driver swerved through traffic, and her body swayed with each sudden lurch. Maybe Rami was right. Tahrir wasn't the place for women. She'd read enough news to know better. If this taxi would just slow down—give her time to think—but all she could focus on was keeping upright as they swerved between cars. They were moving too quickly. It was like this driver had a gift for finding a path through traffic—the Moses of the road or something. In that case, maybe this was meant to be. But no, that was stupid. They would get there too quickly, not giving her time to *think*.

And just like that, they'd arrived.

"Shukran." Hannah's hands shook as she handed the driver some cash.

They were about a block from the square, but traffic was too congested, so she would have to walk the rest of the way. Maybe the walk would ease her nerves and alleviate the shaking in her legs. She opened the door to the taxi and took a deep breath in, but inhaled mainly car exhaust, and other vehicles immediately honked at her to get out of the way. As soon as her feet hit the pavement, the taxi began to move again, and she rushed to shut the door, which the driver didn't even seem to notice, or care, was still open.

If the protests seemed violent, she could always turn around. It wasn't too late to go back. But she'd come all this way, and she wasn't one to just give up. She had to go in, see the people, understand their passion. And also prove Rami wrong. This could be a space for women. It had to be.

Her knees shook as she stood in place, and the only way to make them stop was to move. Her mom would say this was stupid, going in alone. Sure, she'd been involved in the women's rights movement, but she probably hadn't done anything like this. And it *was* stupid. But life was pointless enough as it was—in Egypt, in America, it was all the same. Maybe Tahrir was the wake-up call she needed—something to clear away the daily fog so she could see again.

As she walked, she kept her head down, and the shouts grew louder: incoherent chants, muddled and angry. Her heart was beating fast. Maybe she should just turn back. But her legs kept moving, as though something in the crowd pulled her forward, an invisible magnet forcing her body closer.

The mob was mostly men, but there were a few women on the outskirts, and soon she was among them, close enough to smell their sweat. It would be good to get pictures—some kind of documentation. This was history in the making. She pulled her phone discreetly out of her bra and started to snap photos and videos. They weren't super clear, as she was being shoved around a little, and the men surrounding her were all taller. Others had cameras too, and some men held their phones above the crowds, filming. After a few more snapshots, she shoved her phone back into her bra and tried to move into a less dense area. No one really paid any attention to her, and she kept her head down, doing her best to blend in.

There were tents set up along the sides, people going in and out. Someone was playing the tabla. Army and police surrounded the square. The crowd was starting to get more aggressive the farther in she walked, and the air smelled only of sweat and musky cologne. There were now no more women around either, as far as Hannah could tell. She hadn't meant to go this far, but it was almost like she'd been pushed here by an uncontrollable momentum moving the masses.

The weather was nice that day, a cool breeze in the air, but from her spot in the crowd, she couldn't feel it. The men's sweat rubbed against her, and she began to sweat as well. Maybe if she lifted her head and looked up, she could get some fresh air—or at least get the scent of their body odor out of her nostrils. But they were all so tall, and even with her head raised high it was suffocating.

Someone nearby fell to the ground, creating, briefly, an open space in the crowd. Hannah took a sharp breath in as the disturbance seemed to rile up the people around her. The shouting intensified, and the person on the ground—a teenage boy—was lying prone. Hannah gasped in horror as the people around her stepped on his hands, paying him no mind as he struggled to get up, tears in his eyes. Someone had to help him. She bent down and reached her arm out, but a group of men pushed her in the other direction, and she stumbled back, managing to keep her balance as someone else pushed her from behind. Hannah could hear the boy's screams now, at an octave above the din of the crowd, and it tore at her heart. People trampled over him as he tried to move. It was getting harder to breathe again, the crowd growing dense as the boy's screams pierced the air.

"Help him," she shouted in Arabic, realizing immediately after the words left her mouth the mistake she had made.

They'd heard her voice. Her unmistakably feminine voice. Worse still, the pushing and shoving continued, and the boy was still screaming, but he was out of her line of sight. She had to look out for herself now. As she pushed her way back out, she hit a wall in the form of a large man's chest. She looked up just as he looked down, and their eyes met—his dark and filled with rage.

"Inty bint?" he said as he grabbed her shoulder.

He knew. Hannah tried to shake free from his grasp, but his hand was too strong. The pepper spray. She dug into her pocket and felt the small plastic bottle in her hand.

"Look, here's a girl pretending to be a man," he shouted in Arabic.

He shook her by the shoulder as she took her hand out of her pocket, and the pepper spray slipped from her grasp. She watched it drop to the floor, and as she bent down to try and grab it, a man stepped forward, crushing the bottle beneath his feet. Soon, a group of men surrounded her. Someone pulled at her hat and her bun came loose, letting waves of thick black hair fall over her face. One man pulled her toward him, and she screamed.

"Leave her alone!" she heard a woman's voice shout in Arabic.

A group of women wearing yellow vests and holding sticks and tasers approached. They were all different ages, some in hijab and some not, a group of about ten. They might as well have been a group of ten thousand given the relief that flooded Hannah's panicked senses at the sight of them.

"Let go of her," one of the women said, turning on her taser as a threat.

He let Hannah go, pushing her toward the woman and shaking his head.

"Women shouldn't be here," he said, echoing the words of Rami and his friends.

He pushed his way in the opposite direction, the other men following. One of the women pulled Hannah toward her and grabbed her hand.

"Stay with us," she said.

Hannah followed the woman, gripping her hand tightly. Her own face was wet with tears. She hadn't even realized she'd been crying. The women surrounded her, using their sticks to push through the crowds, tasers in plain sight. Rami was right. She should have known better. She was smarter than this. She could hear her dad's voice in her head now, asking what she was thinking, how she could be so stupid. If something happened to her, it was her own fault for being there in the first place. She thought she was invincible—that her disguise would be enough to protect her. It was so naive. If these women hadn't shown up, anything could have happened.

"Come on, let's get her out of here."

They kept pushing through the crowds, the women with sticks batting their way against some of the men that wouldn't let them through. They shouted the entire time. *"Move, let us through, get out of our way."* They formed a circle around Hannah, guiding her out of the square. As they made their way through the final layer of people, a burst of cool, clear air filled her lungs. She could breathe. Hannah gasped, as though she'd forgotten how to take in air. Her legs began to shake again as the woman holding her hand let go. She couldn't stop it—couldn't move herself now that she was out, and any second, her legs might collapse altogether. She leaned forward. She would fall to the ground, right here on the dirty Cairo streets.

But another woman grabbed her arm and held her up, stopping her from simply collapsing.

"We have to keep going," she said. *"To get you out of here."*

Hannah nodded. The women pulled at her arms and guided her farther from the square. They eventually reached a small café about a block down and went inside.

"Sit, drink water," one of the women said in Arabic.

The woman who was practically holding her up looked younger, probably late twenties or early thirties, and her hair was covered, but loosely so that strands fell from the sides. She handed Hannah a bottle of water.

"Thank you," Hannah said, her hands shaking as she took the bottle. "I mean, shukran."

"You are not Egyptian?" one of the older women said, pulling a chair out for Hannah to sit.

"I am, but American. Egyptian American."

They all sat down around a large circular table.

"Oh, this makes sense. This is why you were in Tahrir. Most Egyptian women don't go anymore. Too dangerous. But Americans—you think nothing is dangerous. You think always everything will be okay."

Hannah shrank from her frank observation, but she couldn't deny that it was true. She'd gone into Tahrir that day with a sense of American entitlement—like she belonged there, like nothing bad could happen. Her mom wouldn't have been proud of that.

Hannah looked around. There were seven women, three older, in their forties or fifties, all wearing hijab, the rest younger, some without the hijab. Twenties and thirties probably.

"Thank you for helping me," Hannah said. "I shouldn't have been out there."

"No," another one of the older women said, her accent heavier. "We wish it can be safe, but it's not."

The woman who had held Hannah's arm spoke up to ask for her name, inviting Hannah to introduce herself. They asked what she was doing out there alone, and she tried to explain as best she could, but as she spoke, her answers felt silly and naive.

"I needed to see the protests for myself." Hannah looked around at all of them. "I know it was stupid, but I wanted to do something, and I didn't know what else to do."

"It's not stupid," one of the younger women said.

"It is very stupid," countered one of the older women. "She can die. They can rape her."

"She wants to help," the young woman said. "We go to the square every day."

"We are prepared."

"Sorry, can I ask, who are you?" Hannah said. "Are you OpAntiSH?"

Hannah had recently read about Operation Anti-Sexual Harassment. They were a coalition that had formed fairly recently to protect women in Tahrir Square. When she'd first read about them, she was reminded so much of what her own mother's activism had centered on.

"Some of us work with OpAntiSH," said the woman who had held her up outside the square. She introduced herself as Manal. "We also work with Tahrir Bodyguard. We fight for women's rights in Egypt, and we go to Tahrir to protect the protesters—usually women but sometimes men too."

The boy who was trampled. Had anyone helped him? No, they were likely far too late for him. Hannah sipped her water. This was the kind of group her mom would have been a part of, had it been around back then. She wouldn't have gone rogue to prove a point.

The women told her they had been involved with the original protests in 2011. It was still dangerous for women back then, but there were more of them, and the stories of sexual assault in the square were less rampant.

"But then the Muslim Brotherhood came," Manal said. "And we didn't know what we were fighting for anymore. They took over the protests, they took over the government, and we had no voice. No women in government. No women to make any decisions."

"So what are you fighting for now?" Hannah asked. "What are you trying to do?"

She asked because she truly didn't know. They wanted the Brotherhood out, that was clear, but what was the alternative?

"We fight for freedom," said one of the women who hadn't spoken yet. "For women's rights. But I think we don't know anymore. The old regime and the army—they are coming back, controlling everything. The lights and the power. This is so they can show us the Brotherhood is no good, but they are both no good."

"We come back to Tahrir for the women," one of them said. "We want women's voices in Egypt."

Her mom had wanted that too. Not just in her youth. When the original protests had begun, she'd been so happy, so proud of Egypt. They'd been on the phone, watching the news from different states.

"Finally, the Egyptian people are doing something," her mom had said. "And look at all the women who are protesting. This is amazing for Egypt."

She was seeing the work she'd done in her youth finally coming to fruition.

The women told Hannah that there were more of them and that they were organized and growing.

"These men," one of the women said, "they come in groups. They attack women on purpose because they don't want us in Tahrir."

They listed off all the injustices that had been occurring. The sexual assaults were a concerted effort—the result of groups of men attempting to keep women from gaining power.

"Is there anything I can do to help?" Hannah looked from one person to the next. "I'd like to be involved. I know going into Tahrir today was misguided, but I want to do *something*. My brother is a journalist in America. Maybe he can write about your organization. And my mom used to be a part of AWSA."

"AWSA?" one of the older women said, an inquisitive look on her face. "This was a very long time ago. What is your mother doing now?"

"She . . . died recently." Hannah looked down and began to peel the label off her water bottle.

"Istukhfurallah," the woman said. "Salamtik."

The others looked at one another, thoughtful expressions on their faces.

"Who does your brother work for?" one of the women asked.

"He works for a Philadelphia paper," Hannah said, omitting his recent firing. She looked back up at them. "But he's looking to move on to something else, if he can."

"If the Americans hear about us, maybe they can help," one of the women said in Arabic to another.

They probably thought she didn't speak Arabic, didn't understand what they were saying.

"The Americans don't care about Egypt," the woman said in response, and Hannah couldn't help but interject, undeterred by their shared look of surprise at her comprehension.

"We can make them care. And if they don't, I care, and I still want to help."

They looked at her. *"You speak Arabic?"* one of them said.

"Yeah."

"Okay," the woman said. She grabbed a napkin and began to

jot down an address and phone number, and she told Hannah to stop by their offices this week. This was her chance to do something for Egypt. This was what she was looking for.

Zain

Zain was lying in bed, looking down at his phone. Emily deserved a real apology. He sat up and clicked her name. After two rings, the call went to voicemail. She was ignoring him. He'd expected as much. He'd just leave a message.

"Emily," he started, unsure of himself. "I know you don't want to talk to me, but I need to see you. I don't like how we left things. I miss you, and I know I have no right to say that, and you don't owe me anything, but I just have things I need to say, and after that, you never have to see me. If you don't call me back, I understand."

A few minutes later, he got a text from her that, despite everything, sparked a small bit of hope.

I can meet you after my rotation. Green Line at 5?

Zain drove into Philly that afternoon and got to the Green Line Cafe early, picking out a table by the window. He didn't plan out what he would say, and his leg shook up and down as he tapped his hand on the table. A girl sitting nearby turned her gaze from her computer to him, and he stopped. But still his heart was racing. He'd never been nervous around Emily before.

She walked into the shop in her blue scrubs, her light brown hair pulled back into a messy bun. There was no pretending with her, no attempts to glam herself up to show that she'd won the breakup. That wouldn't be like her. She sat down across from Zain without saying hello and just looked at him, waiting for him to speak.

"Do you want to get coffee?" he asked.

"Not really." Emily gazed at him absently, her expression impossible to read. "But feel free to get some if you want."

She was going to make this difficult.

"Well, one of us probably should," he said.

She nodded, so he stood. "You sure you don't want anything?" She shook her head.

He ordered and returned with his drink.

"What did you want to tell me?" she asked.

"Just—that I'm sorry." He paused, wrapping his hands around his warm cup.

"That's it? Seems like something you could have said over the phone." She just kept staring blankly at him.

"No, I mean, for everything. Since college. I've taken you for granted and treated you like shit. I don't know why you put up with it."

She leaned back in her chair and crossed her arms. "I don't really know why either. I guess I felt bad for you because your mom died."

He wished he'd prepared some kind of speech or something. He'd keep going, though. He'd apologize for everything, all the way back to when they first started dating.

"When we broke up that first time," he said, "that was the biggest mistake of my life. It hasn't been the same since, and I don't know why it's taken me so long to realize how awful I've been."

She squinted and looked confused. "I mean, you haven't been awful until recently."

He told her that when they broke up the first time it was because he was scared they were getting too serious too young.

"I didn't want to be bound to my college girlfriend for the rest of my life."

But he was stupid back then. He hadn't realized at the time that he was making a mistake.

"This 'no labels' bullshit," he continued, "I was keeping my options open, is all."

"Maybe I wanted to keep my options open too," Emily said.

"What?"

"I didn't want to commit to you yet."

He simply stared at her across the table. He'd assumed the reason they'd never had the relationship talk was because of him. He'd never considered that she didn't want one either.

"But just because we were both noncommittal," Emily continued, "doesn't mean we weren't together. Like a couple. We weren't seeing other people, and you know that."

Now that, he couldn't argue with.

"I know, I fucked up. Without you I have no one, and I'm not saying that so you feel bad or to get you back. It's just the truth, I guess. And I deserve what I get now."

She didn't say anything, her arms still crossed over her chest. At that moment, a phone went off at a nearby table, briefly blasting a familiar song—an Egyptian one by Amr Diab that his mom would play in the car when he was younger. In an instant, Zain was brought back to childhood, sitting in the front seat of his mom's car, Hannah in the back, as she drove them to school, music playing softly through the speakers.

He almost couldn't believe it, but Philly had its fair share of Arabs, so perhaps it wasn't that strange to hear a popular Egyptian song on someone's phone. Sometimes, in the car with his mom, Zain would complain, wanting to listen to the radio instead—American music that he wouldn't be embarrassed to have his friends hear at drop-off. Now he regretted ever feeling embarrassed by his mom's music. The thought was quickly interrupted, though, as the woman at the nearby table answered, a harsh "Hello" grating through the song.

"What do you want, Zain?" Emily said, snapping him back to the present.

There wasn't really any answer to that question. He didn't even know what she meant, exactly. He wanted his mom there, not just a memory of her sparked from a familiar song.

"I—want to be a better person, I think." He took a sip of his coffee, which was getting cold in front of him.

"Bullshit." She rolled her eyes.

"Excuse me?"

"If you want to be a better person, then be a better person, and stop feeling bad for yourself."

"I'm not—I'm apologizing to you. I'm not feeling bad for myself."

"This is not a good apology."

"What?"

Emily tilted her head to the side and laughed. "Do you think this is a good apology?"

"I don't—I mean . . ." He looked down at his cup.

"You're trying to clear your own conscience. This is classic Zain."

"Classic Zain?" He raised his eyebrows.

She smiled and uncrossed her arms, gesturing with her hands now instead. "Yeah, you're all, like, 'Oh, I have no one without you. I made the biggest mistake of my life, poor me, I'm Zain the fuckup who's trying to do better.' Like, goddamn,

Zain. *Be* better, and stop saying you *want* to be better."

"I wasn't trying to—" He wanted to defend himself, to show that he was being genuine—that it was about *her*, not him, but as he stuttered to find the right words, he feared she was right. Maybe the better thing to do was to leave her alone, not force her into this meeting so he could bumble his way through a series of sorrys.

"I don't care what you were or weren't trying to do, because we're not together anymore," Emily said. "It's none of my business. We're not even friends anymore. So just move forward."

Her words stung, leaving behind a burning sensation in his chest. She was absolutely right. They weren't friends anymore, and that loss, that realization, meant he was truly alone.

"I moved back home, you know," he said, changing the subject and storing the hurt away on a shelf in his mind.

"I heard. Get a new job. Move out."

"Yeah." He took another sip of his coffee. "My dad tried to explain himself yesterday."

"What do you mean?"

He looked down at his cup. "Like, he tried to explain how everything with that woman happened."

Emily leaned forward. "Jesus, why would you need to hear about that?"

Her tone was different then, and for a moment, it was like they were friends again.

"His therapist told him to."

"You have to get out of that house." Emily shook her head.

"I'm trying."

"I don't think you are," she said, leaning back again. "Just the fact that you told me that story is you feeling sorry for yourself again and wanting me to feel sorry for you instead of *doing* something. Anyway, I don't even know why we're having this conversation. We're not a couple. We're not friends."

Again, she was right. They weren't friends. He didn't even know what he was thinking, telling her about his dad like that, still hoping she'd comfort him like always. They were both silent for a moment. He sipped his coffee and looked out the window. A group of college students walked past, all of them laughing, like a picture out of a Penn brochure. He turned to face Emily again.

"Em, is this it?"

"I think so." She looked down.

"Okay." He nodded. "I just want you to know how sorry I am. I don't need you to forgive me or anything, but I just needed to apologize because you deserve at least that."

"Okay," she said. "Thank you."

They put on their coats and said goodbye, hugging outside before they turned and walked in opposite directions. He wanted to turn around and follow her, embrace her in some romantic gesture like in the movies. Say something sappy that would make her want to stay with him. But that was stupid. That wasn't like him or like her or like their relationship had ever been. It probably wasn't like any relationship. He didn't turn around and instead just headed toward his car.

There were Penn students with backpacks everywhere, most of them well dressed and perky. They didn't have that postgrad despair yet. He unlocked his car and got inside. It sucked that he had to leave Philly and make the hour-long drive back to Jersey. Crossing the Walt Whitman Bridge again felt like leaving something behind. His entire life was across that river, but that stage had ended. He didn't know what would come next.

Hannah

Hannah was safe now, but her heart kept pounding, her hands shaking slightly, droplets of sweat still on her brow. Those women—they were some kind of dream sent down to rescue her just in time. The protest itself felt unreal, like she'd walked into a hellish pit of violent men who were sent to create a sense of danger. What was the point of them being there? What was the point of them wanting to attack her?

Her phone buzzed. A text from Zakaria. She hadn't seen or heard from him since the night of the drunken sheesha. She figured she'd wait for him to reach out in case he thought of her differently now or didn't want her around. She was the American girl who didn't follow the rules of Islam, and yet, in the text, he invited her to dinner with his family. If he was okay with her meeting his traditionally Muslim family, then maybe his religiosity was a farce too. It was hard to tell what anyone really believed.

"I break the same rules sometimes. It's okay," he had said.

The same rules. Maybe he was just like her. Or maybe he lived with the same hypocrisy as her dad. But Zakaria was different. He hadn't been judgmental at all that night.

Hannah was raised with the idea that Egypt was the motherland—wholesome and innocent—but maybe that wasn't the case at all. She didn't even know if her parents really believed that idealization of Egypt. Zakaria was Muslim, like her, but he didn't follow all the rules or pay attention to every tenet. And what about the men in the square? They were Muslim too—in name, at least.

The taxi pulled up to her apartment, and once inside, she shot a quick text back to Zakaria, agreeing to meet his family that night. He would pick her up, he said. But what did all this mean? Picking her up, introducing her to his family. He'd been so kind to her ever since she'd been here, and at times, she thought he might like her—a small crush, perhaps. But they were friends.

In the meantime, she needed to shower and wash Tahrir from her body. The sweat of those violent men had infused her clothes, her skin, her hair. She could still feel them grasping her sweatshirt, their rough hands grazing her forehead as they ripped her hat from her head. She could smell their cologne, the pungent, musky odors barely masking the scent of day-old sweat. But at least she was home, finally. Or some version of home that she'd created since coming to Egypt.

She slowly made her way to the bathroom. In the tub, the water fell in uneven streams, the heater building up to a piercing screech like a teakettle—like that boy screaming as he was trampled. The women hadn't gotten there in time for him. She reached her hand out mechanically to grab the loofah, but then didn't move and just stared at the white porcelain below her feet. Her brain felt disconnected from her body, transporting her back into the square, back to the sight of the boy on the ground, her hand reaching down, the pepper spray being crushed. She was just another stupid American who thought they were invincible, going into Tahrir Square like that. *How many women aren't rescued? How many die?* She brought her arms together, holding them over her naked chest as she hunched over. She opened her mouth to scream, but nothing came out except for frantic breaths of air.

She wanted her mom. She wanted to cry as her mom held her. She wanted to be a kid again. Her mom would have said going to Tahrir was stupid and dangerous—but maybe some small part of her would have been proud. Proud that her daughter was like her, among the women who wanted to make a difference. But there was nothing to be proud of. Going into that square was a bad decision, and that was all there was to it.

She let the water wash the tears from her face and began to scrub her body, but at the shoulder, a soreness coursed through her back suddenly. Had someone hit her there? She couldn't remember. Maybe they had as they'd shoved her around, pulling at her hair. She would wash all that off. Her shoulder would bruise, but other than that, there couldn't be any reminders of what happened in the square—of what could have happened in the square.

Once out of the shower, she barely recognized herself in the mirror. Her face was the same as always, sure, but it was like looking at a stranger. This whole time in Egypt, it was as though she were watching herself from the outside, like her body was something separate that went about life detached from any true emotion. But now there was this tightness in her chest, like everything she had been running away from was right there above her heart, crushing her.

When Zakaria came by to pick her up, he acted the same as always, not making mention of the last time they were together, when he'd seen her drunk on the streets at night. Maybe he wasn't thinking about it. Or maybe he didn't care. It was on Hannah's mind, though. In the car, she cleared her throat, preparing to bring it up, hoping to clear the air before she met his family.

"Last time I saw you, when you said you make the same mistakes sometimes, what did you mean?"

He didn't say anything for a few seconds as he drove.

"I just mean I'm not a perfect Muslim," Zakaria said. "Nobody is."

They began to slow down, hitting the usual Cairo traffic. A disheveled-looking man was walking between the cars on the road, a spray bottle and a rag in his hand.

"But do you drink?" Hannah asked. "And, like, break other rules?"

"I have." Zakaria kept his eyes on the road, even though they weren't moving. "Nobody is perfect."

He was right. And he only proved what she already knew. That Egypt wasn't the land of wholesomeness that her parents had tried so desperately to make her and Zain believe it was.

The man in the street approached their car and without asking, quickly started spraying their windshield and wiping it down. Zakaria rolled down his window and began to shout.

"La, shukran. *No, thank you.*"

The man was determined, though, and kept wiping as Zakaria shouted, until the window was free of dust. He walked over to the driver's side and demanded money, arguing with Zakaria until he shelled out two one-pound notes. Zakaria shook his head in frustration as Hannah watched the man amble away.

"Guess he really needed the money," she said.

Zakaria laughed. "My friends really liked you." He glanced over at Hannah in the passenger seat.

"Oh, nice." She turned to look out the window again at the other cars sitting in traffic next to them. "They were cool."

Traffic started moving again, and they made their way down the congested road.

"Yeah, they said we should get married." Zakaria laughed, and Hannah shifted her body nervously in the front seat.

It was like he was testing her reaction or something, and playing it off as a joke. She'd seen this coming. This meeting-the-family thing was a classic Arab move—introduce your parents to the girl you're interested in before anything really happens. But he hadn't even talked to her about it. Maybe he thought they were on the same page—that all the one-on-one hangs meant she liked him too. She should have known she was leading him on. It wasn't just Egyptian boys. American boys, too, often misinterpreted friendship for something more. But none of them went so far as to introduce her to their parents. They had different ways to make a move in America.

As they drove, Rami kept popping up in her mind. She was herself with him, not hiding away the parts of herself she kept from her family, or from Zakaria, even. She and Zakaria were different people from different worlds, and even though he wasn't a perfect Muslim, he still wasn't like her. She wasn't really Egyptian, like him. She was too American for Egypt, and not American enough for America—she and Rami had that in common. With Zakaria, she couldn't really even explain it to herself, but there was some mental block preventing her from being real, from being herself, in a sense, with him.

This day was too much—the protests and now meeting his parents. She shouldn't have agreed to this dinner. Zakaria's family lived in Maadi, the same neighborhood as her mom's family. It was quieter there, the streets less busy, but it was still a part of the city. The roads along the way were familiar—streets she'd traversed with her family. She'd managed to stay out of that neighborhood since arriving in Cairo—there was not much to do there, anyway, and she couldn't risk running into any relatives. A moment later, they turned onto the street of her grandmother's apartment, and Hannah held her breath. There was no way. He couldn't live here. But they passed the building, and she let out a deep breath. Zakaria might know them—her mom's family—given how close they lived. They pulled up to a building another block away, and he stopped. When they got out, she kept her head down, in case any relatives of hers might be passing by.

The smell as they entered the apartment brought her back to dinners at home, her mom's Egyptian cooking filling the kitchen, garlic and onion permeating the senses. If she closed her eyes, maybe she could go back, pretend she was home, waiting for dinner to be ready. Maybe she could exist there once again, the smell of Zakaria's house transporting her across the flat plane of time. But she was here, and his family welcomed her like they'd known her for years—like they were her family too. She was sure to disappoint them all.

As soon as they arrived, Layla and Zakaria's parents led them straight to the dining room, where they'd prepared a spread of foods Hannah looked forward to every time she went home—stuffed grape leaves, macarona béchamel, eggplant in tomato sauce, and okra—or bamya—all cooked in those familiar Egyptian spices Hannah never bothered to learn.

"Kooly, kooly," Zakaria's mom repeated when Hannah declared she was full.

"Shukran," Hannah said.

For dessert, they had baklava with mint tea to drink, the baklava not nearly as good as her mom's. She finished her tea, and Zakaria's mom poured another glass, though Hannah insisted she'd had enough.

"You have to have more," she said, like all Egyptians, not taking no for an answer when it came to food and drink.

Zakaria's family was just like her own: two kids, an older brother, younger sister. On the couch, she sipped her second cup of tea and floated back to a time before her mom died, when they were a happy family—or so it had seemed.

As the parents cleaned up in the kitchen, Hannah talked to Zakaria and Layla about movies and TV shows, and occasionally, Layla would break off from the conversation to look down at her phone and smile.

"Who are you texting?" Hannah said.

"Boys, probably," said Zakaria as he rolled his eyes.

Eventually, they started to talk about Tahrir, though Hannah didn't tell them how she'd spent her morning.

"Do you think you'll ever go back out there—to protest, I mean?" Hannah asked Zakaria as she sipped her tea, leaning her elbow on the gold trim of the couch, decor that was distinctly Egyptian in taste.

"I don't think so," he said. "It's dangerous now. I can't do that to my family, not after Ali."

Ali. The friend who'd died. Hannah didn't know what to say. She'd been so privileged as to think going into Tahrir would be okay. She hadn't experienced what Zakaria had experienced—or what any Egyptian had experienced. Tahrir, for them, was serious—not a childish ploy to prove a point.

"I'm so sorry." Hannah turned her glass teacup in her hand and looked down. "That's just awful what happened."

"Mama and Baba are always worried." Layla looked up from her phone. "They won't even let me go see my friends alone anymore."

"Yes, they make me take her everywhere," Zakaria said.

"Are things very different than they were a year or two ago?" Hannah placed her cup on the white marble-top coffee table in front of her. "Like, in your everyday lives?"

"There is more harassment," Layla said. "I don't know why, but the men are worse now."

"And people are getting kidnapped," Zakaria's father said, re-entering the room with more tea. "It's very dangerous to be out. You have to be careful." He topped off each of their cups as they all quietly thanked him.

Later, Zakaria offered to drive Hannah home, but she insisted she would take a taxi. He said he would at least walk her downstairs. She felt queasy suddenly, and as they stepped into the elevator, her chest tensed with anxiety. She had no idea what Zakaria would say or do next, but he was sure to make his feelings known now, and the idea of rejecting him, of causing him pain when he'd been so nice to her, manifested in a building sensation of nausea.

She said nothing as they rode down in the elevator, with Zakaria standing close.

"My parents loved you."

Hannah smiled. "Yeah, they were great. So sweet. You have to thank them again for me."

He smiled too, now, looking at her in a way she recognized—in a way other men had looked at her in the past. In a way that she sometimes wanted Rami to look at her.

She stared at the floor, and the elevator stopped. She stepped out first, and her heart was beating faster now, awaiting what was sure to come.

"Thank you again for the invite," she said once they were outside.

She wanted him to leave, to go back upstairs without waiting for her to get a cab. The truth was, she wouldn't be getting a cab at all. She wasn't going back to her apartment. She would walk, instead, to her grandmother's place. She had decided in that short elevator ride that it was time to see family.

But Zakaria didn't leave.

"Hannah, I like you a lot," he started, just as they stepped outside.

Her heart sank.

"I like you too." She feigned ignorance. "You've been such a good *friend*."

She almost added "You're like a brother to me," but then thought better of it, not wanting to twist the knife even further. But he didn't take the hint or understand her tone and began to lean his face toward hers, closing his eyes, pursing his lips, and before she could even think, she swerved out of the way, leaving him to kiss the air instead.

"Zakaria." She thought she might die of awkwardness. "I'm not—I'm sorry, I can't . . ."

He fumbled back. She didn't know what to say, her mind frozen and untethered, like she'd forgotten how to use words.

"Sorry," Zakaria said. "I didn't mean to—"

"No," Hannah said. "It's okay. I just—I don't—it's—"

"I thought because you're American, it would be okay. I didn't know."

She paused. "What?"

"I should have asked," Zakaria said.

"Asked if you could kiss me?"

"Yes, but we can go slow. It's okay."

He wasn't getting it. He thought he was moving too fast for her, the kiss coming as a surprise she wasn't ready for—a surprise he thought he could get away with because she was American, not an overly conservative Arab girl who wouldn't even kiss. He thought she was innocent.

"Zakaria." Hannah faced him. "I'm not—look, I think you're a great friend, but you don't really know me."

"I want to get to know you," he said.

"No, I just mean, I'm not the person you have in your mind."

He shook his head, as though confused. "What does that mean?"

She wanted to explain that the idea he had of her wasn't actually her—that she would never be someone his family would approve of.

"The other night, I was drunk," Hannah said. "And I'm not saying, like, I get drunk all the time, but that's just a part of my life right now. And I—"

She wanted to tell him about Rami, about how she was walking back from his place that night, but that would only serve to hurt him, when the point she wanted to make was that she wasn't the innocent Muslim girl he thought she was.

"Hannah, I know this. I saw you. I walked you home."

"I'm not, like, this nice Muslim girl." She gestured with her hands as she spoke. "I'm not someone you want to bring back to your family."

That was not something she'd ever thought she'd say. By most standards, she was exactly what parents would want for their sons. But here in Egypt, it was a different story. They were playing a different game altogether.

"I don't understand."

"You're . . . so nice," Hannah said. "And you're religious. You go to Friday prayer. And that's great! That's so good. But it's not where I'm at right now. I'm not trying to be in a relationship or be, you know, the kind of girl you're looking for. I wasn't raised here."

She looked down and kicked at some dirt under her feet.

"Hannah, I know you're not raised here," he said. "I know you're different than the other Egyptian girls. This is why I like you."

She didn't believe him, though. He liked the idea of her, but he didn't know her. She could never be what he actually wanted.

The streetlight over the sidewalk flickered, and she could hear a group of stray cats meowing in the distance. She felt far from the real world in that moment, floating through space as Zakaria stood before her in another dimension. She wanted to keep floating—to float away from this moment, this conversation.

"I'm sorry." She pulled herself back. "My life is just too messy right now. I don't want a relationship. But I hope we can still be friends."

Zakaria nodded. "Okay," he said.

"Thank you for inviting me to dinner," Hannah said. "Your parents were so nice."

He nodded again. "Bye, Hannah."

"Bye." She waved as Zakaria walked back inside.

She wasn't floating away anymore, instead tethered to the ground once again, the weight of guilt and pity holding her down. Had she lost him as a friend? She couldn't say, exactly, why she didn't want to be with him, why, instead, she was drawn to Rami, a man who was only interested in her when they were both drunk and ready for bed. She'd told the truth, though, that she didn't want a relationship. But even if she did, there was something about Zakaria that wouldn't work—some way that they were incompatible.

She worried now that he wouldn't want to see her again. That he was only spending time with her because he was romantically interested. Or maybe after this, friendship would just be too difficult for him.

The cats in the distance were meowing again—a cue for her to get going and head to her grandmother's place. The crisp, cool night air smelled of dust, with a slight hint of mint wafting past from a nearby shop, only to be replaced by an animal scent as a man in a galabiya trudged past her with a donkey. There were some stars in the sky, a rare sight in the city, but this area was dimmer and less polluted. When she reached the building, the same young boy that had carried their suitcases up after her mother's funeral sat outside. It didn't seem like he recognized her, but she avoided eye contact and headed in. She climbed the concrete stairwell again, which was cooler now that the weather had changed. Last time, the sun had shone in through the windows, lighting the path, but now, only moonlight guided the way.

She knocked. Inside, there were voices. Of course other people were in there. It was a building full of family. The doorknob began to turn as Hannah cracked her knuckles and bit her lip. Her heart banged inside her chest, ready to jolt out.

Her uncle, Mohamed, was the one who answered. He stood for a moment in silence then said, "Ya Allah," pulling her inside.

He shouted into the apartment that he had a surprise for everyone—that they wouldn't believe who was here. Inside, her grandmother and her aunt Hebah were drinking tea. They were happy to see her, but it was clear they were distraught too. They probably thought she was uncaring and selfish for not reaching out all this time, and as soon as she walked into the room, she was back at the funeral all over again.

Her grandmother, aunt, and uncle asked about her time in Egypt—where she was staying, what she was doing. She told them about her job at the café, about the neighborhood she lived in.

"I know that café," her aunt said. "I work right down the street. I can't believe I never saw you."

They talked some more until the hours passed and the conversation hit a lull.

"You'll spend the night here," her grandmother said.

Hannah didn't protest. It was easier not to.

"Tomorrow," said her uncle, "I'll take you on my boat. We can go down the Nile. It's beautiful."

When Mohamed and Hebah left, her grandmother gave her a toothbrush and some pajamas to wear—pajamas purchased in America during her last visit. Her grandmother kept asking question after question, even after everyone left. She wanted to know more about Hannah's stay in Egypt and why she was there in the first place. Hannah didn't know what to tell her, so she repeated the same story she told everyone. That she didn't want to attend law school, that she wanted to learn more about the country. She hesitated.

"And everything that's been going on since the revolution." Hannah adjusted herself on her grandmother's couch as she sat with one leg underneath her. "I just wanted to understand it."

"Stay away from the politics." Her grandmother waved a hand in front of her. "It's dangerous right now."

"Well, it's just interesting, I think." Hannah tilted her head.

"What's interesting? We get rid of one president and we have another one that's the same. And now, the garbage doesn't get picked up, and the lights go out, and nothing changes." The expression on her face was one of irritation and disgust, her frown digging into the wrinkle lines around her mouth.

"Was my mom involved in politics?"

Her grandmother shrugged and stood up.

"Because I saw some pictures," Hannah continued. "She was in AWSA?"

"AWSA," her grandmother said, picking up the empty teacups on the coffee table, "was very silly. Her friends were no good, and they made her join."

"Noha and Hamada?"

Her grandmother stopped what she was doing then and looked at Hannah. “How do you know them?”

“They came to the mosque after the funeral.” She didn’t tell her grandmother that she and Noha had been in touch since that time.

“They want Egypt to be better for women.” Her grandmother held the cups in her hand still. “But Egypt is already good for women. Yes, we have men in the streets yelling, and sometimes it’s better to walk with a man, but this is life. Life is dangerous. We shouldn’t fight the government. It’s too dangerous. And for what? To be like America? No.”

Hannah stayed up a bit after her grandmother went to bed. She perused the photos along the wall of her mom, aunt, and uncle as kids. There were photos of her grandfather too. He’d died her freshman year of college, midsemester, and her parents hadn’t wanted her to leave school for the funeral. They’d gone to Egypt themselves, without her and Zain. Hannah had always assumed her mom didn’t want them to attend because she thought they couldn’t handle a funeral. To her, they were always children, even when they weren’t.

Eventually, she made her way into her mom’s old room with the two twin beds and sat down on the hard mattress. Whenever they’d visit Egypt, Hannah always complained about the hard mattresses. It was like people in Egypt preferred to sleep on wooden boards. She looked around the room. Maybe there was more to be found—more insight into her mom’s past. Hannah opened the closet. It wasn’t an in-wall closet like in America. Instead, it was one of those large wooden wardrobes. The inside was filled with old clothes that her grandmother, for whatever reason, hadn’t gotten rid of over the years. One side of the closet was her mom’s and the other side her aunt’s, but it was unclear which was which. She riffled through both, taking in the scents of must and a flowery perfume still lingering on the dresses and shirts.

On one of the shelves was a binder with "YASMEEN" written in large capital letters across the top and then underneath, written again in Arabic letters. Hannah grazed her hand across the thick plastic, transporting herself back in time—back to the version of her mom who doodled on binders. The binder itself held school notes, mostly in Arabic, with more little doodles along the margins. Triangles in the corner. A drawing of a cat. Repeated swirls all up and down the pages. In the inside pocket, there was a photo. Her mom with Noha and Hamada, smiling all together at the beach. Hamada had his arm around her mom.

Hannah threw the binder up on the bed and continued rummaging through drawers filled with shoes and purses. One of the purses held a dried-up tube of red lipstick, a color she was sure she had never seen her mom wear. All the way in the back was an old shoebox, which Hannah grabbed and opened. Inside, there were letters—yellowed envelopes with *"Yasmeen"* written across them in Arabic. Hannah opened one of the letters. It was all in Arabic, the handwriting almost incomprehensible to her. Hannah could read Arabic at a rudimentary level, but she was used to textbook font, the lines and dots clearly drawn. But here, the letters flowed together, the dots turning into shapes, jumbling up into vaguely familiar symbols. She could make out a word here or there: "habibty," "gameela," simple things like that. She got only a few lines into the letter before giving up and flipping to the back to see who it was from. It was signed "Hamada." Hannah flipped back to the front and looked at the date. It was the same year they'd moved to America, just six months before Zain was born.

1983

Yasmeen

Yasmeen sat next to Hamada on a bench, in a quiet part of the nady where they probably wouldn't run into friends or family. They were sitting close, their legs touching.

"I'm marrying Yousef," Yasmeen said, looking down at the grass beneath her feet. "I wanted to tell you before you find out from someone else."

Hamada didn't say anything, so Yasmeen looked up to see that he was staring in front of him, at the soccer field in the distance.

"Is that really what you want?" he finally said.

"He's a good man," said Yasmeen.

"But do you love him?"

She let out a single laugh, mostly out of discomfort and not knowing how to answer. How could she tell Hamada, her first love, who she'd known since first grade, that she loved someone else? And how could he ask her that? Did he think she'd just marry someone she didn't feel any love for?

"Hamada—"

"I'm serious, Yasmeen. Do you love him?" He turned his head to face her, peering directly into her eyes, and she looked away.

"Hamada, you and I broke up already."

"But you still love me." He smiled knowingly.

She swung her head in his direction, her eyes wide with irritation now. Hamada was always so entitled, acting like he knew everything about her.

"It's okay," he continued. "You don't have to admit it, but I know it's true. We wouldn't be here if you didn't."

Two days earlier, she'd kissed Hamada under a tree just a few feet away from where they were now. She'd already known then that she and Yousef would be getting engaged, but she couldn't bring herself to say it, instead letting Hamada press his lips onto hers as he hugged her waist, and she'd kissed him back, his lips a familiar comfort. A part of her wished she could take it back. She'd known that it was wrong and that she was risking her relationship with Yousef, but she hadn't cared.

"Hamada, we have to stop this," Yasmeen said.

"Stop what?" He looked at her again, and she felt his piercing stare and looked away.

"I shouldn't have kissed you the other day," she said. "I'm marrying Yousef. It's wrong."

"I don't think you even love him."

"Why would I marry him if I didn't love him?"

Hamada shrugged. "Your parents love him."

A week earlier, her mom had caught her and Hamada on the phone. She'd picked up the receiver and heard the two of them talking. Yasmeen didn't even remember what the conversation was about—probably just their day, or maybe they'd made plans to meet up. But shortly after, her mom had barged into her room and told her she should be ashamed.

"Yousef is coming to dinner tonight, and you're flirting with another man over the phone," her mom had said. "Haram. It's shameful. You have to stop this now."

Yasmeen had defended herself and said she and Hamada were just friends, but she knew her mom was right. She knew she couldn't let this go on any longer.

"I'm sorry, Hamada." She looked down at the grass again, moving her foot in small circles until she'd created a flat patch beneath her.

"It's okay. I know we'll just be back here next week having the same conversation again." He smirked.

"This is the last time we're having this conversation," Yasmeen said. "It's over now."

Hamada nodded, that smirk still plastered across his face, and she wanted to punch him. She hated that he knew her so well, and she hated that she still wanted him to kiss her. But she wouldn't let that happen again. She was getting married now, and she needed to be faithful to Yousef.

FALL 2012

Hannah

Hannah woke up in her mom's old bedroom and found herself pulled back to the week of the funeral, when she'd still hoped to wake up and find this was all a dream. Now she wanted to leave, to go back to the comfort of her own little apartment, away from this sadness.

But she had the boat ride with her uncle, so she had to get dressed, only she didn't have anything to wear, not having planned to spend the night. She went through her mom's closet again, picking out a blue-and-white-striped shirt with a little white Peter Pan collar. Something about it felt nautical, perfect for a boat ride. The shirt smelled stale with lack of use, but underneath that smell was her mom. Hannah looked in the mirror, and for a moment, she saw her mom standing there in front of her. She recalled Noha that day on the Nile, saying they looked alike, but Hannah couldn't always see it. She didn't have the same tiny arch in her nose, and her lips were slightly fuller, her cheekbones more angled. But her eyes—they were her mom's—dark and round, curving up in the same way when she smiled. As Hannah stared at herself in the mirror, it was like her mom was staring back out of those same large eyes. Hannah looked back down at her shirt. She never wanted to take it off, draping herself in the memory of her mom, and for a few seconds, at least, it was like she was there with her.

When her uncle arrived, she met him outside, and the two of them rode to the nady. Pretty much everyone in Egypt had a membership to at least one nady—a social club of sorts, but really just a local hangout, with a café and playgrounds and sports teams for kids. They were going to Nady el Yacht today, where her uncle had his boat parked. Her grandmother had been holding on to Hannah's membership pass, a pass purchased when she was five that was somehow still valid and had a picture of her from that time. Hannah held it in her hands. She couldn't remember the picture being taken. Her hair in the photo was wild and frizzy and looked like it hadn't been brushed, but there was a little pink bow on the side, keeping everything but the strands of baby hair out of her face. She and her uncle didn't talk much on the drive. They'd never had much of a relationship outside her mom, not having spent time together without the rest of the family, but Hannah answered his questions and made small talk.

As they entered the club, her uncle took the pass from her hands and handed it to the guard at the front gate. He quickly looked it over, looked at them, and then handed the passes back, as though he saw the little girl in the picture and knew it was her.

The country club overlooked the Nile, and boats of various sizes lined the docks. They walked toward one of the docks and stopped in front of a speedboat, which her uncle began to untie.

"I've never taken you on this boat before, have I?" he asked as they boarded.

"No, you had that bigger boat before." Hannah took a seat near the middle.

When her family would visit, he would take them out on his pontoon. They never went too fast because her mom would get nervous and feel seasick. That was years ago, though. Hannah was still in high school back then. She'd always want to go faster and would pout when her mom said no. Now she'd give anything for a slow boat ride with her.

"I sold that one." Her uncle untied the rope attaching them to the dock. "I wanted something faster."

He started the engine, and they began to pull away from the dock. On the river, the sunlight reflected against the water as they sped forward. Across from them, she could see skyscrapers, but before that, palm trees all along the river's edge. Her uncle looked out in front of him. He was wearing sunglasses, so Hannah couldn't see his eyes. The wind hit her face and made her own eyes tear up slightly. She blinked and looked down. They were far from the dock now, away even from the confines of the yacht club.

Her uncle began to slow the boat.

"That shirt—is that your mom's?" He looked in her direction.

"Oh, yeah. I found it in her closet."

Was he upset that she'd worn it? She'd lost her mom, but he'd also lost his sister.

"I remember her wearing that."

He looked back at the water. He and her mom had the same sharp jawline.

"What was it like?" Hannah said. "Growing up here together? What was *she* like?"

Her uncle shook his head. "She was a pain. Always telling me what to do." He paused and brought the boat to a stop, turning the engine off and letting them float. "But she was always there for me," he continued. "Anytime we needed anything, Hebah and I could count on her."

"Did the three of you get along?"

"Not at all." He laughed, leaning back in his seat. "We loved each other, but we fought all the time. When one of us did something wrong, we would all know about it because we went to the same school and knew all the same people, so we'd threaten each other. 'If you don't do this, I'll tell Dad.'"

Hannah smiled. "Did you know her friend Noha?"

Her uncle looked at her and squinted, the sun in his eyes. "You met her at the funeral," he said.

"Yeah, and after."

She told him she'd reached out to Noha, that they were in touch. He didn't seem at all surprised to hear about their meetings.

"Your mom was very headstrong," her uncle said. "And she wanted all women to have independence. I was young, but I knew our parents didn't like her being friends with Noha and Hamada."

"I thought she was engaged to Hamada."

"Noha told you?"

Hannah nodded.

"It didn't work out." Her uncle looked at the palm trees in the distance. "Our parents were always angry because of AWSA, and eventually, she listened to them, and this caused fights between Yasmeen and Hamada. They broke off the engagement."

"Did you like him?" Hannah asked.

The boat swayed with the current as they sat still on the water. It was almost unfathomable that her mom had had this whole other life before—that maybe marrying her dad and moving to America, abandoning everything she'd fought for in Egypt, wasn't the life she'd wanted.

"I guess so," her uncle said, as though unsure himself. "Hamada was a nice guy. We knew him since we were kids." He paused. "You know, when Yasmeen started seeing your dad, she didn't tell our parents, and I found out about it from a friend."

"I never knew that." Hannah was taken aback slightly.

She wasn't that different from her mom, it turned out. Keeping secrets from the family.

"Your mom and I got in a big fight that night." Her uncle smiled. "But I was stupid back then. I didn't like that she had a secret boyfriend. We didn't do that in our family. Or I had an idea that girls shouldn't do that. Because I had secret girlfriends, but it was okay for me because I was the boy." He shook his head. "I don't think like that anymore. That night, though, I confronted your dad, and I hit him."

Hannah laughed and leaned forward. "What? You're kidding. You didn't *actually* hit him?"

"I did," her uncle said. "Punched him right in the face." He motioned toward his own face with his fist. "He didn't even fight back. I wanted him to, but he said he loved Yasmeen. Your dad's a good man. They told our parents about the relationship the next day."

Her chest ached again, and she wished the river would just drown them, pull her down into the depths of the motherland. A good man. If only he knew. Maybe she should just tell him. There was no reason to keep it a secret. It was like she had been trying to preserve her dad's honor, even though he didn't deserve that.

Hannah looked out at the water, endless in expanse. "My dad is not a good man."

"Hmm?" Her uncle looked at her with some confusion.

"He had an affair. Right before Mom died."

Once she'd said those words, she couldn't stop herself from

spilling everything out, the story of her dad's indiscretion flowing from her mouth like the river beneath them. She told her uncle about Vivian and about where her dad was during the heart attack. She told him that they weren't speaking but that Zain had had to move back home after losing his job.

"My dad tries to call me every week," she said. "But I don't answer. I haven't talked to him in, like, three months."

Her uncle listened to the whole story without speaking, and when Hannah finished, they sat in silence for a few moments.

"Ibn el kalb," her uncle said. "I knew it. I never trusted him. Maybe there were others. Maybe it's not only this one."

It was like being hit in the chest, the aching now turning into a sudden thump. Hannah looked up.

"I don't know," she said. "I guess it doesn't matter anymore. But—what do you mean you never trusted him?"

He shook his head and slammed his palm on the steering wheel. "In my gut, I knew something was wrong. I never said anything because I had no evidence, but I just didn't trust him."

"But you said he's a good man."

"Of course, because he's your father. I had to say that."

There was a sudden impulse now to defend him. He was her dad, after all.

"I mean, he's not—like, he was always good to me and Zain." Hannah shifted a little in her seat.

"Of course." Her uncle looked over at her. "That's not what I meant."

Hannah didn't say anything.

"You and Zain," her uncle said, "if you ever need anything, I'm here for you. If Zain needs money—"

"Thank you," Hannah said. "We're okay, I think. Zain might be visiting soon."

They sat on the water for a little while more, neither of them speaking. The sounds of the city had faded away, no more car horns or loud music, and the air around them smelled of fresh moss, with whiffs of fish as the wind blew. Telling him felt like releasing a weight that had been pulling her down for months. Like finally, an adult in the family knew. Not that she and Zain weren't adults, but they were the kids of the family, and now she was unburdened.

"Do you think it was a mistake that she married my dad and broke off her engagement with Hamada?"

She fidgeted with her hands, meticulously cracking each knuckle. She wanted to ask about the letters, but he probably didn't know about those. Her uncle didn't say anything for a few seconds, then shook his head.

"We can never know," he said. "But everything happens for a reason. It's what God wants."

There it was again. What God wants. God's plan. God. Everyone just attributed everything to God, but God gave people free will. Her mom had chosen a life that might not have been the best one for her.

"Did my mom seem happy to you?" Hannah asked.

"Happy?" her uncle said. "I don't know."

"She always said you were close." She didn't know why she was asking him this, or what she was looking for.

"We were close when we were kids, but then—well, in high school we kept secrets."

Secrets. There were so many.

"What kind of secrets?" Hannah brushed her hair out of her face with her hands as the wind blew.

"Girlfriends and things like that. And like I said, your mother and father were a secret, but that was much later—after high school."

Another boat passed and the driver waved. Her uncle waved back.

"Were there other secrets?" Hannah asked.

"Like what?"

"I don't know. You tell me." The letters, she wanted to say.

Her uncle laughed, then told her about an incident when he'd seen his sister outside smoking cigarettes with her friends in high school.

"My mom smoked?" Hannah smiled. She'd never known her mom to smoke a single cigarette in her life.

"We all smoked. I started in high school, but of course we didn't tell our parents. And I never told Yasmeen I saw her that day. I don't know why. Maybe because I always thought of Yasmeen as the perfect goody-good, and that was the first time I realized she wasn't. I liked that. And then she joined AWSA, and I knew one hundred percent she was not a perfect goody-good. But after your parents moved to America, we talked even less."

"After she broke off her engagement, did she stay friends with Hamada? Like, did they talk at all still?"

Her uncle looked over at her. "Why are you asking?"

"I'm just wondering. I'm trying to understand."

"Understand what?"

Hannah paused. If he didn't know about the letters, she didn't want to change his view of his sister. But it seemed like he wasn't telling her something.

"I don't know," Hannah said. "I just want to understand her life."

"Yasmeen and Hamada knew each other for a very long time," her uncle said. "Your dad came much later."

Hannah waited for him to say more, but he was silent. "What does that mean?"

"They still saw each other sometimes," her uncle said. "I told her it was disrespectful to Yousef, but you know, they knew each other for so long, it's hard to just cut it off. But they were just friends."

He was looking out in the distance again, in the direction of the palm trees over the water. Her uncle turned the boat's engine back on, and Hannah tried to picture her mom back then, cigarette in hand, choosing between two men and two vastly different lives.

"I really miss her." Hannah let the wind blow her hair over her eyes, covering the tears that were beginning to well up.

"Me too."

She looked on at the river, at the palm trees and the city, as the boat moved forward. The sun shone down on them, but still, a wave of darkness and melancholy churned within her. The pain was endless, and her mom was everywhere, grief flowing all around with the Nile. Sadness settled in the corners of her mind, and some days felt worse than the funeral. Here on the boat with her uncle, she couldn't help but feel the full force of that grief, and living almost didn't seem worth it if it meant walking through life with this feeling hanging over her. She missed her mom. She missed talking on the phone, telling her about her day, hearing her voice. And there was so much that they didn't know about each other.

After her uncle dropped her off at the apartment, Hannah texted Manal to see if she could come by the offices of the women's group that day.

Yes of course, Manal wrote back.

Their offices were filled with people—mostly women, but

a few men—all sitting at desks, moving around, typing, filing, chatting. When Manal saw Hannah, she quickly rushed to the front of the office to greet her. Hannah faked a smile, the conversation with her uncle and memories of her mom still fresh in her mind. Manal showed Hannah around the office and explained the work they were doing. They were tracking assaults and working on projects to reduce street harassment. They were training people to go out in the square, but always in groups, and they encouraged women to file police reports if anything should happen to them. Most of the time, the police reports went unanswered, but it was something, at least, to have a record. And then there were teams of people trying to get the word out, trying to spread awareness.

"How can I help?" Hannah asked.

Manal told her she could start small. Come into the office and volunteer in her free time, help with paperwork and menial tasks just so they could gauge how involved she wanted to be—and how much they'd even need her help.

"Whatever it takes," Hannah said. "I just want to do *something*."

She would take up the work her mom started so many years ago. They were, after all, more alike than she ever knew.

WINTER 2013

Zain

Zain made the impulsive decision that he would visit Hannah in Egypt. He needed to get away, and he'd been saving a little bit of money with his barista job to buy a last-minute ticket. Of course, it helped that he didn't have rent to pay.

As Zain exited the airport, there was no surge of heat like last time. This was new, the air cool but still stagnant and filled with the smell of cigarettes and car exhaust, mixed with that very Egyptian dust, pollution, whatever it was that told him right away this was Cairo. There was no reason for his heart to be racing, for these nerves over visiting Hannah, except for the fact that she seemed to be in better shape than him, with some stability on her own in Egypt. As the older brother, he was supposed to have his life together. On top of that, he and Hannah had never been really close before, so she didn't know about Rachel, and she barely knew about Emily. That wasn't the kind of thing they talked about, and if he told her everything that had been going on, she'd view him in the same way she viewed their dad.

His eyes scanned the faces of people waiting outside, and there she was—a familiar smile, a wave. Hannah looked different. Her skin was darker—tan from all that Egypt sun—but her face also seemed fresher. Happier, maybe.

"Zain," she shouted.

He pushed through the crowd, past families embracing one another at the doors, and reached in to hug Hannah. The weight that had been clawing at his shoulders subsided, the tight grip of grief letting go, briefly.

"I can't believe you're here," she said amid the shouts of reunited friends and families on the sidewalk. "How was the flight? How are you?"

He tried to match her enthusiasm, smiling back.

"I'm good," he said. "This is wild. You're, like, a real Egyptian now."

"Not really." She laughed.

Her energy was different, somehow. They walked toward the line of taxis, approaching a driver who was shouting at a tourist couple, imploring them to ride in his cab, but the tourists were hesitant, so Hannah waved her hand to catch his attention, and he waved back, guiding them toward his vehicle as the tourists looked on. Zain watched as Hannah maneuvered her way around with such ease. Cairo was her space now.

She asked the driver, in broken Arabic, to take them to her address, and Zain remained quiet so as not to reveal himself as a tourist and get the prices jacked up, but Hannah began to speak in English anyway.

"So I have a bunch of stuff planned. Whenever we're here with Mom and Dad, we don't really get to explore Egypt, and I feel like you should get more of a Cairo experience, you know? Not like dinners at fancy hotels or whatever. And you have to meet Noha. She reminds me of Mom, kind of."

"Yeah, that'd be dope," he said, and looked back out the window, the sight of Cairo airport growing smaller in the distance.

On their last taxi ride in Egypt, headed back to the airport, they hadn't spoken at all. At the time, he hadn't known if they'd ever get past their mom dying, and with the grief still so heavy in his heart, it felt like he barely had. But what about Hannah? Did she not see their mom everywhere?

Cairo belonged to their parents. Back in America, their parents had been one unit. They'd functioned together, and though they were separate people, they hadn't acted independently of one another. But here, they'd been different. His mom would go her own way, seeing old friends, while his dad would do the same. They'd both just always seemed more alive here, and now it seemed that was becoming true for Hannah.

On the taxi ride, they passed the same familiar billboards he'd noticed a few months back. They sat in the same chaotic traffic, and he listened to the horns honking and people shouting. He inhaled the dust and car exhaust coming in from the open window, only this time, there was a nice little breeze, the air not so still.

Hannah turned her head to face him. "Is there anything you want to do?"

"Not particularly. Just happy to be here and see you." He could tell his tone was sad sounding, not as excited as Hannah's. He didn't know how to match her energy, how to pull himself into enthusiasm when life still seemed so bleak. He told himself being far from home should be enough, as though here, his problems wouldn't exist. Out of sight, out of mind. Wasn't that what Hannah was doing here?

The taxi pulled over in the middle of a congested street, and Hannah announced, "We're here." It was different from their grandparents' neighborhood. More lively. Maadi was nothing like this—instead it was filled with apartment buildings, maybe a small convenience store here and there. This was a side of Cairo they'd rarely ventured through, the sidewalks lined with shops and restaurants. From across the street he could hear an outdated Katy Perry song blasting.

Her apartment was clean—unlived in, almost. A plain blue couch leaned against the wall, and a small black coffee table sat in front of it. Besides that, the room looked fairly empty, like this wasn't her place. The walls were bare. She hadn't put up any pictures or decorations. This seemed almost like a temporary space for her—she hadn't committed yet. Maybe she'd be coming home soon.

"So I figured since you just landed," Hannah said as he put his bags down near the entryway, "today would be a chill day. We could just, like, hang out locally. Maybe get lunch at the café where I work?"

"Yeah, that sounds good," Zain said.

Something felt off, like they were being too superficial. He was on edge, afraid that at some point Hannah would ask him why he'd gotten fired, what he'd done, and for now, all he could do was act fake and happy. At the funeral, it had seemed like they'd broken down some walls, but maybe they hadn't. Maybe the sharing of secrets had only made them more distant.

Zain asked to shower before they did anything, wash the flight off him. Hannah pointed to a door on the left where he could get changed—her bedroom—and he headed in with his bag. Her room was neat. This orderliness wasn't the Hannah he knew. Growing up, her bed was never made unless there were guests over and their mom insisted. There was nothing on the dresser, all of it cleared and cleaned before his arrival, probably.

He opened the closet, and then, this was the Hannah he knew. Clothes were thrown in there. Piles of shoes not alongside their matches. Purses hung haphazardly. He shut the door and smiled. That felt real.

In the bathroom, he fiddled with the shower settings. The temperature wasn't adjusting quite right, but his body would just have to get used to it, and then, darkness. The water kept running, but he couldn't see anything, the bathroom having no windows.

"Hannah," he shouted.

"Sorry, the power's out!"

He'd forgotten about the power outages from the last time he was here, lasting exactly one hour on the dot. He had soap on his body, so he let the hot water keep flowing and washed it all off in the dark. It was still pitch black when he stepped out of the shower. His eyes hadn't really adjusted, though there was a faint sliver of sunlight coming from underneath the door. He could vaguely make out the shape of a towel hung on a rack and grabbed it.

"You okay?" he heard Hannah say.

"Yeah," he said. "I'll be out in a minute."

"So the power outages haven't stopped?" he shouted from the bedroom. He was standing with his towel wrapped around his waist, the sunlight from a nearby window making him squint slightly.

"Nope," Hannah said.

Without the fog of the funeral this time around, the journalist sense for a news lead that had long lain dormant in Zain's mind was piqued. No one was covering these outages.

He quickly got dressed, putting on a pair of jeans and a flannel over a white T-shirt. He rolled up his sleeves and glanced at his tattoo. Maybe better to keep the sleeves rolled down. But no, they weren't seeing family yet. It would be okay.

Hannah was lying on the couch with her eyes shut when he came out.

"Yo," he said.

She sat up. "Sorry. I was out late last night. I'm just a little tired."

"Is that safe?" Zain almost cringed at his own words—it was such a parent question, but in all the times they'd visited Egypt, their own parents had ingrained in them the idea that they couldn't go out alone at night. The streets were filled with danger.

"Yeah, it's fine." Hannah got up off the couch. "I'm never alone."

They quickly left to get lunch, as Zain hadn't eaten since the plane—crummy airplane food that was neither filling nor satisfying. Outside felt like spring in Philly. Only it was louder here, with a light brown dust covering the streets and buildings. He pulled out his phone and took a quick snap. A group of men leaned against a nearby wall as a woman carried a basket of bread down the block. Some kids ran past them on the sidewalk, in the middle of a game of tag, and in the street, cars stood still in traffic, the harsh sound of car horns slicing the air.

"The café I work at is just up ahead." Hannah pointed to a newer-looking storefront with glass doors.

They walked inside, and suddenly, Zain felt like they were no longer in Egypt. The clientele was a mix of obvious tourists and Egyptians, with more white people than he'd ever seen in Cairo. Surprising that Hannah would surround herself with people like this here when she could have just stayed in America.

"I know this is, like, so not Egypt," she said, as though hearing his thoughts. "But I just wanted you to see where I work."

"Hannah," a girl at the front said. "Is this your brother?"

Hannah introduced the girl as Vanessa, who she'd mentioned to him a few times over the phone. Vanessa shook his hand and said she was excited to finally meet him, leading them to a nearby table.

As they looked over the menu, people kept coming up to the table and saying hello. It seemed that Hannah had built herself a nice network of friends here in Egypt. It was good that she had people, that she wasn't alone. But still, they were mostly American. What was she even doing here?

"The hummus here is really good," Hannah said as Vanessa came back to take their orders.

The food arrived quickly, and Zain dug into his hawawshi just as another server came by to greet him and Hannah.

"Why does it seem like most of your friends are white Americans?" Zain asked as Hannah's friend walked away.

"That's not true," Hannah said. "Vanessa is only half white. And there's Zakaria. I've told you about him. And some of the girls at the center I volunteer at." She paused. "It's just, like, hard sometimes. I don't feel like a real Egyptian, if that makes sense."

It made perfect sense. They weren't real Egyptians, and they weren't real Americans either. The two of them existed in this in-between world, living in the middle of two cultures in a realm that most people they knew wouldn't understand. Before he could say anything, Vanessa approached the table.

"Did you tell him about the women's protest yet?"

"No," Hannah said. "I have not."

"What women's protest?" Zain looked from Hannah to Vanessa as he held his sandwich.

"Oh, Hannah is, like, a revolutionary now," Vanessa said.

"No, I'm not, I just—I went to a protest. That's how I met this group of women I've been volunteering with—"

"Hannah, what?" He set down his food. "Not in Tahrir?"

Zain sat irate as Vanessa shot Hannah a look before excusing herself to check on her other tables, leaving the two of them to discuss Hannah's *revolutionary* adventures.

"That's extremely dangerous. Why would you do that? Do you know how much assault has been happening at those?"

"I know." Hannah leaned back in her seat. "It was stupid. I guess I just wanted to see. To experience it."

"You could have been killed. Have you been watching the news?"

"Okay, *Dad*. I'm fine."

She shouldn't have put him in this position—the responsible one who had to tell his younger sister to be safe. He was never the responsible one. There was something else, though, something he could tell she was gearing up to say, as she continued swirling her hummus around with her bread.

"I had an incident," Hannah finally blurted out.

She told him that she went dressed as a man, and he felt his nostrils flare in further frustration—he was in sheer disbelief that she could be so stupid as to think that would keep her safe and told her as much. Hannah didn't back down, though, and defended herself with the fact that she'd made it out unharmed, saved by a group of women.

"Now I'm just, like, going to their office and helping out," Hannah said.

"You got lucky."

There wasn't much else to say as he searched for the words to make her understand—he couldn't handle another loss. But what was done was done, and Hannah didn't listen to anyone anyway. She just did what she wanted—always. Like the way she'd stayed in Egypt without considering anyone else.

"I'm not planning on going back into the square." Hannah took a bite of pita. "I'm just working in their office."

"Why didn't you tell me?" Zain asked.

"I don't know," she said. "I knew what you would say, and I guess I thought it would be easier to tell you in person. Honestly, I wanted to do something Mom would be proud of."

Zain begrudgingly nodded. That he could understand—the desperation to make their mom happy, to make her proud even in death. And their mom *would* be proud, not about going into Tahrir and putting her life in danger, but she'd be proud of her involvement in this group. She wouldn't be proud of him, though. Fucking up his whole life, all the choices he'd been making. He felt that scratch of anxiety in his chest again.

"It's stupid," Hannah continued.

"No." Zain looked back up. "I get it."

The next night, he and Hannah headed to their grandmother's place. The day had been spent wandering around Cairo, mostly. They hadn't talked about their mom, but she'd been all around them, haunting the streets, breezing past in the sandy wind.

"I don't know that I'm ready for this," Zain said as they exited the taxi.

Flashes of the funeral replayed in his mind as they neared the building—that foreboding walk up the hot stairwell, the pain of that day racing through his body like an electric shock.

"I sort of know exactly what you mean," Hannah said. "We

don't have to do this. I'll make up an excuse. I mean, you know how long it took me to actually come here."

"No, we should just get it over with."

He inhaled, taking in the stuffy air like a salve before they headed inside.

His grandmother's apartment hadn't changed since his last visit, only this time, no one wore black. They all sat in the living room, his grandmother serving them tea, his aunt and uncle smiling and thanking her. He tried not to play the scenes back in his head, the days that passed after the funeral, when no one spoke, really, but they walked through the apartment—within the walls of his mom's childhood—like ghosts.

"Why didn't your dad come with you?" His grandmother was sitting on the couch across from them. "Next time he has to come. To see Hannah."

"He's probably very busy," his uncle said as he looked down and took a sip of his tea.

Hannah cleared her throat and shifted in her seat.

"Too busy to see his daughter?" their grandmother said.

"Mama, enough," said his uncle.

Does he know? Zain looked at Hannah, who was looking down.

His grandmother asked more questions about how his dad was doing, how they both were doing. She didn't know that Zain had been fired and was living with him, so she asked about his job and if it was possible to move closer to home so that his dad wasn't alone. Hannah remained silent, and Zain answered as though he were still living in Philly, still working for the newspaper. He couldn't let them know what his life was actually like. Hannah would understand the compulsion to continue keeping secrets and lie, both of them having been doing just that for years. Most of all, though, he couldn't say his failures out loud in his mom's old home. She was everywhere, and she would be listening.

When they left, after their uncle dropped them off back at Hannah's apartment, Hannah asked him why he'd lied.

"I don't know." He leaned his head back as they sat on the couch. The blanket, sheets, and pillow Hannah had set up for him were piled neatly at one end. "I didn't want to get into it."

"You know, I don't even really know what happened," she said. She had her back against the arm of the couch, her body facing Zain, who sat at the end with his bedsheets. "You never told me."

"Does Mohamed know about Dad?" he asked, eager to move the conversation away from his own abysmal situation. Luckily Hannah took the bait and began to tell Zain about the day on the boat, their uncle's reaction, and what he'd said of their dad.

"And there's another thing," she added. "I don't even know if I should be telling you this, but I found these letters."

She told him, then, of the letters she'd found in their mom's old room, stacks of them, all from Hamada, the most recent one dated just six months before Zain was born. Then she told him what their uncle had said—how Hamada and her mom had kept in touch and had still been friends. Zain recalled the conversations with his dad and with Hasan. He hadn't told Hannah about those, but the dots were beginning to connect.

"Hannah, I think that's why Mom and Dad moved to America."

He told her everything he knew, then.

"Holy shit," Hannah said. "Do you think Mom was still seeing him after she married Dad?"

Zain shook his head. "I have no idea."

Their parents had more secrets than he could even imagine. Zain didn't want to be like them—either of them. He was sick of lying, of hiding things. Maybe he and Hannah could be honest with one another, at least. They talked a bit more, commiserating about how little they knew of their parents' past, until Hannah's phone buzzed, and she grabbed it to read a text.

"Hey, I don't know how tired you are, but my friends are hanging out at this bar if you wanna go," she said.

He was jet lagged, but he was also only here for a couple of weeks, and it might be cool to see inside Hannah's world and meet her friends and see the version of Hannah who spent her time in bars, and the version of Egypt that included bars. But a familiar, anxious tug began to pull inside him. He and Hannah had never drunk together, and breaking down that wall might be weird. Still, he agreed, but his tone must have been hesitant because Hannah insisted they didn't have to if he was too tired.

"Also, we've never been *out* together, so I don't know if that'll be weird," she said.

So she was thinking the same thing.

"For sure it'll be weird." He laughed. "It was awkward when we smoked together."

Hannah laughed too. "Maybe we shouldn't go."

"No, we should. I think we need to get to know each other better."

If they continued to exist only in the way they had been around their family, they'd never become close. He'd never really know his sister. Sure, going to a bar with her wouldn't magically break down the wall they'd both built, but it was a start. He needed Hannah, as she was all he had left, so he would learn to be himself around her.

On their walk over to meet her friends, the smell of sheesha wafted through the air as they passed a street of coffee shops with people smoking outside. They kept walking and turned a corner. A group of teenage boys leaned against a wall, laughing. They looked at Hannah, and one of them made a remark in Arabic that Zain couldn't really make out, but Hannah ignored them and kept walking, so he followed her lead.

Finally, they stopped in front of a posh-looking building playing Arab music and walked in. A group of people sat at a table in the corner, and Zain recognized a few of them from the café. Once they sat, Hannah ordered a whiskey ginger.

Zain hesitated. "I guess I'll have the same."

He hadn't had any alcohol since the night he'd thrown up outside Emily's, but he was ready to reintroduce the habit into his life, just as long as he didn't use it in the same way as before—as a way to forget his problems and drown his sorrows in drink. Here, now, things were different. He couldn't pass up the opportunity to catch this rare glimpse into Hannah's social life. Hannah introduced him to everyone he hadn't met yet, and when their drinks came, he watched as Hannah took a sip of hers. Growing up, they'd both always been careful not to let their worlds collide—keeping friends and family separate—and now, everything was overlapping. He took a sip of his drink and felt the effect immediately, that momentary, instant rush of alcohol, straight to his head. He'd missed that.

They were on their third round of drinks when Hannah finally asked about his job.

"So are you ever gonna tell me why you were fired?"

"Oh, shit, Hannah getting to the real questions." Vanessa smiled.

Zain laughed. "Are we really doing this here?"

"Yeah, I mean, who cares? These people don't know you." Hannah gestured at everyone sitting around the table.

He couldn't tell her that he'd slept with his boss and cheated on Emily, and that all of that had led to his life falling apart, especially not here, in front of these strangers.

"There was just some shit that went down between my boss and me." He folded his hands together and separated them again, then looked away toward a nearby table, where a group of Egyptians were laughing.

"That's the vaguest answer anyone could possibly give," Vanessa said.

"She's right," said Hannah.

"Hey, who wants another drink?" He gestured to the waiter.

Hannah didn't say anything, but he could feel her looking at him, so he kept his eyes turned away. She would ask again—maybe not here, with everyone present, but at some point on this trip, he'd have to tell her.

It was late when they left, and his head was spinning from the alcohol. The streets were quieter, though many of the shops still had their lights on and people remained outside, smoking and eating and laughing.

"I haven't had a drink in a while," Zain said as he and Hannah headed back to her apartment.

It was cool outside, dust blowing in their faces as they walked, but it didn't bother him, and he could smell hints of garlic and spices coming from an open window they passed. He was surprised how content he felt taking this all in, even absorbing the look of surprise on Hannah's face at his admission.

"I've stopped drinking."

"Oh, were you, like, trying to stay sober? Should we not have gone out tonight?"

"No, I mean, it's fine. I was just trying to get my life together.

Figured I would take a break from drinking and smoking to stay focused."

Hannah said nothing, and they continued to walk in silence as Zain's anxiety grew. Maybe he shouldn't have told her that. She would think he was an alcoholic. Maybe he was. He wanted to disappear in that moment, or teleport back to America, away from this walk and Hannah's judgment, her questions. They turned onto her street, and the shop across from her apartment was dark now, no longer blasting music.

"Do you walk this by yourself at night?" Zain asked.

"No, I usually ask someone to walk back with me, or I take a taxi. If Vanessa walks with me, she'll usually crash here, or I go to her place."

"That's good," he said.

"How much were you drinking before, Zain?"

He wished they were inside already so that he could just go to sleep, like hitting a reset button in which he shut his eyes and shut off the world. He could see her apartment building up the block.

Hannah continued, "I just mean, if you felt like you had to stop, it must have been a lot, right?"

"I think I was relying on alcohol instead of trying to figure out my life," Zain said. "After Mom died and I got fired, it was all too much to handle."

"You getting fired," Hannah said as they entered her building. "Were you like, drinking at work or something?"

"No, nothing like that," Zain said. "But I think after, I started to fall apart." They stepped into the rickety elevator, which shook as it took them up to the third floor. "Actually, I was falling apart before, and I just did some really self-destructive shit that led to me getting fired."

"What did you do?"

Even drunk, he wasn't ready to answer that question. "It's not important."

"You're really not gonna tell me?"

He didn't say anything and let the silence grow between them as they left the elevator and entered Hannah's apartment. He went straight to the couch, allowing the cushions to encompass him. He wanted to melt into it—to turn into a puddle of goo that would simply seep into the fabric, away from this moment, this conversation.

"Come on," Hannah prodded. "How bad could it be? Did you kill someone?" She laughed.

"I slept with my boss." Zain looked at the floor, unable to look her in the eye, to answer the next question he knew was coming.

"Were you still seeing Emily?" She was standing over him.

"Yeah." He looked down.

Hannah didn't speak.

"I don't . . . think I'm a good person," he continued.

"Why did you—"

"I should go to sleep," he said. "This is a lot for me."

As he tried to sleep, he tossed and turned under his covers, sweating despite the cool air. He was aflame, fueled by shame and guilt—a burning disappointment leaving ash and destruction in his wake. And now Hannah knew too. Eventually, he slept, the alcohol helping him drift off. But his sleep was restless, and at four a.m., he woke, hungover, thirsty, and hungry. He got up and grabbed a bottle of water out of the fridge. Maybe Hannah had some food. But when he opened the cabinets, they were mostly empty, as though she didn't actually live there. Hannah was like this, always eating out. Her refrigerator in New York had been pretty sparse too. She wasn't one to cook. He found some cereal and milk and poured himself a bowl.

Zain sat down on the couch and checked the news on his computer. Protests were picking up and becoming more violent, and the thought of Hannah in Tahrir jostled him once again. She should've known better. The violent images playing across his screen made him resolve to somehow talk her out of going to whatever other protest she had planned.

He had fallen back asleep by the time Hannah came out of her room a little after nine. The sound of the bathroom door shutting woke him. His hangover had mostly subsided, and he took his empty cereal bowl to the kitchen. The conversation from the night before brought a rush of blood back to his face, and shame once again erupted inside him. He shouldn't have told her. He heard the toilet flush and the sink turn on, which meant he'd have to face her any minute now.

"How long have you been up?" she said as she entered the living room. He finished folding up the blanket and sheets he'd been using and sat down.

She asked if he'd eaten and if he wanted to eat again, not bringing up the previous night's conversation at all.

"Hannah," he said from the couch. "Last night, what I told you—"

"We don't have to talk about it," she said, walking toward the kitchen.

"No, but I feel like I need to."

"Okay," Hannah said, turning around and sitting down next to him on the couch.

"I'm afraid I'm like Dad."

"Did Emily ever find out?" Hannah asked.

"Yeah. I told her everything."

"Then you're not like Dad at all." She paused. "You fucked up, but at least you came clean."

That was what their dad had said. Somehow it seemed more believable coming from her.

She looked at him for a moment. "What are you gonna do?"

"About what?"

"I don't know. Everything."

"I'm looking for jobs." He started to crack his knuckles.

"Are you and Emily speaking?"

Zain shook his head. "What about you and Dad?" he said. "Do you think you'll ever speak again?"

Hannah's leg began to shake up and down. Their mom used to get on them both for shaking their legs as they sat, the entire couch shaking with them.

"Enough," she'd say, pressing her hand down on their legs to steady them.

"I don't want to talk about Dad," Hannah said.

2009

Zain

They were in Egypt for vacation, once again visiting the pyramids, as though they hadn't been here a hundred times before. Zain had taken time off work for this visit, at his parents' insistence, even though he was saving his time off for a trip to Europe with friends over the summer. He figured he might still be able to swing it, as long as he didn't take any more days the rest of that year.

The family had just climbed the hot stairwell to the inside of the pyramid, and once again, they stood together in the dark, empty room.

"I hate it in here," his mom said once they were inside the large stone tomb.

She hadn't even wanted to go in in the first place, but Hannah and Zain had insisted she come. She had, after all, made them take this vacation.

"Why?" Hannah asked as they walked around, their voices echoing against the bare stone walls.

"It's just dark and depressing, and there's nothing in here," said their mom.

"I like it," Zain said. "It's creepy."

Their mom laughed. "Maybe we'll put you here when you die, then."

"Yes, definitely," said Zain.

Once out of the dark tomb, their mom's mood brightened, the sunlight once again bringing a smile to her face.

"Should we ride camels now?" she asked. They did that on every single visit too.

Not long after, Zain watched his mom's countenance change from cheerful to irritated as she argued with the camel guide for a lower price.

"Mom, it's not that big a deal," Zain said.

Hannah stayed out of it, and Zain could tell she was horrified that they were creating a scene. If it were up to either of them, they probably would have paid the price he was demanding and not even questioned it.

"No, it is a big deal," their mom said. "He's trying to steal money from us. It's dishonest."

"Yasmeen, let's just pay him," their dad said.

"You call yourself a Muslim?" she said to the guide.

She won in the end, as she almost always did, paying the price she thought was fair.

WINTER 2013

Hannah

At the entrance to the strip of desert where the pyramids stood, she and Zain were alone, left to be their own leaders. There were two lines: one for Egyptians and one for non-Egyptians. The Egyptian tickets were significantly cheaper, so she waited in that line, hoping her accent wouldn't give her away.

"Two tickets," she said in her best Arabic as they approached the window.

The man didn't look up, merely handing her the tickets and taking her money.

She didn't say a word as they trekked into the desert, memories of her mom and dad swirling through the sand around them. She could see vestiges of their past selves everywhere, younger versions of herself posing for a photo, her mom telling them all to smile as she squinted in the sun, her dad rushing to the pyramid as though they were pressed for time, like the pyramids would disappear if they didn't go in right away, and her mom shouting behind him, beckoning him to slow down.

"This feels a lot different without Mom and Dad," Zain said as they entered the gate.

Hannah looked down at the smooth desert sand, then back up, squinting again in the sun. She should have brought sunglasses.

"I was just thinking about that."

This was the family trip—oftentimes the one fun Cairo excursion—but now she and Zain were like shadows of their past selves, grasping for a happy memory that had long faded. They stopped in front of the largest pyramid, and Zain pulled out his phone to take a picture.

"We should get a selfie," he said.

They stood next to one another, and Hannah smiled as Zain held his phone out in front of them.

He looked down at the picture. "It's good. Definitely one for the 'gram."

She laughed, looking up at the looming monument before her. They walked up closer and began to climb the few stone steps to the entrance up above. Hannah had to pull herself up and jump for some of the larger stones. She wiped her hands on her pants, leaving sandy streaks along her clean blue jeans, but something about getting dirty—the dusty sand now on her hands, face, and clothes—felt cleansing, like a form of wudu that made them a part of the earth with their mom.

They reached the entrance to the inside of the pyramid and paid another fee to go in. This time there wasn't a separate ticket for Egyptians and non-Egyptians.

The first few steps into the pyramid consisted of more large stone blocks, but now in a narrow, claustrophobic hallway. Deeper in the pyramid, they reached an upward incline, like a ramp with built-in steps for them to walk on and handrails all along the side. They climbed the dark, creepy tunnel leading into a pharaoh's tomb. She didn't even know which pharaoh. There were no signs, guides, or information of any kind. Typical Egypt.

The tunnel was steep, so they had to crouch down or they'd hit their heads on the stone ceiling. It wasn't very hot out, but in here, she began to sweat, the lack of air creating a sticky, humid feel, making it difficult even to breathe.

She and Zain hadn't talked much the entire day, not since their conversation at breakfast. For whatever reason, she didn't know what to say to him. She didn't know how to act or even what to think of what he'd told her. He was her brother, but it was like she didn't really know him. They'd left the conversation of this morning hanging, and now the air felt stagnant, like it was waiting for them to push the story forward.

Eventually, they reached the top of the steps, and she could breathe again. The sweat that had started to trickle down her chest stopped mid-drip, sending goose bumps up through her spine, spreading out to her arms. They entered a cool, dimly lit room—a few lights in the corners, without which they'd be in complete darkness. It wasn't clear where the air was coming from or why the humidity had disappeared. The walls were bare, any sort of color or hieroglyphic worn and faded from a lack of preservation over the years. No one spoke, and aside from the sound of breaths and footsteps, the room remained silent.

The place looked familiar and unremarkable. A few people stood around a stone box in the center as Zain and Hannah walked around the space in silence. They approached the tomb, silently squeezing their way through as people turned to exit. It was empty. Just a large gray stone box. Nothing ornate. No gold or colorful designs like you saw in pictures or museums. She remembered this emptiness from their first visit inside. She didn't know what she'd expected back then. Mummies, dead bodies, piles of gold cursed by the pharaohs. Nothing of that sort was in here—all looted or taken to museums, as if there was any difference. It was all so anticlimactic. It's not like suddenly there'd be a mummy inside, but there was the possibility—or hope—for something more.

"Looks pretty much the same as last time," Zain said, piercing the silence in the room.

Hannah laughed, the sound echoing through the empty space.

Others began to speak as well, as though they were simply waiting for someone to break the spell.

"Yeah, I mean, I figured they might have added some new decor, you know?" Hannah said, looking around at the bare stone walls. "Something to spruce the room up a little bit."

"They're going for the minimalist aesthetic. You just don't get it."

Hannah smiled. Whispers suddenly filled the room.

"There was a mummy in here once," a man said to his little girl.

"What happened to it?" the little girl asked.

"Probably in a museum. We'll see some tomorrow."

Something about the room—this tomb—brought back the funeral. How long had the mummy been in here before someone had found it and raided the place? Put it on display somewhere. Maybe the way they'd done it with her mom actually was better. No embalming or anything, just leaving her in the ground to decompose. Better than being behind a glass case, your body forever a spectacle, forced to endure packs of staring strangers every day.

They retraced their steps back down, walking again through the dimly lit tunnel, sidling out of the way of other tourists coming up. Somehow, the air in the pyramid felt like it flowed more on the way down. Once outside, the sun hitting their faces again, nothing needed to be said, really, but something *felt* different. Did they always need to be near a tomb to feel close again?

"We should ride camels," Zain said. "Family tradition."

"Yeah, obviously."

They flagged down a man in a galabiya and white head wrap, leaning against a stone wall and holding a rope connected to two camels.

"Can we ride?" Zain asked in Arabic.

His Arabic was always better than hers, spoken with less of an accent, but he'd been letting Hannah do all the talking up to this point. Before she knew it, they were both negotiating the price of the camel ride, and it was more fun than anything else—this back-and-forth, she and Zain trying to bargain.

"We're *Egyptian,*" Hannah said in Arabic.

She looked up at the two towering camels that he held on to via rope. They seemed blissfully unaware of the exchange.

"This is the price for Egyptians," he said.

Hannah shook her head. He lowered the price slightly, and she looked at Zain, who shrugged.

"Let's just do it," he said to her in English. "Dude's just trying to make a living."

So they agreed, and Hannah watched as the man tugged on the camel's rope, and the animal began to kneel. The man gestured for her to climb up, and she walked around to the side, raising her leg over its back, steadying herself over the saddle and holding on to the handgrip in the front. The camel began to rise, lifting its hind legs first, forcing Hannah's body to plunge forward. She tightened her grasp, and once she was up, their guide instructed Zain's camel to do the same. The guide led them around the pyramids and past the Sphinx, and Hannah recalled the photo in her parents' living room of the four of them standing in front of the Sphinx, smiles on their faces. They were young in the photo, and she barely remembered that day, but it was hot outside then and her parents had had to coax her into smiling, the heat making her moody and irritable. The weather today was cool. Their family had never visited in January, and so this was her first winter in Egypt.

The whole camel ride lasted about half an hour. They paid the man and tipped him, then began to walk, the wind blowing sand into their faces.

"I kept thinking of Mom," Zain said as they walked quietly through the desert. "On that camel ride."

Hannah didn't look up. She squinted to keep the sand out. In the distance, she could see a Pizza Hut, almost comical in contrast to the sandy frontier they walked through now.

"Remember that time she fought with the camel guy?" Zain continued.

Hannah nodded and laughed.

They walked a little longer, taking a few more pictures before deciding to go on a search for food in the area. The community near the pyramids was slightly less congested and populous than the neighborhoods of Cairo they knew. There were more women in loose, long dresses and hijabs and more men in galabiyas. The roads were somehow dustier, sand blowing freely in the wind. Despite all that, chain restaurants still lined the streets.

They decided on a small café down the way.

"Hannah," Zain said right as they sat down. "I just logged on to the Wi-Fi and got a bunch of news alerts about Egypt."

"Did something happen?"

She was sitting across from him at the table and pulled her own phone out of her bag.

"There's thousands of people protesting today. All over the country."

On her screen, there was a prompt for the Wi-Fi password, which she hadn't paid attention to when Zain asked at the entrance.

"It's all happening right now," said Zain.

He scrolled through his phone, not looking up at Hannah, whose own American iPhone was just a brick with no connection to the outside world. He told her people were live tweeting about the police using tear gas—not just in Cairo, but in other cities across Egypt as well. Hannah was leaning over to see his screen when her Egyptian phone, which didn't have internet access, began to buzz. A call from Noha.

"Hannah, where are you?"

"I'm near the pyramids with my brother."

"Did you see the news?" she asked. "It's too dangerous to be out. Come to my house, both of you. You know the address?"

"Oh, okay, yeah, let me just talk to Zain, and I'll call you back."

Hannah told Zain what Noha said and asked him for the Wi-Fi password so that she could log on with her American phone and check the news herself. Tweet after tweet reported on the protests. *The New York Times* was providing live updates. Tens of thousands were protesting against Morsi, his newfound powers, the new draft of the constitution, and the police or the army or both were getting violent.

"This is pretty bad." Hannah's nerves mounted as she scrolled.

"It's the police," Zain said. "They're the ones attacking people."

"Police under Morsi's orders?" She raised her eyebrow.

"I don't know." He put his phone down, shaking his head as he stared absently past her.

"Maybe we *should* go to Noha's?" Hannah said.

They left the restaurant without ordering, and on the way to Noha's apartment, her grandmother and uncle called too, and Hannah assured them they were safe. Zain talked for most of the taxi ride as Hannah listened. He ranted about the use of force by the police and the army, about how police were no different no matter what country you were in. He talked about Morsi's presidency, about the Muslim Brotherhood, about the Egyptian people who'd voted them in in the first place.

"Egypt is secular, and now they have a religious ruler," said Zain. "Of fucking course it's gonna be a shit show. This is gonna end with the army taking over until they appoint someone just like Mubarak, and it'll take years for them to recover, if they ever do."

"You should write about this," Hannah said as she rolled up her window to stop the dust from blowing in.

"What?"

"Write an op-ed. You care about this."

He paused. "Maybe."

"You used to be so motivated, Zain," Hannah said. "Remember when you were in college? You wanted to work for *The New York Times* or something. It was always kind of impressive, because I never really knew what I wanted to do. I still don't."

"Yeah . . ." Zain looked out the window.

Hannah's Egyptian phone buzzed again, blowing up with texts from the group chat for the women's organization. They were lamenting the news and discussing how to move forward, whether it was even safe for them to move forward.

What can we do? someone said.

We have to go to the square together, someone wrote.

It's too dangerous, said another. We can't fight the army

And then, a text from Vanessa:

Hey just checking in. Did you see the news? Are you home safe?

The only person she hadn't heard from was Zakaria, who hadn't reached out since the awkward incident outside his home. Hannah had figured she'd give him some space—let him come to her. But now, in the silence that followed their last meeting, she wasn't sure she'd ever hear from him again. Something about that pained her. He was the first friend she'd made here—the only real Egyptian friend she had. With Zakaria, she felt somehow closer to her roots, closer to understanding the culture she came from. She could hardly explain it to herself, but losing Zakaria as a friend felt like losing some connection, or understanding, of Egypt.

Maybe she should have been herself with him sooner, not treated him as an extension of her parents—someone who would judge her choices. But he wanted a relationship, and she didn't. That was why Rami was perfect for now. They were in the same place, in a sense. And with Rami, there was some element that was missing from her interactions with Zakaria—something that drew them together despite their better judgment. She didn't expect anything from Rami, though. A text from him asking if she was okay would be weird, given the nature of their relationship, but Zakaria was supposed to be her friend. He was supposed to care.

"Who keeps texting you?" Zain asked as her phone buzzed again.

"It's the group text for the women's group I'm in."

She told Zain about the messages and read a few out loud. He asked for more detail on the organization, so Hannah described what she knew and explained her involvement. So far, she'd only been helping out with paperwork. It was difficult because her Arabic reading skills weren't strong enough to help with most of it, but she went through what she could in English. Mostly, she was reading reports of assaults and organizing them into groups by date so they could compile their statistics. She wasn't a part of the groups of women that were out in the square, defending and protecting whomever they could. Those women were trained.

"It's awesome that that group exists," Zain said. "Because no matter what administration takes over, women are not the priority. So Egypt needs this. You absolutely should not go back to Tahrir, though."

Hannah nodded. Despite the danger of the current situation, she was at least happy to see Zain actually listening to her. He was right, and she knew she wouldn't go back to Tahrir.

Zain

"I'm so glad you came." Noha opened the door to a spacious apartment, the aroma of garlic and cumin seeping into the hallway, hints of parsley too. Standing there in the doorway brought him back home—back to the signature scents of his mom's cooking.

Zain recognized Noha immediately from the funeral, but she introduced herself anyway.

"You look like Yasmeen," said Noha, ushering them inside.

Her kids were watching cartoons in the living room,

seemingly unaware of the day's events. Noha's eyes appeared glossy and pink as she gestured for them to sit down.

"Is everything okay?" Hannah said.

"Yes, why?" asked Noha.

"You just look—never mind."

Hannah and Zain sat. The furniture in the apartment was pretty typical Egyptian furniture—not comfortable-looking, but like something straight out of the Renaissance, gold trim and intricately designed fabric. Egyptians, for whatever reason, liked gaudy gold furniture and crystal chandeliers. Their own parents had even had a few chandeliers shipped over from Egypt years ago, and they were still hanging in the house back in Jersey.

Noha told them lunch would be ready at any minute.

"Oh, you didn't have to make us lunch," Zain said.

"Of course I did. You are Yasmeen's kids."

To his delight, Noha's food was just like their mom's—the same rich garlicky flavors in her grape leaves and mulukhiyah. But something was off. Noha barely spoke. This wasn't the woman Hannah had described—the one so much like their mom. Hannah must have noticed too, because again, she asked if everything was okay.

"I'm sorry I'm not being a good host." Noha wrung her hands at the dining table. "But I can't reach my husband."

She told them, in hushed tones, that he'd left that morning for work but hadn't been answering his phone all day.

"I'm so worried," she said. "The police and the army—they're just killing people. What if he was outside in the wrong place at the wrong time? I didn't tell the kids."

Zain looked over at her kids, still watching TV across the room. He didn't know what to say or how to be reassuring. Before, he'd just read about the events in Egypt from afar, his day going on uninterrupted, but now, here, people were suffering. Being faced with the reality of it all was like being awake for the first time.

"Maybe his phone just isn't working," Hannah said. "Wasn't that happening in the protest before? Too many people in one place."

"Maybe," Noha said.

Zain's phone buzzed on the table.

"Dad is trying to FaceTime me."

"You should answer," Noha said, "so he knows you're safe."

He nodded and went into another room. Hannah didn't say anything, so he knew she wouldn't want to talk to him.

Zain answered the call from the kitchen, where the smell of freshly cooked chicken overwhelmed his senses.

"Zain, did you see the news?" his dad asked. "Are you safe?" He was at home, it looked like, the sound of CNN blaring in the background.

"Yeah, yeah," Zain said. "We are. We're inside."

"Okay, good. Are you at Hannah's apartment?"

"Uhh, no, a friend . . ."

"What friend?" his dad said.

"Just a friend of Hannah's." He couldn't exactly tell his dad that they were currently in the home of the man his wife had almost married. Zain started to bite his nail as he leaned against the counter.

"Okay, well, you should both come home right away. I can buy your tickets now." His dad had his face close to the screen, as though that would bridge some distance between them and get Zain to agree to come home.

"No, Dad, it's fine. We're staying out of trouble."

"It's too dangerous to be there. You have to come home."

Zain leaned his head back and sighed, feeling himself revert back to his frustrated teenage self with his dad. "I can't have this conversation right now. I'll come home in two weeks like I'm supposed to."

"And what about Hannah?"

"Hannah is her own person. She can decide when she wants to come home."

"This isn't a joke," his dad said. "You don't know Egypt."

Zain told his dad he had to go—that they were guests at someone's house and he couldn't talk for long. He managed to get off the phone with the promise that he'd stay safe and update his dad on his whereabouts.

The air in the apartment remained tense that afternoon, all of them constantly checking the news on their phones, watching footage of protesters being tear-gassed and trampled. Anytime anyone spoke, it was simply to break the spell of doom floating around them. But Zain didn't really know what to say, simply commenting on whatever new piece of news he could find online, like a purveyor of information. Noha tried again and again to call Hamada, but his phone kept going straight to voicemail. She paced the living room as Zain fidgeted with the small tear beginning to form in his jeans.

Finally, around seven p.m., they heard keys jangling in the hallway, the doorknob turning. Everyone stood. The man that had come to the funeral walked in, and Noha practically ran to him. It was like a breeze swept through the room, pushing out all the stale, nervous air.

"Oh my God," she said, "Alhamdulillah. I've been trying to call you."

"My phone isn't working." Hamada held up his Android.

He couldn't get through, with the cell lines all jammed, like Hannah had said.

Hamada introduced himself to Zain, saying it was a pleasure to meet him again. As Zain shook his hand, he couldn't help but picture his mom, as her former fiancé stood in front of him now. This could have been her life in Egypt.

1985

Yasmeen

Zain had finally gone to sleep when the phone rang, and Yasmeen practically ran to answer it before it woke him. He'd been up crying all night, and now, finally, she had a moment of reprieve.

"Hello?"

"Yasmeen?"

She knew the voice right away. "Noha! Izayik?"

Yasmeen spent most of her days alone with the baby in their cramped one-bedroom apartment, while Yousef went to work. They were only supposed to live there temporarily, until they got settled in, but it had been a year now, and life in America had been harder than she'd expected. They didn't really have friends here, and while Yasmeen had met a few people at the mosque, she didn't really click with any of them. Most of the women were older than her and much more conservative than her friends back home. She'd thought America would be different. So hearing Noha's voice on the other end brought with it a flood of relief and a feeling of warmth that she rarely ever felt anymore.

"I miss you so much," Yasmeen said.

"I miss you too," Noha said, but the enthusiasm in her voice was lacking.

"What's wrong?" asked Yasmeen, sensing something was off.

Noha paused. "I need to tell you something."

"Okay . . ."

"I don't really know how to say this," Noha started. "And I didn't intend for this to happen. You're my best friend, and I love you."

Yasmeen heard a whine from the other room—Zain stirring—and silently pleaded to God for him not to wake up.

"Noha, what's going on?"

"I think I just have to say it."

"Say what?" Yasmeen said, growing more alarmed by the second.

"After you left, Hamada and I started to spend a lot more time alone together. I didn't have you here, and Hamada was my close friend too."

Yasmeen could feel her palms starting to sweat as she held the receiver, and then another little whine from Zain. A sinking feeling took hold, like a ball of stress in her stomach.

It was like she blacked out after that. Noha said something about her and Hamada being "together," or something like "we've been seeing each other." Yasmeen couldn't even process the words before Zain let out a piercing scream, the sound reverberating through the tiny apartment. She pictured Noha back in Cairo, probably sitting in her dad's study, where she used to hide away and talk on the phone, her and Yasmeen chatting for hours about who knows what, despite the two of them having hung out earlier in the day. They hadn't been talking much in the year that Yasmeen and Yousef were living in America. Long-distance calls were expensive.

"Yasmeen, can you hear me?" Noha said, jolting Yasmeen into reality.

"Yeah, I can hear you."

"I wanted to tell you before you found out from someone else."

"Does everyone know?" Yasmeen asked, picturing all their friends with Noha and Hamada—the new couple. She felt sick.

"Well, not everyone."

Yasmeen didn't know what to say.

"Are you still there?" Noha asked after a moment of silence.

Zain was still screaming in the background. "I have to go," Yasmeen said. "Zain is crying."

She hung up without saying goodbye and rushed into the bedroom to tend to Zain. She picked him up and sat down with him in the rocking chair next to his crib, rocking back and forth with him in her arms as his crying subsided. Silent tears streamed down her cheeks, a year of pent-up emotions flooding out of her. Zain eventually fell back asleep in her arms, but she kept rocking and crying and rocking and crying, until it felt like there were no tears left.

WINTER 2013

Zain

"What do we do now?" Zain said when they arrived back at Hannah's apartment.

"What do you mean?" She sat next to him on the couch.

"Well, Dad wants us to come home."

"Yeah, I'm not doing that." Hannah looked down at her phone. "But feel free to go if you want."

Every time he brought up their dad, Hannah got hostile.

"I didn't say I was leaving."

"Then what are you saying?" She looked at him expressionlessly.

He didn't know. He wasn't sure anymore what was right.

"I just wish you'd stop bringing up what Dad wants," she said.

"I'm sorry."

They were silent for a moment, and Zain began to scroll through Twitter on his phone, unsure of what to say and sensing Hannah's rising irritation.

"I can't move past this," she finally said.

"Past what?" He looked up from his phone.

"Everything that's happened. Mom and Dad. I keep trying to distract myself and forget, but I can't. Everything reminds me of her."

This whole time in Egypt, it had seemed as if Hannah had moved on. That she had a life and friends here and had forgotten. Zain, meanwhile, thought of their mom constantly, though he tried to fake a sense of ease and enthusiasm so that he didn't ruin the trip. He hadn't realized Hannah was faking it just like him.

"Me too," Zain said.

He leaned his head back on the sofa and shut his eyes, enveloped in the memory of his mom, who was everywhere, coursing through him whether he wanted her there or not. They put the TV on, avoiding the news as they watched reruns of old American sitcoms—the only English-language channel they could find.

A week later, the violence had died down slightly, but people were still protesting, and every couple of days, they'd hear about a new protester being dragged and beaten by the police.

Being in Cairo was like being in two worlds at once. While the political mess raged on, Zain consumed every last bit of news, picturing himself among the protesters, reporting on the movement. But he was a tourist in this country—Egyptian, sure, but a tourist nonetheless—and while people were dying in the streets, he was eating kebab by the Nile. Hannah simply continued showing him around Egypt, avoiding any areas where people were protesting, for safety's sake. They'd gone to Luxor, Sharm El Sheikh—all the must-see spots. They met up with her friends, who talked about what was going on, but then they also talked about their personal lives, like nothing was *really* wrong. He easily compartmentalized these two worlds—a cognitive dissonance that shocked him sometimes, but what could he do?

That night, even, they were meeting up with Hannah's friends for drinks at a restaurant a ways off from her apartment, in some posh neighborhood where the residents likely didn't concern themselves with the protests, instead remaining happy about the status quo they'd maintained. The restaurant overlooked the Nile, and everything on the menu was a little more expensive than other places they'd gone, but still cheaper than American prices.

Four people sat at a table outside. They were all familiar, but he couldn't for the life of him remember their names—except Vanessa, but that was because Hannah talked about her the most. Two hours in, they'd all had several drinks, pretending like everything was fine, like Egypt wasn't in disarray, and it was almost too easy to forget.

Hannah at this point was blatantly flirting with someone she'd introduced as Rami. Or at least it seemed that way. Seated next to him, she leaned her body toward his. Zain winced, never having thought about Hannah's romantic life before.

"Is that a thing?" Zain whispered to Vanessa, who was sitting next to him. He pointed his chin toward Hannah and Rami.

"What do you mean?" Vanessa said.

"They're just really flirty."

Vanessa turned to him and smiled. "Uhh, I mean, what has Hannah told you?"

"Okay, so yes it is." Zain laughed.

"I'm not trying to blow up her spot." Vanessa also laughed.

"I'm just not used to seeing my sister, like, flirt with people, you know? It's weird."

He couldn't even explain what he meant. Hannah was just acting differently. Like her voice was higher pitched or something, and everything Rami said seemed funny to her, even when it wasn't.

"Wait, so are they *dating*?" Zain whispered.

"No," Vanessa said. "Just—well, you can ask Hannah yourself."

He wouldn't ask her. They didn't talk about those things, not really.

"I don't particularly like Rami," Vanessa said slowly and in a whisper.

"Why not?"

She glanced at Rami, then back at Zain. "I don't know. He's kind of a little shit."

Zain laughed and asked why, but he wasn't surprised. Rami was good-looking and had the attitude of someone who knew he was good-looking. Zain could recognize in Rami the same charm that people saw in him, and he knew instantly that Rami was the type of attractive nice guy that wasn't actually very nice.

"Sorry, I shouldn't be saying anything," Vanessa said. "I sound like an asshole. We should talk about something else. Like, you're a journalist?"

"Yeah, sort of." He took a sip of his drink.

"What do you write about?"

He told her about his most recent job, writing news he didn't care about until he eventually got fired. He left out the details of why, and she didn't ask, probably remembering the last time they'd all talked about it, when he wouldn't divulge any information.

"What do you *really* want to write about?" Vanessa asked.

He paused for a moment to think, remembering the ambition he'd once had in college—the plan he'd had for his life. When he'd taken his job at the *Philly Inquirer*, he'd thought it would be easier to move up in the ranks and eventually get a serious reporting job in New York or DC. But then he'd stopped trying, for the most part phoning it in at work. Meanwhile, people he'd gone to school with got jobs at *The New York Times* or *The Wall Street Journal*, while he watched from afar, wondering why he couldn't make it himself.

"I thought by now, I'd be writing more substantial stories—things that mattered, you know?"

"Like what kinds of things?"

"Articles about world issues, foreign policy, social issues . . ." He glanced around the restaurant, and in that moment Egypt's two worlds seemed more stark than ever, as rich Egyptians sat around them without a single care. "Something that would make a difference. Like what's going on in Egypt. This is where my family is from, and I want to be able to make them proud—or make my mom proud. Everything that's going on now is just so incredible. I'd love to be a part of it, a part of history, through my writing."

"I'm actually writing about Egyptian politics and the revolution for my dissertation," Vanessa said. "But I've also been publishing pieces with a few news outlets—like op-eds and interviews. If you're interested, I can put you in touch with some people I know."

Zain felt his face light up. "That would actually be awesome," he said. "Yeah, I mean, anyone I can reach out to or anything. I just need to get back out there. Thank you so much."

Goose bumps traveled up and down his arms, waking him up to the possibility of hope. If Vanessa could do that, he could maybe get his foot in the door somewhere—even just get an introduction.

Vanessa asked for his email and said she'd reach out the next day.

They joined the others in conversation after that, and he noticed that Rami had his hand on Hannah's leg now.

"So you're also Egyptian?" Zain interrupted their conversation.

"Yeah." Rami removed his hand suddenly. "Grew up in America, but I'm just hanging out here for a while. Working."

Rami talked about his job and his time in Egypt. Every once in a while, Hannah would interject, as if she seemed uncomfortable, like the two of them talking bothered her.

"So you been keeping up with what's going on in the square?" Zain mixed the ice around in his drink with his straw.

"Yeah, it's wild," said Rami.

"Rami doesn't think women should be protesting," Hannah said.

"Oh no, here we go." Vanessa leaned her head back.

"What do you mean?" Zain said.

Rami adjusted himself in his seat and looked at Hannah. "That's not what I said."

"He thinks the women who get assaulted deserve it for being there in the first place," Hannah said.

"Are you kidding?" Zain furrowed his eyebrows.

"Oh my God, that's not what I said," Rami repeated.

"You did say that," said Vanessa.

Rami started to gesture with his hands as he spoke, nearly knocking his drink over. "All I was saying was that for a woman to go into the square right now is stupid *because* of all the assaults that are happening."

"I mean, yeah—" Zain started to say.

"And therefore it's the woman's fault if she gets assaulted," Hannah interrupted.

"Stop twisting my words," Rami said.

"You know Hannah went to a protest?" Vanessa said to Rami.

"It's a good thing I didn't get assaulted, though," Hannah said. "Because then I'd have no one to blame but myself."

"You went to a protest?" Rami looked at Hannah.

Hannah told him then that she'd gone to Tahrir, and he told her that was dangerous, his voice somber now, almost worried sounding.

Hannah smiled. "What? Are you suddenly concerned about me?"

"No—I mean, yes, I'd be concerned about anyone. Why would you do that?"

Zain and Vanessa watched this exchange without saying anything.

"Honestly, it was stupid," Hannah said. "You were right."

Rami leaned forward in his chair and faced her at the circular table. "No, I'm not. You don't deserve to be assaulted. Wait, you weren't—"

"No, I just said I wasn't." She took a sip from her drink.

She told the story again of the women who'd rescued her.

"I didn't know until I got here," Zain said once she'd finished her story. "She never told me. If she had, I would have told her not to go."

Eventually, they circled back around to Rami's thoughts on women protesting, and before long, the entire table was attacking Rami for his views. It was honestly impossible to tell anymore what the dynamic was between Hannah and Rami.

"So is this what you do every day?" Zain said when he and Hannah arrived back at her apartment later that night.

"No, not every day," Hannah said. She took a seat on the couch.

Zain went straight to the couch too, and started to lie down, with his legs bent so that his feet sat on the cushion next to Hannah. He knew if he fell asleep now, he'd wake up hungover, but he started to let his eyes close anyway. Every time he drank he promised himself he wouldn't get drunk this time, that he'd only have a little bit and wake up refreshed. He'd thought Egypt would help him stay on track—that America was the problem—but Egypt had all the same temptations, and he'd been waking up hungover more often than he would have liked. Maybe the problem wasn't America.

"What's the deal with you and Rami?" Zain asked, his eyes still closed, head leaning back.

"What do you mean?"

He opened his eyes and looked at the ceiling. "Are you two, like, a thing?"

"Did Vanessa say something to you?"

He angled his head to look at Hannah. "Actually, Vanessa said very little when I asked. She is a true and loyal friend."

"He's just—we're not a thing. Rami is an asshole. It's not important." She was looking down, picking at something on her hand.

And there it was. The wall again. Before their mom died, it had seemed unfathomable that they'd even be in this place—where they could have a real conversation—but there were still some things neither of them wanted to talk about because they'd grown so used to hiding.

"We're a real mess, aren't we?" Zain shut his eyes again. "Mom would be proud."

Hannah laughed. "For sure," she said. "I have this moment of panic every day where I'm like, *What would she think?*"

He opened his eyes and sat up slightly. “You know, back home, I’ve been praying.”

Hannah looked at him. “What?”

He shouldn’t have said that. She wouldn’t get it. Or maybe she would. He told her about the day he’d prayed in his room for her, for their mom, for his own life to improve. He’d needed to believe in something, to believe that someone was watching out for him, and he wasn’t so alone.

“Did it help?” Hannah asked.

“I don’t know. It just sort of feels like she’s listening. I can’t explain it.”

He wasn’t suddenly religious now, not even close, but talking to her, believing she was out there—it felt like floating sometimes, like the weight of life could lift off him for just a short while.

“It feels like I can finally be honest with Mom.” Zain sat up fully now. “You know, since I never was before.”

“Yeah.” Hannah nodded. “I get that.”

Neither of them said anything for a minute, and he leaned his head back against the wall.

“Didn’t you say you also had Egyptian friends?” he said, breaking the silence. “Like, born and raised in Egypt?”

“Yeah . . .” Hannah’s voice trailed off. “I thought I did.”

He looked at her. “What does that mean?”

“Well, there was that guy, Zakaria, who helped me out my first day here.” She brought her legs up on the couch.

Hannah told Zain about the awkward exchange outside Zakaria’s apartment.

“It kind of sucks,” she said. “I feel like I lost a friend.”

“Jeez, I’m sorry. I was just asking because, like, I don’t know, you said you wanted to get to know the real Egypt, but . . .”

"But all my friends are American."

"Yeah, I mean, there's Rami, I guess . . ." Zain said.

"Rami is American too, though. But maybe the reason I keep—or, like, the reason I hang out with him is that he's like me. Like us, if that makes sense."

"Caught between two worlds." Zain's fingers glided along the armrest, and he pulled at a loose string sticking out from the edge.

He understood exactly what she meant. With Rami, Hannah could be herself, fully. Like them, he knew what it was like to be stuck between cultures, belonging to neither.

"Exactly," Hannah replied. "I like Zakaria, but he's just—I don't know. I couldn't be myself. But then maybe the problem is me."

This was the most honest Hannah had ever been with him, sharing a part of herself that he understood well. In America, he hung out with other Americans—people who didn't really get his upbringing. He always hid that part of himself in order to fit in. He'd never considered how relaxing it would be to just find someone like him. Not Egyptian, necessarily, but someone who, deep down, never really belonged anywhere, stretched thin in opposite directions.

They said good night, and Zain fell asleep quickly. In the morning, he woke up hungover like he'd predicted and chugged a bottle of water. An email from Vanessa waited in his inbox. In it was a list of editors and their contact information, all people he could pitch stories to, but he had too much of a headache to even think about that.

He couldn't keep doing this—this cycle of drinking too much and waking up hungover, with no energy or motivation to start the day. He'd never become a real writer if he kept this up. He planned to get serious now. He would stop drinking. He'd pitch whatever he could. Eventually, someone would publish him, and then more people would publish him, and surely that would lead to some regular work. The lights inside him turned on again, goose bumps trickling all over. Bolts of electricity jolted through his brain, waking him up, finally.

Hannah

In the weeks since Zain left, protesters were still being beaten, tear-gassed, even shot at, and each new day in Egypt felt more disillusioning than the last. At the women's organization, they were working to tackle street harassment. The group was shooting a commercial in a few weeks aimed at showing the danger of harassment for women, and they were creating an app with user data that would tell women which streets to avoid. It wasn't the best solution—women shouldn't have to avoid anything—but it was a start.

"What if we also create some kind of school campaign?" Hannah had suggested at one meeting.

"What do you mean?" someone asked.

"I just mean, for a more long-term solution, we can start educating kids early that harassment is bad. Like let's have speakers go to schools, explain what it's like for women—really get it in the kids' heads."

There were a few whispers around the table. Maybe she shouldn't have said anything. It wasn't her place. She was new. But then people began to nod.

"That's a good idea," one person said.

From there, Hannah had become part of the team making a plan, putting together some kind of curriculum, and she'd thrown herself fully into the project, unable to rest for even just a moment. But she was just a volunteer, stretching herself thin between her paid job, her friends, and this work. If she could do activist work like this and get paid for it—that was what she wanted.

Meanwhile, she put Zain in touch with people she'd met while volunteering—with protesters who had been tear-gassed who'd come into the center looking for guidance, or someplace they could report their stories. He was freelancing now, writing mostly about Egypt. He told Hannah excitedly every time he pitched an article, and it was nice seeing him doing something, finally, and seeing how it changed his whole demeanor from someone feeling sad and sorry all the time to someone who had something to work toward. He'd reached out to the editors Vanessa had connected him with and interviewed the protesters Hannah had given his info to. People in America needed to know—not that America ever really proved much help with anything.

"What do you want to do with your life, Hannah?" asked Manal one day as they were working on plans for the women's march happening in just a couple of weeks.

Hannah and Manal were sitting alone at a conference table, and Hannah was jotting something down in her notebook, when she stopped suddenly at Manal's question. Manal was older than her, in her early thirties. While she volunteered at the women's center, she also had a job at an education nonprofit.

"I don't know," Hannah said. "I was supposed to go to law school before I came to Egypt, but I just didn't."

"Why not?"

Hannah wasn't quite sure how to answer, as she didn't know the reason herself. Was it all just a reaction to her mom dying?

"I think I applied for the wrong reasons," Hannah said. "My mom wanted me to go, but I didn't really put any thought into *why* I was going, or what I wanted to accomplish."

"Well, what do you want to accomplish?" Manal pressed on.

Hannah squirmed in her seat. "I'm not sure. I like the work we're doing here. Like, activism."

"But this is a volunteer job."

"I know," Hannah said. "But I just want to do something meaningful—something that could help people, or bring about change."

Manal didn't say anything at first, seemingly lost in thought.

"I know that's not specific at all," Hannah said. "I guess I just need to think about it more."

"I know some people at AUC," said Manal.

"AUC?"

"American University in Cairo. I want to put you in touch with them. I studied public policy there, and I'm close with some of my professors. I know some people there studying human rights law too, if you want to talk to them."

"Oh, um, yeah, sure."

Hannah hadn't considered going to school in Cairo. Since she'd been here, she'd felt like she was floating along, not really in control of her own life. Anytime she thought of what would come next—or of going back to America—she'd feel that twinge of anxiety and compartmentalize those thoughts away into the back of her mind. Sometimes, she felt like she had no options, no way forward. Meeting Manal and these other women seemed like a miracle sometimes. Maybe she needed a lifeline like this, someone to push her in the right direction.

"You should reach out to them," Manal said. "There's so many things you can do, and I think they can help you."

"Thank you so much," Hannah said.

Manal smiled, and they went back to planning for the women's march. Hannah was supposed to march too, though she hadn't told Zain yet.

Later that afternoon, Vanessa warned her not to go, fearful that it would prove dangerous, like many of the other protests happening around the country.

"They're taking precautions," Hannah said as the two walked by the Nile. The air was breezy and cool, the sun beating down in just the right spots.

Vanessa remained unconvinced of Hannah's safety, trying instead to convince her of the unpredictability of an event of that size. The protest was supposed to be completely peaceful, with hundreds of women involved, ensuring a sense of safety in numbers—protection from men like the ones who assaulted women in the square. Still, though, Hannah couldn't guarantee anyone's safety from the army or the police sent by Morsi to quell the protests. She couldn't really assure Vanessa, or anyone, really, that they'd be safe.

Her family and Noha were also warning her lately that it was becoming more unsafe to walk alone, day or night. As a woman living alone, though, that was impossible to avoid. She walked to work and walked home and walked to meet friends. She took taxis alone, and sometimes, even the drivers would tell her she should have someone with her—a man, preferably. Yet here she was with Vanessa, two women walking alone. It was true that there was always an element of feeling watched, men leering at them or yelling comments their way, but still, she never felt like she was ever in any real danger. She did find a shop that sold pepper spray, though, and bought a second bottle after the first was crushed in Tahrir.

The Nile shone as sunlight beamed down, reflecting off the water. In the distance, they could see palm trees and boats docked at the nady ports.

"Just be careful," Vanessa said. "Don't go to anything that might be dangerous."

"Everything could be dangerous," Hannah said. "Even just standing here, with you."

They walked a little while more and stopped for some ice cream nearby.

"Have you still not heard anything from Zakaria?" Vanessa asked as Hannah licked some mango ice cream off her spoon.

"No, I don't think I ever will," Hannah said.

"Are you upset?"

"I mean, yeah. We were friends, and now we're not. But, like, I don't know." She paused and looked out at the river, where a boat full of tourists passed by, traditional Arab music blaring from its speakers. She looked back at Vanessa, who scooped up a spoonful of ice cream from her cup. "It's just awkward, and if he really liked me, then maybe it's too hard being friends or whatever."

"Out of curiosity"—Vanessa wiped away some ice cream that had dripped onto her hand—"why didn't you like him?"

"I don't know, I just never saw him that way."

She had been racking her brain for a while now, looking for the answer to that question. There was nothing wrong with not liking him, or not being attracted to him, but she wondered if the reason behind it was this hang-up she had of him being born and raised in Egypt, when she herself didn't feel fully Egyptian.

"You know, I don't really want to date anyone right now, anyway," Hannah said.

She looked up, briefly making eye contact with a man walking in their direction, staring at the two of them, and then looked down.

Vanessa laughed. "Yeah, except Rami."

"Rami and I are not dating." Hannah looked back up at Vanessa.

The man that was staring was right in front of them now, not moving out of the way as they approached, and Hannah and Vanessa had to swerve slightly to avoid bumping into him as he pressed forward. Hannah glared at him as they walked past.

"But, like, if he *did* want to date you, would you?" Vanessa said as they kept walking.

"Neither of us wants a relationship." Hannah took in another spoonful of ice cream and let the mango melt over her tongue slowly.

Vanessa squinted. "You sure about that?"

"Yes," Hannah said, smiling now between bites. "I am in no place to be in a relationship. I'm literally in Egypt running away from my life."

"Okay," Vanessa said. "Well, either way, I'm sorry that you lost Zakaria as a friend. That really sucks. *But*, you still have *me*. And I would never abandon you, even if I were in love with you and you didn't love me back."

Hannah laughed. "Thank you. That means a lot, truly. Anyway, I gotta go soon. Dinner at my grandma's."

"Be safe," Vanessa said as they split off in different directions. They found themselves saying that more than ever now. "Be safe," as though the words alone could protect them—a cry of sisterhood shielding them from the growing danger of Cairo.

Egypt felt hopeless sometimes, like it would never be safe for women, or kind to those in need, the wealth gap growing larger by the day, despite the Muslim values the nation ascribed to. And yet, Hannah couldn't imagine leaving anytime soon. Something about Egypt beckoned her, told her she had to be there, at this time especially.

A little while later, she pulled up to her grandmother's apartment in a taxi.

"Hannah," her grandmother said once they were at the dinner table. "I called your father yesterday."

Hannah looked up from her plate and quickly swallowed the food in her mouth. She shifted her eyes toward her uncle and took another bite.

"Mama," he said. "We said we weren't going to talk about this."

Hannah put her fork down as she chewed. The wooden dining table was covered with a white frilly tablecloth and, on top of that, a thick clear plastic tablecloth. Hannah looked down and played with the plastic hanging over her lap, her fingers tracing the smooth material, back and forth, avoiding her grandmother's gaze.

"Quiet." Her grandmother waved her hand toward her son and then looked at Hannah. "Why aren't you speaking to him?"

"Mama, leave her alone," her uncle said.

"No, she has to talk to her father. Haram."

Hannah swallowed and looked up. "I don't know what you mean," she said.

Maybe she could just pretend it wasn't true—that she and her dad talked all the time. Her uncle said nothing, and Hannah looked straight at her grandmother. Maybe if she maintained eye contact, she could keep up the lie.

"He said you're not speaking," her grandmother said. "Why aren't you speaking to him?"

"What did he tell you?" Her voice was calm and steady, though her mind was scrambling, trying to come up with the right lie.

"Just that he calls you and you don't answer, and you haven't talked to him in months."

It was funny, really, that he would tell her grandmother that bit of info without telling her the reason why, making himself out to be the victim and Hannah the callous, coldhearted child.

"We got in a fight." Hannah looked down at her plate again. She dug her nails into the thick plastic tablecloth held between her fingers, creating an indent she couldn't take back.

Her grandmother began to lecture her on the importance of family. She told her she was being selfish, that she was hurting her father. He was alone, she said, and Hannah needed to speak to him, to show that she was there for him. Her grandmother said that he was her father, and he'd done a great deal for her over the years, and that she was being unappreciative and heartless. How could she do this to him after her mother—his wife—died?

"Mama, khalas," her uncle said, his tone quiet and tired sounding.

With her fork, Hannah moved the food around on her plate and avoided eye contact. She wanted to stab the chicken in front of her repeatedly, her fork piercing the meat over and over, scratching against the plate in a screech that would mimic the angry screams in her head. Instead, she moved the chicken from side to side, keeping her breath at an even pace. Her grandmother didn't know the truth. Of course she thought it was insensitive—the mark of a bad daughter.

"Are you going to talk to him?" her grandmother said finally.

Hannah looked at her uncle. "Do you want to just tell her?"

"Tell me what?" Her grandmother looked from Hannah to her uncle.

"Only if you want me to," her uncle said.

She nodded. And so her uncle explained. He told her grandmother everything Hannah had told him that day on the boat. He talked about the affair, about the day of the heart attack, about Zain finding out. Her grandmother listened and said nothing, the expression on her face remaining stoic—no reaction whatsoever. Maybe she was in shock, all the grief and anger hiding behind a facade. When her uncle finished speaking, the three of them sat in silence for a few seconds before her grandmother stood up. She left the table, the room, and then Hannah heard a door shut.

"She just needs to process," her uncle said. He began to clear the table, so Hannah got up to help.

She couldn't imagine what her grandmother was thinking, learning that this man she'd known for years had cheated on her daughter. But after they brought the dishes to the kitchen and put the food away, her grandmother came out of the bedroom. Hannah was wiping down the table with a small towel.

"Hannah, you still need to talk to your father."

She stopped what she was doing then and didn't say anything.

"This happens with men," her grandmother said, her hands leaning over one of the dining chairs. "It's not good, but it happens, and we forgive."

It felt like she'd been hit over the head, because everything blurred in that moment, a dizzying dream that couldn't be real.

"What?" Hannah stepped back slightly.

"Men do this," her grandmother said, shaking her head as though shaking off a silly inconvenience. "It's in their nature."

Hannah stood still, the towel she was using gripped tightly in her hand. "Are you joking?"

Her uncle came out of the kitchen. “Mama, stop.”

“No, she has to talk to her father. So what? He’s with another woman. This is what happens. She has to understand.”

“He cheated on your daughter,” Hannah said. “On my mom.”

“This happens.” Her grandmother gripped the back of the chair now.

“I have to leave,” Hannah said. “Right now.”

She dropped the towel on the table and stepped away. If she didn’t get out of there she’d say something she’d regret. She couldn’t even fathom the sexist mentality it took to think like that—to forsake your own dead daughter like that.

“I’ll drive you home,” her uncle said.

Hannah left the room and waited in the building’s hallway. Her uncle said something to her grandmother as she walked out, but she couldn’t make out the words. She paced the dark hallway, each step back and forth banging her rage into the floor. A moment later, her uncle came out.

“I thought you left,” he said. “Come on, let me drive you.”

“How could she say that?” she said once they were in the car.

“She’s from a different generation. She thinks differently. Anyway, don’t pay attention to what she said. I’ll talk to her.”

He drove in silence for a few minutes, the lights from the city shining down into Hannah’s lap. The windows were open just a crack, the smell of car exhaust from the surrounding cars seeping into their vehicle. Now that they’d left the apartment, Hannah could also smell the spices from her grandmother’s chicken in her clothes and hair.

“I can’t talk to him.” Her voice cracked. “I just can’t.”

“You don’t have to.”

“He’s my dad, though. Everyone thinks I’m being cold and unforgiving.”

Her uncle stayed focused on the road, swerving in and out of lanes to avoid traffic like only an Egyptian could.

"Do you think the reason you want to stay angry at your dad is so you don't have to be sad about your mom?"

Hannah leaned her head back and groaned. "I forgot you're a psychologist."

Her uncle laughed. "Well, do you think that might be it?"

"Obviously," Hannah said. "I can understand that much. I just—I can't help it. I *am* angry."

It took her grandmother a matter of minutes to excuse her dad's actions. Something that men did? Jesus fucking Christ.

"You probably don't remember this, but when you were four or five, you were visiting Egypt and you got very sick," her uncle said. "We had to take you to the hospital. It was a bad virus, and you couldn't stop throwing up."

Hannah looked up at her uncle as he drove, unsure where he was going with this story.

"Your father didn't leave your side," her uncle continued. "I don't think he slept for three days."

"What about my mom?"

"She was there too, but she also had to take care of Zain, and Yousef was the one who insisted on staying in the hospital with you, making sure the doctors were doing their job and nothing bad happened."

He went on to describe the three-night hospital stay, how sick Hannah was, and how worried her dad was the entire time.

"He never left the hospital while you were there." Hannah didn't say anything, but her uncle continued. "I'm telling you this story to show you that your dad loves you. What he did to my sister was horrible, but I know he loves you and Zain. And it's okay if you never forgive him for what he did. I won't. But it doesn't mean you can't have some relationship—when you're ready."

At that moment, they pulled up in front of her apartment.

"Thank you for driving me." Hannah didn't know what else to say as she unbuckled her seat belt.

"I'm not saying you have to talk to your dad now, but you can think about it."

In her apartment, she continued to pace back and forth. She had to get out or distract herself in some way. She texted Vanessa.

Hey you free?

Vanessa responded right away.

Ahh no, sorry! I've got a writing deadline, and I need to get this done tonight

Her mind was on fire, burning, burning, ready to turn to ash if she didn't find something to tame the flames. Who else was there? Maybe she could call Zain. They could FaceTime, and that might help. But before she got to the letter *Z*, her hand hovered over Rami's name. She shouldn't text him, but he was a good distraction.

Hey do you wanna hang out tonight?

She pressed send.

"Fuck," she mumbled out loud to herself.

But then three dots appeared on the screen, indicating that Rami was typing.

Yeah sure. What do you want to do?

She suggested a place they both knew, and they made a plan to meet in an hour.

"It's just, like, how could she say that?" Hannah said. She was on her second drink in the dimly lit bar. Rami sat next to her and listened as she told the story of what had transpired at her grandmother's apartment. There weren't many people there, so the space was quiet, couples and small groups huddled together in private conversation.

Rami listened as she spoke, responding at all the right moments, his face evoking concern and sympathy. Maybe he wasn't so bad, after all. He was here when she needed someone, and he helped her forget. Around him, she could escape her grief for just a little bit.

Rami ordered another round of drinks for the two of them. He paid, even though Hannah pulled out her wallet and insisted on paying herself.

"You're having a rough night." He pushed her hand away. "Let me get it."

"Thanks."

"I don't think you should have to talk to your dad if you don't want to." He turned back to face her. "The guy's an asshole. He did this to himself. Like, I get it, he's your dad, but you don't owe him shit."

"Thank you," Hannah said, surprised at his understanding, but her mind also went back to the story her uncle told her.

Rami took a sip of his drink, then looked back at her. "But at the same time, are you ever planning on talking to him? Or are you just done?"

"I don't know." She twirled her straw around in her glass, looking down. She imagined her dad sitting at her bedside in the hospital and felt the grip of guilt squeezing her body. She looked up at Rami, who was nodding in understanding. She expected him to be more antagonistic or to take the side of her grandmother, but he just got it. That's when she realized that she didn't know anything about Rami. Sure, she knew his uncle, she knew what he did for a living, and she knew he had four siblings, but other than that, Rami never talked about himself. And she never asked.

"Are you close to your parents?" Hannah said.

"I'm close to my mom."

"Are your parents married?"

"They're not, and my dad was never really present, you know?" He swirled the ice in his glass around with his straw before taking another sip.

Rami began to open up. His parents divorced when he was young, and his dad lived in another state. They hardly saw him. There were visits on holidays and school breaks, but he said he never got the sense his dad really cared.

"We actually got in a big fight right before I moved here." Rami didn't look at Hannah when he said this.

"About what?"

"A girl." He paused and shifted his eyes, looking down at his drink. "Yeah, um, I was in a pretty serious relationship, and, you know, she wasn't Arab or Muslim, and when I told my mom about it, she just, like, freaked out. She said I couldn't marry someone who wasn't Muslim, and then she called my dad, and he said the same thing, and I was just like, 'What right do you even have to say anything to me?' He wasn't in my life, and now he thought he had a say in who I ended up with?"

Hannah listened, and she could tell this wasn't something he talked about often, as he usually kept things superficial. This side of Rami was new and one she wanted to see more of.

"And then what happened?" Hannah asked.

"I told my dad that I didn't want to speak to him again, and he tracked down my girlfriend's parents and said we couldn't be together. I was furious." He took another sip and shook his head.

"Holy shit," Hannah said. "Even *my* parents wouldn't do that."

"And then she broke up with me not long after, so I left the country."

Hannah looked at him, but he avoided looking back and scratched at the stubble on his face before taking another sip.

"I'm sorry," Hannah said. "I had no idea."

"No, I mean, how could you? You never asked." He looked at her and smiled then.

His words were like a smack in the face, a sudden wake-up call to the fact that all this time, she'd slowly unloaded her own crap, unprompted, on Rami, and never once had he done the same.

"Oh," Hannah said. "I'm sorry. I didn't know—I mean, we don't hang out that much."

"And yet, I know all about *your* family drama," Rami said.

She didn't know what to say.

"I'm messing with you." He laughed. "It's totally fine. I get it. You're the main character of your life."

Hannah laughed too. "Okay, so I'm a little self-centered. I will definitely work on that."

They ordered another drink, and a little while later, Rami walked her home. They pretended like they didn't know how the night would end, like he was just being nice by making sure she got home okay, but when they arrived at her apartment, she invited him up.

"Why did you text me today?" Rami said as they lay in bed later that night, Hannah's head resting in his neck. "Do you even like me?"

She laughed, mostly because she wasn't sure how to answer

that. She did like him, but at the same time, she knew she shouldn't, that if she let herself get caught up in him, he would only hurt her in the end.

"I mean, I wouldn't text you if I didn't like you," Hannah said. "I guess I knew the night would end with us hooking up, and I was in a bad place and didn't want to be home alone." She paused, worried she'd given too earnest an answer. "And then it turned out that I actually enjoyed your company too."

He laughed. "Wow, so glad you enjoyed my company."

"Okay, come on, do *you* even like *me*?" Hannah said.

"Yeah, I wouldn't be here if I didn't."

"You're here because you knew we'd have sex. Both of us knew how this night would end."

He laughed again and ran his fingers gently over her back, sending chills down her spine. "I guess I was just surprised that you texted me," he said. "When we hook up it's usually because we were awkwardly hanging out with the same group of people."

Rami had his arm around Hannah, while her own arm rested on his chest, her head on his shoulder.

"I just didn't want to be by myself tonight," Hannah said.

"Yeah, I figured."

They stopped talking. If she could just hold on to this moment, just pause her life right here, she would. She didn't need the guilt that her grandmother had put on her tonight. It was easier to be here, her skin against Rami's, his arms around her, existing just as a body.

Zain

Zain pitched the story about Egypt's power outages to every editor on Vanessa's list. Most of them didn't even respond, so he followed up, then followed up again. Finally, he got a couple of standard replies: "We're going to pass on this, but feel free to pitch me again." He was just about ready to give up on the piece entirely when an editor at *The Guardian* finally answered. She liked the idea but wanted to know more. Who were his sources? How could he prove it was the government causing the outages?

He couldn't really prove that, he responded. He could only speak on the accusations the Egyptian people were making, and report on the outages themselves, which had gotten no real coverage yet, but he named a few sources he could speak to, which he'd gotten from Hannah and Vanessa. He hit Send and held his breath, as though waiting for an instant response—an instant rejection he had to brace himself for.

He didn't actually get a response until two days later, when he checked his email while in line at the grocery store. She was interested, she said. The assignment was his. Zain smiled to himself as the cashier waved him forward. He tucked his phone into his pocket and sped home, eager to answer the email and get started. Maybe this would be the start of something—his first big story to launch his career.

For three days after the piece came out, Zain's phone would not stop buzzing: pings from likes and retweets, people commenting on the article, both negatively and positively, but even the negative comments brought with them an endorphin rush—actual haters to prove he was finally making it. Each like, each retweet, each positive reinforcement, was like a shot of dopamine straight into his veins, a high so different from the one he was used to that he was flying now, not floating, but sprinting through the air and grasping nothing, trying not to fall. He wanted to text Emily, to tell her all about it and ask if she'd read the article. She must have seen it. They still followed each other on Instagram and Twitter. But he wouldn't reach out. He'd promised her.

He also couldn't let this moment sit, though, and knew he had to keep the momentum going—to pitch again and get his name out there before he was forgotten. So he contacted Hannah, asked her about the women's protest she was helping organize. He needed sources he could talk to, something he could scrape together to pitch.

Once he put together a pitch, he simply sat at the desk in his bedroom, his leg bopping up and down like an addict waiting for his next fix. But all he could do now was wait.

Praise for his writing was great—a distraction from grief, keeping him from drinking away his problems, but each moment of happiness, each ping sending a chemical joy into his brain, wouldn't last, as the grief would creep back slowly, consuming his body and mind like an infestation. Alcohol, drugs, and sex never really eased the pain. The small success of the article helped, but the scourge of grief remained, feeding on what little joy he had until there would be nothing left. This way of life was manageable for now, but not sustainable. And so he prayed. It didn't really make sense—he openly defied Islam's laws but still felt the need, lately, to pray. Something about the act of prayer calmed his nerves, stopped the uncontrollable jitters of his body, as he forced himself to sit still and focus on one thing. He still wasn't sure what he was praying for, or if there was even a God out there listening, but saying words out loud helped. Maybe it was just a form of meditation. He asked for his life to get better, whatever that meant. He didn't want to feel this way anymore, but at the same time, if he let himself feel joy, did that mean he'd forgotten about his mom? Perhaps grief never ended and people just learned to cope.

Later, he was sitting in front of his computer, browsing job listings in New York—someplace he could start fresh and become a real journalist—when there was a knock at his bedroom door. It was his dad.

"Have you talked to Hannah lately?" his dad said from the doorway.

Zain was actually about to FaceTime with Hannah in a little bit.

"Yeah," Zain answered from his desk. "Why?"

"Is there any chance she'd talk to me?" His dad scrunched his face, concerned-looking, and Zain noticed the wrinkles in his forehead, deeper than he'd remembered. Had the grief aged him, or had he looked like this before?

"I don't know," Zain said. "Don't involve me in this."

His dad pleaded after that, saying he hadn't spoken to Hannah in months, asking when she'd ever reach out—if she'd ever reach out. They had this same conversation every couple of weeks, but truly, Zain didn't know what to do.

"She just needs time." Zain swiveled back and forth in his desk chair, facing his dad now.

"Well, what about *you*?" his dad said, stepping into the room now. He took a seat at the edge of Zain's bed so that Zain towered over him slightly in his desk chair.

"What *about* me?"

"Will we ever have any kind of relationship again?"

Zain couldn't help but chuckle to himself. It's not like he and his dad had had much of a relationship before. He'd always been closer to his mom, and his dad was just . . . there. Despite that, a familiar heaviness plunged into his stomach. Guilt—like he was the one in the wrong, the bad son.

"I don't know what you mean." Zain looked down at his hands and began picking at a piece of dry skin.

"I'm trying really hard," his dad said. "I love you and Hannah so much, and I feel like I've lost you both."

Zain didn't say anything for a few seconds and kept looking down. He couldn't exactly walk away from this conversation, because it was happening in his own room. There was nowhere to go.

"I'm trying—just, not to be so angry with you," he finally responded, "and this is the best I can do right now. I'm sure Hannah will speak to you again at some point. I don't know when. Maybe if Mom hadn't died—if we'd found out about this while she was alive—it would be easier."

"If you could just tell her that I love her." His dad stood up now, probably realizing there wasn't much more to say.

"Dad, I don't want to be in the middle of this." He looked at his dad then, who nodded and walked away.

Just like in the aftermath of every one of their interactions, Zain's stomach remained heavy with guilt, his whole body infested with grief. Then the turbulent thoughts raced through his mind: Should he have been kinder? More understanding? Made more of an effort to connect? To forgive? His dad was also grieving, and his and Hannah's behavior, in many ways, made that grief worse.

One thing was for sure, though: He needed to get out of this house. He couldn't actually work through his feelings about his dad if he was living here like a high schooler still—conflicting feelings of guilt and resentment constantly churning in his gut. Maybe he would just leave, head to New York, where all the real journalism jobs were, and work part-time at a restaurant or something while he freelanced. Just until he found something more permanent. All he knew then was that it was time to leave.

That night, he began looking at New York apartment listings, mostly around Brooklyn. He could afford a place with roommates with what he'd saved up. He'd been working consistent hours at the coffee shop, freelancing, and barely spending a dime. He wasn't going out anymore, had no rent to pay, and his dad was even doing all the grocery shopping. He really was living a privileged life here in the suburbs.

He messaged a few people who had listings up saying they needed a roommate. The apartments looked nice enough, and even though it was New York, living there with roommates was cheaper than his Philly apartment, where he'd lived alone.

All three people he messaged responded quickly, telling him he could come by the next day to look at the place, but they had other prospects coming too. Zain didn't expect such a quick response, but friends he knew in New York always told him apartment rentals moved fast there.

Tomorrow. He had a shift in the morning, but he could head into the city after.

Hannah

The International Women's Day protest was a week away, and Hannah was deep in preparation. She volunteered at the organization every day, helping assign roles to all the different people involved. She kept herself busy in an attempt to ignore the nerves that were building up inside her, flashes of that first protest popping up in her mind like an unwanted guest, sending pangs of post-traumatic shock through her body. But there were going to be bodyguards at this one, people handing out food and water, handing out goggles in case of tear gas, carrying milk for the same reason. There were organizers set up to lead the march, standing at the front and risking their lives in case of police or army interference. This protest was meant to be different—a protest for Egyptian women, all peaceful. They wouldn't be going to Tahrir, to avoid the violence there, and instead they planned to take a different route—one that hopefully the government wouldn't intercept.

Hannah ignored the warning signs in her body, the panic attacks that happened now and again, as though that first one had opened the door for more. Noha, despite her husband's protestations, wanted to attend too. Vanessa was still on the fence, and with her status as a journalist, if she were arrested—well, it was hard to say what would happen.

That morning, as Hannah scrolled Facebook, seeing vestiges of her past life—friends back home, parties, New York nights she'd left behind—she paused over a photo Zakaria had posted of him and his sister. She still hadn't heard anything from him since that awkward night, and she felt bad about how it had all played out. Aside from losing a friend, she also felt like she'd lost something more. Maybe it was because Zakaria's family seemed so much like her own—he gave her a glimpse into what her life would be like if her parents had never left Egypt.

Maybe it was on her to reach out to him. It's possible he was too embarrassed, or thought that she was the one who didn't want to be friends. With this protest coming up, there was some sense of urgency—like she had to tie up any loose ends before she went and marched the streets of Cairo.

Hi how are you?

Her heart raced as she typed the message, for fear that he wouldn't answer, or maybe he'd say he didn't want anything to do with her. If he couldn't have her as his girlfriend, then maybe he didn't want her as a friend.

Good, he wrote back not even a minute later. How are you?

She told him she was okay and asked if he wanted to talk or get coffee soon. He said he was free that afternoon.

Hannah arrived at the coffee shop early and sat down at a table outside. The sun was shining, the weather perfect for an outdoor café. Zakaria smiled and waved as he approached, like he didn't have a single care or worry in the world. He sat down with a sense of carefree ease.

"Hannah, how have you been?" he said.

"Good, I'm good." She smiled.

Her heart was beating fast. She didn't want another awkward encounter like last time. At that moment, a waiter came over to take their order, and once they were left alone again, she took a deep breath.

"Look," she said. "I just want to say I'm sorry, about, like, our last conversation. I didn't mean to—"

"It's okay," he said, waving his hand in the air. "We can be friends. I shouldn't have said what I said."

"Oh, okay."

She didn't know what to say next, having prepared for a longer conversation about why she only wanted a friendship. They could talk as if everything were normal, but that didn't feel right, and as they got their coffees, something inside her said that this was all fake. They'd sit and drink coffee and make small talk, but after today, Zakaria would maintain his distance, and they'd be acquaintances, not friends. That was usually the case with straight men and women, wasn't it? You could never become too close because one person would always fall in love.

"Is it okay, though?" Hannah said. "Are you okay?"

"Hannah, we don't have to talk about this."

She could tell he was uncomfortable and wanted to move on. "Yeah, no, I'm not trying to make things awkward. I just want you to know, it wasn't about you. It was about me. And I know that sounds like a cop-out. Like that 'It's not you, it's me' thing—"

Zakaria laughed and added cream and sugar to his coffee.

She leaned forward. "But, like, seriously, it really is me. I'm not in any place to be dating anyone. My mom died, and I moved to Egypt, and then I found out about my dad's affair . . ."

He looked up at her then. "Your dad's what?"

"Oh God." She leaned back in her chair. "I haven't even told you about that."

She told him then, for the first time, everything she had been dealing with since coming to Egypt. Avoiding her family, not speaking to her dad. She sipped her coffee as she spoke, realizing she'd kept so much of herself from Zakaria and that the person he liked was a person that she'd created. Of course he had fallen for her. She showed him a self who was catered specifically to him, and now, finally, she was shedding that character, coming to the table as her true self for a change.

"I didn't know," Zakaria said. "But I understand." He paused. "My dad too—well, he was with another woman."

"*Your* dad?" Hannah put her cup down.

Their families were even more alike than she'd thought. They seemed so happy and wholesome. Maybe it was all projection, again, of what Egypt was like. Her parents had made her believe that families here held on to their values—that God came before everything else. When she'd seen Zakaria's family, they were exactly the image she'd expected—the image her parents wanted their own family to be. It seemed that Zakaria's life was no different. It wasn't surprising, really. After all this time in Egypt, she knew that the stories her parents told about this country were fairy tales. No one was happy and wholesome.

Zakaria told her about discovering the affair and confronting his dad. He told his dad to end it or he'd tell his mom. At the time, his dad cried and begged forgiveness. He said he'd end it right away. But then, a year later, it happened again. That time, Zakaria told their mom.

"But she already knew." He turned his cup around in circles on the table. "She told me not to say anything to Layla and to just pretend everything was okay."

"I'm so sorry," Hannah said.

He sighed. "My dad still sees other women, and we just pretend like nothing is wrong. Like we're good Muslims."

She understood now why he liked her. He must have seen in her the same damage he saw in himself—the result of parental turmoil and hypocrisy. He didn't come from a perfect family, nor was he a perfect Muslim, as he'd already made clear.

"My parents"—Hannah squinted slightly as the sun moved over her face—"if Zain or I did anything wrong, would always say things like 'We'll send you to Egypt. Maybe then you'll learn.' And then, like, my dad never thought we were religious enough. And we're not. Zain and I don't pray, we drink, we smoke, I've had sex and I'm not married . . ."

Zakaria raised his eyebrows at that last part. Maybe she was sharing too much. He wasn't *exactly* like her. He went to Friday prayer, after all.

"Anyway, my dad doesn't know all of that," she said, "but he sees that we're not religious, and he would always say things like 'Maybe we shouldn't have come to America. Maybe we should have raised you in Egypt.'"

"This is stupid." Zakaria shook his head. "Egypt is just like America."

"Is it, though?" Hannah said. "Because when you tried to kiss me—"

"I'm sorry about that," he quickly interrupted.

"No, it's whatever, but you said something like you thought it would be okay because I'm American."

"I shouldn't have said that." He looked down at his cup.

"But you have the same ideas I do. That America is—I don't know—looser?"

Zakaria didn't seem to know where Hannah was going with all this, and truthfully, she didn't even know herself.

The waiter came back, fresh coffee in hand, and poured them each another cup. Hannah took a sip, the strong Egyptian roast filling her senses, waking her up to the conversation at hand. What was she trying to say?

"I think what I mean"—Hannah crossed and uncrossed her legs—"is that I was never myself around you. I was so hung up on this idea of you as a good Muslim—not that you're not, I mean, I don't know—but I created this person in my head based on everything my parents instilled in me about this country, and it was wrong. And I acted a certain way because I didn't want you to judge me or something. Because that's all I know of Islam. That you have to follow these rules, and if you don't then you're not Muslim, and you're . . . not good. I didn't want you to think of me as bad, you know?" She gripped her cup tightly and looked to Zakaria for a response.

He shook his head. "This is wrong. This interpretation of Islam. My parents are like this too, and many people in Egypt think like this. That if you break one rule, you go to hell, and the haram police tear you apart."

"Yes," Hannah said. "Like it's all or nothing."

That mentality was why she could never really embrace Islam in the first place. She was constantly made to feel unwelcome, her lifestyle and ideologies not meshing with the words that were preached.

"My family is Muslim, and look at them," Zakaria said. "Your family too. And I also have drunk before, and I smoke sheesha and hashish—everyone in Egypt smokes sheesha, but really, it's haram. I have been with other girls too—Egyptian girls, not from America. They are like you, like me. Nobody is perfect."

It was like a fog had cleared and she could see Zakaria for the first time, and through him, she saw herself too.

"I think maybe we should start over," Hannah said. "As friends, if you're okay with that. Maybe, like, we could just be ourselves now."

"Of course," Zakaria said.

She sipped her coffee and told him about the women's march she was attending the next week, and he asked about the organization and what they'd been working on.

"Just be careful," he said, echoing the words of her brother and Vanessa. "I told you about my friend that died."

"Yeah," Hannah said. "I know. I'm being careful."

Zain

Just days after looking at apartments, Zain was packing up his things, having seen several places in Brooklyn all at once and deciding to sign a lease. He'd be living with two roommates—people he didn't know, but they seemed okay. The last thing he needed to do before he left, though, was see his Philly friends again. One more night with the old crew.

They were out at their usual spot, his whole group of friends minus Emily. Everyone was ordering the eight-dollar beer-and-shot special.

"Let me get you a drink," James said as they approached the bar, but Zain hadn't had a drink since coming back from Egypt. He hadn't even stepped foot in a bar.

"Uhh, you know, I think I'm just gonna get some soda water and lime for now."

"Really?" James asked.

"I'm sort of taking a break from drinking," said Zain. "I don't know for how long, but I'm not really ready to go back to it."

"I think that's great," James said.

The place smelled like it always had—sour, sweet, and wheaty all at once, like the sticky, stale beer that coated the floor. He remembered the last time he'd been here, sitting at the bar with James, confessing his sins over the phone to his dad because he no longer cared. Nothing had mattered anymore. He'd wanted to die then—to let the alcohol course through his system in waves, drowning him in a golden, foamy grave just so he didn't have to face the reality that his life had imploded entirely.

Tonight was different, though. He wasn't happy, exactly, but he had something to look forward to—a new chapter ahead. He'd never been to this bar without going home drunk at the end of the night, and as he watched his friends ordering drinks, he was tempted to do so himself, afraid that everyone would ask questions about why he wasn't drinking. But no one asked or seemed to care at all, and when he said he was sticking to soda that night, the responses he got were "Oh, nice" or "That's cool."

"Hey, have you talked to Emily lately?" Zain asked James as they stood in line for the bathroom.

James hesitated before answering. "Yeah, we hang out sometimes."

"How is she?"

"She's good. She's better."

Better. "Better" implied that before, she wasn't good. He had hurt her. Zain just nodded, but something in his nod must have concerned James because he immediately followed up with "Look, I don't know if I should even tell you this, but she's been seeing someone." Then, gently, he added, "You should just leave her alone."

Instantly, a sense of dread and anxiety took over Zain's body. It felt like someone had dropped a bomb inside him.

"I am leaving her alone," Zain said.

"Yeah, no, of course," said James. "I just didn't know if

you—well, like, I know what happened last time we were here."

"Yeah." Zain felt his cheeks flush with the shame of that night. "I was going through a lot."

"I know," James said, patting Zain on the back.

The bathroom door opened, and Zain went in. He wanted a drink badly as he thought of Emily dating someone else. He'd known she would start dating again, but he didn't want to hear about it. He didn't want to know that she'd moved on. A part of him that he knew too well was saying that one drink wouldn't hurt. One drink would ease his nerves and get his mind off her, but instead, he washed his hands and walked over to the table where the rest of his friends were seated and sat down next to them, no drink in hand.

As the night went on, he tried to push away any thoughts of Emily and push away his grief. He laughed, he slept at James's, and they all got brunch in the morning to say goodbye—just like he'd planned. He wouldn't let things get out of control anymore.

Three days later, he was packed and ready to go. His dad offered to help him move, and had picked up the U-Haul early that morning. Most of the drive was spent in silence, Zain waiting for his dad to say something as they drove down the turnpike on their way into Brooklyn. Zain fidgeted in the passenger seat, looking out the window at the big green signs pointing to the next exit. As a kid, he'd always assumed if they were in sight of a big green sign, then they still had a long way to go on their drive—far from home on a journey of undetermined length.

"Zain, I'm proud of you." His dad broke the uncomfortable silence. "You're fixing your life."

"Thanks," Zain said.

He wasn't sure how else to respond, or what else to say, the chasm between them having grown so large. He wanted to make peace with his dad but simply didn't have the words. He couldn't just flat out say that everything was okay—that they were good—because it wasn't and they weren't. But at the same time, now, in this moment, his dad was trying his best to mend their relationship. He was grieving, and his kids had turned their backs on him, and so he was grieving that too. Grieving the consequences of his own choices. But Zain didn't say anything, instead sinking farther into his seat, into the silence, with only the swish of passing cars filling the quiet void.

They reached the new place, in a nice sunny area not too far from Prospect Park and the Brooklyn Museum. After parking the truck, they focused only on moving—lifting the bed, the dresser, the desk, working together as a unit. The air was crisp, with spring not too far off, and he could smell someone grilling on a rooftop nearby.

"Should we have lunch somewhere?" Zain said as they stood next to the empty truck.

His dad looked surprised almost, a small smile forming on his face. They found a nearby Palestinian restaurant and got some falafel, saying little between bites, but it was nice—the beginning of something.

"You're okay?" His dad stood next to the truck after they ate.

"Yeah, I'm good," Zain nodded. "Thank you. For all of this."

His dad stood in silence for a few seconds, his hand on the side of the truck, before responding. "You're welcome."

It was like he wanted to say more, but he didn't have the words either, didn't know how to bridge the gap that had built in the past months. Zain wasn't sure what prompted him—maybe it was the look of sadness on his dad's face, his eyes beginning to well up, his brow furrowed in distress—but he reached in for a hug. His dad, as though stunned, held his arms awkwardly in the air for a second before reciprocating.

"See you soon," Zain said as they pulled apart.

Hannah

It was the night before the protest, and Vanessa was in Hannah's apartment helping out with posters. The living room floor was covered in poster board and cut-up cardboard boxes. The plan was to hand out signs for people to carry, with various slogans in Arabic and English—something newscasters could capture in their photos or on TV.

"Are you ready?" Vanessa asked, sitting on the floor across from Hannah.

"Yeah, I think so." Hannah put the cap back on a black Sharpie. "Are you sure you don't want to come? There's gonna be so much protection in place."

"I don't know," Vanessa said. "I'm a little nervous, given everything. I almost want to talk *you* out of going, but I know you won't listen."

"Yeah, no. Not after all this," Hannah said, gesturing to the posters sprawled around her living room.

Hannah hadn't told Vanessa that the panic attacks had kept coming after that first one. She hadn't told her about the nightmares with the men in the square either, or about the boy who was trampled. Some nights, Hannah would wake up and feel like the air had been sucked out of the room and she was gasping for breath. Other days, it felt like water was filling her lungs, and she was sinking, sinking, sinking, her skin wet and clammy like she'd been dropped into the Nile.

"This just feels important." Hannah gathered some of the posters into a pile. "Like something I have to do."

She wasn't sure if she was trying to convince Vanessa or herself.

"I know." Vanessa reached out to help. "I'm not trying to talk you out of it. Just be careful."

They piled all the posters together and placed them in a corner, then gathered the markers on a table. Someone from the women's group was stopping by later to pick them up.

"So"—Vanessa sat on the couch—"were you planning on telling me what the deal is with you and Rami? I have to hear from him that you two have been hooking up still?"

"It's nothing." Hannah shook her head, taking a seat on the opposite end of the couch. "It's not a big deal."

Rami felt more like a bad habit than anything else.

"Okay," Vanessa said. "I mean, he's hot, so whatever. Just as long as you're good."

"It wouldn't have happened if you were free to hang out the night of the fight with my grandma." Hannah adjusted herself on the couch, tucking one foot underneath the other.

"Oh shit, that was the night you two—" Vanessa paused. "Okay, that makes sense. I didn't know you were going through an emotional crisis. If you'd told me what happened I would have made time."

"No, it's okay," Hannah said. "I'm fine."

"Wait, so, do you two, like, talk? Or is it just hooking up?"

"It's, I don't know—both? It's casual. We're hooking up, but we also talk."

Being around him also made her forget that her life was in

shambles. She was using him—using sex with him—as a coping method, but it felt harmless. No one was getting hurt.

Hannah and Vanessa talked for a bit more, until a woman came by to get the posters. Vanessa stayed for a little while after, then left around eleven, and as Hannah got ready for bed, her phone rang—a FaceTime from Zain. She was tempted to not pick up, sure that he would try to talk her out of going to the protest, but on the last ring, she relented.

Zain

"Hannah," Zain said. "I was afraid I wouldn't catch you before you went to bed."

He was in his new place, sitting at a desk in his bedroom, boxes he hadn't unpacked yet still nestled in the corner. From his window, he could see the sun beginning to set over the apartment buildings across the way. He was freelancing more regularly, and he'd picked up a few shifts at a restaurant in his neighborhood to supplement his cash flow. He felt like less of a failure now, and when he spoke to Hannah, he no longer wanted to hide away the parts of his life he was ashamed of.

"Are you calling to tell me not to go tomorrow?" she asked.

Zain smiled. "Yes and no."

That *was* why he was calling, but he knew she wouldn't listen to him. Still, he called anyway. That was his job as the older brother.

"I know you've seen the news," Zain said, "and I know you know how dangerous this is." He watched himself on the screen and adjusted some stray hairs atop his head.

"It'll be fine. I'm with a large group, and I'll have protection. I can't *not* go."

He knew all this, but he was worried. He'd lost too much already.

"I just don't want anything to happen to you," he said. He was serious now, the smile gone from his face.

"I know."

"Dad is always asking me when I think you'll talk to him again."

He wasn't sure why he'd brought this up now. It wasn't the time, but it was like something compelled him to say it—like it might be the last chance.

Hannah took a few seconds to respond. "What do you tell him when he asks?"

"I don't tell him anything." Zain looked to his right, outside for a moment, where he could see through a neighbor's window in the distance. "I just say I don't know."

He looked back at the screen and couldn't exactly read her reaction, her face blank, becoming pixilated at one point. She didn't say anything, her eyes avoiding the camera.

"I have this guilt," Zain said. "All the time."

"Guilt about what?"

"Dad."

His stomach was always in knots now, his appetite coming and going, depending on when he'd last spoken to their dad. On the days they didn't talk, he was okay, able to forget and instead focus on his new life in New York. But then his dad would call, a concerned parent asking how he was doing, what he was up to, and always, Zain heard the sadness in his voice—the longing to go back to a time when everything was happier, less complicated. After the call, he'd feel heavy for the rest of the day, like the air had become thick and he was wading through molasses, trying to move forward. Eventually, he'd give in, lying in bed and letting the viscous weight hold him down, as though he were glued to the sheets, with someone pressing on his chest to keep him there.

Hannah

She understood exactly what he meant. For her, the guilt had gotten worse since that conversation with her uncle in the car. She couldn't help but picture her dad alone at home with no one to talk to.

"He's still our dad," Zain said on the other side of the screen. "I feel like I'm being a bad kid, like ungrateful, and I know he's hurting, but I just don't know how to handle this or move past it."

"He did this to himself." Hannah sat up more in her bed.

"Do you not feel guilty, though?"

Anytime the thought of her dad even entered her mind, her chest tightened and she had to remind herself to breathe. If she didn't focus on breathing, it felt like someone was squeezing her lungs, suffocating her with guilt. She'd never not talked to her dad for this long. And now, she missed him. She missed both her parents. The loss of them formed an emptiness that grew and grew each day. But there was nothing she could do. Her mom was gone, and her dad was someone she didn't know and didn't like. She missed the version of him he used to be—or that she thought he was. But did she ever really know either of her parents? Maybe her mom had had an affair too, back before she'd even had time to give their marriage a chance. Maybe it was doomed from the start.

"I *wish* things could go back to the way they were." Hannah leaned her head back on the wall. "I mean, of course I feel guilty. Mom died, and I cut Dad out of my life. I know that must be killing him."

The pressure on her chest returned. Zain was making her feel worse than she'd felt in a while—like she'd abandoned her dad in his time of need.

"I get it, and I'm not trying to make you feel bad," Zain said. "I just . . . thought you should know, you know?"

Zain

Their dad just wasn't the same man anymore. There was darkness, and a deep, deep depression—that was clear. Zain was worried, now that he'd moved out. It was hard to tell what Hannah was thinking, though. Maybe he shouldn't have said anything.

After he hung up, he leaned over to open his bedside drawer and ruffled through some socks. Underneath was his ziplock bag of weed and rolling paper. He didn't smoke as often these days, but sometimes he needed that immediate sense of calm after smoking, a sensation that pushed away the swirling, static-like anxiety in his chest. And it was better than drinking. He didn't lose control of his life when he smoked.

He sat down on his bed and rolled a joint. As he took a hit, the high traveled through his body and head quickly, like a blanket of calm falling over him. Nothing would ever be the same with his dad. Too much had happened. But he could build something, maybe. He wouldn't be able to forgive him, but they could attempt to get along.

Hannah

Hannah couldn't sleep. As soon as her head hit the pillow, her mind began to race—a hamster wheel in her brain spinning and spiraling. If her mom were around, she would tell her not to go.

But it wasn't just the march. It was also what Zain had said over the phone about her dad being depressed, both his kids hating him. She did hate her dad, but she hadn't become indifferent. She hadn't thought much about how long this anger would last or how long she would ice him out. Her mind was always on the present, with some assumption that one day they'd speak again.

She looked at her phone. It was almost midnight, and she had to be up at eight. She could text Rami to distract her. They'd hook up, and she'd be able to sleep. But she paused to think.

It was 4:45 p.m. in New Jersey. She thought then of calling her dad. Maybe it was time. But she couldn't bring herself to actually do it, instead balling her sheets up into her fists as she kicked her feet underneath her—just as she'd done as a kid when she was angry or frustrated. She wanted to scream, to release all that emotion and feel nothing, but instead, she texted Rami, like she knew she would.

You up?

Lol, he responded.

Rami was in her bed less than an hour later. She would be tired the next day, but a part of her needed him there, his body near hers. Otherwise, she would have cried herself to sleep.

"I have to get up really early tomorrow," Hannah said as they lay next to one another.

"Are you kicking me out?"

She laughed. "No, I'm just saying I'm gonna set an alarm for eight."

"Eight? What are you doing tomorrow?"

She hadn't told him about the women's march, his words from months earlier still ringing in her head. She didn't need to hear from him that she deserved to get assaulted if she went. But now, just hours before the protest, with him in her bed, she had to tell him.

"Oh God," he groaned, "don't be an idiot, Hannah."

"Excuse me?"

"Didn't you already do this?"

"Do what?" She started to sit up slightly, keeping the blanket over her naked chest.

"Go to a protest and get attacked and have to be rescued."

"Yeah, but this is different."

He turned to his side to face her and gently ran his hand down her bare arm. "Yeah, this is even dumber now that the police are out there tear-gassing people and shooting them down every other day."

"This one is organized," Hannah said. "We're not going to Tahrir. It's a large group of women. It's completely peaceful. There's no reason to open fire on us."

"Do you hear yourself? This is so stupid. You absolutely shouldn't go."

"You have no idea what you're talking about." She pulled her arm away from him and pulled the blankets up farther as she sat up straight now.

"Okay, I'm not trying to get you mad. Let's just go to sleep. Or we can have sex again," he added, laughing.

"I think you should leave," Hannah said.

"What?" Rami sat up.

"Now I'm kicking you out."

"Oh, come on, I'm kidding. I'm sorry." He smiled at her.

"Look, Rami, I actually am getting up very early, and I think it would be better if you left."

She didn't want him there when she woke up, making her feel the way she felt now. That sense of glumness when someone shits on something you're excited about. She had thought she needed him next to her so as not to feel so alone, but now she was just irritated.

"You're serious?" he said.

"Yes." Hannah didn't look at him, instead staring up at the ceiling.

"Okay. I am sorry, though." Rami stood and put his clothes on. "I wasn't trying to offend you."

"You can just be an asshole sometimes." Hannah reached for her shirt on the ground.

"Yeah, I know."

She put on a T-shirt and sweatpants and walked Rami to the door.

"Are we . . . cool?" he said before walking out.

"I don't know. I'll text you later." She gave him a hug goodbye just before shutting the door.

It was like he came and went in a flash, manufacturing an argument for no reason, making her question herself and leaving a sense of gloom in his wake. Maybe she needed a break from him and the energy he brought into her life—an energy that, while comforting at times, too often depleted what little joy she had.

In the morning, she didn't dress like a boy. She put on a pair of jeans and a blue T-shirt, her green jacket over it. She left her hair down and didn't wear a baseball cap. She brought only her phone, with some cash tucked into her bra again. This protest would be safer, but it couldn't hurt to be careful. No need to bring more than what was necessary. She pushed the memory of the first protest out of her mind, just as she'd pushed Rami out too.

The plan was to leave from the office of the organization. Rather than going to Tahrir, a place now filled with danger, they would start at Talaat Harb Square a short distance away, and from there, they'd march to the High Court, demanding rights for women. When Hannah arrived at the office, it was already packed, and Noha was waiting for her outside with Hamada.

"You made it!" Hannah said. She looked over at Hamada. "How did she convince you to come?"

"It's important," he said. "I know that. I was just worried because of everything that's happening. But you're Yasmeen's daughter, so of course we want to support you and support Egypt."

Yasmeen's daughter. She'd never know for sure if her mom had cheated on her dad with this man, but she didn't care anymore. Maybe her parents' issues didn't need to concern her so much. She wouldn't exactly forgive her dad, but maybe their problems weren't hers to deal with.

Hannah felt genuinely grateful. Standing there with her mom's best friends from youth was like having her mom by her side, somehow.

They went inside, and the center was packed. She took a quick photo, then pushed her way through the crowds over to her desk, where some of the organizers were taking head counts. The room was vibrant, women everywhere holding posters, laughing, ready for the day ahead. She took a few more pictures—something to post on Instagram and send to Zain later. She stood between Noha and Hamada in the crowd as people shuffled across the office, grabbing their posters.

Hannah's phone vibrated in her pocket. Vanessa was calling.

"Hannah," she said. "I'm coming, wait for me!"

"No way, really?"

"Yeah, I'm in a taxi now, really close by," Vanessa said. "I just felt like I had to be there with you. Plus, I've got a pocket knife with me just in case."

"Dude, that's awesome. I'm in the office, but hurry up."

As she hung up the phone, she felt a tap on her shoulder and turned around to see another familiar face.

"Layla!" Hannah said. "What are you doing here?"

"We're both here," a man's voice said from behind her.

Hannah looked up to see Zakaria as well. She'd never expected him to come. She hadn't even asked him to.

"We didn't tell our parents, obviously," Zakaria said, "but we wanted to be here."

"We want to do this for Masr," Layla said.

Hannah hugged them both. She smiled, and in the distance, someone shouted her name above the chaos in the office. It was Vanessa, and soon they were all ready to go, ready to march.

At the front of the office, a woman with a loudspeaker stood on a chair.

"We will leave soon," she said in Arabic, *"but before we go, find a group—your friends, family, people standing next to you—whoever. Make sure you know each other's names, and stay with your group. We don't know what will happen today. Inshallah,*

we'll be safe, and this will be a peaceful protest, but we never know what the army will do. So stay with your group. Make sure you're never alone."

She proceeded to explain the route they would take. She said others were already there or on their way—that this would be even larger than they'd estimated. The same tension Hannah had felt in her stomach right before she went to Tahrir returned. She turned to look at Vanessa, who smiled.

"We'll be okay," Vanessa said, and Hannah nodded, linking their arms together.

It took another fifteen minutes to leave the office, as they were surrounded by groups of people, many holding posters with Arabic writing scrawled across the front, all trying to squeeze through the doors to get outside.

Once outside, they moved slowly down the street, and people began to chant in Arabic. A woman in a purple hijab stood near them, both hands in the air raised in peace signs as she chanted along with the crowd.

Walking in this group of protesters was so different from that day in Tahrir, when each step had brought more and more danger. Here, the sun shone down on them, and the energy in the crowd was one of overwhelming glee and excitement, and she felt safe. Hannah relaxed her muscles, loosening her arms and her grip on Vanessa. They marched down the street, one strong cohesive unit, and no one bothered them. Men didn't circle around or try to attack, try to remove them from the group. Avoiding Tahrir altogether was a good idea. The army hadn't planned for this and couldn't stop them—couldn't twist this into a narrative of violent protest.

They made their way from the square to the High Court and stood outside chanting, Arabic words muddled together, demanding the fall of the regime and more rights for women.

Hannah couldn't even make out the words exactly, her own Arabic language skills not quite up to par with political vocabulary, but she smiled along anyway. Maybe this wouldn't work. Maybe it wouldn't change anything. But it meant something that they'd pulled this off. The crowd was tightly packed, and there was some pushing and shoving, but nothing too extreme. No one fell to the ground. No one was trampled.

Maybe this was home now—these people and this country—a place her mom had once called home. She wasn't alone here.

Suddenly, it was over. Hannah watched as her friends recounted the events of the day while they grabbed lunch at a restaurant. She connected to the Wi-Fi from her American phone and was about to FaceTime Zain when her phone buzzed with an incoming call from him.

"Zain, I was just about to call you," she said. "It went so great. They said there were over a thousand people in attendance. Vanessa came. Zakaria and Layla came. Noha and Hamada too."

She moved her phone to the sides, showing the whole group as they waved at the screen, then turned back to look at Zain, his face solemn as he stood against a white backdrop.

"Wait, where are you?" Hannah said. "Shouldn't you, like, just be waking up?"

"Hannah, Dad had a heart attack."

Zain

That morning, Zain awoke to three missed calls and a voicemail from a number he didn't recognize. Still in bed, he hit play on the message and learned that his dad had been taken to the hospital overnight, that he was alive but he'd suffered a heart attack.

His stomach dropped, and he practically jumped out of bed, envisioning for a moment that both his parents could be gone. He called his dad's phone, but he wasn't picking up, so he instead called the hospital back. He threw some clothes on without showering, got into his car, and drove straight there.

"Dad," he said, leaning over his sleeping father in the hospital bed.

His dad slowly opened his eyes, looking confused for a moment before a smile of recognition washed over his face.

"Zain. Thank you for coming."

Hannah

Noha and Hamada drove Hannah home immediately, where they sat with her as she booked a flight back to America. She hadn't spoken to her dad in months. She'd thought she had time. Time to think, time to decide, time to figure out how she felt. Vanessa came to help her pack, and Noha drove her to the airport that night.

The day was a blur, and the flight even more so. Hannah tried to sleep but couldn't, so instead she watched one movie after another, until she couldn't keep her eyes open anymore. And even then, her sleep was plagued by violent nightmares—images of her mom and dad alongside fire and destruction.

When she landed at JFK, Hannah trudged her way through the airport, to the subway, then to NJ Transit, where she took another train into Jersey, then an Uber to the hospital. She didn't know, at that point, how many hours she'd been traveling, but she wanted to collapse and cry. Maybe from exhaustion or maybe from the thought of losing her only living parent, or maybe from the anxiety she felt about seeing him again.

Once inside the hospital, she took the elevator to the fourth floor as Zain had instructed and slowly dragged her suitcase down the sanitized hallways until she reached her dad's room. Hannah paused for a moment, briefly wondering if she should just turn around—head back to the airport, back to Cairo—but a nurse quickly approached before she could fully formulate her thoughts.

"Are you Yousef's daughter?"

Hannah stared at her and didn't say anything.

"You flew here from Egypt, right?"

"Um, yeah," Hannah said.

"Your dad and brother are inside," said the nurse. "You can go right in."

Hannah opened the door slowly, taking a deep breath at the sight of her dad, frail-looking, lying on a bed in a hospital robe, wires sticking out from his chest.

Zain

When the door opened, Zain looked up to see his sister's nervous face as she stood in the doorway with her suitcase. He knew she didn't want to be here—that she'd been in Egypt to get away, to avoid these problems back home. But he was glad she'd come. He couldn't keep dealing with everything alone.

His dad sat up in bed and smiled.

"Hannah," he said. "I'm so happy you came."

"Hey, Dad," she said. "Zain called me. I—what happened?"

"My heart." He moved both hands up to where his heart was. "But I'm alive."

Hannah nodded and didn't say anything. Zain could feel the tension and wished he could open a window or something, let all the still air out of the room.

"I'm so happy to have both of my kids here," his dad said, seemingly unfazed by Hannah's stiff demeanor.

The three of them sat for a while as their dad asked Hannah what she'd been up to in Egypt and Zain listened to her reluctantly open up without giving too much detail or insight into her life. Hannah was trying not to be too open, he could tell.

"Are you hungry?" their dad said to Hannah, and before she had the chance to answer, turned to Zain and added, "Take her to the cafeteria. She just got off the plane, probably didn't eat."

Zain was happy at the opportunity to talk to Hannah alone, and the two of them left their dad momentarily to get food.

"How are you doing?" Zain asked once they were out of earshot.

"Uhh, you know, I've been better," Hannah said.

"Can you believe Dad had a heart attack just to get you to come back? Pretty dramatic, if you ask me."

Hannah laughed and shook her head as they walked down a hallway that smelled of rubbing alcohol and plastic. "So extra."

"I'm happy to see you," Zain said.

They made their way to the cafeteria and stood in line behind a group of doctors and nurses.

"How have you been?" Hannah asked.

"I think good, up until now. A lot better than when you last saw me."

He told her about his move to New York and how he was building a new life for himself. He was working hard, he said, not slacking off like before. Zain bit his lip, unsure if he should tell her about quitting drinking again, for fear that she'd look at him differently. Like when he'd told her about cheating on Emily.

"And I stopped drinking," said Zain. "Officially. I still smoke weed, but alcohol is out. California sober at the moment."

One of the doctors in front of them in line turned his head, as though curious to put a face to the conversation he was listening in on.

"Oh, that's good, I think," Hannah said. "I know you said you were taking a break before Egypt, but like, did something happen when you got back?"

"I think it was actually being in Egypt that made me realize I needed to stop."

"What do you mean?" They took a few steps forward as the line moved.

"I thought I just needed to handle my alcohol better—like, drink less when I went out—but every time we went out, I got pretty drunk," Zain said. "I couldn't control myself. I woke up hungover most mornings. Did you not notice?"

"Oh, I mean, yeah, I guess I did notice, but I thought maybe it was because you were on vacation."

"That's kind of what I told myself," Zain said, still nervous about how his sister would view him. "But I was just doing exactly what I'd been doing. Drinking to avoid my problems."

They reached the front of the line and each ordered a sandwich before paying and making their way over to the cafeteria tables. They chose a table by the windows and sat down.

"You probably think I'm, like, some fucked-up alcoholic now."

Hannah scrunched her face. "What?"

"I don't know, like I'm someone that needs to quit drinking, otherwise my life gets too out of control. It's embarrassing." He leaned back in his seat and looked out the window.

"Zain, I'm not judging you," Hannah said. "It takes a lot of courage to admit something is a problem and then actually make a change. We've both been through a lot this year, and you've changed your life so much. You should be proud of yourself."

Sometimes, it shocked Zain that Hannah was the younger one. He looked down at his plate and nodded.

"Thanks, Han. I appreciate you saying that."

Hannah

Hannah meant what she said. She was proud of Zain for how much he'd changed. He'd fucked up a lot of things in his life, but he'd picked it back up and he was moving forward. Hannah, meanwhile, was feeling a little stagnant, and now, back in America, she felt more confused than ever.

She didn't know how to act or what to say. She was still so angry at her dad, but she also missed him. When her mom had a heart attack, she was just gone—no second chance at life. Her dad, though, was here. He'd survived. And yet, Hannah didn't know what to do with that. The universe seemed to be giving her an opportunity to reconcile, but the idea was so daunting—so unfathomable—that she wished she could just leave again.

"I have to have a real conversation with Dad, don't I?" Hannah asked Zain as the two of them ate their sandwiches, surrounded by doctors and nurses eating together in their white coats and scrubs, alongside tables of other visitors, all seated in the same gray cafeteria.

"Yeah, I don't think you can run away from this one," Zain said.

"I wasn't running away, really," Hannah said. "I mean, I was, but I think I needed to figure some stuff out."

"Did you figure it out?"

"I'm getting there." Hannah thought of the list of contacts Manal had given her, still sitting on her nightstand in Cairo. "I'm thinking about applying to grad school."

"Do you think Columbia would let you take your spot back?"

Hannah laughed. "No. I'd have to reapply probably, but that's not even what I mean."

She told Zain about her conversation with Manal, and about how she'd started looking into the public policy master's program.

"And they also have a master's program for human rights law. Maybe I could be an organizer, or work for a place that's trying to help women or refugees, or just helping create policies that get people out of poverty."

She knew she was all over the place, but that felt okay. She didn't need to know exactly where she wanted to work just yet. That was the whole point of grad school—to learn and figure things out.

"I think that's great," Zain said.

Hannah smiled. "Really?"

"Yeah, that would be sick, and I think you'd be good at it."

"I haven't told anyone yet, but I want to stay in Egypt, and if I can get into AUC, then I'd have a reason to be there."

"No, that's really cool, Hannah. I think you should apply."

"What do you think Dad will say?" Hannah asked.

"I think he'd just be happy you're talking to him."

On the plane ride over, she had been thinking about what to say to her dad and how to accept him into her life again. She thought back to the conversation with her uncle on the boat and to the letters in her mom's closet.

"Maybe it's unfair how I've been treating Dad," Hannah said. "Maybe Mom cheated too."

Zain

Zain had just taken a bite of his sandwich, and he slowly finished chewing. He thought of their conversation back in Egypt and the conversation with Hasan—about how his parents left Egypt because of his mom's former fiancé—and then later, the conversation with his dad about that very topic.

"I don't think we'll ever know," Zain said after swallowing his bite. "Maybe it was innocent between her and Hamada—just friends."

"Or maybe not," Hannah said.

"Maybe it's better not to know."

Hannah looked down at the now empty plates in front of them. "We should probably head back upstairs," she said.

Hannah

Once back inside the hospital room, they all resumed their positions, until Zain left Hannah and her dad alone for a moment as he went to get water. Hannah could feel her heart beating fast, and the only other sound in the room was the ambient beeping of her dad's heart monitor. She didn't know what to talk about with Zain gone. Here she was, in front of this man she thought she knew, but it turned out she didn't at all. And really, he didn't know her either, given all the secrets between them.

"How are you?" her dad asked.

"I'm good." She nodded and leaned forward in her seat.

"I'm so glad you're here," he said.

Hannah didn't say anything and simply nodded again.

"I know you're still upset with me," her dad continued. "And that's okay, I deserve it. I'm so sorry, Han."

Her dad looked so small, lying down in his plain blue hospital gown. She thought back to the story her uncle had told her—of her dad spending every moment by her side in the hospital. Now here they were again. Tears began to pool in her eyes, and she bit her lip to keep from crying. She said nothing, knowing that as soon as she opened her mouth, her voice would crack and the tears would stream.

"I just want you to know it means a lot to me that you're here," her dad said, "and I hope one day you can forgive me."

"I just don't know how to not be angry with you," Hannah said softly. "You cheated on Mom, and then she died."

"I know. I understand."

"But also, when Zain told me about the heart attack—I don't know what I'd do with you gone too."

She was openly crying now, and her dad sat up in bed and tried to reach over to hug her.

"No," Hannah said. "You shouldn't get up."

Zain

In the days that followed, Zain found himself back home, once again sleeping in his childhood bedroom. Hannah was home too, and it was almost like they were a family again. Of course, nothing was the same without their mom there. Dinners were quieter, and Zain and Hannah were doing all the cooking. Healthy meals their dad could eat.

It was awkward at first, the three of them together, acting as though everything was fine, not wanting to stress their dad out in the slightest. But it wouldn't last forever. Zain had to get back to the city, and Hannah planned to fly back to Egypt.

"It's so much different here without Mom," Hannah said one day over dinner.

They were all thinking it, but no one had said it yet.

Zain looked down at his plate and poked at the grilled chicken.

"She would be happy to see us all together," his dad said.

They sat in silence for a moment, no one taking a bite of their food, no one knowing exactly what to say.

"If Mom were here, she would have been like, 'This chicken is terrible,'" said Zain, breaking the silence. He was the one who'd made the chicken.

Hannah and their dad laughed.

"Well, it kind of is," Hannah said, sticking her fork in the bland chicken and holding it up for them to see.

"It's healthy," Zain said. "For Dad."

"I think it's great. Thank you, Zain," their dad said.

After that, they were able to talk and laugh a bit more freely, recalling memories of dinners with their mom over the years, and for a little while at least, they could forget their anger and pain.

Hannah

It had been three weeks, and Hannah was packing to head back to Cairo. In her time away, she'd heard from Noha, Vanessa, and Zakaria—all checking up on her, making sure everything was all right. Now, as she packed up her things in her childhood bedroom, standing next to a bulletin board fully pinned with photos of her and her friends from high school, a text from Rami came through on her phone.

Hey I just heard from Vanessa about your dad. Wanted to check in and see how you're doing

Also I'm sorry about how we left things

She hadn't really thought about Rami since she'd been back

home, and she realized then how little he even factored into her life. Was she happy to hear from him? Excited that he was checking on her? Or did she just feel nothing? She wasn't sure and didn't even know yet how she'd respond.

Hannah finished packing and dragged her suitcase down the carpeted stairs, each step reverberating in a dull thump.

"You ready?" her dad said.

Hannah nodded. Since she'd been home, she'd told him about her idea to apply to grad school in Egypt.

"I think it's great," he had said. "I'll miss you, of course, but I'll come and visit."

The two of them loaded into the car and began to make their way to the airport. The ride began in silence, and Hannah looked over Rami's text again.

Thanks, I'm ok, she responded. I'm actually flying back to Egypt today

She didn't know if she'd keep in touch with him when she got back, but she figured that answer was good enough for now. Maybe her romantic life would remain a mess, but that was okay. She had other things on her mind. She'd go back to Cairo, continue working at the café, and keep doing the work she was doing at the women's organization. But she'd go to grad school too, and eventually, she'd make a difference in the world.

"Maybe Zain and I can come visit you in Egypt in a couple months," her dad said as he drove.

"Oh, yeah, I'd like that."

"I'm really glad I got to see you, Hannah."

"Yeah," Hannah said. "Yeah, me too."

She meant that this time. Though still angry with him, she wouldn't ice him out completely anymore. She'd let him back in slowly.

Zain

Back in New York, Zain was unpacking from his stay with his dad when he heard the ping of a new email on his phone. It was from a name he didn't recognize, but the domain was nymag.com, and the subject line read, "Staff Writer Position," so he opened up the email right away.

An editor from the magazine had seen some of his articles and said she was "very impressed." Zain's eyes sped through the email, so excited that he was barely taking in the words, so he had to reread it more slowly. It wasn't a job offer quite yet, but they wanted to set up a meeting—an unofficial interview. He'd still need to submit an application as a formality, but they asked if he was interested and what his availability would be.

Zain could hardly believe it. His hands were shaking as he responded, trying not to sound too eager or include too many exclamation marks. This was what he wanted—what he'd moved here for. Nothing was certain, of course, as this was only an interview, but this was far more than he could have hoped for after the way he'd fucked up his life.

Smiling to himself, he lay back in bed, staring up at the ceiling. He wondered if his mom could see him. She'd be proud, finally. Zain looked back at his phone and opened iMessage. He scrolled back and back and back, all the way to the last text from his mom last summer.

What's the Netflix password? he had written, to which

she'd responded, ZainHannah1234, something anyone who knew her could have figured out. He laughed quietly to himself and scrolled back even farther. Most of their texts were logistical—what time he'd arrive, what he wanted for dinner when he came home for the weekend, things like that. But in between logistics, there was the occasional Love you, Miss you. He sat up and looked out the window, at the trees on his block, at the sun shining down. Was she watching him? Could she see him now?

He typed "Miss you, Mom" and hit send. He waited a minute, as though expecting some response, or some sign. The text went through in blue, not green, meaning the number was still active. Maybe his dad hadn't stopped paying the bill, or maybe the number belonged to a stranger now. Then, another ping. The interview had been set up. He would be heading over to the *New York* magazine offices in just one week's time.

Hannah

At the airport, as Hannah waited to board her flight, she opened her phone and scrolled back through all the photos of her time in Egypt. She stopped at a picture of her mom. She had taken the picture from an old photograph she'd found at her grandmother's house on the day of the funeral. Her mom was young, wearing too-bright lipstick and a big goofy smile, leaning against a railing with the Nile in the background.

A moment later, boarding began, and people began to stand and form makeshift lines in front of the gate, but Hannah still looked at her phone, at the photo of her mom. She was probably the same age Hannah was now, back in Egypt before she knew how her life would turn out—back when she used to go to protests and marches. Would she have ever guessed that one day she'd have a daughter doing the same?

Hannah kept looking at the picture until she heard her zone being called. She locked her screen and shoved her phone into her back pocket as she got up and grabbed her backpack. Somehow, as she made her way to the gate, she could feel her mom close by, as though she was watching over her, both of them heading home.

acknowledgments

I've been thinking about my book acknowledgments for years—who I would include, what I would say—and now, sitting on an airplane trying to write this, I don't know how to start in a way that's authentic. Anyone who knows me knows that I'm not an overly sentimental person—that I'd rather jump off a cliff than say my feelings out loud. But here we go.

I worked on *Dust Settles North* for nine years. I want to thank so many people in my life from that time. First, I need to thank my parents, who have always been encouraging and supportive—sometimes emotionally, sometimes financially—about my dreams and desire to be a writer. I want to thank them for not forcing me to go to medical school, like their parents did to them. And I know that my choices didn't always make sense to them, but they never discouraged me or told me to give up in all the years I was working on this book. And thank you to my brother, Omar Mohtady, for your constant support.

Thank you to my writers' group: Angela Chen, Lilly Dancyger, Jeanna Kadlec, and Nina St. Pierre. Through them, I learned to be a writer in New York. And more than anyone else in my life, I could count on them to understand the struggle of trying to get a book published and survive in this city. Thank you for your feedback, your encouragement, your advice, your brainstorming sessions, and all the ways you showed up for me as a writer.

Thank you also to my friends here in New York, without whom I would have had multiple mental breakdowns in the years I was working on this book. Thank you to the "Mommy Issues" group chat: Josephine Adamski, Sarah Elnahal, and Percia Verlin. Thank you to Micaiah Johnson, for being my most optimistic and encouraging hype person. Thank you, Juliana Roth, Julianne "Gigi" Adams, Wesley Boyko, and everyone else in "The Main Chat" who I already mentioned.

I especially want to thank my agent, Monica Rodriguez. You believed in my book from the first moment you read it, and you've gone above and beyond your role as an agent. The submission process was brutal and stressful, and many times disheartening, but you never gave up on me. You kept up the hope even when I felt completely hopeless, and I'm so grateful for that. I can't imagine having gone through that process with anyone else.

Thank you to Jananie K. Velu, who saw potential in my book and went on to sign me with Bindery. Watching your videos, it's incredible to see someone speak with so much enthusiasm and excitement about this story I wrote. Thank you so much for bringing my book into the world and sharing it with your followers.

Dust Settles North started out as a short story I wrote for an MFA workshop, which later expanded into my MFA thesis, so I would like to thank my professors and peers in the Rutgers-Camden MFA program. In particular, I want to thank Patrick Rosal and Lisa Ziedner. Pat, one of the best choices I made during my time in the program was asking you to be my thesis adviser. You pushed me to understand the emotional stakes of my characters in a way that I would not have otherwise. Above all, you made me realize why this story was so important to me. Lisa, your craft classes and workshops taught me so much, and

I am a better writer because of you. I started this novel in your class, and I am immensely grateful for your feedback in those early days.

Thank you to my MFA cohort: Katy Callahan, Kate Catinella, Kevin Dorn, James Faccinto, Cherita Harrell, Caroline Rash, Alex Ruiz, Shelby Vittek, Brock Warren, and anyone else I'm forgetting.

Thank you also to my old roommate, and friend, Alexis Ayala, who got me through Covid quarantine, and who was always supportive of my work.

Thank you, Ciara Bhattacharyya and Mary Hesson, for being friends with me for so long and listening to me talk about this book and all my anxieties around it for years.

Thank you, Alan Drew, my first creative-writing instructor. Your classes in undergrad made me realize that this is what I want to do with my life, and I'm forever grateful for that.

Thank you to the whole team at Bindery for your support in bringing this book into the world. Thank you, Matthew Patin, for your wonderful edits. You really saw the characters and understood the story in a way I didn't expect, and you gave my book that final, necessary push to become what it is now.

Thank you, Charlotte Strick, for my beautiful cover. I absolutely love how it turned out, and thank you to the original illustrator, Cecilia Carlstedt, for allowing us to use your art.

Thank you, CJ Alberts, Kim Kent, and the rest of the team at Bindery and Girl Friday Productions, and thank you to my publicist, Brittani Hilles.

Most of all, thank you to my cat Sasha. Without you, I could not have survived this long, and I can't imagine my life without you in it.

thank you

This book would not have been possible without the support from the Boundless Press community, with a special thank-you to the Associate Publisher members:

Jayson Messenger
Kia Borner
Monica Yvette Maldonado
Tabita Aitonean
Books2readilse
Lesli
hannahtrehm
CassidyAscione

about the author

© Sylvie Rosokoff

DEENA ELGENAIDI is a writer and editor based in Brooklyn, New York. She holds her MFA in creative writing from Rutgers University–Camden and her MA in English from Villanova University. Her writing has been featured in *Vulture, Nylon, Salon, Lit Hub,* and more. *Dust Settles North* is her first book.

Boundless Press is an imprint of Bindery, a book publisher powered by community.

We're inspired by the way book tastemakers have reinvigorated the publishing industry. With strong taste and direct connections with readers, book tastemakers have illuminated self-published, backlisted, and overlooked authors, rocketing many to bestseller lists and the big screen.

This book was chosen by Jananie K. Velu in close collaboration with the Boundless Press community on Bindery. By inviting tastemakers and their reading communities to participate in publishing, Bindery creates opportunities for deserving authors to reach readers who will love them.

Visit Boundless Press for a thriving bookish community and bonus content:

boundless.binderybooks.com

© Jaclyn Vogl

JANANIE K. VELU is a Toronto-based content creator and marketer who raves about her favorite books on her channel thisstoryaintover with an audience of over 100K subscribers across YouTube, Instagram, and TikTok. As the founder of Boundless Press—an independent publishing imprint with Bindery Books—Jananie aims to uplift new voices and stories that reflect the beauty and flawed complexity of human nature.

VISIT @THISSTORYAINTOVER ON INSTAGRAM, YOUTUBE, AND TIKTOK.